FOR ALL THE WORLD

CULLEN'S CELTIC CABARET - BOOK 1

JEAN GRAINGER

To my wonderful readers, who have stuck by me all these years. Without you, I would not have this wonderful life talking to people who never existed and recounting things that never happened.

All the world's a stage; and the men and women merely players; they have their entrances and their exits, and one man in his time plays many parts.

William Shakespeare

CHAPTER 1

DUBLIN, IRELAND, JANUARY 1917

ETER

HE FELT it as much as heard it. The deafening pounding of stamping feet on the wooden floor of the Gaiety Theatre, the rapturous applause that never wavered in intensity as the entire cast took their second encore, and then got even louder and warmer as the other actors slipped back into the wings, leaving only Peter and the actor playing Macbeth standing side by side on stage, their arms held out to the audience.

It was intoxicating, the waves of sheer love coming from the full house, the calls of admiration ringing down from the gods. He couldn't believe he'd actually pulled it off, playing a leading role at only seventeen years of age.

He'd been seven when he'd first sneaked into the Abbey in the shadow of a lady's dress. He was small for his age, and she'd had so many hoops and such a large bustle, the doorman never spotted him scuttling past on his knees. It was the opening night of John Millington Synge's *Playboy of the Western World*, and there was all kind of commotion because of a reference to Pegeen Mike, the girl of the place, being in her nightie, which sent the ladies and gentlemen of the audience into a right spin altogether. Little Peter had watched, enthralled, as the audience rioted and the Dublin Metropolitan Police had to be called.

He sneaked into lots of shows after that, and though none of them were quite so eventful, he learnt to love the theatre.

By the time he was eight, he was running errands for the stage manager, Mr Griffin, fetching and carrying in return for watching the shows for free. Mr Griffin gave him the odd penny, and the regular cast adopted him as their mascot and let him come backstage. He made himself useful, listening to them say their lines and correcting them if they went wrong. He wasn't much good at the books – he'd left school too young – but he had an incredible gift for recall. If he heard a poem spoken, or a prayer or a song, he could remember it straight off, not a bother in the wide world. And if he heard an actor read their part just once, then he'd know it by heart, better than them. Not only that, he could mimic the exact way they said the words – the women's voices just as well as the men – which made everyone laugh.

Mimicking people was why he'd left school before he'd learnt much of anything. He'd gone to a little national school up on North King Street, St Michael's, where there were no desks and forty children in each class in the room. The brothers who taught there were cruel, and one day one of them caught him imitating Brother Constantin to amuse his friends. The brother picked him up by the hair and dangled him until he cried – he was only seven – and then asked him why he was crying. Peter shouted at him, 'Because you're hurting me, ya big thick eejit!' And he got a beating for being cheeky, and so he never went back after that.

He spent the next years trying to help his mother, giving her the few secret pennies he earned at the theatre to buy bread when his father had drunk his wages down the pub, like he always did. He begged shops for half-rotten vegetables, ran to the pawnbroker and the money lender, trying to keep the show afloat. At last he turned ten and was old enough to get a proper paid job as a messenger boy at the Guinness brewery, where his father worked.

Peter liked his job. He started at five in the morning and finished on the dot of one; another messenger took over then. It meant he got to meet all kinds of people and knew the city like the back of his hand. And it gave him the rest of the day to hang around the Gaiety Theatre. As he grew older, he even got to be on stage, carrying a spear or a pitchfork if a crowd of soldiers or angry peasants were needed, and for that he was paid sixpence, which also went secretly to his mother.

A week ago he'd had his first real break. The actor who played the porter in *Macbeth* had gotten too much into character and was so drunk he could hardly stand up. The director, Louis O'Hare, had heard Peter mimicking the porter's lines, and the next minute, he was being dressed in the porter's costume. He was rigid with fright, but he tried out the piece of advice he'd heard given to the cast by Arthur Shields, Dublin's best-known actor, who had popped in one day to see how rehearsals were going. Like Arthur said to do, he breathed deeply in and out, and the nerves left his body with every exhale.

When he walked out on stage, any remaining fear he'd had just melted away. He wasn't Peter Cullen playing a drunken porter. He *was* the drunken porter. O'Hare was so pleased with his performance that the original actor was relegated to being Peter's understudy and sat in the wings sulking for the rest of the run.

Until tonight, when a different actor had let Louis O'Hare down.

Christine Kemp, who acted Lady Macbeth so brilliantly, that afternoon lost a baby she didn't even know she was carrying and was in the hospital haemorrhaging half to death apparently. He'd heard the women gossiping before they shut the door on his flapping ears. He'd been sad to hear it; Christine was lovely, and sometimes if she got flowers, she gave him one to take home to his ma. Everyone was mad about her. But the show must go on. Except Christine's understudy, who had never once been called upon, had disappeared for a last night of passion with her soldier boyfriend, who was being shipped out to France tomorrow. Peter was sent out to search every pub and place she might be, but he returned alone with only fifteen minutes to spare until the curtain went up.

'I'm so, so sorry, Mr O'Hare. I can't find her.' He was nearly in tears of disappointment himself. This was the night his siblings were coming to see him play the comic porter. The tickets were two shillings each, but Mr Griffin had given him four free tickets on the proviso he didn't say a word. Even cast members didn't get free tickets when the show sold out, and this one had filled the theatre every night. And now they had no leading lady.

Instead of howling and tearing his hair out, Louis O'Hare looked Peter up and down. 'You know this whole play backwards, don't you?'

'Yes, Mr –'

'Millicent!' barked the director over his shoulder at the make-up girl. 'Take Peter here and dress him up as Lady M, and tell Joe he's back on as the porter.'

'Mr O'Hare!' Peter was horrified. What would his brother and three sisters think if he pranced around up there in women's clothing? 'Mr O'Hare, I can't! I'm a boy!'

But Louis O'Hare was a man with his back to the wall. It was the last night of the show, and he needed the ticket money to turn a decent profit. 'Don't matter a rattlin' damn if you're a gorilla. You're doing it. Besides, all the female parts were played by boys back in Shakespeare's time, when women weren't allowed. I've heard you imitate Christine – you have her to a T. Now off you go to the dressing rooms. I'll make it worth your while if you don't make a dog's dinner of it. There's a good lad.'

The strange thing was, even though he was a boy, as soon as he set foot on the stage, he changed into Lady Macbeth, every bit as much as he'd been the comic porter. And the applause…on and on and on. The theatre in all its forms was a drug, and he was addicted. This was what he would do for the rest of his life.

* * *

LATER, after the whole cast had congratulated him – they knew as actors what a hard thing he had done, to play someone of the opposite sex with such conviction – he sat and gazed into the mirror, wiping the greasepaint from his face.

He was in Christine Kemp's dressing room, and it wasn't the cramped cupboard he'd had to put up with when playing the porter. Here the mirror had the bulbs all around it, like he was a proper star. The golden wig was hanging carefully on the hook – Millicent in costumes told him she'd batter him if it got a tangle – the scarlet and gold velvet dress so wretchedly uncomfortable that he wondered if women really wore such garments was draped over the back of a chair, and Lady Macbeth's stiff white ruff was in its box.

It was taking him a while to come back to himself, but with each wipe of the cotton cloth, Lady Macbeth disappeared and seventeen-year-old Peter Cullen came back into view: floppy blond hair and navy-blue eyes, a symmetrical face, a dusting of freckles over his nose, straight brown eyebrows, a delicate but square jaw. He suspected it was because he could pass as a girl that Louis O'Hare had risked giving him the part. Without the ruff, his Adam's apple showed, but that was the only sign of his manliness. He didn't care. He was surrounded by big strong fellas all day, who just cursed and fought and drank, and he had no desire whatsoever to emulate them. He wasn't puny himself, far from it – he was lithe and athletic – but he still had some growing and filling out to do. His beard, before Millicent shaved it off, had been soft and fair; it would coarsen in time.

Anyway, he was glad he looked nothing like his father, a swarthy man, strong from a lifetime of rolling Guinness barrels in the brewery. Kit Cullen was handsome in his own way, but Peter hated him, and so he was happy when Ma said Peter took after her brother, Anthony, who died of scarlatina when he was twelve. Same cupid's-bow lips, she said.

Peter had no idea what that meant, so he asked Kathleen, his older sister, and she explained. He wasn't sure having bow-shaped lips was a good thing at first, but it seemed it was. Women liked it anyway; he'd discovered that. His pouting mouth drew their attention. The girls in the canteen and the laundry would tease him when he came delivering messages from the bosses at the brewery, calling him their lover boy, offering to kiss him, saying how they'd like to take him home.

One old woman who worked in the tannery, with thread-veined cheeks and hands like sandpaper, told him that if she had him, she'd put him in a glass case and throw sugar lumps at him. He'd told his ma and Kathleen this, and they'd howled laughing, explaining it meant she thought he was nice. But he thought it sounded daft.

He was relieved May wasn't here tonight. They'd been walking out, nothing serious. She was a nice enough girl. She'd come to the theatre when he was playing the porter and waited at the stage door to get his autograph; somehow it had ended up with him offering to walk her home.

She was too middle class for him. It turned out she lived in Ranelagh in a lovely red-bricked double-fronted house with a garden out the back, and she told him her father was high up in the bank and her mother from a big farm down the country, so he decided not to tell her about his own background; it would only shock the poor girl.

She was mad about the theatre, knew all the actors and was always talking about this production or that one. She said she'd been in a few productions, amateur, but her parents didn't approve.

The theatre had widened his vocabulary and given him a range of accents to choose from. His fellow actors were all what his father would call toffs, from places like Rathmines and Ranelagh. The fella playing Macbeth was English but lived in Seapoint, and Duncan and Banquo were from Dún Laoghaire, which was fierce posh. So he'd let May believe he was from somewhere like that, and now he was stuck with the lie.

Luckily there was a drive once a year by the wives of the Guinness bosses; they brought in all the clothes that didn't fit or were too worn for their husbands and sons and let the workers take what they wanted. This spring he'd found a pair of black trousers and a smart white shirt that were nearly new, and Kathleen took them to work with her and had them washed and pressed with one of the laundry's heavy irons. He'd even found a pair of proper shoes, a little big for him but fine with two pairs of socks. So he was able to look respectable when he took May out for a cup of tea or a walk in the park.

And so far he had managed to avoid being introduced to her parents, who might ask more searching questions, and he'd make sure to finish with her before she found out where he was really from.

As he finished changing into his one set of good clothes, which he now wore to the theatre instead of his workman's clothes and hobnailed boots, the dressing room door burst open and his sisters, Maggie, Connie and Kathleen, came running in, followed by his older brother, Eamonn. The girls were bubbling and laughing with excitement.

'Holy Moses, Peter, was it really you?' Eight-year-old Connie's eyes were shining with wonder at it all. 'We was lookin' for ya in the porter's dressin' room, and the man said you was in here, and he said not to say, but it was you playin' that woman. I swear I never knew it was you! I couldn't believe it when he said you was playin' a mot.'

'Shh, don't be tellin' anyone. I wouldn't normally be doin' it, but our lead actress is sick, and I had every line of the play off by heart, so Mr O'Hare – he's the director – he made me do it at the last minute. And it's good you didn't know it was me.' He glanced at Eamonn apologetically as he buttoned up his white shirt. 'I'm not plannin' to make a career of playin' women, just so you know, and maybe better to not say anything about it at work. Wouldn't want Da findin' out.'

Kit Cullen already thought theatre people were all 'pansies' and had shown no interest in coming to see Peter playing the comic porter. He'd forbidden Peter's mam to go either, and she was so downtrodden, she hadn't dared defy him. God knew how Kit would react if he found out his son had been playing a woman.

'Ah, it's grand, Peter,' Eamonn said, with a wave of his hand. 'I never copped it was you, so I'm sure no one else did either, so don't be worryin' about that. C'mere to me, I hated all that stuff in school. Remember Jonesy tryin' to teach me poems and all that? Couldn't get outta there fast enough. But you were somethin' else up there, and whoever they thought ya were, they all were glued to ya.'

Peter grinned at Eamonn fondly. His brother's strong working-class Dublin accent was incongruous in these sumptuous surroundings, but he had made the effort to come and was doing his best not to mind that his brother had played a woman up there on the stage. Eamonn took after their father, but only in his looks. When it came to personality, Kit was surly and often drunk and communicated mostly with his fists or slurred nonsense. But Eamonn, who was a couple of years older than Peter but had stayed at school a while longer, was a great laugh and could rattle off stories nineteen to the dozen with a cigarette hanging out of his mouth.

'And you were amazin', even if you were havin' to act being a lady – that must have been really hard,' fourteen-year-old Maggie added, hugging him. 'Like, I never knew yer wan was you, but when she was goin' on about the blood on her hands, "Out spot," I was on the edge of me seat, I swear.' Her china-blue eyes and copper curls made her look fairly theatrical herself, Peter thought.

'Lady Macbeth was desperate altogether, wasn't she?' piped up Connie. 'Poor auld Macbeth, ya'd feel sorry for him, wouldn't ya?' She was so sweet, with her blond pigtails and her best frock on, a faded blue one that had been Kathleen's and then Maggie's.

'Ye would not! The big eejit, believin' all that rubbish outta them witches, and his mate Banquo after tellin' him not to trust them, but he wouldn't listen 'cause he was dyin' to be the king.' Maggie's mad mop of curls was loose; their mother would have a fit if she saw her out without a hat. 'He was just a greedy bas –'

'Maggie Cullen!' Kathleen gasped, ever the older sister. 'Do *not* use that language in here.'

Maggie giggled. Their ma would wallop her for cursing, but all the women in the button factory where she worked said desperate things, and Maggie picked it up like a sponge.

'And you're not supposed to say the name of that play in a theatre anyway. You're supposed to call it "the Scottish Play", 'cause it's cursed and terrible things happen to people who say that word…' Peter spoke in a spooky voice that frightened Connie and made Eamonn laugh.

The door flew open again, and this time it was Mr Griffin, the stage manager. He was fat, with a huge bushy moustache and a shiny bald head. He could be snappy, but Peter knew he had a heart of gold under the gruff interior, and tonight he was beaming as he handed Peter a brown envelope out of the pile he was carrying.

'Your wages. Three weeks as the porter and an extra bonus for playing Lady M. It was a mad idea, but you did great. Well done, son. You pulled it off, and no one noticed you were a young fella. Louis had to rush off to the hospital to see poor Christine – we're hoping she'll pull round. There's a great lady doctor there, Kathleen Lynn. Anyway, he wants you to know you really pulled his fat out of the fire this time, Peter, and when we audition for *Hamlet*, you're to show up and he'll find you a part.'

'Thanks, Mr Griffin.' Peter was almost dizzy with delight. Visions of playing the Dane himself danced through his mind…

'Maybe he's got you pegged as Ophelia,' joked the stage manager, before he rushed off to deliver the other envelopes, leaving Peter smiling ruefully. It wasn't the dream to be playing women, but he was on stage and he was acting and that was all that mattered.

'Well, go on…open it,' Eamonn urged, and Peter realised the eyes of all his siblings were fixed on the envelope. He'd been so excited about O'Hare's offer to join the troupe that he'd forgotten about the money. And in fact he had no idea what to expect. When he'd been told to play the porter, no one had mentioned wages. Lady Macbeth had come out of the blue. What did actors earn anyway? Did they make a good living?

Money was always tight in their house, and the Cullen family lived week to week, even though everyone except Connie and Ma worked. These days Eamonn rolled barrels with Da in the Guinness brewery, Maggie worked in the button factory and Kathleen as a seamstress in Arnotts in town. But Kit Cullen still threw his own wages down his neck in the form of the very stuff he spent the week slaving to make, and any of his children's wages he could get his hands on as well.

Peter felt the envelope before he opened it – no coins, which he found strange. He eased the gummed flap of the envelope open, reached in and felt paper. His heart sank. He hoped it wasn't a cheque – only rich people had a bank account – but more likely it was an IOU; he knew well Louis O'Hare was big on owing money to people. He extracted the rectangle of paper. It was a ten-pound note.

'Ten pounds? For three weeks' work?' Kathleen was astonished. 'That's not right surely?'

'Maybe it's a mistake?' Peter said, as amazed as his siblings. He got nine shillings a week as a messenger boy, which was less than two pounds a month, so could he really have earned so much in three weeks? Is that what the theatre paid, for doing something that wasn't hard work for him at all?

'Don't say a word, even if it is,' Maggie said wisely. 'Wait till you see if he asks ya for it back.'

'Yeah, maybe I'll do that.' It was wonderful to have so much to give to Ma. She could squirrel it away and use it all for herself and her children, unlike all the other wages coming into the house from Eamonn and the girls, which her husband bullied out of her. He felt an urge to celebrate first, though.

'Will we go for a wan and wan?' He grinned at them.

The suggestion made his younger sisters squeal with delight, but Kathleen looked cautious. As the oldest daughter, she carried the burdens of the family on her shoulders.

'We shouldn't. The gas man is callin' Thursday and Da emptied the meter, so we need all the money we can get...'

'Ah, Ka.' Eamonn put his arm around his older sister. 'It's only a few chips and a bit of fish. We can surely do that after Peter's big night, so will we let him enjoy himself?'

'All right, but three between the five of us, right?' Kathleen smiled and raised an eyebrow.

As they set off for Burdocks, the fish and chip near Christ Church Cathedral, his siblings chattered on and on about the money and the play, but Peter tuned them out. He was an actor, a proper paid actor. It was incredible. Nobody he knew was anything like that. Everyone was a docker or a cooper or a driver or something like that, but he was an actor. And not only that, he was making proper money – money his da need never know about. Things were looking up for the Cullen household.

CHAPTER 2

 ETER

THE FIVE OF them crept up the tenement stairs in the dark, avoiding the rotten floorboards that made it a treacherous climb. Their rooms on the third floor of Number 11 Henrietta Street were all they could afford, and those rooms were leaky and cold and miserable. Peter tried not to rub his elbows on the walls. They were painted with Raddle's red and Ricket's blue, which killed the germs, they said, but your clothes were destroyed if you rubbed it, and he wanted to keep his one good shirt clean.

It was hard to believe the grand Georgian townhouses of Henrietta Street were once home to Dublin's elite, toffee-nosed lords and ladies who thought of Dublin as the second city of the British Empire. Traces of old magnificence still remained: large and wide front doors, brass boot scrapers set in the granite steps, decorative fanlights, intricate coving and ceiling roses, sweeping staircases with elaborately decorated banisters. But these days Henrietta Street housed Dublin's poorest of the poor, broken men and beaten-down women squashed into every room like sardines, their shoeless children dressed in rags and living on bread and watered-down porridge.

His mother did her best for them all, feeding them better than most, washing and scrubbing, hanging out her family's laundry to dry on the wires that crisscrossed the street, anchored in the brickwork by five-inch nails. But with only one toilet and one tap in each house, shared between all the families who lived there, it was a struggle, and the pervasive smell of human waste assailed Peter's nostrils as he climbed to the third floor. A hundred people in a house meant for one family could make for terrible smells.

Eamonn, who had gone ahead, stopped and turned, shushing the chattering girls with his finger to his lips. Lying across the stairs, the stink of porter strong off him, was Larry Maguire, their father's most hated neighbour. And that was saying something, because Kit Cullen hated everyone.

Larry was fond of a drop, as they said, but that wasn't why Peter's father despised him. The reason was, Larry regularly mocked Kit Cullen's claims that he had fought in the Post Office last year with Pearse and Connolly and the rest of the men who signed the Proclamation of Independence, declaring Ireland to be free of the old enemy. The valiant rebels fought for over a week, and the British hammered them back, and everyone feared there'd be nothing left of the city by the time it was done. Peter and Eamonn couldn't get to work. Henrietta Street was on the north side of the Liffey, same side as the Post Office, where most of the fierce fighting took place, and at any time, they might have had to evacuate. Ma made them stay inside – well, Peter and the girls. Eamonn slipped out when Bridie Cullen wasn't looking.

Peter's father had turned up four days after the fighting began, claiming all sorts of heroics. Nobody believed him, but fearing his meaty fists, they kept silent. Only Larry Maguire was brave – or rather drunk – enough to jeer him, telling everyone Kit Cullen was in the back room of O'Donnell's pub out in Drimnagh for three days and nights during the Rising that saw the city in flames.

'Is it not a great wonder,' Larry was heard to remark often and at great volume in the halls of the house, 'how the English were draggin' every last man jack of the Volunteers in for questioning, but they never so much as raised an eyebrow at our brave Kit, and he such a hero for old Ireland? 'Tis for all the world like a miracle, so it is, and aren't we lucky such a bright star of a free Ireland is still here to tell the tale?'

Larry had two enormous brothers who could batter Kit Cullen in three seconds flat if he challenged Larry to a fight, so Kit pretended to laugh it off as the ravings of a drunkard and took out his bad temper on his family instead, doling out even more insults and digs than usual to poor Bridie and his children.

Peter sighed as Eamonn stepped carefully over Larry, trying not to wake him. This was so stupid, such a Neanderthal way of going on. Getting plastered, battering people, working like a dog for a bite in your mouth and to pay the rent to a landlord who enjoyed fine port and a feather bed in the leafy suburbs of Dublin, well away from the inner city. If only people used their brains and not their fists, or guns for that matter, things would be so much better. He longed to get out, get away from here. He loved his ma and Eamonn and the girls, but he wasn't like them, he knew that. They couldn't see a life beyond this place, this poverty. They believed it was all they deserved. Peter didn't necessarily believe he deserved better, but he was determined to get it anyway.

He would be eighteen in the summer, and he'd been giving his ma all his wages since he was ten, but as he followed Eamonn over Larry's snoring body and turned back to lift little Connie across with Kathleen's help as well as give a hand to Maggie, he decided for the first time in his life to tell his mother a lie. He'd say he was sure Mr Griffin had made a mistake and only meant to give him a one-pound note, not a tenner, so he would have to give him back the rest. And then he'd use the other nine pounds to do something different for himself. He didn't know what the future held for him yet, but it didn't involve staying in the tenements and drinking himself into a stupor every night, that was for sure.

Eamonn eased the door of their rooms open; it was really just one big room of the original house divided into three by thin partitions. The living room, if you could call it that, was where they cooked and ate, and also where he and Eamonn shared a settle bed that was pulled out at night and folded away during the day. The second space was their parents' bedroom, and the last, which was tiny, had a double bed the three girls shared. Despite his ma's best efforts, the whole place smelled of damp and body odour.

Peter's heart sank as he entered the living area. It was after midnight and he just wanted to sleep – he had to be up at half past four for work – but his father was still awake, sitting on the settle that his sons needed to sleep on, dressed only in his vest and trousers, his braces hanging down and his forearms on his knees. He didn't look up as they entered. The gas lamp was lit, and there was a bottle of stout on the table next to an empty glass.

The girls slipped away into their room, all their happy chatter and good spirits evaporating into a scared silence.

Eamonn approached Kit the way you might stalk a wild animal, cautiously, making no sudden movements. And Kit Cullen was like an animal, thought Peter. He was hairy like an ape, and his shoulders and arms were huge.

'We might just pull out the settle there, Da…' Eamonn said quietly.

Kit didn't move.

Peter and his brother exchanged a look. This could go any way. Kit could just stand up and go into his own bed, and they'd pray not to hear the animal sounds of him forcing himself on their mother through the thin partition. Or he could try to pick a fight and batter them. Or he could be all bonhomie, demanding his sons drink with him and listen to endless rambling and entirely fictitious stories of his great bravery in the face of the English. If he got started on his hatred for England, they'd be there until it was time to go to work.

'Da?' Eamonn tried again. Their father sat with his fists clenched in his lap.

Peter tried then, leaning down to speak. 'Da?' He hated how meek his voice sounded, but he knew the slightest intonation that displeased Kit could result in carnage.

15

This time his father looked up, and his hard, unblinking eyes were full of hate. 'Tell me, Peter...' His voice was gravelly, menacing, but not slurred, so he hadn't taken much drink, not enough to slow him down. 'Tell me what made ya think that ya could make a show of me like that?'

Peter glanced at Eamonn in alarm. 'What? I don't –'

The next thing he knew, he was pinned to the inside of the door, his pressed and washed shirt in a ball in Kit's fist, his father's scarlet face inches from his.

'Shamin' me on purpose, was it?' Spittle landed on Peter's cheek, the horrible stench of his father's breath turning his stomach. 'Makin' a fool of me, dressin' up like some kind of a faggot, so the whole place can burst their arses laughing when Larry Maguire goes shouting up and down the halls about Kit Cullen's young fella prancing the boards painted up like a tart?'

The sweat of fear poured from Peter, running down his back. Larry... He should have thought of Larry. The theatre bar was one of the few places left that hadn't barred the old drunk, and he often hailed Peter from his stool at the counter. 'Peter Cullen, son of the famous war hero! Ha, ha, ha!'

'Da, it wasn't like that...' he managed, but his father was pressing hard on his windpipe and he couldn't force any more words out. It was nearly impossible to breathe.

'Da, let him go!' Eamonn tried to intervene but got his father's elbow in his face, sending him reeling.

'Down the docks till this time, were ya?' roared Kit, jabbing Peter in the stomach with his fist as his right hand tightened even more around his son's throat. 'Got a few bob for that skinny little arse of yours, did ya?'

'We were at Burdocks chipper, Da,' Eamonn protested, scrambling back to his feet.

Kit ignored his older son and jabbed Peter in the stomach a second time. 'Or up in Monto? With the rest of the brassers?' He hocked a ball of phlegm and spat into Peter's face, and as Peter, winded and choked, tried in vain to take a breath, he could sense the foul globule sliding down his cheek and onto his chin. He started to think it was the last thing he would ever feel, because the lights in his brain were going out one by one...

'Kit!' His ma's voice cut faintly through the roaring in his head. He could see her; she was in her long nightdress, her hair loose.

'Stop it! Leave him alone! You're killing him!'

'That's right, defend yer little girl!'

'He's your son!'

'He's no son of mine.' With an evil grimace, Kit Cullen tightened his already deadly grip on Peter's windpipe and leant in closer, bright scarlet with rage. 'No son of mine is a nancy boy. No son of mine gives Larry Maguire a reason to make a laughing stock of me!' He drew back his meaty fist again, but this time Eamonn grabbed the heavy iron kettle off the top of the pot-bellied stove and swung it as hard as he could, catching Kit on the back of his head.

Bridie let out a shriek as Kit went down like a sack of spuds, and Peter slid weakly to the floor, gasping for breath. Eamonn dropped the kettle, the girls appeared, and all the Cullen family just stood and stared at their father, motionless on the threadbare carpet. He was face down but awkwardly twisted in the middle because his fat belly had forced his hips to roll to one side. A trickle of blood leaked down his neck from the back of his head.

'Is he dead?' asked Connie in a breathless little voice, and Bridie Cullen let out a wail of horror.

'What will we do, what will we do?' she groaned. She had fresh bruising on her face, Peter could see as his vision cleared. His father had obviously taken his rage out on her before he and the others got back from the theatre. This was all his fault for agreeing to play Lady Macbeth, and now his older brother would be hung for murder.

Eamonn knelt on the floor, his fingers on their father's neck, feeling for his pulse; the brewery had sent him to a first aid course last year. 'Stop crying, Ma. He'll live, worse luck.'

'But what will we do, what we will do?' she kept on asking, standing over him, wringing her hands. 'He was trying to kill Peter! He was trying to kill his own son.'

'I know, Ma. Kathleen, get somethin' to bandage his head. The cut's only shallow. If we wrap it tight, we'll stop the bleedin'. Maggie, clean that kettle. Wipe it and scrub every bit of blood off it. We'll tell him he was drunk and fell and hit the back of his head off the floor. With a bit of luck, he won't remember any of it. Connie, go back to bed and go to sleep. We never heard nothin' nor saw nothin', right?'

'But he was trying to kill Peter, his own son,' Ma kept repeating in a bewildered voice. 'Kit said he'd swing for him. I didn't believe him – he wouldn't kill his own son. But he did. He tried to kill him.'

Her husband stirred and groaned, and Bridie Cullen let out a terrified shriek. 'Oh God, what will we do!'

'Get Peter out of here, that's what we're going to do,' said Eamonn, getting to his feet after tying up their father's head wound with a piece of cloth Kathleen had ripped from her own skirt.

Peter pushed himself into a sitting position against the door. 'You want me to leave here?' His voice was hoarse, his windpipe so bruised.

Eamonn came to help him up. 'Yes, and not just the house. You have to get out of Dublin, Peter. He's tried to kill you once, and he'll try to kill you again. We have to tell him you've left the country – it's the only way.'

'But where will I go? It's the middle of the night. And I was going to audition for another part...'

'I know, but ya can't do that now unless you want to be dead. Ya have to get out of here, as far as you can go. Maybe that young wan of yours – May, is it? Hide out at her place till the mornin'.'

'Ah, Eamonn, I can't go running to her. She hardly knows me.'

'Well, you have to get out of here anyway. And listen, when you've got where you're going, send a message to me. Not here or at the brewery. Maybe send it to Kathleen in Arnotts. She'll see I get it. Tell me where you are, and I'll let ya know how things are goin' here. But go now, y'hear me?'

Peter knew his brother was right. He'd no idea what to do, where to go, but staying here wasn't an option. Never had he seen such murderous hate as was in Kit Cullen's eyes tonight. His father had intended to kill him, and he would try again, and if his mother or Eamonn tried to stop him, he'd kill them too.

His mind raced. He had the money Mr Griffin gave him in his pocket, a whole ten pounds, less the fish and chips. He'd already been thinking of moving on. But not like this, so fast, with no plans.

Where were his hobnailed work boots? He needed to pack a bag…

Kit Cullen moaned and started to push himself up before collapsing back again, muttering to himself.

'Peter, just go. Quick!' his mother begged him, tears running down her bruised face.

There was no time for him to pack; Kit was coming round too fast. He hugged Kathleen and Maggie briefly – 'Say goodbye to Connie for me' – and held his ma for a long second, whispering in her ear, 'I'll write.'

She clung to him, sobbing. 'Take care, Peter. Take care. Please God, we'll meet again in this world.'

Eamonn clapped him on the shoulder, and Kathleen tried to push his father's donkey jacket on him, but he shook his head. He wanted nothing of Kit Cullen's. His father groaned again, and his mother gasped and gave him a frightened shove towards the door.

In the hallway, he stepped over the still-unconscious Larry Maguire, the man who had started all this trouble, made his way cautiously down the rotting stairs and let himself out into the starry Dublin night.

CHAPTER 3

CORK, IRELAND. 1917

ICK

THE HONOURABLE VIVIAN NICHOLAS SHAW – third son of Walter Vivian Shaw, the fifth Baron de Simpré, and his wife, Harriet, a second cousin of the Earl of Perthshire – was sitting alone in the bar of the Metropole Hotel in Cork, drinking a stiff gin that he had wheedled out of the night porter and writing the last letter he would ever address to his unloving parents.

Dear Mother and Father,

By the time you read this letter, I will have joined the king's forces. As you have repeatedly reminded me, I am not officer material, so I will be signing up as a private soldier under an assumed name. So now your patriotic duty is done, Father, and you can keep Wally safely by your side and the future of Brockleton will be secure.

He paused, his pen raised, picturing the old estate house just a few miles from Cork City, set in the lush green slopes of the Lee Valley. Three storeys high, but ugly and dour, built of dark-grey granite. He wouldn't miss it. He didn't even care if he never set eyes on the place again. The rooms inside might be beautifully appointed, but they were formal and cold. There was only one corner he would miss, and that was the music room on the third floor, which had a Steinway grand piano. It was where he spent all his school holidays hiding from his brothers, playing the piano and singing his favourite songs.

His grandmother was also musical, and she had spotted his talent at an early age and engaged a music master for him at her own expense. The diminutive Maestro Zarela always arrived with a basket of his wife's delicious little cakes, which Nicholas loved and ate lots of, but on the downside, the little man always cried with joy when he heard him singing, which disconcerted the young boy because he had been taught that men don't cry.

Maestro Zarela had since gone back to Italy with his kindly wife, after spending only three summers in the cold Irish climate. The teacher would arrive for so many lessons soaked to the skin, his straw hat dripping, and the look of sheer disappointment on his little face made Nick feel responsible for the wet Irish weather. After the teacher left, Nicholas's voice had broken; he'd gone from a pure soprano to a light tenor. But he still loved singing, because it was the only time he could come out with whole sentences without stuttering.

Nicholas's stammer was the bane of his life, and it was the reason his father so often reminded him he would never be officer material. It wasn't too bad when he was relaxed, but when he was nervous – which was often – he could hardly get a word out. And then his brothers would bully him and his school mates would mock him, and that made the whole thing worse.

'Oh, for goodness' sake, boy, just say the damned word,' his father would bellow as young Nicholas stood before him, fighting to speak. The baron was tall and broad, with a huge belly. Though an aristocrat, he had the physique of a wrestler, his lion's mane of salt-and-pepper hair brushed back from his wide brow; in his youth he'd been nick-named Bruiser at school.

'I'm sorry, F-F-Father…'

'And I'm sorry you're such a F-F-FOOL!' roared Walter Shaw. The fifth Baron of Simpré did not suffer fools gladly and clearly counted his youngest son among the ranks of the most foolish creatures God ever created.

'I'm s-s –'

'Urgh. Get away from me. You disgust me.'

Nicholas sat in the dark lobby, blinking back tears. They had hurt him one time too many. It was over now.

Everything had been done to put a stop to his stutter. He'd been dunked in ice baths, been beaten at home and at school, made to stand in the corner for so long he'd wet himself, because he wasn't allowed to move until he could recite 'Ozymandias' by Shelley without a stammer – which of course he never could. Then came the so-called experts. A doctor who smelled of fish stuffed Nicholas's mouth with marbles until he was in tears, terrified he'd choke to death. Another made him spend hours trying to speak with the tip of his tongue pressed against his palate – the latest miracle cure that had no effect whatsoever.

Once, his father was told by some fellow at his club that boxing was the best cure, so Nicholas was taken to an instructor in Killarney who tried to teach him the art of hitting people. Fourteen-year-old Nicholas was not a natural, to say the least – he was a stocky child, slower on his feet than the others. But it helped that he was strong at least, and he did manage to win a few bouts by pretending his opponent was his father; it was an outlet for his anger. But alas, he continued to stutter…

Except when he was singing.

His parents weren't interested in music, and the room with the Steinway was so far from their own rooms that they couldn't hear him, so they never really noticed he had a talent. And he had no intention of asking them to listen to him; he was sure it would ruin things and he would start to stammer even when he was in mid-song.

Though he didn't mind when his grandmother, Alicia Shaw, who he called Floss, mother of the baron, came in to hear him play. Somehow he could cope with that.

The dowager was a cool, quiet woman, but Nicholas loved her. She came from a rich merchant family in Boston, Massachusetts, the place where the rebels had flung all the tea into the sea, and the fourth Baron de Simpré had married her for her money. She had married him because her parents were social climbers and determined to have a title in the family. She never lost her American accent and was mischievous and funny. She found the stuffy ways of the British upper classes ridiculous, and Nicholas often giggled when Floss got some point of etiquette wrong on purpose.

She would have loved to have been a singer herself when she was younger, but of course that was completely vetoed in favour of finding a suitable husband.

She'd ask Nicholas to sing some of her favourite American songs, 'The Battle Hymn of the Republic', 'Camptown Races', 'The Stars and Stripes Forever'. She missed her home country so much. He'd promised her he would take her back one day, when he was grown up. Was that a promise he'd have to renege on now? The thought made him so sad.

She didn't make him nervous in the way his own parents did, and she was kind to him. When he went back to his hated boarding school, Moorbury, she would give him sugared almonds to bring with him, which he used to eat quietly in the night.

Please give my love to Floss, he added to the letter in his copperplate schoolboy hand, the one thing that had been successfully beaten into him at Moorbury. *And tell her that one day, I will keep my promise to her.*

Yes, he would miss his grandmother, and he knew she would miss him as well.

Unlike Father and Mother.

Vivian Nicholas Shaw hadn't realised how thoroughly his parents despised him until only a few days ago. Up until then, he'd just assumed they weren't that interested in him. And why would they be? He wasn't the heir. Roger had that honour. Roger would inherit the title, Brockleton and its extensive grounds and their father's seat in the House of Lords. He was a dashing, handsome boy, athletic and brilliant; he would make a wonderful sixth Baron de Simpré. Mother adored him, although Father seemed to think him a bit of a bore. He liked reading; that was probably why.

His parents had had a serious falling out when Father decided to send Roger off to war. Or rather, allow him to go, because Roger was very excited to get stuck into the Hun. Mother argued strongly against it – there was no conscription in Ireland, and they were under no obligation – but Father was a loyal British subject and had to hold up his head in his club in Mayfair, where he intended to spend his own war. Roger, he assured Mother, would be perfectly safe as an officer.

After a short but glittering military career with the Royal Navy, poor old Rog was torpedoed in the North Sea a few weeks ago. He'd lived for a few hours, it seemed, but died in the lifeboat before rescue came. They were spared the terrible telegram, as a friend of Father's at his club delivered the sad news, and Father came home on the ferry to tell Mother, arriving back last Thursday.

Harriet Shaw was always perfectly groomed, her treacle-black hair pinned back expertly every morning by her lady's maid, Agnes, and her slim figure dressed in the latest trends of London and Paris. That was how she looked when she went to greet her husband in the lofty entrance hall of Brockleton. But as her husband delivered the news of her son's death, she turned from an elegant lady of the manor into a wailing banshee.

Reeling around, she railed and screamed and tore at her hair and clothes. The servants beat a hasty retreat, but Nicholas, sitting on the marble cantilevered staircase, on a level with the black cast-iron chandelier that hung over the three storeys of the atrium, watched numbly from above as his mother raged, blaming her husband, screaming that he had sent her son to be slaughtered when there had been no need. He'd wished his grandmother was there, but she was spending a month in Brighton with old friends.

Father tried to comfort Mother. 'I've already sent a telegram to Wally, Harriet, and he's on his way back from China, so you will have him here with you all the time. I only found out about poor old Roger myself ten days ago.'

'Ten days!' she screamed. 'You've known my child was dead for ten days, and I'm only hearing it now?'

'Well, yes, I'd promised Monty Pilkington I'd go down for the grouse and –'

She ran at him then, trying to scratch his eyes out.

'Harriet, please, control yourself! You're frightening the servants. Wally is on his way and…' His father's voice trailed off.

Wally, the second son, was tall and powerfully built like Nicholas, though nothing like him in temperament. He had fashioned himself the life of a playboy, ostensibly managing the family's interests in Shanghai while drinking a lot and getting himself into tricky situations with other men's wives, which had to be then sorted out by their father. Walter Senior seemed to not mind his middle son's rakish ways. 'Chip off the old block,' he would growl as he dashed off another cheque. 'Reminds me of meself when I was a lad.'

'Wally?' Mother screamed in fury. She was so shrill and sharp, her voice hurt Nicholas's ears almost as much as it hurt his heart, but still he watched. 'You think Wally can comfort me for the loss of my darling Roger?'

'He's also your son,' Father said, offended.

'He's *your* son, the one you love, the one you care about.' Her green eyes glittered dangerously with grief and pain.

'Surely you care for him too,' Father spluttered indignantly, his bushy eyebrows furrowing, trying to understand the woman he only ever called 'your dear mama'.

'I mean, he'll make as good a baron as your precious Roger, better maybe. He's a chip –'

'I know, I know, a chip off the old block, worst luck.' His mother spoke more quietly now, but there was a snarly smirk to her lips that frightened Nicholas; it was mean and cruel. 'And what is your genius plan for your favourite son, Walter? Send him off to war as well so a German can put a bullet in him, will you? Or keep him at home, because you always loved him better than my darling Roger?' Sarcasm dripped from her every word.

'Well…I… No… Well, obviously Wally will be expected to do his bit. The men at the club…good patriots. Bad enough my mother is American, and her bloody country is doing nothing to help us…'

'So you'll send our second son to die, like Roger?' Her voice was even lower now; Nicholas had to strain to hear.

'But…but they know we've lost Roger.' He was floundering, totally out of his depth. 'They'll make sure Wally stays safe behind the lines. He's good officer material…'

'You fool! You blind fool!' She was screaming again, her skin blotched and her eyes blazing with sheer hatred, her face only inches from Father's. 'So you'll send your Wally to die as well! And then who will be left to us? Nicholas! N-N-Nicholas!' She threw back her head and cackled as she imitated her third son's stammer. That horrible laugh. He would never forget it. Never. To his dying day. 'Nicholas the imbecile. Nicholas the idiot. So Nicholas is going to be your heir?'

His father looked utterly horrified, as if this awful possibility hadn't crossed his mind. 'God would not punish us that way, Harriet –'

'And why wouldn't God punish you with Nicholas, you old goat! You punished me with him! I nearly died pushing him out into the world! No wonder I can't bear to look at him.'

'Harriet, I know you're upset…'

'You had your heir and you had your spare, and Roger was mine and Wally was yours, and were you content with that? No! You had two fine sons to show the world what a virile man you were, how you could service your wife as well as *that woman…*'

Father checked nervously around the hall for servants, decided they were alone and dropped his voice. Nicholas remained frozen in his spot. Who on earth was 'that woman'? He could still hear his father loud and clear, though, because even when the baron whispered, he couldn't help booming. 'Harriet, dear, please. A little decorum. That's all water under the bridge now.'

His mother ignored him and went on. 'But then you had to force yourself on me, again and again, knowing I hated it, hated you, until once again I was bearing another of your spawn.'

His father stopped trying to calm her down, grabbed her by the arms and shook her. She rattled in his grip like a rag doll, her carefully arranged hair coming even further undone. She shrieked and tried to kick him, even baring her teeth to bite him, but his father, though many years her senior, was stronger.

'Stop it now!' His father shouted for the first time since this exchange began. 'Control yourself, woman!'

She reached up and scratched his cheek, drawing blood, and he reacted by punching her in the face with his closed fist, sending her flying against the rosewood and ivory hallstand.

Three floors above, Nicholas sat as still as a mouse, a very large mouse, the tears streaming down his face. It was horrible. Everything was horrible. He knew for sure now his parents didn't love him, no more than they loved each other. He'd never dared to imagine they cared for him like they cared, in their separate ways, for Roger and Wally. He knew he wasn't in the same league as his older brothers, but he'd always assumed they did love him a little bit.

He was wrong.

Now, sitting in the late-night bar, he drained his gin, folded the letter into the envelope the hotel porter had given him and addressed the envelope to *The Baron and Baroness de Simpré, Brockleton, Coolroe, Cork, Ireland.*

It was hotel stationery, so they would know where he had been when he wrote it, and that would be further proof of him not being officer material. He recalled some friends of his father's saying the Metropole in Cork was a fine place for the middle classes but not a place one would want to be seen personally. Staying in hotels was frightfully bourgeois; the upper classes stayed at their clubs.

Nicholas didn't care. By the time his parents received this letter, he would be in war-torn France.

CHAPTER 4

 ETER

'YE ALL RIGH', love?' A few women gathered around a brazier on the corner of Westmoreland Street and Grafton Street in Dublin's city centre laughed as he passed. He fought back tears. He had longed to get away, that was true, but not like this. He wanted to save up, to leave properly, to take his ma for a cup of tea and bun to Bewley's like a proper lady, to have a plan. Now he had nothing except some money and the clothes he stood up in.

He'd have to leave the theatre he loved, where his career had been just about to take off, his family, his ma... As he walked, the reality of what he was facing sank in. It was coming up to one in the morning, he was a fugitive from his own father, and he didn't even have anywhere to sleep.

Maybe Eamonn was right that he should go to May's. He shouldn't leave without telling her anyway, he supposed. It would be wrong not to let her know, because she liked him, he knew that, and she was nice.

He walked, hands in his pockets, over the Liffey, all the way up Grafton Street to St Stephen's Green, over to Baggot Street across the canal and on to Northbrook Road in Ranelagh. He remembered the number of May's house because he had walked her home that first night, and he had perfect recall of anything that interested him. He hoped she wouldn't be too upset when he told her he was leaving. But someone from such a fancy address shouldn't be going out with a lad from Henrietta Street anyway. She wouldn't have looked twice at him, he was sure, if he hadn't let her think he was middle class. So maybe it was all for the best, a way to break up before she found out.

By the time he reached the Gallaghers' house, it was close to two in the morning, which was no time to call on anyone. He would have to hang around until May left for work; she had a job in the munitions factory out Parkgate Street. In the office, of course, not on the factory floor. May's ma didn't like her daughter having a job at all. She thought the only point of May's expensive education was to make her a suitable companion for her future husband and a good mother to her children, so she'd flatly refused to let her daughter be a nurse, which was what May really wanted, and had only given in on the office job because it was for the war effort. May's parents were big supporters of John Redmond, who had made some kind of deal with the British that if Ireland joined the war, then they'd give them Home Rule, so they didn't agree with the rebels trying to get the same thing by force of arms. Eamonn said people like May's parents were blind as bats if they thought the king would ever go home nicely and leave them in peace as a thank you for helping out against his cousin the Kaiser.

May's brother, David, had already joined the British army and gone off to the Great War, and her parents were so proud of him apparently.

And that was a thought… There was no conscription in Ireland, but the British army were recruiting anyone they could get their hands on, and at least it would mean money in his pocket, food, somewhere to sleep and a pair of good boots instead of these uncomfortable shoes.

Eamonn would have a conniption; he hated the British. But so did Mr Redmond under all his calm delivery, and he said it was the right thing to do, to join an Irish regiment to fight the war. And it wasn't like Peter had a lot of options. He was a fugitive, no idea where or what to do next. Joining up would get him out of here quick smart, and it might even be a bit of fun. He'd heard tales back, men who'd joined the Royal Dublin Fusiliers or the Irish guards, that things were rough over there, but that might all be talk, just them boasting about their bravery, the same as the way his father went on about the Rising last year.

Yes, he would tell May he was joining the army.

He was getting cold, just standing around. Maybe there was a shed behind the house and he could sneak in there and sleep for a few hours? He opened the side gate, and thankfully it didn't creak; Michael Gallagher wasn't the kind of man to allow his gates to be creaky apparently. He crept down the side of the house and into the large back garden. Sure enough, the shed was in the far corner. It was small and stacked with forks and spades, a lawn mower, an old bicycle, bags of compost and some tins of paint. One day, he promised himself, he would have the luxury of a house and garden that would require all this stuff, but for now, cold and homeless, he squeezed into the narrow space just inside the door, sitting on the floor next to the lawnmower, and tried to get comfortable. There was no blanket or even an old bit of sacking or anything to cover himself with, but as he heard the pitter-patter of rain on the roof, he was grateful to have shelter at least. It was going to be a long night, though; he'd never be able to sleep…

He woke to the sound of a woman shooing a cat. He eased the shed door open a fraction with his foot and peered through the crack. The sun was just coming up – it was probably half six or seven in the morning – and the woman stood at the back door of the house, crossly flapping her apron at a ginger tabby. She was square and stocky and dressed in a grey uniform, so Peter thought she must be the Gallaghers' housekeeper, Madge, who May said was very sour and complained constantly about her bunions.

Having got rid of the cat, the housekeeper retreated into the house, leaving the back door open. Peter saw his chance.

Creeping out of the shed, he nipped across the garden, keeping close to the hedge, and stuck his head in the back door. If the house-keeper saw him there, he'd pretend he was a delivery boy or something. But she was in the kitchen at the range with her back to him, so he tiptoed quickly along the carpeted hallway and up the stairs, his heart pounding. The landing at the top of the stairs had four doors leading off it, all painted white, with brown Bakelite handles. One of them must be May's bedroom, but which?

The first door was ajar, and he peeped in. It was a bathroom, and Peter marvelled at the idea of having a whole room to yourself to get washed in, one that smelled of freesias and sunlight soap and not a hair astray anywhere. He would have a bathroom all his own one day, he promised himself.

He listened at the door of the next room. No sound, no movement. He turned the handle very softly. The room was empty, a bed made perfectly and some rugby pennants on the walls. The brother, David, off fighting the war, making his parents proud.

So that left the parents' room and May's.

As he approached the next door, he heard movement behind it and retreated into David's bedroom, where he stood with one eye pressed to the crack of the door frame. A tall, paunchy man with grey hair standing on end, dressed in navy striped pyjamas and his feet bare, padded past, bleary-eyed and yawning, and went into the bathroom, closing the door after him.

Without wasting a second, Peter nipped down the landing to the last door, slipping in and closing it behind him. As he leant against it inside the darkened room, his heart beating almost out of his chest, he heard Mr Gallagher padding back to bed. He exhaled slowly, then took in his surroundings.

The curtains let in some of the morning light, and the room was decorated in such a pretty way, he knew his sisters would have swooned if they'd seen it. A dressing table held a mirror, a jug and ewer in delicate china with pink peony roses on them, a brush and comb set in pewter and some glass jars. There was a pink velvet upholstered stool in front of the table, with a fringe of maroon tassel around the bottom. The single bed was covered with a quilt embroidered with flowers, and there was May, fast asleep, her head turned to one side, eyelashes resting on her dimpled cheeks, her pink mouth very slightly open, her rich blond curls fanned out across the pillow. Her hair was much longer than he'd realised; she always wore it neatly pinned under her hat. He thought the curls must reach nearly to her waist.

He crept across the pink silk rug and gently touched her shoulder. She gave a little sigh but didn't stir. 'May,' he said in her ear, giving her a slight shake. 'May, wake up.'

She groaned and tried to settle again, but then her brown eyes flickered open and she murmured dreamily, 'Oh...Peter... What...'

'Shh.' He touched his finger to her lips.

She came to properly then and sat bolt upright, her hands pressed to her chest, staring at him in shock. 'Peter, what are you doing here?' she hissed. 'You shouldn't be in here! Supposing my parents find you?'

'Shh, shh! I'm so sorry to burst in on you like this, May. I just had to see you.'

'But why? What's happened?'

'I came to say goodbye.'

'Goodbye? Why?' Her brown eyes widened with horror.

'I have to go away. Something happened last night with my father. He attacked me because...' He didn't want to tell her about Lady Macbeth or the truth about his family. 'Because I told him I was joining the army. He was furious and threw me out on the street with just the clothes I'm standing up in.'

'Oh my goodness, Peter, you poor thing.' May's confusion changed to that soft look she reserved for him, and she reached up to place her hand against the side of his face. 'How awful for you. He should have been so proud! He's not a republican, is he?'

'I'm afraid he is.' Peter tried to look ashamed. 'He even fought with the rebels in the Post Office.'

'Oh, Peter, that's so awful. What will you do?'

'Join up straight away. I was going to wait until I could tell you properly, but now I've no choice. I've no clothes, no money...' He decided not to mention the nine pounds in his pocket; she might suggest he stay in a hotel so they could have a last day together or something. She'd been born with a silver spoon in her mouth and even had her own bank account, and she wouldn't understand that once his money was spent, there was no more where that came from.

'Oh, Peter.' Her mouth trembled and tears gathered on her lower lids. 'But what about your acting? You're so good at it.'

'The play has finished its run, so I'm not letting anyone down. Maybe if you're at the theatre again soon, you could tell Mr Griffin I've joined up? Just so they know.'

'Of course I will. But, oh, Peter, I don't want you to go.' She sobbed for a moment, wiping her eyes with her sheet, then gave a little shiver and seemed to pull herself together, raising her chin and taking a deep breath. 'But I won't stop you from doing your duty, and I'm going to be so, so proud of you even if your father isn't. You'll have to let me know where you are so I can write and send food and socks and things, like I do for David. And I promise I'll be true to you, and I'll be here waiting for you when you come home.'

He was taken aback. 'Oh, May, that's lovely of you, but...' This wasn't going quite as he'd planned. He hadn't expected May to want to carry on as his sweetheart after he'd joined up. He barely knew her really – and she certainly didn't know him. 'I could be gone for years, and if you meet someone else, well, I'm not going to hold you to anything.'

'Don't be silly. I'm your girl, and I promise you I won't even look at another boy. There's no one in the whole wide world as handsome as you, Peter.' And she smiled bravely at him, though her big brown eyes were still swimming with tears.

Touched and flattered, he leant down to drop a light kiss on her rosy lips. 'I need to get going, May. Supposing your mother or father come in.'

'No, don't go yet. Wait here,' she whispered, glancing at her alarm clock. 'It's seven o'clock already. Mother is in Kildare visiting her sister, but Father will be getting ready for work. I'll go and have breakfast with him and act like I'm poorly, and he'll insist I stay home from the factory for the day, and then I'll bring you up some food. You'll be all right in here. Madge hates the stairs, and she goes out after breakfast to do the shopping, and it takes her hours because of the bunions.'

'Well, all right...' It felt a bit risky, but maybe she was right; she seemed to have it all planned out.

'Just sit on the bed and read or something, and I'll be back in half an hour.'

She put on a pink dressing gown and sheepskin slippers and left the room. Her father must have come out of his room at the same time, because a muffled conversation ensued, her voice and then a deeper one, disappearing together down the stairs.

Left alone, Peter stretched out on her single bed, luxuriating in the softness of the mattress and pillows, and this time it was May who woke Peter, with a tray of tea and toast and bacon and eggs. 'Hi, sleepyhead! Everyone's gone out, so we've got the house to ourselves.' She set the tray on her dressing table and made him sit on the uphol- stered stool to eat while she left the room again. This time she returned with a small brown suitcase and an armful of clothes.

He watched in the dressing table mirror as she placed the case on her bed, then put into it three white shirts, two pairs of flannel trousers, a dark-green pullover, a tie, a tweed jacket, a belt, some underwear and socks and a pair of black lace-up shoes. 'What are you doing?' he asked, wiping his mouth with the napkin she'd given him, though he suspected he knew. Eamonn was right – girls were very helpful when they were sweet on you.

She closed the lid, buckled up the leather straps and clapped her hands together. 'Now you're all packed!'

He pretended to protest. 'Oh, but I can't take all those things!'

'You can and you will,' she replied cheerfully. 'They're David's. He's a bit bigger than you, so the trousers will need the belt. You can bring them back when you come home.'

She set the case by the door, then came to stand before him. 'Now you will come back for me, won't you? I want to wait for you, I really do.' And she looked so innocent and sweet, and she was being so kind, and the breakfast had been so delicious, that he couldn't say anything but what she wanted to hear.

So he smiled at her and said, 'I will, of course. I'll write and tell you where I am and...' He stood and went to take her hand, but she moved towards him at the same time and wound her arms around his neck. Instinctively his arms slid around her slender waist, and the sensation of her warm, young body so close to his caused him to exhale and try to move back. He didn't want her to be horrified at how his body reacted to her. They'd kissed a couple of times, but this was different, here in a bedroom, with her dressing gown fallen open and only her flimsy white nightie between him and her body.

But though he tried to move away, she held him tighter, pressing herself against him. She kissed him then, not an innocent peck on the lips like before, but an urgent, longer-lasting kiss. He ached to open his mouth but didn't dare. And then he didn't have to. Her tongue parted his lips and he was kissing her, fully, like he'd seen people do in the alleyways when they thought nobody was looking. Her hands pulled his shirt out of his trousers, and he could feel her hands on his back, hugging him even tighter as on and on they kissed. There was no mistaking his reaction to her now, but instead of recoiling, she pushed herself against him. He groaned. It took every fibre of his being to pull away, but he had to.

'May,' he said huskily, his ardour unfamiliar to him, 'I... We mustn't...' May was such a respectable, demure young girl, so religious, Sunday Mass and benediction on Sunday evenings. This was totally out of character for her, and he was worried she'd regret it.

'My father is gone to work.' She ran her hands through his hair. 'Madge has gone shopping. We're all alone.' She drew him towards her again, and this time he was powerless to stop her, and he found he didn't want to. And the many liaisons his older brother, Eamonn, had boasted to him about seemed very dull by comparison as May Gallagher undressed and caressed him.

Afterwards, when he was shocked, spent and panting, she looked down at him and smiled, a satisfied little smile that made her rosebud mouth curve at the edges. 'I just needed to make sure I was what you wanted – you're always so gentlemanly. But I did wonder…and now I don't.'

'What?' Peter was still trying to process what had just happened.

'I was worried you didn't like me as a sweetheart but more as a friend.'

'I like you…in every way,' he managed.

'Good. Then I'll wait, and when you come back, we'll get married properly and carry on where we left off?'

'Married…'

She giggled coquettishly. 'Of course we should have done it first, but nobody need know if we don't take too long about it. All the girls at the tennis club are doing it. Their boys are joining up, and it's not right to send your chap away without some experience, we all think.' She pushed off the bed and went to her dresser, where she extracted a bundle of notes from a jar.

He lay there feeling confused and dizzy. He'd come to see May to say goodbye, and now she was talking marriage? Yet it seemed wrong to object after what they'd just done, and the suitcase of clothes was wonderful, and now the rolled-up bundle of notes, which she was placing into a side pocket, was going to be very useful. Besides, she was lovely and he really liked her.

She came back to sit on the bed. 'I think you'll look so handsome in uniform.' She smiled lovingly at him. 'And you know, there's a lot of entertainment in the army. David wrote to me that they had a sort of concert where he was, given by other soldiers, with singers and magicians and everything – it sounded smashing. You're so talented. You could be one of those, and then you wouldn't have to fight and I wouldn't have to worry about you so much.'

He laughed. 'I'm not a good singer, and I can't do magic.'

'Peter, you're so talented, you could do anything,' she said firmly, and she stopped his objections with a kiss.

CHAPTER 5

ICK

THERE HAD BEEN a nice man called Mr Gerrity who came to tune the Steinway piano every year, and Nicholas Shaw thought it as good a name as any other.

At first he worried the recruitment officer in Cork would demand some kind of proof of his identity, but to his surprise, everyone was happy to take his word for who he was. And so Nick Gerrity, born on the 12th of April 1898, with a father who once owned a small grocery store, deceased, and a mother from Waterford, also deceased, was recruited into the Royal Irish Rifles, provided with a uniform and told to show up at the docks the following day to be shipped out to France, and not another question asked. The Honourable Nicholas Vivian Shaw, youngest son of the fifth Baron de Simpré, was no more.

Afterwards, he went to a branch of the Royal Bank of Ireland and produced his bankbook. He asked to withdraw fifty shillings, and also for the rest of his savings, about a hundred pounds, to be transferred into the account of his grandmother, the Honourable Alicia Shaw. He signed, *The Honourable Vivian Nicholas Shaw.*

It was the last time he ever intended to use that name.

The clerk made no remark when he handed back the bankbook with the cash, but as Nick was turning to leave, the manager came after him. 'Ah, your…er…your… Sir…' He was most obsequious in his manner.

Nick's heart sank. It looked like he would have to use his old name one more time or be accused of fraud. 'Shaw, N-N-Nicholas.' He turned and shook the man's outstretched hand politely.

'Ah yes, your father is the Baron de Simpré, is he not? I had the honour to make the baron's acquaintance at a reception last year.'

'That's right.' He would keep this short.

'Well, just to say, sir, that…well, that anything we can do to assist you, then we'd be happy to do so.'

Nick nodded. 'Thank you. B-b-but I'd rather you kept my visit to yourself p-p-please.'

The man was now making 'that face', the one Nick had had to put up with all his life, whenever his nervous stammer overcame him – pity mixed with condescension. 'Of course I will. Say no more, sir.'

'Thank you.' Nick shook his hand a second time and left.

Back out on the streets of Cork, he walked north towards the Metropole Hotel, where he would stay for his last night of luxury.

It might have been considered bourgeois to stay in a hotel, but the room he had booked into was lovely. It had a large double bed, with a big comforter and feather pillows, and the mattress was so comfortable compared to the cold dormitory in boarding school or the horrible ancient horsehair mattresses at Brockleton. Apparently aristocrats led very uncomfortable lives compared to the self-indulgent middle classes.

It had been such a fast process at the recruitment office that the hotel was still serving breakfast, and as he dined on kippers, poached eggs and toast, he felt a contentment pass over him that was unfamiliar.

All his life, for as long as he could remember, he'd been tense.

Trying to avoid his brothers' teasing, trying to gain his father's approval, trying not to see his mother's disdain for him. Then at school, more bully avoidance. He was a reasonably able scholar; he did all right at his books but nothing spectacular. His old French master, Monsieur Moreau, said he had a good accent, and he actually found it easier not to stammer in French; maybe because when he was speaking it, he felt like a different person altogether, someone handsome and suave. He wondered what his former French master would make of him heading off to France tomorrow.

He would never know what Monsieur Moreau thought about it. He was never going to go back to his old life, never go back to that school. And that knowledge was wonderfully relaxing...apart from one thing.

Transferring his money into his grandmother's account was his way of saying to her that she wasn't forgotten, but he hated the idea of never seeing her again. Saying goodbye to her for the last time had been very painful.

Alicia Shaw had arrived home from Brighton the day after the baron, returning to comfort her son and his wife over their loss as soon as she'd heard of her grandson's death. Nick had already made up his mind to run away but had stayed on for an extra day to see his grandmother one last time.

He hadn't intended to wake her when he'd slipped into her bedroom early the following morning. It was coming light outside, but the room was darkened, as the heavy drapes were drawn. Floss was still sleeping, and with a rush of affection for the old woman, he had leant down to kiss her dry papery cheek as he blinked back his tears. It was the last time he would ever see her, and he did love her, and she loved him in return.

As he straightened up, ready to creep out, her eyelids fluttered.

'Nicholas, darling, is it you?'

He stopped and turned back, caught out. 'Yes, Floss.'

She felt for her spectacles on the bedside locker and put them on. 'Are you all right, Nicholas? Open the curtains please.'

He did, letting the pale morning light into the room as she pushed herself up against the pillows. She was a tall, fine-looking woman, with long blond hair streaked with silver and grey and cool grey eyes.

'What is it, Nicholas? Why are you here?'

'I've decided to join up, Floss.'

'Oh, Nicky, must you really?' She held out her hand, and he came to sit on the side of her bed. 'Your parents have already lost one son. Supposing they lost you too?'

'Father wants one of his sons to be fighting the war. He's a patriot and likes to show it. But I don't think it should be W-W-Wally. If he died, that would break Father's heart.'

She looked fondly at him. 'My darling boy, that is so good of you to think of your father's feelings. But you know he loves you every bit as much as he loves Wally.'

Nick smiled at her, and she dropped her gaze, because they both knew it wasn't true. 'I don't want you to go to war, Nicky,' she said softly. 'I'm so very fond of you.'

'I don't want to either, Floss, and I'm fond of you too, but I have t-t-to go. Besides, everyone I know is going, lots of the boys from school, or their older brothers.' He stood up and moved towards the door. 'Goodbye. Try not to worry about me, and take care of Mother and Father and don't let them argue too much, and tell Wally to mind himself and enjoy looking after Brockleton.'

She threw back the covers then and padded in her bare feet and long white nightdress towards him. She was nearly as tall as him, but thin. She placed one hand on his broad chest and the other on his face.

'Be careful, Nicky. Don't take unnecessary risks or act all brave like I'm sure Roger was doing. I want you to keep your head down and come home safely, do you hear? Have you let your parents know you're going?'

'Not yet. I'll write t-t-to them.'

'Why not tell them face to face?'

He smiled at her. 'Because Father will only remind me I'm not officer material.'

'Oh my dear, don't pay any attention to him – that's just him being in a bad mood. Of course you're officer material. You're his son, the son of a baron. Hold up your head like a good boy and don't let anyone tell you otherwise.'

'But my stammer, Floss...'

'Don't be silly. I've heard a great deal worse in the officer ranks, I can assure you.'

He didn't argue with her. When he was around his grandmother, he barely stammered at all, compared to how he was with everyone else. So she wouldn't understand. 'Goodbye, Floss,' he said simply.

'Make sure to write, my darling.'

'I will – I promise.'

Now, sitting in the hotel, he blinked back a tear as he remembered that parting, and how he realised at that moment that she was all he had in the world. And now he had no one, because even if he survived the war, there was no way he was ever going back to Brockleton or the parents who despised him. Even to see his darling grandmother.

He was going to join up as a private, disappear from view and never go home.

He placed his knife and fork neatly side by side, and the waitress took his empty plate and gave him a shy smile. He blushed. Having only brothers and going to a boy's boarding school, he had no experience whatsoever of girls and found them terrifying. And he had absolutely no desire to have a relationship with one, not after being raised by two parents who clearly hated each other. Why anyone would enter into the state of matrimony was, to him, bewildering.

CHAPTER 6

NORTHERN FRANCE, JULY 1917

 *ETER*

WHEN PETER JOINED up at the Dublin recruiting office, he was assigned to the Royal Irish Rifles and shipped out to Flanders straight away. He'd been surprised at how easy it had been at the time, not much in the way of paperwork. They didn't ask for any identification, and now that he was here, he could see why. It was a slaughterhouse, nothing short of it. The lads from the Royal Dublin Fusiliers had not been exaggerating.

Starving, disease-ridden, absolutely exhausted men, in hellish conditions, awaiting the instructions of some fat officer sitting in a London club with a belly full of steak and brandy, puffing on a cigar and pushing soldiers around a board like it was a game.

It felt like years they'd been stuck in these positions, a few hundred yards won or lost, and it seemed like nothing would ever change.

Maybe he'd still be here when he was twenty-five, or thirty, or fifty. Going up and down the bleedin' line.

It wasn't even something one could get used to. He was terrified every time he heard that whistling sound, followed by the earth-moving boom of a German mortar landing. And the fact that the Hun were trying to blow his trench to bits daily was only one of his endless sea of troubles; the mud, the bloody endless rain, the lack of rations – those things would have been bad enough even if no one was shooting at him.

To say nothing of the rats.

Being from Henrietta Street, he'd thought he was used to them, but in the trenches, they were huge and they were everywhere. You had to be so careful not to let any food out – the disgusting creatures could find it no matter where you stashed it – so whatever you got, you ate standing up, there and then. It turned his stomach when he saw them gorging on the dead bodies out in No Man's Land, poor young lads lying there waiting for a gap in the fighting so their remains could be rescued and buried.

And it wasn't just dead bodies that the rats liked. One night, in the bunk beside his in their foxhole, Jethro, a lad from Bournemouth, woke screaming that he'd been bitten, and sure enough he had – a rat had taken a chunk out of his forearm. Jethro got blood poisoning and had to have his arm amputated from the elbow down, and everyone agreed he was a lucky bugger, getting to go home.

Trench foot was another curse to be avoided. Peter had learnt to try to keep his feet dry, to change his socks as often as he could, to take care of his body inasmuch as was possible on short rations. Thank God for May, who sent him boxes of hand-knitted socks and huge food parcels every week, which he would retrieve when he was behind the lines. The girl was an angel, she really was.

The Third Battle of Ypres was meant to be the turning point of the Great War. Since last July the fighting had been fiercest around the town of Passchendaele, which was located on the last ridge east of Ypres and more or less on the supply line that the Hun used to get food to their troops. The theory was that once Passchendaele was captured, then the German 4th Army was going to be absolutely banjaxed and the crushing defeat of the Kaiser would soon follow. But they'd heard a lot of this old guff before.

The battle should have been won already, everyone kept saying, except it never stopped bloody raining and tanks just sank in the mud. Rumour had it that the top brass were fighting among themselves, with Lloyd George wanting to wait for the Yanks but Haig, the leader of the British Expeditionary Force, wanting to press on with the same stupid tactics, and what harm if his men were slaughtered daily? He was some eejit, that Haig, and Jellicoe not a hair better. Easy for them, sitting in London. They wouldn't last ten minutes on the front line.

Peter got the job of messenger in the army, just like he had been for the Guinness brewery in Dublin. He had followed May's suggestion that he tell the recruiting officer he was an actor and really interested in getting involved in the entertainment of the troops, but the man had just laughed at him and asked him what his day job was. Peter had told him 'messenger', which had gone down a lot better.

He'd been trained in map reading and reconnaissance, and now he wore a red armband and was known as a runner, delivering messages up and down the line. The other privates thought he was lucky, having the freedom to roam around. But mostly it was an awful job, running out in the open along the duckboards, the raised platforms over the sodden ground, trying to avoid being shot or bombed, and he wished he'd known before he signed up what he was getting himself into.

The English lads hadn't had a choice; they'd been conscripted. And everywhere, miserable half-starved boys crowded on top of each other, huddling for what little food or warmth there was in this hell on earth. Peter saw men carted off by stretcher who'd endured gas attacks, those who were blinded, those who'd lost bits of their faces, their limbs and worse. Then there were those who'd just gone barmy, couldn't take it. Last week some Geordie lad just calmly, without a word to anyone, climbed out, up the ladder, over the sandbags and walked straight out. Kept walking till the sniper bullet got him. He'd had enough.

Everyone said they knew how he felt.

Not everyone was as bad off as these poor sods, though, left to rot in the waterlogged, rat-infested dugouts, scrambling for a few bits of bread or dry biscuits. Even here in the trenches, the class structure the English were so fond of was alive and well. The officers, captains and lieutenants somehow stayed dryer, and ate, if not good grub, then at least enough.

One bunch of officers about two miles up the line had quite a nice set-up: dry bunks, warm blankets and even an odd bottle of the local wine. When Peter delivered messages there, he loved to just stand for a while in their dugout. There was a little stove, so it was warm, and they sat around playing cards, braying 'top hole' and 'jolly good show' and going on about Oxford and Cambridge rowing races and Lady this and Viscount that. Posh twats. It wasn't right that just because they were higher born than him and his mates that they had such a cushy time of it while the poor privates rotted in the cold and wet. They even had a Decca gramophone and a whole pile of records, some classical, some popular music of the day.

He often lifted some biscuits or a pair of socks when they weren't looking. And last week he'd decided to relieve them of the gramophone, and he did it without compunction.

He wasn't a thief at home; he liked to play things straight, and he despised his da for being lying and conniving. But life in the trenches had changed him. He had realised that being good, doing the right thing as dictated by people who saw themselves as superior, wasn't necessarily the right thing. The officers didn't care a jot about him and the other privates. The common soldiers were just numbers to them, and it mattered nothing to the top brass in England who lived or died so long as the war was won. That realisation could make one bitter, or it could make one resourceful. Peter chose the latter.

He introduced himself to the officers in the swanky dugout as Pat Murphy, and listened patiently to all their jokes about Paddies, pretending to take it all in good humour. Some of them had even served in Dublin during the Rising and as a result held his fellow countrymen in very low esteem, but Peter assured them he was different to his duplicitous, murderous fellow countrymen – wasn't he here fighting for England's cause? – and they came to trust him.

Tonight the four officers had finally invited him to play poker, something he'd been angling after for weeks.

Peter brought two things to the game with him.

One was his stake, a bottle of cherry brandy, which he'd lifted from a different officer's set-up in a local hotel; the man was so soused, he'd never know. It was one of the perks of being a messenger – he could go anywhere, any time, no questions asked. He regularly delivered messages to the brothel in Poperinge, as one of the captains was obsessed with the madame and more or less lived there. The poor girls in the brothel were always hungry, and many of them had children, so sometimes he brought them a packet of biscuits, and soda bread too if May had sent it. It was often stale by the time he received it, but it was better than nothing. They offered him their services in return, but he politely declined. Too many of his fellow soldiers had fallen victim to VD, which was what everyone called venereal disease for short, and he wasn't going to be next.

The second thing he brought to the game was a grenade.

One of the lads up the line used to play a practical joke on his comrades by pulling the ring on a grenade and sending everyone diving for cover, then using the opportunity to filch their smokes or dirty postcards. What he'd done was taken all the explosive out so the grenade was empty and then put it back together. People were wise to him now, so the lad was happy to let Peter have the hollow grenade in return for one of the packets of cigarettes sent over by May.

That night, as he studied his cards, Peter held the grenade in one hand, idly flicking the pin up and down.

'I say, old chap, you're making me nervous. Put that down, would you?' asked a frightfully posh-sounding fellow with a pencil moustache and a livid scar from his temple to his jaw.

But Peter just smiled. 'Don't worry. This one should have got me yesterday, landed right beside me but never detonated. It's my good luck charm. I don't want to lose my brandy.'

'That doesn't mean it won't detonate now, for God's sake. Stop flicking it, Paddy,' another of the four complained; he had emerald-green eyes that slanted arrogantly.

Peter studied all their haughty patrician faces, grinned widely and pulled out the pin. With yells of fright, they instantly jumped up and ran, shouting expletives as they scarpered, upending the table and knocking over the empty ammunition supply boxes they'd been using as stools.

The grenade of course did nothing, but the toffs were gone far enough away down the trench not to notice, and at that precise moment, the Hun decided to land a bloody great shell about fifteen feet away, sending sand and earth flying. In the ensuing melee – whistles blowing, barked orders to retaliate, smoke and gunfire everywhere – Peter grabbed the gramophone and the records, shoved them in one of the ammunition cases and ran up the line away from the action. His red armband marked him as a messenger, which meant he was never questioned as another private would have been had he been caught running away from an engagement.

When he arrived back at his own dugout, panting and delighted with himself, he found it empty.

Damn. He'd been looking forward to playing the records for his mates. He didn't know what type of music they liked, if any, but surely anything would do to break the terrifying monotony of war.

He changed his wet socks for another pair May had knitted for him, took one of his precious remaining cigarettes out of its packet and went out for a smoke. He never used to smoke back at home, but here it was something to do, and it took the edge off the hunger. The sun was low in the sky, and he went around the side of the dugout. One of the previous occupants, dead now, had constructed a kind of platform there, which was a good place to sit. It was high enough that your feet were out of the water but low enough that your head was beneath the parapet, because otherwise – well, it was curtains.

He was happy to find Enzo Riccio there before him, a lad around his age. Lorenzo was his real name, but everyone called him Enzo. He was from London, and spoke in a strong Cockney accent, but his father was Italian, an ice cream maker, and he was named for him. He had so many stories about his romantic conquests, and Peter believed them all. He had dark kiss-curled hair, flashing dark eyes and sculpted cheekbones, and he reminded Peter of a statue he'd seen in Glasnevin Cemetery in Dublin, where his father's parents were buried. He'd no idea who it was, an angel or something. The day they buried his granny, Peter had been bored by the priest droning on and he'd studied the face of the statue over the tomb of some bigwig. He didn't fancy lads, he knew that, but he admired that sculpture, and he admired Enzo too. Like the way you would a piece of art.

On the far side of Enzo was another soldier, tall and broad who Peter didn't recognise.

'Alrigh', Paddy?' Enzo greeted him by shifting his behind along the platform. Peter was used to being called Paddy now, though he didn't like it. The English called all Irishmen Paddy as far as he could tell.

'Not bad, Enzo. You?' Peter said, pulling himself up to sit on the plank.

'Apart from freezin' my whatsits off, 'alf starved to death and being wrinkled like a prune from the bloody wet you mean?'

Peter laughed. 'Yeah, apart from that.' His feet were dry, but his stomach grumbled. The tinned bully beef and hard biscuit ration was gone. He'd nicked a bit of bread from the officers' dugout along with the gramophone, and ate it as he ran, but it hadn't filled him at all; he was still starving. But then two fat rats ran along the sandbags, bloated from dead men's flesh, and his appetite faded.

'Well, I've just been making friends with our new lodger here. He's a Paddy like yerself, God 'elp me.'

'Go way outta that. You're glad enough to have us fighting the Hun beside you.' Peter lit his cigarette and leant across to the other Irishman, holding out a hand to shake. 'Peter Cullen, Dublin. Runner.' He tapped his armband.

'N-N-Nick Gerrity, W-W-Waterford.' The young man winced; his stammer clearly annoyed him. He had a round face, a broad chest and innocent blue eyes framed by long dark lashes. Peter thought he could have been any age really. He had brown curls that had been cut off by the army but which were now stubbornly growing in whorls around the brim of his hat.

'How long you been at the front, Nick?'

'F-f-f-forty years.' He smiled, and Peter warmed to him.

'F-feels like that anyway. In reality, three weeks. I was at a station out at C-C-Calais, but we got moved in here for the Big Push. Lost the rest of my platoon t-t-two weeks ago, got shoved across here, into your dugout. They said you had a spare bunk.'

Peter sighed. 'Yeah, that was Norris. He was shot by a sniper last night.'

'Poor kid,' added Enzo, and the three of them sat and smoked in silence for a while, thinking about how short life was. Their section was quiet for a change, and Peter rested his head against the boards that covered the side of the dugout behind him and looked up at the sky, usually a dull monotonous grey but now streaked with pink and crimson. It was nice to see a bit of colour for once. The sandbags that lined the top of the trench and formed the walls below, only interrupted by ladders to climb over the top, were all dun-coloured. Uniforms of khaki, bunks with dark-green blankets, black earth churned up from shells, boots and grenades, tank traps and barbed wire, and the whole lot covered in a blanket of dark-brown mud. There was no colour in this war, nothing to brighten the miserable, sodden landscape, except this sunset.

'It's so b-b-boring, isn't it?' Nick said suddenly. 'Petrifying and b-boring in equal measure.'

'You scared of death?' Enzo asked casually.

Nick appeared to consider his answer. 'Not of being dead,' he said eventually. 'That'll be fine. But the d-d-dying bit...'

They both knew what he meant. Last night it had been poor Norris, groaning out on No Man's Land, injured, unable to move; on and on he'd moaned and cried. The stretcher bearers made several attempts, to be fair, but he was too close to the German line and the German snipers were watching and waiting and peppered them every time they came close. The captain in the next dugout was a crack shot, so eventually he'd crept up the ladder and fired, and the moaning stopped.

'It was nice of you to give Norris your chocolate ration yesterday morning, Enzo,' Peter said lightly.

Enzo shot him a sharp look. 'Don't start that again, Paddy. He was sad about his sweetheart dumpin' him. I just reckoned the poor bloke needed cheerin' up, that's all.'

'Start what again?' asked Nick, interested.

'Enzo here is the seventh son of a seventh son...' began Peter, grinning widely.

"Ow about you shut yer cakehole or I'll shut it for ya?' Enzo said darkly, and Peter slung his arm around his mate's shoulders, gave him an affectionate hug.

'Ah I'm sorry Enzo, I'm only sayin''.

The rumour about Enzo having second sight was partly his own fault; he'd made the mistake of telling several people about the seventh son thing, which was actually true. But then two brothers, the Davidsons, were sent on a reconnaissance to a section of No Man's Land, and Enzo had given them his last cigarettes. They trod on a mine and were blown to smithereens.

Then he'd helped another private, Bennett, to write home, and the boy was killed a few hours later.

After the Bennett thing, the other soldiers started acting nervous around him, especially if he offered them a cigarette or something, and Enzo realised everyone thought he knew whether they were going to die and got quite upset about it. He was still living the whole thing down.

'So what d-d-did you two do before this funfair?' asked Nick, tactfully changing what was obviously a sore subject. 'Peter?'

'I'm an actor.' The recruiting sergeant had laughed when he'd said that, but he'd be damned if he'd let his dream go forever. If he survived this war, and that was a big if, he wouldn't be running messages for anyone ever again; only a right eejit would go backwards.

Nick didn't laugh; he looked impressed. 'Would I have heard of you?'

'Nah, I was just starting out, then this happened. But if I live, I'm going back to the theatre.' He removed his arm from Enzo's shoulders, smoked the cigarette down to the butt, then tossed it in the murky water below. 'What about you?'

'I worked in my p-p-parents' shop.'

'Oh? What kind of shop?' Life was so short here that it was normal to ask a lot of questions straight away. Friendships in the trenches grew fast and were often intense. Nobody knew when it might all be over. And this big fellow Irishman intrigued Peter. He was somehow too soft for here, not classically handsome like Enzo, but there was something compelling about him, a sort of quiet confidence despite the stammer.

'G-g-grocery.'

'In Waterford?'

Nick nodded, and Peter let it go. He had an ear for accents, and he'd known Nick was lying as soon as he'd said he was from Waterford. And as for working in a grocery shop…very unlikely. Enzo might not be able to tell the difference between one 'Paddy' accent and another, but Peter could, and he knew that Nick Gerrity, or whatever his name was, did not come out of a lowly grocer's shop, and he also suspected Nick belonged more with the officers in their cushy dugout up the line than down here with him and Enzo. He decided not to ask for any more information, though. Nick's business was his own.

'How about you?' Nick asked the Londoner.

Enzo shrugged. 'My old man had an ice cream van – he had it off his father – and I worked for 'im, but 'is family are circus people, performers, so I reckon I'm more like them.'

'Seriously?' Nick looked impressed all over again.

'Yeah, all my father's family were circus people, all my aunties and uncles and cousins, my *nonno* and *nonna* too. My *nonno*, 'e was one of the best clowns you'd ever find. 'E was mates with the family of the great Joseph Grimaldi, you know? The most famous circus clown what ever lived. Nonno used to 'ave 'em rollin' in the aisles, 'e did.'

'In England?'

'No, Italy. I spent all my summer 'olidays travelling wiv me *nonno* and *nonna*. They had me doing acrobatic shows ever since I was a littl'un, my cousins throwing me about like a rag doll, and then they got me on the trapeze and tightrope when I was older, no safety net. Not that my mum knew – she'd 'ave blown a gasket. And sometimes I rode on the circus ponies.'

Peter pricked up his ears; it was the first time he'd heard Enzo talking about the ponies. 'What other animals did they have?'

'A dog that could count to three – he was smart. We had an elephant for a while, but 'e was really old when we got him and 'e died.'

'Anything else?'

'A huge fat bloke who pretended to be a giant, and a woman with a beard – she was boring. My *nonna* was a fortune-teller. She read palms and 'ad an old crystal ball, all of that...' He saw Peter grinning again and scowled fiercely. 'She was good at readin' people's faces, Paddy, that's all. She just got these feelings, OK, sort of based on what they were telling her.'

A distant patter of Jerry guns, hitting a section of trench much further up the line, made them lift their heads, and they sat listening as their own guns returned the fire. The sunset had faded to night now, and the stars were beginning to appear in the sky.

Then Enzo made a sudden show of offering Peter a cigarette, and he went into peals of laughter at the horrified expression on Peter's face. 'Don't get your wind up, Paddy, just messin'.' He chuckled.

Peter's heart was thumping, but he laughed too. 'Very funny, Enzo. Don't be doing that, OK?'

'You'll be fine. Want to know the feeling I have about you? That you'll survive, and you and me, we'll be chums forever. Nick here as well if he likes.'

Nick coloured. 'I d-d-do like.'

Enzo nodded and lit the cigarette he had pretended to offer to

Peter, the glow from the match illuminating his handsome face. 'A bloke needs 'is mates out here, that's for sure. So we'll all three look out for each other, what do you reckon?'

'Like swear an oath of f-f-friendship?' Nick looked at them hopefully, and there was something so open, so innocent about his request, Peter felt a wave of affection for him. He must have been to a posh kind of school, though; nobody at Peter's school ever swore an oath of friendship – they were more likely battering each other.

'Mates,' said Enzo seriously, putting his hand out, palm up.

'M-m-mates,' Nick echoed, placing his hand on Enzo's.

Peter placed his hand on top of theirs. 'Mates, to the death.'

To his surprise, there was nothing awkward about it. They were sealed in friendship now, and that was that. It was something he'd never really experienced before. He'd played with Eamonn and the girls when he was a small lad, and all the others in Henrietta Street, and he knew a few of the delivery lads at the brewery and some of the actors, and of course May. But actively making a new friend for the purpose of friendship alone was something he'd never considered.

A flare went up closer by, and a volley of machine-gun fire, followed by a scream, then the thumping crunch of a shell landing. 'Them bloody whizz-bangs. I 'ate them ones.' Enzo rubbed his ears. He'd been complaining of tinnitus all week. 'At least the bloomin' coal boxes don't wreck yer ears.'

Answering machine-gun fire came from further down the line. It was always so noisy at the front. A moment later, out in No Man's Land, a shell squealed and landed with a bang that sent the earth in the trench shuddering, dislodging a bank of sandbags only thirty yards along. That would be someone's job tomorrow, filling and lugging heavy sandbags down here to replace the ones blown out. Even at this distance, the impact sprayed the three of them with damp sand, and Peter wiped grit from his streaming eyes. There was an ominous scurry of rats too, disturbed by the explosion.

'Right, lads, I'm out of here. This is getting too hairy for me.' He hopped down off the plank, followed by the others.

Back inside the dugout, he lit a candle, opened the ammunition box and set up the gramophone on his flat, hard bunk.

'Where did you g-g-get that?' Nick asked in astonishment.

'Ah, some friends of mine didn't want it any more,' Peter said silkily, placing a record on the turntable and winding the handle. The volume wasn't much good – it was a bit low – but the unmistakable sounds of Vesta Tilley's 'Jolly Good Luck to the Girl Who Loves a Soldier' filled the night air. Enzo knew the words and sang along at full volume, completely out of tune.

'Reminds me of one of me old girlfriends,' he said, when it came to an end. 'Last time I was on leave, she announces she don't love 'er husband no more, and she's goin' to leave 'im for me, so I knew it was time for me to 'oppit, and I cut me leave a few days short.'

Enzo had told this story before, and there was one chap in the next-door dugout, a Scotsman, a big brawny chap with red hair, who couldn't believe his ears when he heard Enzo boasting about it. 'When I get leave, I dinna hardly have time to get to Glasgow, let alone do anything I shouldna be doing,' he'd said, and he explained how by the time he'd made it to Calais, then Folkstone, then London, and finally all the way to Scotland, he barely had time to kiss his girlfriend, Betty, and have a cuppa with his mother in the station café before he had to get on the next train to be back in time. His gorgeous Betty, the woman of his dreams, was a strong-minded girl, and she didn't like him spending any of his precious time with his mother, who was also a formidable character. The way he described them slogging it out and dragging him to and fro between them on the platform was hilarious; he'd had Peter and Enzo rolling around. Everyone called the Scotsman Two-Soups because his name was Baxter Campbell. He had a ready smile and a ridiculous number of jokes at his fingertips, and Peter had been very sorry when a shell had exploded on top of the dugout and Two-Soups had been dragged out unconscious and carted off in an ambulance, probably never to be seen again.

'So you d-d-didn't love her?' asked Nick, curious.

'Gawd no. And it wasn't just the married one, to be 'onest,' confessed Enzo. 'Romantically speaking, things was getting a little 'ot and 'eavy all round, 'cause, well, she wasn't the only one, if you get my meaning? So I thought, time to bugger off sharpish. Coming back to this' – he waved his hand around the dugout – 'wasn't my finest idea, though, in 'indsight.'

The three of them laughed, and Peter put on another record, 'Keep the Home Fires Burning' by Stanley Kirkby, and they all roared the words out in unison. The patriotic lyrics and the upbeat mood of the music was so incongruous with the reality of their lives, it added to their mirth, and they ended up in stitches.

After that, Enzo stopped singing and just listened. 'I know I can't sing – you know I can't. My old mum said I couldn't carry a tune in a bucket, and she was right.'

They didn't try to persuade him otherwise.

The next record in the pile was 'It's a Long Way to Tipperary', which Peter and Nick sang quite mournfully, thinking of Ireland, and the one after that had a funny-looking label, but Peter put it on anyway. A beautiful tenor voice drifted out, singing in a lilting and exotic language he didn't understand, and the laughter in the dugout died down.

'*Che bella cosa 'na giornata 'e sole L'aria serena doppo 'na tempesta...*'

'It's in Italian,' breathed Enzo, his eyes shining.

Just then an officer's voice Peter recognised as belonging to Major Stubbs, a sadistic brute of a man, boomed in the darkness. 'Lights out and no smoking, you horrible little lot! Jerry's getting active tonight!'

Peter removed the needle from the record. It wouldn't do to draw attention to themselves with Stubbs for any reason.

As the major's strident voice carried on away down the trench, Enzo went on speaking, his voice lowered now. 'I miss hearing that language. I miss everything about Italy, the sunshine, the beautiful ladies, the wine, the olives. Sometimes in my dreams I can almost taste the gelati and the focaccia. I dunno when I'll ever see it again...' His voice conveyed a wistful sadness so powerful, Peter felt a lump in his throat.

Then from beside them came Nick's voice, not like they'd heard before, stammering and shy or singing along loudly and comically with Peter, but a melodious resonant tenor.

'*Che bella cosa 'na jurnata 'e sole L'aria serena doppo 'na tempesta...*' He sang softly, with no hesitancy.

'*Pe' ll'aria fresca pare già 'na festa Che bella cosa 'na jurnata 'e sole. Ma n'atu sole cchiù bello, oi ne'. 'O sole mio, sta in fronte a te. 'O sole, 'o sole mio, sta in fronte a te. Sta in fronte a te.*'

Nick finished and turned and smiled at his companions, who stood dumbstruck.

'You know Italian?' Enzo asked, wiping a tear from his eye.

'No, afraid n-n-not, just the words of the song.'

'That was amazing. I never heard as good,' said Peter truthfully. 'And you never stammered once.'

'I d-d-don't when I sing.'

'*Grazie amico,*' Enzo said seriously, patting Nick's shoulder. 'I don't know much about singin' and that, but that was outstanding. You need to be on the stage, my friend.'

CHAPTER 7

 AY

MAY STRETCHED out in her comfortable little bed, staring at the white ceiling, making her plans for the day, which was a Saturday.

She needed to stitch buttons onto the new shirt she had made for Peter on her mother's Singer sewing machine, which was operated by a foot pedal. Then finish up the long letter she'd been writing to him all week. Go to the shops to buy Barry's tea, sugar, lots of packets of biscuits, sweets, chocolate and cigarettes, and put it all into a big card-board box with the shirt and the seven pairs of socks she had also made that week. Deliver Peter's latest letter to his sister Kathleen – not in person, just by leaving it with one of the floor walkers in Arnotts where she worked behind the scenes – and check if there was any word from her to him, then take the box to the post office and post it to France.

On top of all that, she had to come up with a plan to help Peter's new friend.

The letter Peter had sent said he hoped she was well, and he'd thanked her for the socks and everything. It was all a bit too friendly and formal for her liking; she would have loved some romantic stuff, but he wasn't that kind of chap.

He'd asked if she could work out how to help a fellow called Nick Gerrity, who needed to get in touch with somebody who lived or worked – she wasn't sure which – in a big house called Brockleton in Cork, and whether May could find out a way to get a letter to this person without going through the post. It was a challenge, but May loved running errands for Peter, being his representative while he was away bravely defending them all. Maybe she could talk to her friend Harriet from the tennis club who had a housekeeper called Molly whose son lived in Cork...

She thought she'd better get up and get started; it would take her hours to do everything. She only hoped Mother wouldn't decide to skip her church flowers meeting and stay home to fuss over her and force her to stay in bed. May had made the mistake of sneezing when she came home from work yesterday, and her mother had acted like she had TB and made her go straight to bed with a hot water bottle, when all she'd wanted to do was finish off Peter's shirt in the sewing room.

At least she'd been able to knit him another pair of socks on the quiet, in between her mother popping in to make sure she was resting. May was very quick and nimble with her needles, and she was able to send Peter a lot of socks these days because she was no longer knitting them for David. Poor David. He was missing in action, and she knew her parents feared the worst, even if they wouldn't say it. That's why they had her wrapped in cotton wool all the time. And she did sympathise and understand, but her mother especially could be so suffocating.

May was upset about David as well, but she was sure he would come home alive. She'd prayed to God to keep him safe, and God was good about answering her prayers, which is how she'd known from the start that she was going to marry Peter, the minute she saw him up there on the stage, looking so handsome, even with all the make-up and having to pretend to be drunk because he was playing that funny porter fellow in 'the Scottish play'.

A tentative knock on her bedroom door interrupted her thoughts, and she sat up in bed in her nightie. 'Morning, Mother,' she said brightly as her mother entered with a tray of tea and toast. 'I'm feeling so much better. You didn't need to bring me breakfast in bed.'

'Oh, but, May, love, you look terribly pale. I really think I should send for Dr Gleeson. I'm so worried about you…'

Olive Gallagher was a plain woman; May got her good looks from her father's side. Her father's sister, Auntie Marie, was stunning, and everyone said May looked just like her. Olive had a broad face, mousy-brown hair, light-blue eyes and a nose a touch too big. She wasn't fat, but she was soft and shapeless, and her personality was sort of soft and shapeless too.

'Not at all, Mother,' May said firmly. 'I haven't sneezed once in all this time I've been awake, so I really think there's nothing wrong with me at all.'

'Are you sure, dear? I wish you weren't mixing with all those common people, with all their awful illnesses. I know, I know. They are fine people, I'm not saying they're not, but living on top of each other in the tenements like that, well, disease spreads, doesn't it? And then they come into work, and they might pass it on to you.'

'Now, Mother, you know we all have to help the war effort, and it's not like I'm on the factory floor with the women from the tenements.'

May was determined to keep her job at the shell factory on Park-gate Street, where she did typing and filing in the office of the general manager, Mr Swift. It was tedious and harder work than she'd expected for a white-collar job, but it was still better than sitting at home with Mother, day in, day out. She was gradually getting more responsibility and was proving herself to be a good organiser, and Mr Swift was impressed.

'But all that going to and fro in all weathers,' fretted her mother. 'Lydia Carney got a terrible wetting a few weeks ago. The three o'clock tram never came, and then the next one was too full and whizzed past so she got drenched, and it turned into a chill, then influenza, and eventually she was put in hospital with pneumonia. She's lucky to have survived, Deirdre was telling me after Mass yesterday. She had the Mass said for her recovery, and Father O'Reilly joined us afterwards and said there's a lot of nasty bugs about.'

May knew she'd have to head her mother off, because if she went down the road of the gospel according to Father O'Reilly, they'd be here all day. She threw back the bedclothes and jumped out of bed. 'I promise you, Mother, I'm as fit as a fiddle. I think I'll get dressed now.'

'Oh no, don't, May, please don't do that.' Her mother looked like she might cry. 'You really were very poorly last night, and I think a day tucked up warmly in bed will do you the world of good. Father had to go and see a man in Kildare about the lawnmower, but he left word you were to rest today. He's worried about you too, and he'd never forgive me if you didn't. Get back into bed, May, while I let in some sunshine.'

Mother set down the tray on the dressing table and opened the pretty floral curtains she'd had made to match the coverlet and pillowcases on May's bed, then brought the breakfast over. 'I just worry about you, May,' she said fretfully, standing with the tray in her hands while her daughter reluctantly climbed back beneath the blankets.

May felt a pang of pity for her mother, so terrified of losing both her children. It had been David's twenty-first birthday last week, and that day had felt like it would never end. They'd gone to Mass, had it said for him, and then afterwards the three of them had stood in the churchyard, not knowing what to do next.

For birthdays since they were little, Mother would bake a cake and there would be a candle to blow out and a gift, and other children would be invited to tea and to play pin the tail on the donkey. But what did you do for the birthday of your only son and brother who was missing all the way over in France? Ignore it? Have cake? Sit around talking about him? It was impossible to know.

'All right, I won't get up, though I'm perfectly capable,' she said, settling back against the pillows and accepting the cup of tea and dainty triangles of toast and marmalade. 'Don't you have your meeting this morning with the ladies who do the flowers for the church altar?'

'Oh, I'm not going if you're ill. Of course I'm not.' The woman looked horrified at the very thought of leaving her sick daughter's bedside.

'Ah, Mother, don't be silly. You must. Otherwise, you know what will happen – instead of daffodils or dahlias, Mrs Cuddihy will think she has free rein and will cover the altar with her own sweet peas and lily of the valley, and poor Father O'Reilly's hay fever will go haywire.' She laughed gaily, and her mother smiled weakly but still looked worried.

'May, I don't know… What if you feel worse?'

'I'm fine, Mother. Look at me. I'm eating like a horse.' She took a big bite of toast. 'But if it makes you and Father happy, I'll relax here for the day, but only on the condition that you go about your business. You know I love it when you do the altar flowers. You're by far the best at it.'

May knew a little flattery went a long way with her mother. Personally, she couldn't care less if they put spuds and turnips on the altar, but she knew it mattered to her mother, and any bit of joy the woman could extract from life at the moment was to be encouraged. Besides, the flower meetings always seemed to last at least four hours, and then the ladies would have tea and scones, so it would all take forever hopefully.

'But what about your lunch if I'm not back in time? Madge has gone to see her sister, who's having her veins done tomorrow – the poor woman is a martyr to the varicose veins.'

This was another conversational avenue to be avoided. Madge's bunions, her sister's veins… Her mother would never leave if she got started.

'If I'm hungry, I'll put on my dressing gown and go downstairs for ten minutes and have some of that soda bread Madge baked yesterday and a cup of tea, and I'll heat up some soup. I'm seventeen, Mother, not nine. I won't starve. Now please, get your hat and coat and go. That's an order.'

'Are you sure? I could rearrange the meeting…'

'No, definitely not. Off you go. I'll be fine, I promise. If you hurry, you won't be late.'

'I don't know…' She was still dithering. It was honestly exhausting, but May did her best to remain calm and kind.

'Oh, Mother, on your way back – I know it's a bit out of your way, but would you get me one of those cream horns from McGettigan's? I'd love one with a cup of tea this afternoon? Maybe get one for you and Father too, and we can have a little treat when he comes home?'

St Catherine's Church was on Albany Road and the bakery was well past Gonzaga College, so it would take her a good half an hour extra to walk there and back, giving May even more time.

Glad to have a justification for her departure, her mother relaxed. 'Of course I will, pet. That's a great idea. We'll all have one – your father loves McGettigan's baking too. I know Fitzgerald's do them as well, but they're not as good at all.'

'Thanks, Mother, you're the best. See you later,' said May, relieved. She held her breath as her mother left the room, wandered down the stairs and fussed around in the hall, and she didn't really fully exhale until she heard the front door close.

She waited another five minutes, just to be safe, then set the breakfast tray aside, jumped out of bed, got dressed and hurried down to the sewing room to begin her day.

SHE LEFT FINISHING her letter to Peter until she had shopped at the corner store for all the things she knew he needed and packed them in the box along with the shirt and socks.

Most of what she'd written already was just about how much she missed him, and how proud she was of him, and reminding him that he needed to apply for that bit of the army that went around entertaining the troops.

Now she added, *I've been thinking about how to help your friend Nick, and I'm going to talk to Harriet in the tennis club, who has a housekeeper*

whose son lives in Cork, and see if he knows anything about Brockleton. It
must be a really big house if it's just known by its name. Is Alicia the maid
there or something, and she's not allowed to have a sweetheart? Is that why he
has to be so mysterious about it? I do hope so. I adore romance. Tell him to
write her a letter and send it with your next one to me. I'm sure I can get it to
his sweetheart without the mistress of the house finding out.

Now, my dearest Peter, I have to go because I need to drop your sister's
letter to Arnotts and see if she has left any message for you, and then post this
parcel and get home again, all before Mother comes back from her flower
meeting. She and Father still have me wrapped in cotton wool. It's very frus-
trating, but I grin and bear it because they're so sad about darling David. I
am too of course, but I know he's alive out there somewhere – I just wish I
knew where.

My sweet, handsome Peter, I love you so much and I can't wait until you
come home on leave and I can introduce you to my parents and we can get
properly engaged.

I've left a kiss at the bottom of this page, so if you kiss the paper right
there on the X by my name, it will be like kissing me. I had such a lovely
dream about you last night, but I won't tell you what it was because I'm too
much of a lady! It wasn't just about kissing, though. Oh, I'm blushing!

All my love, so much love, love and kisses, love, love, love, I adore you,
Your future wife,
May x

Her letters to Peter were a lot more fulsome than his to her, which
were just short scribbles thanking her for the stuff she'd sent and
asking for more stuff. She forgave him for that, though. Probably his
soldier friends would rib him for writing anything sentimental, and
also she could tell from his handwriting and spelling that he found
writing a bit slow and difficult.

She wasn't surprised about his poor education, because unlike her
mother, May Gallagher had a good brain.

Peter's middle-class Dublin accent had fooled her at first; she'd
assumed he was from somewhere like Dún Laoighaire. But when he
relaxed, he slipped up and said things like 'ma' instead of 'mother', and
then he'd accidentally mentioned about going to school in North King

Street, which gave it away even more. In Dublin, like anywhere, people's pedigree could be immediately identified by the school they attended. Her father and David and her grandfather and his father had all gone to the Jesuits at Belvedere College, which was one reason Father tolerated her having the office job at the factory, because her employer, Mr Swift, also went to Belvedere and played rugby when he was younger.

The way Father and Mother saw it, May's only mission in life was to look pretty and marry a man from the right class, someone just like Mr Swift. Looking pretty was no bother to May – she knew she was a beauty – but if they thought she was going to marry some lumpen-shouldered, cauliflower-eared rugby player like her boss, they could think again. She would marry her handsome Peter, and they would just have to accept it.

She was gradually getting her parents used to the sound of Peter's name. They knew she wrote to him, and they saw his letters arrive, and she spoke about him as much as she could and said how he always asked after their health – which he didn't, but she said he did to endear him to them. Of course they'd asked where he was from, where he'd gone to school, so she'd said something vague about a family in Galway, father a doctor, which Peter had left behind when he got the acting job in Dublin.

They did share that unspoken look when she'd said he was an actor, the one she'd come to recognise, and she knew there was a faint disapproval there. Nothing you could put your finger on, but acting clearly wasn't on the list of professions required for May's husband. So then she explained that Peter intended to own a theatre of his own one day, and that cheered them up a little, because that would be something they could tell their friends. And right now Peter was serving king and country; he was a loyal subject like their own dear David. And at least he clearly had nothing to do with the rebels who had destroyed the city with their well-intentioned but ultimately futile and destructive behaviour during the Easter Rising.

Poor Father. He'd been very confused when Old Belvedere was fired on by the British army during the Easter Rising. He was a staunch supporter of the war effort, but then to see the very army his son was enlisted in firing on his old school really put him in a predicament. He was able to separate the two, though. It was a poor show, but the British had to react to the rebels, many of whom were ruffians and degenerates – her father's words.

They were good people, her parents, not mean or cruel, but they were middle-class snobs and that was just how it was. It didn't matter. Once they met Peter, once they realised he was intelligent and hard-working and all of the things they liked in a person, once they saw how much he loved her and she loved him, they'd warm to him. And until then, there was no need to tell them he'd been brought up in Henrietta Street.

She'd been so shocked when she found out.

She hadn't minded that he was lying to her about his background – it just meant he was afraid of losing her if she found out – but she was a curious girl who liked to know the truth about things. So after their third date, when he'd once again found an excuse not to intro-duce her to his family or to come and meet hers, she'd followed him home at a distance. It was still winter and dark, and she was wearing a dark coat with a hood that she pulled up over her hair so he wouldn't recognise her. But he was wearing a white shirt, no jacket despite the cold, and she could see him ahead of her as he passed under the gas lamps. By the time she saw him enter the street where the once grand homes were now rat-infested, overpopulated slums, she was in a state of horror. She'd been sure Peter was working class as soon as he let it drop where he'd gone to school, but she'd been hoping he at least lived in one of those nice houses Arthur Guinness had built for his workers.

But no, the house Peter went into was the type people complained about. She'd never even been to this part of the city, had never set foot over this way before in her life, and she was astonished and appalled to see children out on the street at this hour, dressed in little more than rags, no shoes on their feet, rough-looking men and women, some drunk, yelling at each other in the strongest Dublin accents she'd ever heard, even more common than those of the women who made the shells on the factory floor.

Could her handsome, talented Peter really have come from such low beginnings? It was hard to believe, but it seemed he did.

Anyway, it didn't matter. She would take him away from there, save him from his old life, and they would live together somewhere lovely once the war was over. He could go back to acting; they were keeping a place for him at the Gaiety – she'd already made sure of that by making friends with Mr Griffin.

When she'd told the stage manager that Peter had enlisted, he'd been very disgruntled, and talked of feeling let down when they were going to offer Peter a good part in Hamlet, maybe even the Dane himself. But May had done her research and knew Mr Griffin's son was in the navy. She told him Peter had wanted to fight because Mr Redmond said it was the way to get Home Rule, and it turned out, as she already knew, that his own son was in the navy for the same reason. So of course Mr Griffin had melted and said Peter could come back to his acting job whenever he wanted.

Hopefully Peter could do some acting in the army as well. There seemed to be a lot of fun and entertainment at the front. It wasn't just what poor dear David had told her. One of her friend's brothers had written home saying how there was a visiting troupe in Ypres while he was there, brought out from England, and it did the men great good. Peter would be superb at that sort of thing. She was surprised he hadn't sorted it out yet, but he'd written to say that the officers weren't interested.

He must have been being too modest. It was a pity she couldn't be there to sort it out for him. Once they were married, she'd make sure nothing would stand in his way. He'd have a theatre of his own one day; she'd make sure of that. He might not be the best at reading and writing, but it was a credit to him he could do it at all, given his background, and she had enough education for both of them. She was on Peter's team now, and she wouldn't let anything hold him back.

CHAPTER 8

 ETER

EVERY WEEK OR SO, Peter and his mates would get sent back behind the lines for what the army called 'rear rest', though it wasn't that restful, truth be told.

First they'd march the four miles back, until the deafening shrieks of moaning minnies and whizz-bangs gave way to a distant, relentless thud and crash. The rear area, when they got there, was a bustle of activity, troops coming, injured men being treated, communications and supplies being fed up the line.

He and the rest of his company would be told to go and get bathed and deloused, a thoroughly unpleasant experience when the water was cold. The carbolic stung the eyes and the delousing powder didn't really work, but like everything in the army, it wasn't a choice. After that they'd be shown to their billets, usually a farmer's barn, where they would sleep on straw and a few horse blankets.

Then there was training all day, a lot of needless marching up and down. The army was worried that drinking and the visiting of brothels was weakening the fighting force, so it insisted on daily drilling and endless kit inspections even when on rest. All the privates hated and despised the boring, pointless waste of it all and couldn't wait to head out to the town of Poperinge to get plastered.

The officers had a different experience of course. Baths with hot water were found for them, and much better food, and billets in local houses were paid for. But the barn wasn't too bad, and at least they weren't being shot at and it was mercifully quiet; the constant thud and crash of the battlefield was far enough away to sleep through it. And in the evening, they could go to the Aigle d'Or, one of the many drinking houses in Poperinge, which served chips and sometimes an egg if a chap had enough money.

And Peter did have enough money, for him and for Nick and Enzo as well.

Every time he got back to the rest area, there would be a huge parcel from May waiting for him; she made this war almost bearable. She sent so much stuff, he was able to do a sideline trading in socks, cigarettes, chocolate, sugar, tea and biscuits, while still having plenty left for him and Nick and Enzo. As a messenger, he was always up and down the communication trenches, so he knew who wanted what, and everyone knew that if they needed something, one of those little luxuries that made life bearable, then Peter Cullen was your man.

At the moment he was sitting on a bale of hay, going through the latest box. Lots more socks – seven pairs! – and another load of treats, and also a shirt that he knew she'd made herself; she'd told him she was going to do it. It was clever of her to make a shirt from scratch, as well as knit so many socks. She was a very capable girl as well as beautiful, and he appreciated her generosity with the treats.

After the first parcel, he'd written saying that she really shouldn't be spending all her money on him, but she wrote back that her father worked hard and provided well for the family, and she was allowed to keep all her wages for herself, and what else would she be spending them on? Such a different life from his own, where all the family wages went down Kit Cullen's throat.

There was a letter from Kathleen in this latest parcel, which pleased him to no end because he'd been longing to hear from home. He had been writing to his sister rather than to Eamonn, who was a fierce republican, because he felt sure his brother would not approve of him taking the king's shilling. He opened Kathleen's letter before he opened the one from May, and with much less trepidation. It wasn't that he didn't like May's letters. They were all full of love and how much she missed him and all of that, and how clever he was and what a great career he had in front of him. And it was nice, but it made him feel under pressure. And anyway he was more keen to know how his mother and sisters and Eamonn were managing without him.

Kathleen had stayed at school until she was twelve, and her hand-writing was easy enough to read. And Peter had been practising his reading in the boredom of the front, working on deciphering the tatty adventure books that got passed around from dugout to dugout until the covers were off and you had to hope the last page wasn't missing. He was still slow at it, though, moving his finger from word to word of Kathleen's letter. Some of her sentences he read over and over, repeating the words under his breath, just in case he hadn't under-stood them properly, because the letter contained astonishing news...

Six weeks ago, Kit Cullen had had an accident at work. He'd fallen off a ladder and crashed headfirst into an empty vat and suffered some kind of brain injury. When he came out of hospital, he hardly knew who anyone was any more, even his own wife and children, and found it hard to talk and had to be helped to walk and everything. The doctors said the damage was permanent. The brewery had been great, because the accident happened at work. Kit and the likes of him hated all the toffs, but Edward Guinness, a baron or viscount of something and the grandson of Arthur, the original Guinness, was a decent man who treated his workers fairly and did right by the city that gave him such wealth. He had built a hospital with his own money, and Kit had been treated there for free, and now they were giving Ma regular payments from a fund for the families of workers who were hurt or died on the job.

What with the pension, and everyone else's wages, and Kit unable to walk let alone get down to the pub or bully their mother, things had never been so good in the Cullen house, Kathleen had written. They were even planning to move out of Henrietta Street. They were on the waiting list for one of those snug little houses the Guinness family had built for their workers, because they had enough every week to pay for that now. And when Peter came home, he'd be able to visit, because Kit wasn't capable of killing a fly these days and there was nothing to fear.

Nick and Enzo looked up in surprise at Peter's massive whoop of joy. He didn't like to say it was because his father had been in a terrible accident, so he just waved May's letter at them instead of Kathleen's and made out it was because he was so happy to hear from her.

'Your May must be some girl.' Enzo grinned.

'D-d-do you love her a lot?' Nick asked.

Peter thought of that morning back in Dublin, how she'd allowed him to do what no nice girl should – and no nice boy should either, come to that – and it was clear that she'd only allowed it because they would marry. Her parting gift to him so that they were marked out for each other. He'd always thought, based on what he'd overheard anyway, that girls didn't really like it but that they let you do it to make a baby, but May was so enthusiastic and made him feel like he was irresistible, her body so delicious in his arms, it was like he'd lost all control. He'd have agreed to anything rather than stop, and afterwards he could hardly just walk away.

'She's very nice and generous,' he said, to avoid answering truthfully.

'Come on, what's she really like?' Enzo asked, the hand gesture indicating he was more interested in her shape than her personality.

'Pretty,' Peter said truthfully.

'But you d-d-don't love her?' Nick wasn't letting it go.

'I'm not sure, really. Not sure what love is at all, I suppose.' He felt weird talking about it like this. Nick often spoke about emotional things, and Peter didn't dislike it exactly, but it took some getting used to.

'How far d'ya get?' Enzo was, as always, more interested in the carnal element of it.

'Mind yer own business,' Peter said, but he couldn't help blushing, his face giving it away that he was a man of the world now, not a child with no idea about such things.

'Woohoo…old Paddy's 'ad a roll with the lovely May,' Enzo teased, then guffawed. 'Just 'ope you ain't goin' 'ome to a surprise in a carriage, me old mucker, and then you'll be done up like a kipper.'

Peter knew what he was talking about, but it had never occurred to him. There was no way May could be having a baby; that couldn't happen the first time…could it?

'What about you, Paddy Two?' Enzo nudged Nick. 'Got someone back there?'

'N-n-no.'

'No little red-haired colleen waitin' for ya then?'

'Alas, no.'

Enzo patted Nick's shoulder sympathetically, then went into one of his many stories about his romantic conquests.

Peter opened May's letter with a feeling of trepidation. It was four pages long and it took him ages to get to the end, but he was happier when he did. There was definitely no mention of anything that sounded like she was in the family way, just lots of love and kisses. She also reminded him to get a job entertaining the troops; she obviously thought he could just snap his fingers and it would be done. Nobody on the home front understood what it was like out here, and he didn't like to tell her when he wrote back – it would give her nightmares.

She said her big brother, David, was still missing in action, but she was happily convinced he was still alive. Peter didn't intend to burst that bubble either, but missing in action meant dead as far as he was concerned. Just blown to bits so badly, they couldn't identify the body. He hoped David had died instantly and not suffered. That's what Peter would reassure her must have happened, if May ever came around to admitting her brother was dead. Although for all he knew, the poor boy had died screaming like poor Norris.

May's biggest problem these days seemed to be that her parents wanted to wrap her in cotton wool and never leave her out of their sights, and Peter couldn't help thinking how nice it would be to be wrapped up in cotton wool instead of being shot at and blown up and chewed by rats. It was impossible to be annoyed at her, though, because it was only ignorance and she was a good girl at heart. She even had a plan about how to get a letter from Nick to whoever it was in this house in Cork he wanted to write to.

'Hey, Nick, May says if you write a letter to this Alicia Shaw, she can find a way to get it to her without anyone else knowing,' he said, smiling across at him.

'Oh, that's so k-kind of her.' Nick beamed from ear to ear.

'Hey, thought you didn't have a girlfriend?' protested Enzo, acting indignant at being lied to.

'I d-d-don't…' Nick turned red. 'Alicia's my…g – cousin.'

'Then wot's wiv all the secrecy, mate?'

'She's married to a rich man who doesn't like her k-k-keeping in t-t-touch with my side of the family because we've g-g-got no money,' stammered Nick, red as a beetroot now.

Peter knew Nick was lying, the same as he'd lied about where he was from, and wondered why, but he could see how uncomfortable the conversation was making his friend and wasn't going to pry. 'Lay off him, Enzo,' he said good-naturedly. 'Not everyone has to have a love life like yours.'

'Still, he needs to get started somewhere. Taffy's gone out with dysentery. 'E said I could 'ave 'is cards. Fancy a look, Nick?' Enzo offered.

Taffy was actually called Owen, but Enzo called him Taffy the same as he called Peter 'Paddy'. Taffy was what the English called anyone who was Welsh. Owen had a whole stash of French postcards he'd won off a fella in a game of cards, on which all the girls were naked and posing provocatively. The cards were famous and had done the rounds of the trench several times. Owen wasn't gone out with dysentery, though, but syphilis. Peter had overheard the C.O. telling one of the other officers about it when he was delivering a message.

Venereal disease was rampant in the trenches because the women in the red-lamp places in the towns were infected. The brothels of the Western Front were one of the many things to surprise Peter back when he was a raw recruit, but despite the note from Kitchener that each soldier got, urging him to resist temptation in the form of wine or women, men who were fit and strong, miles from home and fearing each day might be their last, took comfort where they could. The blue-lamp establishments were for officers, the red for ordinary soldiers, but the pox saw no rank; the top brass went down with it as much as the Tommies did.

'No thanks.' Nick blushed again and shook his head.

Enzo guffawed. 'No need to be shy. Hey, Paddy, reckon we'll 'ave to get our mate 'ere to Madame Picot's in Poperinge. Apparently there's a girl, Odette, who can do things to ya no woman back in Blighty ever even thought of.'

'Yeah, yeah. Or maybe Nick doesn't want to find himself getting arsenic injections and having mercury rubbed all over his bits and pieces.'

'I d-d-definitely d-d-don't.' Nick answered vehemently, and all three of them laughed.

* * *

THE AIGLE D'OR on Rue de Flaubert was a favourite watering hole for the English Tommies, and later that evening, Enzo, Peter and Nick entered the bar, famished after a boring day of sewing on buttons, polishing boots and marching around the parade grounds to the yells of some jumped-up sergeant.

The first person to greet them was a big brawny chap with red hair, who beckoned them over to his table. He was well into a *pichette* of rough red wine, and his empty greasy plate held not a morsel remaining of the egg and chips the owner did so well.

'Two-Soups!' Peter clapped him on the back, delighted. 'How're you doing?'

'We thought you woz dead, mate,' said Enzo, falling into a chair and taking a swig straight from the *pichette*.

'Och, just a wee scratch.' He chuckled. 'A good thing, really, unconscious for a week – best week of the war, no question.'

'How d'you feel being back in action?'

The Scotsman answered with a joke, like he always did. 'What's at the bottom of the sea and twitches?'

'I don't know,' chorused Peter and Enzo, playing along. 'What's at the bottom of the sea and twitches?'

'A nervous wreck.'

All of them laughed, and then Enzo introduced Two-Soups to Nick, who was intrigued by his nickname, not seeming to know that both Campbell and Baxter were brands of tinned soup. Odd for a grocer's son, Peter thought. And he wondered again about the connection to Brockleton, and this woman called Alicia Shaw.

The daughter of the man who owned the Aigle d'Or, a pretty girl of around sixteen called Celine, brought over some glasses and cutlery and stayed to take their orders. Peter did his best with sign language to ask for three plates of chips, then sent his friends – and Celine as well – into fits of mirth by mimicking a chicken laying an egg three times.

'Ah, *oui, oui, monsieur, trois oeufs*,' gasped the waitress, wiping her eyes on her apron. '*Et pour boire?*' She pointed her pencil at Enzo, who pointed at the pitcher of wine and indicated for her to bring another one.

'*Et, monsieur?*' she asked Nick, still dimpling.

'*Un peu d'eau pour accompagner le vin, s'il vous plaît*,' he said, gazing at her with his eyes shining, clearly bowled over by her prettiness.

Peter and Two-Soups stared at Nick, and Enzo demanded, 'What did you just say to 'er?'

'I just asked for some water to go with the wine,' Nick said, blushing and looking startled. 'Didn't you do French at school?'

Peter said quickly, before the others could start asking questions about Nick's unusually good education, 'That's great. Could you ask for a glass of apple juice for me if they have it?'

'*Aussi une verre du jus de p-p-pomme, s'il vous plaît.*' said Nick to the waitress.

'*Bien sûr, monsieur,*' Celine said with a shy smile, and went off to fetch their orders. Nick gazed after her adoringly as she sashayed through the tables in her little black dress and white apron.

'Don't you like wine?' Enzo asked Peter, pouring himself and Nick a generous glass from Two-Soups's pitcher. 'Thought it was just the rum you didn't like.'

Peter always gave Enzo and Nick his rum ration, an egg cup full every day, saying he didn't like spirits. The truth was he didn't drink at all; his father had put him off for life. Now he made a joke of it. 'I'm a pioneer of total abstinence, and my duty as such is to reach out to those suffering from alcohol-related harm.' He smiled beatifically, and his friends hooted.

'Och, alcohol is the least likely thing to harm us here, mate. If the Hun dinnae get ya, one of them over there will give ya the clap and you'll wish you'd got some alcohol-related harm then!' Two-Soups nodded at the collection of straggly dressed women standing up near the counter, eyeing up a crowd of Tommies seated at the large centre table.

Madame Picot's girls were all emaciated, and their hair was limp. They'd done their best, God love them, but the dresses that hung from their skeletal frames were badly in need of a wash. They'd used wine to redden their cheeks and lips, and they tried to look merry – nobody wanted to pay good money for a night with a moping Minnie – but Peter could see the pain behind their eyes.

Celine returned a few minutes later with the water, apple juice and wine. Nick burst into a stream of French that made the waitress smile, then she responded in an equally rapid-fire torrent of inexplicable words. Peter and Enzo didn't bother to ask him to translate; they were distracted by a commotion on the other side of the room, where there appeared to be some disquiet among the crowd of Tommies. A small stage sat in the corner, just a wedge, raised only a foot or so, and an old upright piano stood against the wall. The Tommies were pointing at it. Suddenly the whole table erupted into a chant. 'Marine, Marine, Marine...'

The tall French proprietor with the handlebar moustache and a hangdog look appeared from behind the bar and went up to the centre table, and Peter could hear him pleading with them over the noise. '*Messieurs, je suis vraiment désolé...*sorry...*mais ce soir...*tonight... Marine...*non!*'

'Marine, Marine, Marine!' Jugs were being pounded on tables, cutlery too, boots stamped.

The owner looked like he was about to cry.

'What the 'ell's up with that lot?' Enzo asked as Celine appeared again.

She glanced at him and said to Nick, her green eyes worried, '*Monsieur, dites á leur que* Marine *n'est pas la ce soir...*'

'What did she say?' Peter asked Nick.

'Apparently someone called Marine couldn't make it tonight.' Nick turned to Celine. '*Qui est* Marine?'

'*Une chanteuse et danseuse*, Marine, *elle est en retard, or quelque chose comme ça...je ne sais pas, mais mon Père est très inquiet...*' She nodded in the direction of the very scared-looking owner.

'She's the singer and dancer, and she hasn't turned up,' translated Nick.

'And them geezers look like they're ready to start smashin' the place up if she doesn't show,' said Enzo, frowning.

It seemed like he was right; the atmosphere was rapidly becoming threatening. Men who at home would never have hurt a fly had been blooded out here, and violence, bloodshed and death meant almost nothing to them. They had come here tonight to hear this Marine sing, and they were getting angrier by the second that there was no sign of her.

Peter didn't allow himself any time to think. 'Tell her not to worry – I'll sort this,' he said to Nick.

'You and whose army?' asked Enzo, astonished.

'Never you mind, Enzo. Look, just tell her, Nick, then come with me.'

Nick spoke once again in rapid French, which seemed to relieve the girl.

And then he said to Peter, as Peter took his glass out of his hand and set it down, 'Come where with you? Hey, what are you doing?'

'Saving the day. Come on.' Peter pulled his friend to his feet and drew him through the crowd towards the stage.

'My girl, May, she's always saying I should try and get a job entertaining the troops, and it's given me an idea. We're going to give them a few of the songs we've been singing along to these past weeks, and maybe that will hold them off.'

It was a long shot, and the English soldiers weren't being very welcoming. Jeers and shouts of 'Get off!' followed them as they climbed onto the stage. 'We want Marine, not your ugly mugs!'

One soldier even threw a glass at them. Peter ducked as it missed him by a fraction, smashing a picture of Georges Clemenceau, the French prime minister. This caused hilarity and whooping in the crowd, who were by now mostly very drunk.

'G-G-God's sake, Peter! You're going to get us k-k-killed,' groaned Nick.

Celine's father obviously thought the same thing, as he looked agonised, and young Celine had her hands to her cheeks.

'Sing me a starting note,' said Peter urgently. 'Quick.'

'No need, there's a piano.'

And to Peter's astonishment, his friend sat down at the piano and opened the lid. The keys were yellowed and one or two were missing the ivory, but Nick just said, 'Let's hope it's in tune.' He rested his fingers on the keys, struck a run of notes in the middle of the piano and nodded, and somehow the crowd quietened; it seemed to settle them. 'What will we start with?' he asked, looking up at Peter.

'I...er... Right.' Peter was taken aback. Nick was a young man of many surprises. 'Can you play "It's a Long way to Tipperary"?'

'I can p-p-play anything,' said Nick politely, and he launched into the first few bars of the song and then started to sing, with Peter joining in.

'It's a long way to Tipperary, it's a long way to go. It's a long way to Tipperary, to the sweetest girl I know...'

The piano sounded rough and often out of tune, but Nick had a really good voice. Peter stood with his hand to his heart, then shaded his eyes as if looking into the distance, acting like the soldier who was singing the song, bringing his character to life.

'Goodbye, Piccadilly. So long, Leicester Square. It's a long, long way to Tipperary, but my heart lies there...'

The key changed.

'Pack up your troubles in your old kit bag and smile, smile, smile...'

Peter switched to pretending to pack a bag and sling it onto his back, then marched up and down, and to his intense relief, some of the crowd began to sing as well. Before long every man in the place had joined in. Monsieur was safely back behind the bar, beaming, and Celine was being called for beer and wine.

'My Bonnie Lassie', 'The Girl with the Golden Hair', 'Keep the Home Fires Burning', 'When Tommy Comes Marching Home'...

They had built up a large repertoire from listening to the gramophone Peter had stolen from the officers' dugout, and Nick played on and on as the Tommies sang their hearts out, arms around each other, some openly and unashamedly crying. To his surprise Peter felt a wave of affection for the English soldiers, who had been behaving so badly only a short while ago.

He remembered hearing Eamonn talking about James Connolly, the Irish revolutionary and signatory of the Irish Proclamation of Independence. The British tied him to a chair to execute him because he was so wounded that he couldn't stand. Connolly said that the war should not be country against country, that the Irish poor had more in common with the poor of England or of Russia than the wealthy of their own land. It had never struck him so true as now. These men were working class from the poor streets of London or Birmingham or Liverpool; they knew what it was like to be hungry, downtrodden. And yet he was reared to hate them but feel affinity for the Irish gentry who lived in luxury just because they were born on the same lump of rock.

Celine climbed up on the stage and placed a glass of wine on the piano beside Nick and another of apple juice on the stool beside Peter.

'Give 'im a proper drink!' one of the men yelled.

'I'm a pioneer!' Peter called, mid-song.

There was a loud cheer from a group of Munster Fusiliers.

'God bless you, private,' a man in the uniform of a major called. It was surprising to see officers in the Aigle d'Or. They normally went to the Hôtel Champs Verts two streets away. They didn't care to mix with the lower ranks, and the feeling was mutual.

Peter was getting hoarse and thirsty and stopped to drink the juice. Nick vamped along in between songs, giving his own voice a break. Peter yelled out, 'Anyone have a party piece?'

There was jostling among the men, encouraging each other, and one man was pushed forward.

'What you got for me?' Peter asked, now thoroughly enjoying himself as the master of ceremonies.

'Do "Charlotte the Harlot"!' his mates yelled.

'Do not,' Peter warned. The lyrics were too bawdy, and he didn't want to be reprimanded by the officers who had just entered the bar.

The lad blushed. 'How about "Madelon"?' he suggested.

'Much safer.' Peter winked. The song, translated from French, told the tale of an innkeeper's daughter who was loyal to the whole regiment. A bit saucy certainly, but not obscene like the earlier suggestion.

The boy looked at Nick, who said, 'Sing it, and I'll pick it up as you go along.'

The boy began in a passable tenor voice, with Nick quickly joining in.

'There is a tavern, down in Brittany, where weary soldiers take their liberty. The innkeeper's daughter, whose name is Madelon, pours out the wine while they laugh and carry on. She knows a captain, who twirls a big moustache. She knows a colonel, whose eyes with fury flash. She gives them both the sweetest kind of smile, and stops and chats with both a little while...'

The lad finished to rapturous applause and sat down, being clapped on the back by his mates.

'All right, lads,' Peter said, once the hooting had quietened. He'd just noticed Enzo had been served an enormous portion of chips and eggs and realised he was very hungry. 'Myself and my friend have to eat now, but be thinking of requests for the second half and we'll be with you soon.'

The applause was enormous as the two of them returned to the table, and Peter basked in it. It felt as good as the applause for his performance in Macbeth, the crowd going wild for him. Intoxicating. How he'd missed it. He was born to do this. He remembered what May had said to him the day he signed up, about trying to get into the entertainment side in the army. He didn't think there was any chance of that, but just making tonight happen in a simple bar in front of a crowd of drunken Tommies made him feel wonderful.

'Well done, you two.' Two-Soups shook their hands as they sat down.

'That was smashin',' declared Enzo, with his mouth full.

Moments later the owner arrived with two huge plates of golden-fried potatoes, sausages, bread and fried eggs piled high. '*Merci, messieurs, merci beaucoup.*' He waved away Peter's offer of money as his daughter placed yet more wine and apple juice on their table. '*C'est le moins que je puisse faire.*'

'"Ow comes you can play the piano so good?' Enzo asked Nick, as Nick tucked into his sausages with gusto.

'Just p-p-practise...'

'But did you pick it up by yourself, like?'

While Nick was hesitating over his reply, one of the officers came to their table. Major Billingsley was the adjutant to the commander. He walked with a cane after a sniper bullet relieved him of his kneecap earlier that year, and so he was on administrative duties only. It was only a few months since he'd been released from hospital, and he could have stayed at home – his injuries were bad enough – but he'd wanted to come back to the front, to be with the men. Everyone spoke well of the major. He had a reputation for being straight as a die, no pilfering of rations or giving himself an easier ride than the privates, and he was liked enormously for it.

He also was the one who gave the orderlies the instructions to tell men they were being moved or, better still, going back to Blighty. He was much more generous with relief passes than the adjutant he'd replaced, and seemed to realise that the soldiers were exhausted and spent and needed to recover in between the attacks. People who hadn't got leave for two years were now getting four-day passes fairly regularly.

All four of them stood to attention.

'As you were, soldiers, as you were.' The major spoke in a broad Yorkshire accent and gestured to them to sit. 'That was a fine show you put on there, Cullen and Gerrity. My friends and I normally go to the Hôtel Champs Verts, but as we were walking past, we heard you and thought we'd stick our heads in for ten minutes or so. Done this kind of thing before, have you?'

'Yes, sir. I was an actor in Dublin, sir. And Gerrity here is a concert pianist.' Peter wasn't sure what that was, but he'd heard May use the phrase and it sounded good. Nick blushed but didn't contradict him.

'I see, I see.' The major rubbed his chin with his hand. 'Not the sort of show I'd go and see myself, normally, but it was heart-warming to see the boys enjoying themselves. They could do with more singing and less drinking and what have you. You don't drink yourself, Private Cullen, is that right?'

'Yes, sir. I mean, no, I don't, sir.'

The major tapped his cane on the floor. 'Very good, very good. Come and see me tomorrow, would you? You too, Gerrity. I'd like a word.' Seeing the look of trepidation on Nick's face, he smiled. 'Don't worry, lads, nothing unpleasant.'

CHAPTER 9

DUBLIN, IRELAND AUGUST 1917

*M*AY

SHE SAT at her dressing table, reading his letter again, checking the date he'd given her, as she had every day since it had arrived. It was a much longer letter than anything Peter had sent her before, and the spelling was a lot better than when he first started writing to her. Maybe the army gave lessons? Or his friend Nick had been helping him? Peter was so clever – she was sure once he put his mind to learning anything, he'd pick it up as fast as he was taught. It wasn't his fault he'd been to that awful slum school.

Dear May,

Good news! I've got a four-day pass!

You remember saying I should get into entertaining the troops? Well, I did. Me and my pal Nick put on a show at this place called the Aigle d'Or. The French singer hadn't turned up, and Nick is really good at singing and playing the piano. Anyway, it was great. We sung all the music hall songs and everyone loved us. Best thing, though, is Major Billingsley gave me and Nick a four-day pass as a reward for 'raising the spirits of the troops', so we're coming home for a couple of days! Enzo and Two-Soups are very jealous! I've told them when me and Nick get back, we'll see if can we get another show at the Aigle, and then Two-Soups can tell a few jokes, which he's really good at, and maybe Enzo can hang from the rafters or something – he did trapeze in the circus – then maybe they'll get a pass as well.

So well done for that idea, May. It was you put it into my head.

Can you leave my letter to Kathleen into Arnotts and get Nick's letter to this Alicia Shaw person in Cork? He says thank you very much for your help, by the way. I'll be getting into Dublin on the twenty-first of August and leaving on the twenty-third, and I'll make sure to come and see you. It will be nice.

Sorry David is still missing, but if I was you, I would let your parents mollycoddle you even if it does drive you mad. You don't realise how nice a mother's love is until you don't have it. I might mollycoddle you a bit myself when I get to see you.

Love, Peter

And now it was the twenty-first, and he was coming today, and May was faint with excitement. She'd written back to Peter that she'd taken the three days off from the factory and would be waiting for him.

Her plan was simple. He hadn't said what time he was going to be here exactly, but he only had a couple of days, so they couldn't dilly-dally. As soon as he arrived, they'd go for a walk and he'd propose. She had money to buy a ring, in case he hadn't enough. And they'd come home and tell her parents that evening.

After that, though she hated the idea of sharing him, she supposed he'd want to see his own family. She knew he'd lie to her about where they lived and refuse to take her with him, but she'd whisper to him that she already knew, that she'd found out, but that she still loved him just as much as before when she thought he was middle class. And then he would be so grateful to her, and he'd take her and introduce her to them as his fiancé, and she'd be charming to his mother and sisters, and his brother, not at all snobby, and that would make Peter love her all the more.

Then tomorrow she'd introduce Peter to her tennis friends at a proper little afternoon tea party in the Gresham Hotel – she had it booked already. She couldn't wait for the girls to see Peter. He was so handsome, they'd swoon; she just knew it. They all were crazy for Rudolph Valentino, and he was handsome, but he wasn't a patch on her man. Peter's navy-blue eyes that crinkled slightly at the sides when he smiled, his pale skin with the faint dusting of freckles over his nose, his sandy hair that flopped down over his forehead. And his body... She had to catch her breath when she thought of him.

For a short while, she'd harboured a hope that they could marry instead of just getting engaged. Cecily Fitzgibbon had got a special licence when her boy was home from the front for four days last January. It had cost the extraordinary sum of twenty-nine pounds for the special licence in order for them to marry without the statutory three months' notice to have the banns read, but the reason Mr Fitzgibbon had been so willing to pay the huge sum became obvious a few months later. People were shocked, but nobody said anything, and George and Cecily welcomed a little boy four months after the rushed wedding.

May wasn't going to have a baby, though she'd half hoped she would be after Peter left for the war; it would have been one way to force her father's hand in the event of him being obstinate, and it would be an excuse to get Peter back home again quickly. Surely any soldier going to be a father would be allowed home to make an honest woman of his girl? Still, she had to accept the wedding probably wouldn't be this time; an engagement ring on her finger would have to do. She'd filed and buffed her nails for the last ten days to make sure they looked in perfect condition for showing off her sparkler.

Time to get ready. She'd checked that the boat from France docked at nine each morning at the port, so Peter would be here at ten thirty at the latest.

First, she put on her new brassiere and chemise – she never used a corset, as she didn't need pulling in – and then her new pink shot-silk day dress. She admired herself in the mirror.

May spent most of her wages on sending parcels to Peter, but Mother and Father were generous – they allowed her to have whatever she wanted really – so she'd had this special dress made to her own specifications. It was broad at the hip and narrow at the hem, as *Vogue* said all dresses should be these days; she'd read it in the ladies' reading room of the library in town. It had a large collar with red cherries embroidered on it and a wide ruched belt at the waist; the skirt was full but not overly so, and it was cut to calf-length.

Mother didn't approve of the shorter styles, so May had ordered the dress without telling her. But she had lovely ankles, and the barrel shape really suited her, and she was confident that when her mother saw the dress on, she'd see her daughter was right, like May was right about everything.

She'd also splashed out on a pair of two-tone brown and cream side-buttoned boots to complement her shorter hemline, and when she and Peter went for their walk, she would finish off the whole ensemble with her lovely pale-pink velvet hat with the fashionable turned-down brim.

She pinned her hair and applied a little rouge to her cheeks and lips, not too much to make her look cheap, but just enough. By quarter to ten, she was ready. In her purse she carried the five pounds she had saved for the ring. Today was the day, she thought, as she gave herself one last appraisal in the mirror. Irresistible. Today she would become an engaged woman, and soon, as soon as was humanly possible, she would become Mrs Peter Cullen.

Downstairs, the house was peaceful. Madge was away helping the sister with the varicose veins, her father was at work, and her mother was visiting her childless aunt, May's great-aunt, who lived out in Stillorgan and was very poorly. Mother had wanted May to come with her, especially as the aunt had promised May a small legacy, but May had pleaded a bit of a sniffle, which nearly had her mother staying home to look after her again; May had had to push her out of the door.

She stood at the window of the living room, watching for Peter to come in the gate with his lovely loping walk. She fantasised about taking him to her bed the moment he got here, and maybe it was a bit of a waste of a free house not to do so, but she knew getting the ring was more important. When they were married, she could sleep naked beside him every night. How lucky married people were, to be able to do that whenever they wanted and nobody could complain.

* * *

Ten thirty came.

The late-summer sunshine was warm on her face as she went into the kitchen to make a cup of tea. As she waited for the kettle to boil on the stove, she gazed out into the garden where everything was in colourful, fragrant bloom. Her mother's flowers for the church altar were her pride and joy.

Where would they live, she wondered? She liked looking at gardens but hated doing any work in them, and Peter had laughed that he didn't know a daisy from a dock leaf on account of never having done any gardening himself. She knew why that was – there were no gardens in Henrietta Street – but she'd pretended she thought it was because his family had a gardener at their fine house in Galway.

Eleven thirty. The hands of the clock moved towards noon.

The nagging doubt that always lingered in the darker corners of her mind threatened to burst into her consciousness. Did Peter think she was a loose girl, so not the marrying kind? She hardly believed she'd been brave enough to take him into her bed at all, but he was so handsome and she adored him – not just love but actual adoration – and it had hurt a little but not as bad as she'd feared.

She'd still been very innocent less than a year ago, but at least she had her job at the factory, because otherwise she would have had no idea about how things worked at all. It was overhearing snippets of conversations among the women there that had opened her eyes and her mind to a whole other world, where men and women could have sex without being married as long as they knew they were going to get married in the end.

Peter understood that, didn't he? Surely he must know to look at her that she wasn't the kind of girl who went to bed with a man unless she was sure he would marry her. Of course he'd propose. He was definitely going to. He only never mentioned marriage in his letters because he wanted to do it in person… That was it. He was so romantic, he wouldn't say it on paper.

The clock hands passed noon, then touched one o'clock.

She had the right day, of course she did. Maybe something had happened that he couldn't go, or he missed the boat or the train or something. She wished there was a way to check, but there wasn't.

Two o'clock. Three o'clock.

She almost wished she'd gone with her mother to see her grandaunt Maura however boring she was, instead of being stuck staring at the clock all day and feeling worse and worse and worse.

Four o'clock. Five o'clock. Her parents would be home soon. Dejected, she decided she'd better go upstairs and change out of her finery.

CHAPTER 10

ICK

LEAVING Peter on the bridge in Dublin City, Nick walked purposefully along the quays towards the bus station. He'd told Peter he was catching a bus to Waterford, and he didn't want to disavow him of that idea. In reality he was going to meet his grandmother at the hotel on Sackville Street, although he wasn't sure where that was; he'd never been there before.

He had time to kill, though, so once he was sure he was out of Peter's sight, he turned back up the quays, over the Ha'penny Bridge, back down the other side of the Liffey and then over the bridge once more. Nick had never been to Dublin, and he decided it was a pleasant city despite the fact that several buildings were still in ruins, thanks to the battles of 1916. His father had raved about the upstarts and criminals who had 'riled up the masses' in this city on Easter Monday and was of the opinion that a much firmer hand should have been taken. But hearing Peter talk about the executed revolution leaders, life in the tenements, the city having the highest infant mortality rate in Europe and the third highest in the whole world, the vice-like grip the wealthy British factory owners had on their beleaguered workforce, Nick could understand why they rose up, and he found himself wishing them well when they tried again, as Peter assured him they would.

Still, it was nice that everything was peaceful in the city right now. It was good to be away from the misery of the front, where the days were alternately tedious and terrifying and the whole place was drenched in fear, blood and death. One day you might see the chap you were just sharing a gasper with a few minutes earlier blown to bits in front of your face. Or when you weren't under attack, the days were just repetitive, cold, hunger-filled and exhausting. Filling sandbags, sitting on sentry duty, clearing the trench, patrolling, being inspected, killing rats – it was such a frustrating waste of time. It was enough to make a nun punch a hole in a stained-glass window.

And all the time here in Dublin, there were people just walking around freely and chatting like there was no war, no threat of imminent death. It even felt a bit strange and unnatural, like he was in a play…

It was warm. He turned his face to the bright sunshine as he walked along, his kit bag on his back. He should probably get some civilian clothes, if for no other reason than to avoid confrontations like had happened on the quayside, where a number of republican men had cursed them for fighting with the English. Peter had yelled back something to do with Mr Redmond, and they'd backed off then, but it was hard to be going through what they'd been through and be treated like villains when they came home.

He thought of all the clothes in his wardrobe at Brockleton. He should have asked his grandmother to bring him some… Still, they might not fit him any more; he'd slimmed down a lot in the last few months, army rations saw to that, though he was still pretty broad and barrel-chested.

He had some money that he had assiduously saved from his army wages for his first leave. His fifty shillings had gone straight away, long before he'd met Peter and Enzo, because it had taken him a while to realise that a private's wages were only seven shillings a week, not seven shillings a day. He'd been astonished that seven shillings a week was considered enough to live on, not that he could have said that aloud to his friends.

But how much money did he need for a shirt and stuff?

He'd never bought clothing off the peg before. All of his clothes, before he was kitted out by His Majesty, were made by a tailor who came to the house, and everything was made to measure. He had no idea of the cost of anything. He'd assumed that a career in law or politics awaited him, or indeed just the life of the idle rich, the same as his predecessors. What a privileged little upstart he'd been. 'So well got', as Peter might say if he knew, and yet oblivious to his privilege.

It was incredible how the war had changed everything. It was a great leveller. It didn't care what class you came from, how educated you were. It would blow someone from a big house and with a title to smithereens just as easily as the chap beside him who came from a tenement. It didn't give a damn.

He enjoyed heat on his face as he strolled back up Sackville Street and down Henry Street, for no reason but that shoppers seemed to be coming and going there.

He saw a large shop with mannequins in the windows modelling clothing, the name Arnotts over the door, and went in. The gentlemen's department, he was informed by a pleasant-faced young woman with a Dublin accent, was on the second floor.

Once there he stood and tried to take it all in. Did you ask for what you wanted? Did you need to know your size? How did it all work? Jackets hung from hangers on poles in rows along one wall, pullovers were folded on a platform in the middle of the shop, another one bore shirts, and there were trousers too on smaller, thinner hangers, just a single bar with the legs of the trousers folded over them. Socks seemed to be in drawers, and he presumed underwear as well. Overcoats, shoes, boots and braces covered the back wall of the first floor, and in the middle was a counter with a large and ornate brass till.

'Good day to you, sir.' A neat, dapper, older man, with steel-framed circular glasses and a short, well-trimmed beard, dressed in a navy pinstriped suit approached, a tape measure hanging around his neck. 'Can I help?'

'Em…yes, p-p-please.' Nick suddenly felt vulnerable. In the army everything was new to everyone, so not knowing how things were done was fine until you got into the flow of it, but this was different. 'I n-n-need…'

The man waited patiently as Nick struggled to formulate the words. As usual the stammer was worse when he was nervous. On the front, with his good friends, it was fairly under control now, still there but not that annoying. Back in Ireland, the years of being teased by Roger and Walter, of enduring his mother's thinly veiled wincing or his father's irritated frustration, came flooding back and paralysed his tongue.

'A garment in particular, sir?' the salesman prompted.

He breathed deeply, the way Peter had shown him, to calm his nerves; apparently it was a technique taught by the famous actor Arthur Shields. 'I n-n-need everything. P-p-please.'

'Very good, sir.' The man nodded and smiled kindly. 'Casual or for more formal wear?'

'C-c-c-c…'

'Casual? Lovely. I have some nice flannel trousers here, and perhaps a shirt and a pullover?' The man deftly circled Nick's waist with the tape measure and then his chest. 'We actually have a discount on our shirts this week – if you buy one, you get the second one at half price. Also socks are on special offer. Big demand among lads like yourself, back from the front. I hear 'tis an almighty job to keep the feet dry.'

Nick smiled to himself. Nobody had ever discussed the cost of clothing with him or offered a discount before. He decided he must be doing a good job of blending in with ordinary people who worked for a living, and he was grateful to the man for not criticising him for being a soldier. 'Th-th-thank you.'

In the little room provided, he changed out of his uniform, stuffed it in his kit bag and dressed into his new clothing. He walked out onto the street dressed as a civilian for the first time in months. It felt so nice to have soft warm fabric against his skin, comfortable shoes and socks on his feet. As he stood on Henry Street, he wondered what he should do next.

He wasn't meeting his grandmother for another two hours, and he'd used most of his wages to pay for the clothes. He should probably go to a bank and take out some money... Then he remembered he'd closed his account. He wasn't the Honourable Vivian Nicholas Shaw any more.

He crossed over the tramlines and walked north towards the Gresham Hotel. His grandmother had booked two rooms there, and maybe he could have a rest and some sandwiches while he was waiting.

I know only the middle classes stay in a hotel, darling, she'd written to him, *but seeing as you've been slumming it in the trenches, maybe you won't mind. And it saves bumping into any friends of your father in the clubs. If you get there before me, and you're hungry, order room service. They can bring up food and drink to your room.* Being American, she was slightly more used to hotels. They weren't so despised by the upper classes in her own country apparently.

As he approached the Gresham, he thought the Georgian façade looked magnificent, even nicer than the Metropole Hotel in Cork. The room he was shown to by the uniformed porter was also beautiful, and to his surprise and delight, it had a private bathroom attached, with a clawfoot bath.

He'd asked the man at reception to send up some sandwiches and a pot of tea, which the porter delivered, and he wolfed the whole lot down in minutes, and then felt slightly sick. It was a long time since he'd had that much food. He undressed and hung his new clothes, placing his kit bag in the bottom of the wardrobe, then ran a bath. He poured in the bath salts supplied, which fragranced the water with a bouquet-of-flowers scent.

His feet were blistered and sore from months of being in wet boots and socks, and the flea bites all over his body sometimes made him think he would go mad from the itch, but as he sank into the hot water, he'd never felt such perfect contentment. He lay there for at least an hour, topping up the hot water with his toe by turning the tap, thinking about his friends, Peter and Enzo, and what they'd say if they knew he'd been born to a life of privilege and luxury.

Would they despise him? Reject him? It would break his heart.

Emerging from his bath, he dressed again in his civilian clothes and went down to the resident's lounge where, to his delight, his grandmother was sitting stiffly, very upright, with her hands folded on her cane, her grey-blond hair in a neat bun. Her intelligent grey eyes lit up when she saw him, and she stood to embrace him.

'Oh, Nicholas, my dear boy, look at you.' She held his hand as he sat down beside her on the sofa. 'You look so handsome, different somehow. You've lost weight! Are they starving you? Tell me they're not starving you. Poor Roger always wrote home the food was excellent. Is it different for…soldiers in your situation?' She meant the ones who weren't 'officer material'. Nick had confessed in his letter to her that he was a private, not an officer, and begged her to say nothing to his parents.

'Of course not, Floss. The food is lovely for us as well.' He suppressed a smile at such a blatant lie. 'It's just I've been getting a lot of exercise.' There was a code among soldiers not to tell what it was really like.

'Well, that won't do you any harm. But darling, look at this hand – it's so hard and calloused! And you had such lovely soft hands… I hope it doesn't affect your piano playing?'

'It doesn't at all,' he answered with a grin. It was so wonderful to see her again.

'And you've found a piano to practise on? And you've kept up with your singing?'

'I have, of course.' Alicia Shaw had probably never heard a single one of the songs he'd belted out in the Aigle d'Or two weeks ago on a battered old upright with the cloth hanging off the back. It would make her faint at the sight of it. But however ignorant she was about the conditions at the front, he loved her. It wasn't her fault she had no idea what it was like. No newspaper or radio reported it – it wouldn't have been patriotic to talk about anything but heroism and victory. 'Are you in good health yourself, Floss? How is everything back at Brockleton?'

A waiter was hovering, and Alicia Shaw requested tea and sandwiches, then turned back to her grandson, taking his hands again. 'I am quite well. Walter is delighted the Americans are in the war now – he doesn't have to be ashamed of me at his club any more. But your mother is still grieving Roger. She barely comes out of her rooms. Your father begs her to put on a better show for the servants, but she acts like Roger's death is all his fault. Wally is a bit bored, I think, but Walter enjoys having him home. He somehow managed to get rejected for the army, something your father was appalled by, but Wally seemed delighted. They go off riding with the hounds together, and Walter is trying to interest Wally in things like crop rotation and culling deer and coppicing the woodlands. It all goes over Wally's head a bit – he's not clever like you – but hopefully it will sink in one day. He had a half-baked scheme to go over to see my brother Douglas in Boston – he's quite taken with your cousins, pretty girls they are – but your father refused to allow it.'

'Poor Wally. I don't think he really wanted t-t-to be the heir, did he?'

'Well, he has no choice, I'm afraid. He's the future baron now, and he can't shirk his future duty to Brockleton or the House of Lords. But never mind Wally. How is it at the front for you, darling? I hope you're keeping yourself safe.'

'I am, Floss, I promise,' said Nick. 'I'm very careful.'

She looked relieved. 'I'm glad to hear it. Lady Clarissa's son Edmund was very unlucky – he stepped on a mine and lost his leg. So careless of him, but he never did look where he was going. How long is your holiday?'

'I'm going back the day after t-t-tomorrow.'

She was shocked. 'Goodness, darling, I would have thought they'd let you have at least a month after all you've been doing. I have to go back to Brockleton for the summer party this afternoon – Walter would never forgive me if I wasn't there to act as hostess while your mother refuses to leave her room. I've booked you the room for four nights here, and I was hoping to come back and we could go to Brighton together or something.'

'I'm sorry, it's just a f-f-four-day pass. I might get some p-p-proper leave later in the year.'

'Are you sure you even want to go back to that beastly war? I hate that you're not speaking to your parents. And all this hole-in-the-corner business, getting the gardener to give me your letter. I couldn't understand what Joseph wanted at first. Apparently he'd been given it to give to me by the son of a woman who works as a housekeeper in Dublin for the friend of a friend of a friend of yours… All very complicated. Surely it's far better to be open about everything?'

'F-F-Floss, please don't tell…'

She raised her palm upward in that 'stop' gesture she often made. 'Don't worry. I've told them nothing, just as you asked me. Your relationship with your parents is for you to sort out, Nicholas. But I wish you would. Why don't you come back to Brockleton with me this afternoon?'

'I really c-c-can't.'

'Or if not Brockleton, at least stay here in Ireland, in Dublin, go and live your life, find a lady to marry, have children. You're not the heir of Brockleton, so you can do as you please. You don't need to be out there getting all muddy.'

'I can't just walk away from the army. No one can. Deserters get shot.'

'But you're the son of a baron…' She went quite pale. 'No one would dare to shoot you!'

'War is a great leveller, Floss.'

She looked doubtful but didn't contradict him. Instead she opened her maroon leather bag, extracted something and put it in his hand. He looked down and saw it was a thick wad of bank notes.

'No, that's yours,' Nick protested, and he tried to give her back the money, but she refused to take it.

'Nonsense, Nicholas. It's your money. I know it was you who put this in my bank account.'

'B-b-but…that was a p-p-present.'

'Take it. I'm sure they don't pay you enough in the army. And here, dear boy…' She pointed to a small leather suitcase standing at her end of the sofa. 'This has a few things in there for you – silk pyjamas, books and some of the music you left behind. Mozart, Schumann and Brahms, all your favourites.'

He smiled, thinking of the audience at the Aigle d'Or. 'Thank you, Floss. That's very k-k-kind.'

Their sandwiches arrived then, cucumber and cream cheese, with a pot of Earl Grey tea and sugar cubes with tongs. It was all hilariously far from the maggot-riddled dry biscuits of the front. To be honest Nick would have preferred a big plate of steak and potatoes, but at the same time, this was what Floss always had for lunch, and it brought back fond memories of them sitting together in her drawing room in Brockleton.

Later, after Alicia Shaw's chauffeur-driven car had come for her, he dressed in the new pyjamas she'd bought for him and climbed into the bed though it was the middle of the afternoon. The bed was soft and the pillow smelled of soap and fresh air, but dog-tired as he was, he couldn't sleep. He tossed and turned, the images he'd been forced to witness – men with limbs blown off, bodies being eaten by rats, endless noise and dirt and blood – rolling like a moving picture in his head. Eventually, realising he was in too much comfort – it was too far from what he'd grown used to – he climbed out of the cloud-soft bed and lay on the hard floor, a pillow under his head, and there, finally, mercifully, he slept until late the next morning.

CHAPTER 11

DUBLIN, AUGUST 1917

 *ETER*

'PETER!' It was Connie who opened the door to him, and he picked her up, swinging her around until she squealed with delight. She'd turned nine since he saw her last, but she was still tiny and light as a feather.

And then it was his mam's turn to hug and caress him and say all the things a loving mother says of her son when she hasn't seen him for so long and he'd been in such danger.

Then while she fussed and made him tea and heated up a big pot of Irish stew, Peter stood and looked around him with a smile. His family were still on the waiting list to get into one of the houses Guinness had built for their workers, but in the meantime, even this place was looking so much better.

The rooms were all scrubbed clean, and there were plates and cups without too many chips and lots of knickknacks on the dresser. Ma's late parents had been quite respectable, he knew. Her da had had a job as a postal worker, and Peter remembered as a little boy going to their house and seeing stuff like this, photographs and keepsakes, including a photo of Ma's brother, Anthony, the one Peter looked like, who'd died of scarlatina when he was twelve. Bridie Hegarty had really taken a turn for the worst when she married drunken Kit Cullen, but now even these damp rooms, with mice still scurrying in the walls, were beginning to look like that remembered parlour, with a Child of Prague on the mantelpiece and a picture of the Sacred Heart on the wall. And to his surprise, a photo of himself in army uniform that he'd sent to Kathleen was now in a brown leather frame. He hadn't expected her to put it up in the house. Kit wouldn't like that much, though it seemed he didn't have much say these days, but Peter was surprised Eamonn had allowed it.

'Will you go in and see your da?' Ma whispered to Peter as she bustled by, jerking her chin towards their old bedroom.

He pulled a face, but she smiled encouragingly. 'Don't worry, pet. Your da's no trouble any more. You just go on and see him. He'll only just be sitting there staring into space, not a peep outta him as usual. He doesn't say nothin' nowadays, but his eyes move. You never know – he might know who you are.'

Not sure he really wanted to do this, Peter opened the door in the flimsy partition and walked into his parents' bedroom. Sure enough, Kit Cullen was sitting in a chair squashed in beside the bed, staring blankly into space. Peter stood before his father.

'Hello, Da.'

Kit's eyes moved up and down, taking in the figure in front of him. His lips contorted and trembled, and a bubble of saliva formed in the corner of his mouth, then dribbled down his chin. It was as if the mute invalid in the chair was spitting at him in slow motion.

Peter shuddered and backed away. 'Bye then, Da.'

Back in the living room, his mother asked, 'Do you think he recognised you, son?'

'I dunno really.' His father's ineffectual venom at his son's betrayal by putting on a British uniform wasn't something he was prepared to dwell on. Just one more reason for his father to hate him, on top of prancing across the stage dressed as a woman.

He was more worried what Eamonn might say about him being in the British army, but when his brother arrived home in the next half hour, he seemed delighted to see Peter and hugged him tightly.

'Good to see ya, ya mad headcase. Don't let the Hun get ya, y'hear me?'

'I'm a fast runner, Eamonn.' Peter laughed, relieved his brother didn't see him joining up as a betrayal. 'I can outrun any bullet.'

'Connie, go down to get water for me love.' Their mother gave his youngest sister two buckets. Grumbling, she did as she was told.

'Yeah? Well, keep on running. We want ya to come home in one piece, so we do, and not to be in bits like Harry Bradfield. He's in a wheelchair now, and he can't see nor nuttin', and his ma is mindin' him night and day.'

Peter had seen plenty of young men like that on the boat and train here, sent back on stretchers from the front. Gas attacks, mines, bullets, shells having done their worst on their bodies and minds. There were worse things than dying, that was for sure.

'And you be careful too, Eamonn.'

'I don't intend to have an accident at the brewery, if that's what you mean.' His brother winked.

'Glad to hear it.' Peter waited while Ma put two steaming bowls of stew – plenty of meat for once, as well as carrots and potatoes – on the table, then disappeared into the bedroom to feed a third bowl of dinner to her incapacitated husband. Then he said in a low voice, 'You know what I mean?'

The altercation on the quayside, when he and Nick got off the boat in British army uniforms, had shaken him. And Kathleen had told him in her letters that the Irish Volunteers, what was left of them after the Rising, were gathering. Those who'd been sent to prison in England were mostly home by now, and there was a definite air of threat in the city. The Rising had been just the opening shot across the bow of British rule. The execution of the leaders, the men who signed the

Proclamation, had moved an ambivalent and sometimes hostile Irish public to rally to the Irish flag, and the result was a very jumpy and dangerous British military in the city. The whole place felt like a tinderbox that could go up in flames at any second.

Ever since the Easter Rising, when Eamonn was as much out of the house as in it, Peter had guessed his brother was in the Volunteers, and it seemed there was no doubt in anyone's mind that the Volunteers were mobilising.

'Ah, ya know me, Peter. I'll be grand.' Eamonn laughed it off as he dug into the stew, the tacit understanding obvious between the brothers.

Peter refused to be fobbed off. 'Look, I know better than most the tactics and the methods of the British army, and while I'm over there wearing this' – he flicked his hand at the lapel of his army coat – 'that doesn't mean I've forgotten who I am or where I come from.'

Eamonn looked at him thoughtfully, then nodded. 'Don't worry. I did have a bit of a run-in with them, but you got me out of it.'

'Me? But I wasn't here?'

'They came lookin' for me last month, stompin' up the stairs. One of our boys was picked up, and they tortured names out of him in the castle. Battered our door down – poor Ma nearly had a heart attack. But sure, when they saw your photograph, in full uniform, proudly defendin' king and country, sure they realised they had the wrong house altogether. Thanks be to God, Ma insisted on having it framed and I didn't have the heart to stop her.'

He chortled and Peter laughed as well. No wonder Eamonn had forgiven him for wearing his uniform.

'Still, though, don't you let them take you next nor near that castle, right?'

After Eamonn's story of nearly getting arrested, Peter was even more worried for his brother, who was, unlike their father, the real thing when it came to fighting for Ireland. Dublin Castle, the heart of the British administration in Ireland, was on Dame Street, and it almost pulsated with a threatening throb all around the city. People brought in for questioning rarely came out alive.

'I won't, I promise. You're like an auld one with all your fussin'.'

'Do they have your name?' Peter asked, not convinced by his brother's bravado.

'Sure, I'm registered as Edward Cullen, Eamonn O'Cuilleáin – they never heard of him.'

'Don't be so flippant, Eamonn, I mean it. They're on edge. They'd never say it, but the war is going badly in France and in Gallipoli too. The death toll is much worse than they're letting on and supplies are pitiful, so they're like cornered rats. Maybe once enough Americans arrive, things will change, but it's all so painfully slow.'

Before Eamonn could answer, the door burst open again and Maggie rushed in, followed by Kathleen and little Connie with the buckets. All the wars and bloodshed were forgotten, and Peter's family reunion was complete.

CHAPTER 12

 AY

TODAY SHE WAS WEARING her boring cream day dress, corduroy with a round neck, and though Mother liked it, May felt it did nothing for her. It didn't matter now, she supposed; Peter wasn't going to arrive today either. It was almost one o'clock and the boat docked at nine every morning, so if he'd been on it, he'd have turned up by now.

Either something dreadful had happened to him or he just didn't love her any more and this was his way of showing it. She hardly knew which was worse. She'd already cancelled today's afternoon tea at the Gresham, and though she pretended to her friends nothing was wrong, that Peter had just had his four-day pass cancelled, she could feel their pity coming down the phone lines at her and it was awful.

She heard the key turn in the front door. Her mother was back from the shops. Olive Gallagher bustled into the kitchen, clearly pleased to find May up and drinking a cup of tea and wearing the dress she'd bought her daughter for her birthday.

'Ah, you look lovely, love.' She beamed. 'Now help me with the vegetables. Mrs Joyce could talk the hind legs off a donkey, honestly. I only wanted a few carrots for the shepherd's pie – Madge asked me to pick them up – and the woman would not stop. Between her lumbago and the Kaiser and Father O'Reilly's bad chest, I thought I'd never get away. I went to McGettigan's, and would you believe they only had two cream horns left, so I –'

The diatribe was interrupted by a knock on the front door. Her mother looked surprised – they didn't often have callers – and May started. Was it him? What if it was? And she looking like this? She panicked, and instead of going to the door, she ran upstairs.

'May?' Her mother was confused. 'May, what is it?'

She peeped over the banister as she heard her mother go to the door while muttering to herself, and then saying, 'Hello?' and a familiar voice answering…

It was him. Peter. It was him! He was here! She rushed into her room and pulled off the corduroy dress and quickly dragged on the pink, almost ripping the fabric in her haste. Voices wafted up from downstairs, and more panic set in. What were they talking about? How did Peter introduce himself? Did Mother guess who he was?

She buttoned her brown and cream boots, fixed her hair quickly and ran back downstairs. He was there, standing with his back to her in the kitchen.

'Here's May now,' said her mother, then looked startled at the sight of her daughter in the calf-length dress. 'May, darling, where did you get…'

May ignored her. Peter had turned as she entered, and she almost melted at the sight of him. If anything he'd become even more attractive, more manly. His hair was cropped short instead of boyishly floppy, and his skin was a lot browner, hiding his freckles but making his navy-blue eyes even more vivid. The straight eyebrows were the same, and his cupid's-bow mouth, but his shoulders and arms had got more muscular and he was slightly taller than she remembered – still not much taller than her, but definitely tall enough – and heartbreakingly handsome in uniform.

'Hello, May,' he said in his new cultured middle-class accent, and his voice was deeper and he sounded older, more worldly-wise. She loved it. 'I'm so pleased to see you.' And he did look pleased. He took her in, running his gaze over her body in the shapely pink silk dress with the ruched belt.

'Hello, Peter.' She knew she was blushing. 'Mother, you remember me telling you about Peter Cullen, my friend?'

'Yes, yes, of course...' Her mother was still looking at her in alarm. 'May, darling, where did you get that short dress?'

'I had it made. Mother, have you offered Peter anything yet? He's been fighting the Germans on our behalf, just like David, so I'm sure you want to at least make him a cup of tea?'

'Oh...goodness. Yes, of course.' Poor Olive dragged her eyes away from her daughter's hourglass body and bustled with the kettle. 'What regiment are you with, Peter?'

'The Royal Irish Rifles, ma'am, but we all get a bit mixed in together at the front.' He was talking to May's mother, but his eyes continued to rest admiringly on May, a smile playing on his beautiful lips as she took a chair at the kitchen table and indicated for him to sit opposite her. 'And your daughter, May, has been such a good friend to me, and her letters cheer me right up when I get them, and the socks she sends have saved my feet.'

Olive sighed as she filled the teapot. 'Yes, she used to send so many socks to our boy, David. He was with the Royal Dublin Fusiliers, but we haven't heard from him in so long. We only have a missing-in-action telegram, but they don't tell us whether they're looking for him or anything...'

'I'm very sorry to hear that, Mrs Gallagher,' said Peter sympathetically. 'It's very hard for the family, not knowing. It's harder for those on the home front, I think, than for us fighting the war.'

'Yes, that's true. It's the not knowing – it's awful.' Olive looked so grateful to be understood.

'When you don't know the truth, it's often easy to fear the worst,' he said soothingly.

'I've had such terrible dreams, you see, Peter,' she confided in him as she put the teacups on the table. 'Of my David bleeding and nobody helping him, or being so maimed or blind… You hear terrible things, don't you?'

'Sometimes, Mrs Gallagher. But my advice is, don't dwell on them.'

'Do you think he could be in a prisoner-of-war camp?' she asked, and though Peter thought no such thing, he hadn't the heart to say so.

'He might be.' It was the best he could manage.

'Do you really think so?' Her mother looked gratefully at him. 'How horrid of them not to let him write to us.'

'I suppose the Germans just want everyone to be upset, to undermine morale, so it's important to keep our chin up and not let them frighten us.'

'It's so comforting to hear you say that. He was…is…such a lovely boy, you see, and we love him so dearly. It's just very hard to be brave sometimes.'

A tear rolled down her cheek, and May watched in amazement as her normally very proper mother allowed Peter to stand up and take her in his arms and pat her back as she sobbed gently into his tunic. She'd never even seen her mother do that with her father, and she was selfishly glad that Peter was the one to break through to her.

'I know,' he said soothingly. 'I know. But the war will be over soon.'

'I'm sorry… I really…' She took the handkerchief he offered and wiped her face. 'Please forgive me for talking about my own troubles. I don't know what came over me. Just seeing you in uniform and reminding me of…'

'You'll feel better for having let it out. Tears are good for us, Mrs Gallagher. All that sadness eats away at us inside if we don't let it out, and you'd want to be made of granite not to be broken-hearted by what's going on.'

'Thank you, Peter,' Olive said, her voice strangled by emotion.

May sat in stunned admiration. She had imagined Peter's homecoming so many times, but not like this. He was perfect, knew exactly what to say. She'd been prepared for a big fight when her parents found out she and Peter were getting engaged, but he'd won half the battle for her already. He had her mother hook, line and sinker.

'Now, why don't you two sit here and have a cup of tea,' Olive said, wiping her eyes and beaming fondly. 'I had some at my meeting, so I don't need another cup. I got two cream cakes in McGettigan's, and ye can enjoy them with it and have a nice reunion? I have some things I need to be getting on with in the garden, so I'll leave you to it.'

May was delighted and amazed that her mother left her and Peter unchaperoned, even though she was only in the garden, but still... Suddenly shy, she busied herself with the cake box, untying the string and laying the table with the good china. 'So, Private Cullen, how have you been keeping?' she asked, with a sideways smile at his beautiful face.

'Era, I'm still breathing in and out, so that's something. You look well.' He grinned at her, and she blushed again.

'Thank you.'

As she laid a plate in front of him, he caught her hand, and her breath quickened.

'It's good to see you, May. I meant it about your parcels. They really cheered me up, and I wanted to say thanks so much for delivering all those other letters and things.'

'I don't mind. I love it really, writing to you about all my worries. I feel so alone sometimes. It was kind what you said about it being worse for us on the home front. And did you really mean what you said about David? I feel very sure he's alive, but I do wonder sometimes if he's all right.'

He shrugged and did that lovely thing with his lips that she just adored, pursing them to the side when he was thinking. 'I don't know for sure... But you have to hope, don't you?'

Her heart sunk a little, but at least he was being honest. 'Have you got any way of finding out, I mean, or maybe asking around at the front?'

Peter smiled to himself, with his long dark eyelashes lowered, and she had a feeling she'd said something very silly. But then he looked up. 'Well, there's thousands of men at the front and it's a very long line, so chances of finding someone who knew him aren't great, but I could ask my pal Enzo.'

'Enzo? Is that his real name?' He'd mentioned this friend in letters but she'd never met anyone with that name before.

'Short for Lorenzo. He's Italian – well, a Londoner, but his father is Italian. He's got this weird ability to sort of know things, like who's going to die that day, though he pretends not to so people won't be afraid of him.'

'Really?' May was fascinated with all of that, but her parents forbade any talk of it in the house. People said Mr Yeats the poet was always having séances and he and his friends were mixed up in that, but Father O'Reilly even gave a sermon on it, saying it was satanic and not safe for anyone to be mixed up in.

'Yeah, I think he knows things. His grandmother was a fortune-teller – maybe he's inherited the gift.'

'Did he know about us?' May asked coquettishly. She loved David, of course she did, but they didn't have much time and she wanted to get the conversation around to themselves now. Apart from the grab of her hand when she gave him a plate, the conversation had been very friendly but not romantic.

'He did, of course, but because I told him, not because he heard a whisper from beyond.' Peter grinned and took a bite of the pastry filled with whipped cream and jam. He shut his eyes and moaned in ecstasy. 'Oh, May, you've no idea. You forget that things can taste like this, honest to God you do. The stuff they give us is so horrible, dry, tasteless…'

She didn't want to hear about that. 'What did you tell him about us?' she asked.

He opened his eyes. 'Well, he asked me if I had a sweetheart waiting for me, and I said I had you.'

May felt a surge of relief. Of course he thought of her as his sweetheart. His letters were just friendly because he preferred to keep the intimacy to when they met.

'Will we go for a walk?' she asked, after he'd finished the pastry and drained his cup. 'If you're not too tired after all your travelling.'

'Ah no, it was grand. We slept most of the way. I travelled with my other pal Nick. He's from Waterford, where his parents own a grocery store, or so he claims.' He got to his feet and cleared his plate away into the sink.

'What do you mean, so he claims?'

'I dunno. Something about him. He's not telling us everything, to be honest, so God knows what the story is there. That Alicia Shaw is his cousin, he says, but I'm not sure I believe him.'

'Goodness!' Peter's friends were all so interesting, and mysterious. 'I did wonder if there was a romance there. Maybe he's the son of the house and she's the lady's maid, and they're having a secret affair because he's not allowed to marry her? Oh, I do hope they elope!' She retrieved her coat from the hallstand and pinned on her pink velvet hat with the fashionable brim. She steered the conversation back to themselves again. 'I nearly died when you didn't arrive yesterday, Peter.'

'Oh, I had to go and see my ma and my sisters and my brother. We had a lovely day all together,' he said as he buttoned up his uniform jacket.

Her eyes widened. 'You went to see them before you came to see me?'

The look he gave her then made her instantly regret her words. She'd spoken without thinking; she had been too proprietorial. Of course he went to see his family – why would he not? It was only in her world that his family were in his past and she and Peter were the future.

'I had to go and see my mother, May. She's been worrying about me.'

'Of course you had to.' She backtracked instantly as she opened the front door. 'I was just worried too…that's all.'

He seemed to consider her for a split second, and May feared she'd ruined everything, but then he seemed to relax again, and they moved down the path through the small front garden and out onto the foot-path, closing the gate on its well-oiled hinges behind them.

'So how is your mother, and your sisters and brother? All well, I hope?' she asked. She wondered why he said nothing of his father but didn't push him.

'Ah, they're grand. My mother was delighted when I came in the door. And my little sister Connie was so happy to see me.' His voice caught on the emotion of it all. 'She threw herself into my arms and gave me the biggest hug. It was lovely.'

'That's nice.' They walked beside each other, not touching. She longed to take his arm, but maybe it would be too forward after not seeing him for so long. She dared a sideways glance as they walked; his uniform made him look even more handsome.

'And the rest of them, they were in great form.' He smiled at the memory of his day with his family. 'I took them all out for breakfast this morning.'

'I'll look forward to meeting them,' May said quietly. She'd always imagined just rescuing him from his past, but of course he had his own ideas, and it looked like she was going to have to welcome these people into her life. Never mind – she would help them all to get ahead.

Peter dropped his eyes as they walked on, side by side, through the leafy roads and neat houses with well-kept gardens. 'Yes, well, though maybe not this time...'

'Surely I'll have to meet them sometime. Surely... I mean...when we...before we...'

She stopped walking and so did he, turning to regard her, his face a mask. He had a way; she remembered it from before. It was hard to describe, but he could almost pull a shutter down, and then once he did that, she had no idea what he was thinking.

'Well, before we marry.' There, she'd said it. The words hung between them, and she felt herself redden, but she was glad she'd managed to get it out. She didn't dare look at his face, though, keeping her gaze dropped.

'Marry?' he eventually said. 'May, I...'

She walked off and hoped he'd follow her. She didn't want to have this out on the street. She turned into St Fiachra's Park, a little enclosed garden with a few benches around the perimeter. Apart from an old man walking his dog, it was empty.

He followed her, and she sat on a bench. He sat beside her.

'May, please, I like you, I really do, but we can't get married. May, we're too... It wouldn't be...'

She felt faint. Her whole future was slipping away. But she wasn't going to lose him without putting up a fight. 'You think I let you... That night before you left, you think I'd let someone I wasn't going to marry do that? I thought you felt the same. Otherwise I would never have...'

It was his turn to blush now. 'May, I'm sorry, I should never... And I was afraid all the time you were going to write and tell me you were having a baby, and then of course I would have married you if that was what you wanted. But you're not, and honestly, May, you could do a lot better than me.'

Oh, thank goodness. Her heart flooded with relief. So that was it, just as she'd suspected. It wasn't that this beautiful boy didn't love her. It was because he thought once she found out about Henrietta Street, she would reject him because of his lowly background. He knew she was above him in station and was worried he would insult her by asking her to marry him. He daren't tell her the truth after lying for so long.

It was time to reassure him that she didn't mind, that she knew all about him already. Though it was much too embarrassing to admit she'd followed him home.

'I don't care about where you're from, Peter. I love you. I want to marry you. You said once that you went to school in North King Street, so I know well you're not from Dún Laoghaire. But I don't care if you are from the slums on the north side. I would still want to marry you, and I really mean that. It doesn't matter to me where you're from – it's where you're going. You're clever enough to do anything you want, and with me by your side, you will make it to the top, I promise. And we'll look after all your family as well.'

He sat and looked at her for what felt like a long time, clearly weighing her words. But then he shook his head. 'No. Your ma and da would have a stroke for a start if they thought I was from...where I'm from. You're right about my background. We're from different worlds, May, same city but completely different worlds, and your parents would be right to want you to marry someone much better got than me.'

Now he was worrying about her parents. 'You're not listening, Peter. I don't care about what Mother and Father think. The important thing is, I want you. Me. May. Don't you want me, Peter?'

He looked torn and miserable. 'I… You're very special to me, and I'm so grateful, and I'm so lucky to have you as a friend, but…'

May felt herself colour. This was harder work than it should be; he was being very stubborn. 'You think of me as just a friend?' she said, her voice and expression incredulous. 'A friend? Because, Peter, let me tell you something. I have a lot of friends, and I don't let them in my bed. Oh, Peter, how could you do this to me…' With a gasp of misery, she scrabbled for a handkerchief in her bag. 'I'm ruined, don't you see that? I gave myself to you, thinking that you came to see me that morning because I was the one you loved. How can I ever change that now?' She buried her face in the handkerchief and started to wail.

'Ah, May, please, don't cry.' He sounded terrified.

'All I was doing was waiting for you to come back, for us to be together again, forever, and now you tell me you don't want me…' She sobbed harder. 'That you just used me, ruined me, and now you're discarding me…'

'I'm not saying that, May. I'm not saying that at all. Of course I wasn't just using you…and I'm very fond of you, you know I am…'

She dropped the handkerchief. 'So will you marry me?' she asked.

He sighed and took off his peaked hat and ran his hand through his short fair hair. 'May, if you knew where I was from…'

'Show me.'

'Ah, what? No…' He ran his hand through his hair again and looked flustered.

'Show me where you're from. You can see for yourself if I care then,' she insisted.

'You won't like it,' he said with conviction, but he stood up and took her hand, placed it in his arm and walked purposefully towards the tram stop. One arrived within minutes, and he ushered her on and into a seat, then sat beside her, saying nothing as the tram wound its way through Harcourt Street and Westland Row, over the Liffey and up as far as Amiens Street, where he helped her alight.

This time she linked him as they walked in silence, and Peter led her off the main Georgian boulevards of the city to a part she'd only visited once before, when she'd followed him home. She was very glad now that she'd done that. If she hadn't been prepared, she might have shown her shock, but as it was, she was able to stay cool and gracious as he brought her into the Georgian squares and streets, where poverty and neglect painted everything grey with misery.

It was even worse by daylight, though, so despite being prepared, she had to try hard not to wince at the sight of the outdoor toilets from which the most putrid odour emanated.

Peter was watching for her reaction. 'Two privies between 116 people, and that's just two houses. No running water, nowhere to wash. This is where I was brought up, May. Imagine bringing your parents to meet mine, in this place?'

Some children in rags screeched past them, barefoot, chasing a scrawny pig.

'They're raising it in the yard,' he said, but she refused to flinch and bestowed a charming smile upon the ragged urchins.

They passed women hauling tin baths full of water up stairs and others hanging grey frayed sheets and rows of well-past-use children's clothes on the lines that were strung across the yards.

'Look around, May, really look,' he said, bringing her to a halt. 'This is where I come from. This is all I have to offer, can't you see? If I make it through the war, and that's a big if, when I come back, and then if I'm in one piece, this is what I'll come back to. You couldn't live like this. I couldn't have it, and neither could you. My ma had nine kids, do you know that? And there's five of us left, and she's doing better than most. Babies die here for want of clean water or a doctor. You're used to finer things, a lovely home, beautiful clothes. So forget about me, May. I'm no good for you. Find some fella like that boss of yours at work you told me about, with a future, with prospects.'

She felt so self-conscious in her pink silk dress and her floppy hat; everyone in the street was staring at her. She knew Peter wanted her to cover her little nose with her handkerchief, and get faint, and insist on being taken away, but she refused to give in.

'But you won't be here, Peter. We both know that,' she said quietly. 'You'll make something of yourself. You're going to be living a different life in the future, I know you will, and I want to make that life with you.'

'And how are we to do that, would you mind telling me?' He was smiling now, though also shaking his head in exasperation.

'For a start, you're going to be a famous actor after the war.'

'That's what I want to do, that's true. But actors don't make that much money, May.' He chuckled as he spoke, and she was angry with him now, treating her like she was a naive schoolgirl, blinded by romantic notions. 'Enough for one, maybe, but their families aren't well looked after. They need parents who can bail them out when needed, and that I don't have.'

'I'll bail you out…'

'I'm not going cap in hand to your family, May. What sort of son-in-law does that?'

A sense of triumph stirred in her breast. She was wearing him down. 'I'm not talking about my parents. I have an inheritance coming to me, from my mother's aunt, my great-aunt. She's childless, and I'm all she's got, God be good to her. I'll be twenty-one in three years, and if she's died by then…' She crossed herself hastily; it seemed wrong to talk about her great-aunt's death, but the old lady was very, very old. It was really odd the number of young people who were dying from the flu while her old fossil of a great-aunt lingered year in, year out. 'Then I will have her money. I don't know how much it is, maybe five hundred…' She knew that amount was unlikely, but she didn't care. 'It would be such a great start for us.'

The shutter had come down, his face going blank. 'No, I can't do that. I won't take all your money. Look, May, if I make it, I won't be coming back to Dublin anyway. I might go to England.'

The words cut her so deeply. She'd hoped if she passed this test, let him show her around the slums and kept on smiling, then he'd see how strong she was, as well as beautiful and clever, and would have to admit they were made for each other. But all along he'd just been hoping it would knock the wind out of her sails, that she would have a fainting fit and agree to let him go. She hadn't done that, so he was throwing another obstacle in her way. England.

It was over. She tried her best not to cry. She should let him go, not humiliate herself further by begging. She turned and walked away, hurrying, her buttoned boots splashing through the excrement and mud, lifting her skirts and finally allowing herself to shudder.

'Ah, lads, look at this beauty.' A young man with two others flanking him was walking along beside her, looking her up and down.

May walked faster, her heart racing, but he followed along. 'I'd say you're a bit lost, love. Let me help you home.' He winked at his mates, who leered and laughed.

'She's with me,' said Peter behind them, and May felt weak with relief.

'Is she now, soldier boy? Is she indeed? And you the fine brave lad fighting for the king?'

'Come on, May,' said Peter quietly.

'May, is it? Ah sure, leave the lovely May here with us, soldier boy. We'll see no harm comes to her, won't we, boys? She's one in a million, so she is...'

'So are your chances,' May retorted.

The two henchmen laughed at her rejoinder, and the ringleader scowled; he didn't like being made to look small.

'Now kindly let us pass. We are, as you say, lost, but I'm sure we can find our way out of here.'

The bully stood in front of them, blocking their way, and went to punch Peter on the jaw. But Peter managed to duck and sidestep him, and the young man stumbled over the broken cobblestones, falling forward onto his knees. Before he had time to get up, May whipped the long pin from her hat and stuck it in his bottom, causing him to howl with pain and his friends to howl with laughter. Then she grabbed Peter's hand and the two of them took off down the street, not stopping until they were out of the slums and back on the main thoroughfares once more, mingling with the well-dressed people of the city.

They started to laugh then, bordering on hysterical, while the middle-class women passing looked at May as if to say such behaviour wasn't seemly in a lady as finely dressed as she. May didn't care; she just roared and hooted until she didn't have the breath to carry on.

'And you're going to tell me we're not a good team, are you?' she demanded, wiping the tears of laughter from her eyes. 'I know you brought me there to scare me off, but that's not my future and it's not yours either, Peter. We are good together, so why can't you just survive this war, don't let anything happen to you, come home, marry me, and together we'll take the world by storm?'

He was still smiling, and there in the middle of the street, not caring a jot what anyone thought, she kissed him full on the lips. A moment's hesitation, and then he responded, his mouth pressed to hers, his tongue finding hers, and on and on they kissed, oblivious to the scandal they were causing.

'Is that a yes?' she asked as they broke away for air.

'It's a "we'll see if I make it".' He chuckled.

'Can I have a ring?' She knew she was pushing it, but it was now or never.

'I can't afford one, May. This is what I mean.'

'Put your hand in your pocket,' she said with a giggle.

He looked puzzled but did as she asked and extracted a five-pound note.

'What? Where did this come from? May, I'm not...' He looked so horrified, she had to laugh.

'I saved it from my wages and my allowance. Please, Peter. You've said if you survive the war, we'll get married, and I want to have something to show my friends that I'm not some pathetic girl losing my heart over a boy who isn't interested. I know people laugh at me when I tell them about you. The girls at the tennis club think I made you up. I was going to have them to tea in the Gresham today to meet you, and I had to cancel and it was really embarrassing, and I just want to have a ring to show off. I'm sorry if that makes me sound silly, and I know I should wait until you propose, but you're going back to war and anything could happen, and I just want to be able to tell everyone that I'm your girl.'

He laughed again, like she was the funniest person he'd ever met, and placed his hands on her shoulders. 'All right, you win. Let's do it. But I won't use your money. I'll use my own. So it won't be as fancy a ring as you might like, but it will be the best I can do. And I'll have to speak to your da first, and he'll probably give me a flat no once he hears who I am and where I'm from, but I'll try. Is that fair enough?'

Da. She'd have to get those little words out of his vocabulary. He'd done so well to remove his roots, but a few telltale traces remained. There was no way he could be talking about her 'da' or his 'ma' down in the cricket club or after Mass. She would help him, though. She would hide his background in the slums, his lack of education, his dearth of connections. She would bring him where none of that would matter. She would elevate him.

'That will have to do, I suppose, as long as you don't make a liar out of me.' And when he looked at her quizzically, she explained, 'I said your father was a doctor in Galway and you'd only moved to Dublin because of the theatre.'

'Oh, May...'

She put her hands on her hips and looked him boldly in the eye. 'Don't argue, Peter. You didn't mind not telling me, did you? And you did a lot naughtier things with me than just not mentioning where you were from.'

He reddened then but didn't argue back, and she grabbed his hand with a gleeful giggle. And soon they were strolling together down Sackville Street like a young all-but-engaged couple with not a care in the world.

* * *

PETER MADE an attempt to leave her at the gate, saying he had to get back to his 'ma'.

'Mother,' May corrected him gently, before making him bring her to the front door. Her father opened it, and she thought he might be cross with her for being out so long, worrying her mother, but he greeted Peter with surprising warmth.

'Private Cullen, is it? You're very welcome. Apparently you've been a great comfort to my wife – she's been singing your praises all afternoon.'

Peter shook his hand politely. 'Good evening, Mr Gallagher. I'm sorry to keep your daughter out so long, but she's so pleasant to talk to. Now, I'll –'

'Peter's got something to ask you, Father,' said May firmly. Peter was taking the boat back tomorrow, so this might be her one and only chance. 'Why don't you bring him into the living room, and you can discuss it there?'

CHAPTER 13

ETER

MAY'S father was a stiff-looking man, and he was no doubt a snob like all his type, but he didn't appear unkind. In the living room, he offered Peter a whiskey and soda, and seemed to approve when Peter asked for just soda.

'Not a drinker, Cullen? Unusual for a soldier?'

'No, sir. I have a…had an uncle who was a martyr to the drink, and I've seen the destruction alcohol can do, so that's not something you'd need to worry about.'

'I hope you don't mind if I partake?' The older man poured a whiskey for himself and indicated for Peter to sit in one of the armchairs that faced each other across an embroidered rug, in front of the fireplace in which a few small logs were burning.

Peter sat carefully into the comfortable chair, which had a lace antimacassar, while Michael Gallagher took the one opposite and rested his whiskey on the arm. He had a big red face and a bristling moustache, rather like Lord Kitchener from the famous 'Your

Country Needs You' posters. 'Now tell me, Cullen, why would I need to worry about your habits at all? How do they affect me, or my daughter?'

Peter felt a bit like a rabbit caught in the headlights of a car; this interview was the last thing he'd thought would happen when he knocked on May's door a few hours earlier. But he could hardly let her down, could he? Not after that long walk home, when they'd kissed in every shop doorway and on every corner. She was so attractive, and the way she responded to him, well, she was unusual in that regard. Most of the lads he knew spoke of constant pushing on their part for a glimpse of flesh or a touch of a hand or a kiss and cuddle with their girls, but May wasn't like that. If anything, she was the more forceful one; he'd had to beg her to stop a few times.

'Mr Gallagher,' he said cautiously, 'your daughter is a wonderful girl, but you know that.'

'So what is this question she wants you to ask me, Cullen?' asked Mr Gallagher, taking a sip of his whiskey and soda. 'Come on, boy, don't be shy. Spit it out.'

'Well…I…I suppose it's to ask for her hand in marriage, sir.'

Michael Gallagher didn't seem remotely surprised. He just sat, stroking his big Kitchener-style moustache, gazing at a portrait of his daughter on the wall over the fireplace. May as a little girl in a white cotton frock, a ribbon in her hair and holding a doll.

'I know we've not known each other very long,' said Peter into the silence, 'but her letters have been such a pleasure.'

'You love her, do you?' the older man asked abruptly, and Peter was taken aback by the question.

'Well, yes, of course.' He wasn't sure that he did, but then, what was love? He was eighteen – he had no idea. And maybe what people called love wasn't a good thing anyway. His mother said she loved his father – that's why she'd married so far beneath her – and look where that had got her. May would never drag him down like Kit Cullen had dragged down Bridie Hegarty. She was sweet and he found her funny. He liked her, and he thought she was really, well… attractive. Maybe that was love. 'I do love your daughter, Mr

Gallagher, and I would much appreciate your permission to marry her.'

Michael Gallagher took one last look at the picture, then turned to him. 'You strike me as a fine young man in lots of ways, but if you'll permit me to speak freely?'

'Of course, sir. Speak away.'

Gallagher eyed him over his whiskey. 'She's a headstrong girl, you realise?'

Peter smiled for the first time since May had ordered him and her father into the living room. 'I do. She knows what she wants, all right.' He didn't think that was a bad thing, though. He admired May's drive and her determination; he could see she would be a good person to have on his side.

'And I'm assuming what she wants is you, as she's sent you in here to ask for her hand,' Gallagher added wryly.

'I imagine so, sir. Of course, it wasn't just her idea, sir.'

'Now, listen, Cullen, and don't take offence if you don't like what you hear...'

'I won't, sir.' He felt a slight sense of relief, and then wondered if May would blame him if her father refused to give him her hand, if she'd complain he hadn't tried hard enough. If the food parcels would dry up...

'May is very precious to my wife and me, and while she comes across as very confident and sure of herself, she is still just a girl, and I'm fearful that this...her...determination to...have you...is just her latest fixation on getting what she wants, be it to dress in the latest fashion, however unsuitably short, or take a job in an office that she simply doesn't need.'

'Really, sir?' Peter wasn't sure he liked Michael Gallagher talking about him like he was the latest fashion in clothes. Funnily enough, it made him want to fight harder for May. 'Well, I think I'm more to her than that.'

'Mm. Maybe so. But I'm fearful that she doesn't understand how things work. She is used to a comfortable life, a nice home, fashionable clothes and so on, things girls like. She's an equal among her peers, and we'd imagined she would marry someone where we knew the family, a friend of her brother's perhaps, or the son of someone I know – that was how we imagined it working out. And I just worry that she's not really aware of…well, the huge social difference…'

'The social difference?' Peter asked cautiously. Did May's da already know he came from Henrietta Street? Dublin was a very small place, so it was possible.

'Yes. You can hardly deny it. I know your father was a doctor, Cullen, but May tells us you want to be an actor. Is that still the case?'

'Ah.' How ironic. To him being an actor was this huge step up, but to the Gallaghers, it was clearly a big step down.

Michael Gallagher had the grace to look uncomfortable. 'I hope you're not offended. As I say, you seem like a very nice chap.'

Funnily enough, he wasn't offended at all. May fretted about her parents being snobs, while unconsciously being one herself, but Peter understood about wanting to better yourself, and wanting better for your children. 'I can understand why that would be a worry, sir, and I know I'm not what you and Mrs Gallagher had in mind for your daughter – you don't need to tell me that, or apologise for saying it. And I know being an actor doesn't sound like a very promising profession, but I intend to go far, Mr Gallagher, and May and I…well, we'll be a good team. We have a lot of plans, and I'm ambitious. Of course we'll have to wait until after the war, whenever that is, and even then I don't think we should marry until I can give her, if not luxury at first, at least some degree of comfort. I'm not intending for your daughter to live in squalor, Mr Gallagher.'

Michael Gallagher looked genuinely pleased and interested. 'I'm glad to hear you say that, Cullen. I was worried you were going to push my hand, maybe demand a special licence or something. I bet she's been dropping hints about that, eh?'

'She did mention it, sir…' She had, but he'd said he wanted to do things properly for her.

'And you stood firm. Well done. You've gone up in my estimation just for that, and I must say, you seem to have your head screwed on.

Always thought actors were airy-fairy fellows myself, but you've impressed me, Cullen.'

Peter smiled. He enjoyed this feeling of speaking man to man, promising a father that he would take care of his daughter. It made him feel like he'd arrived in society. Maybe May was right that she could drag him up to this level. He knew how hard it was to break out of the station you were born into, so this was a ticket up. He'd be foolish not to take it.

'War changes a man, Mr Gallagher. It does one of two things as far as I've observed. Either it fills a man with despair, a hopelessness and a belief that everything is doomed, that there is no future, or it makes him feel alive. And privileged to be so. I've seen so many of my comrades die, more than I can ever count, or even remember. It's like a film, reel after reel of death and destruction. I hate it, but it makes me realise that life is precious, that we have to make our own luck, that we have to take chances and trust to fate. And if I survive, then that's how I intend to live. I can't promise your daughter a fine house like yours in the first few years, but I intend to get there, and in the meantime, I can promise her my respect, and love, and that the man she married will never stop trying to better himself.'

Michael Gallagher threw back the whiskey and got to his feet. Peter stood up as well, not sure what was happening. Gallagher shook his hand. 'And you love her and she loves you – you're sure of it?' he asked again, still gripping Peter's fingers hard.

'Yes, sir.'

'Well then, I'll talk to my wife, of course, but I don't think that will be an obstacle. She's quite incapable of refusing May anything.'

'Thank you very much, sir,' Peter said faintly.

'Don't look so shocked, Peter.' The other man smiled kindly. 'Did you really think I'd say no? I'm no more capable of standing up to May than my wife is. I hope you have more luck with her.'

'Yes, thank you, sir.'

'Talking of my wife…' Gallagher poured himself another whiskey, no soda this time, and stood staring moodily into his glass. 'I gather she was talking to you about our boy. David.'

'Yes, sir, and I'm sorry that he's missing. It's very hard for you all.'

May's father turned from the sideboard to face him, the whiskey in his hand. 'Did you really mean what you said to her, about David maybe being a prisoner of war?'

Peter hesitated. He'd felt a bit bad at the time, when May's mother grabbed hold of the hope he was offering her, like a drowning man grasping at a straw. And without doubt, it was false hope. But maybe false hope was exactly what was needed in a situation like this? 'I can't say, to be honest, sir. But it's possible, isn't it?'

'Is it?' He studied Peter for a moment, then swallowed the neat whisky and shuddered. 'I appreciate you comforting my wife. She's been having very bad dreams. One day she'll have to face the truth, I fear, but until then... Well, you take what comfort you can get, don't you? I think of him as an angel in heaven, looking down on us. Maybe he sent you to us. May loves you, and my wife has taken to you. Maybe I will take to you as well.'

'Thank you, sir.' And Peter felt the sad, heavy weight of this family descend on him – not just May but her parents, so desperately in need of a son.

'Take care of our daughter, Peter,' said Michael Gallagher, shaking his hand again. 'And you'll get no argument from me. You're right – war changes everything. And maybe all change isn't for the worst.'

He fixed his future father-in-law with an unwavering gaze. 'I will, sir.'

'Good. Now you go and talk to May, and I'll go and tell my wife.'

* * *

PETER SAW Nick before Nick saw him. He looked well rested, and he leant on the wall of the dock, smoking a cigarette with the sunset behind him. Peter felt a pang, like it was wrong to send Nick back there. He'd survived, he'd got home, so why tempt fate again?

Funnily enough he didn't feel the same way about himself. Connie and Maggie had insisted on walking him to the port. Kathleen had had to go back to work and Ma to go home to mind Da, who had

123

taken a bad turn since Peter came home and kept having little fits; maybe it was the uniform that had set him off. May was with him as well, and Eamonn, and Eamonn had taken May's arm to help her over the ropes and anchors littering the quay because Connie and Maggie had hold of both Peter's hands and weren't letting him go.

Peter was delighted May was getting on so well with Eamonn. Eamonn was the one member of the family he was worried might take against her, because she was so middle class. But May had charmed them all.

She had insisted on treating his whole family to a posh Sunday dinner in the Maritime Hotel, to 'celebrate their engagement', on their way to seeing him off. She'd told him to bring them to meet her there at one, three hours before his boat sailed, and when he protested at her spending her money, she pointed out how much she had saved by cancelling afternoon tea at the Gresham with her tennis friends.

There had been great excitement and astonishment in Henrietta Street when he came home with the news of his engagement yesterday evening, and his fiancé's request to join her for Sunday lunch, which they found almost more exciting than the engagement. Bridie Cullen had never been inside the door of a hotel in her life, nor had the rest of them, and Maggie was even of a mind to refuse. But Peter knew May wouldn't take no for an answer, so he just warned his younger boisterous middle sister to behave herself and to scrub up well.

Kathleen helped their mother to get dressed. Kathleen had a free dress from the stock room in Arnotts. It had been ripped by some woman too big for it trying it on and the manager was going to throw it out, said it was beyond repair, but Kathleen had asked if she could have it and the manager agreed. Ma had stayed up most of the night mending it until it looked almost as good as new.

In the morning, Ma washed her hair and pinned it up under a hat she'd borrowed from Mrs Cussen downstairs – Mrs Cussen played the organ in the church and so always wore a nice hat – and with the dress from Arnotts, she looked lovely.

The girls were in their Sunday best, which wasn't very good but much better than it used to be before Da's accident. And Eamonn wore some clothes he'd got off the Guinness ladies. He looked devilishly handsome, the way Kit Cullen must have looked as a young man, swarthy and muscular and with piercing blue eyes, and rakish with that cigarette always dangling from the corner of his mouth.

Peter wore his uniform; it was all he had anyway. But even despite everything that had gone on since the Rising, Eamonn only grinned at him and winked.

May stood waiting for them at the door of the Maritime Hotel, waving and dimpling prettily. She had a little parasol with her, and she was wearing the silk dress and the button boots. Eamonn's eyes were out on stalks when he saw her, which made Peter laugh, and his sisters oohed and aahed and Ma looked quite frightened.

In fairness to May, though, she put everyone instantly at their ease, making a joke about the stuffy-looking doorman with the top hat and tails. In the restaurant, she took over the ordering – she must have realised none of them had a clue – and they had soup, followed by roast beef with mashed potatoes and carrots and parsnips and then apple tart with cream, and when she called Ma 'Mother', Peter could tell his ma was bursting with delight and pride.

She also explained with a serious face why her own parents weren't there to meet them, that they had to visit the great-aunt all the way out in Stillorgan, that she was at death's door. His ma looked relieved and said she understood, that there was plenty of time for that.

He'd said his last goodbye to May's parents the night before. Olive had shed a tear and Michael shook his hand warmly, and for a second, Peter feared he might hug him, such was the level of emotion. He knew it wasn't all for him; his departure in uniform must be a poignant reminder of them saying goodbye to their only son, for what might turn out to have been for the last time.

Of course the real reason May hadn't invited them to the hotel lunch was because she'd told them his father was a doctor in Galway. He supposed they would have to find out the truth about his parents some day. Also he suspected May wanted to make sure his family was cleaned up a bit first before everyone got introduced.

It might be too late for his mother, but if anyone could drag his sisters up in the world, Peter thought to himself, it was May. The three of them were melting over her, and watching her carefully to see which knives and forks to use, and Eamonn even whispered to Peter in between courses that he could do a lot worse than May Gallagher, which was high praise indeed from his republican brother.

'And when you get married, can I be one of yer flower girls, May?' asked Connie as she licked cream from her lips. She was the least nervous of all of them and already in love with her 'new sister'.

'Of course you can,' said May generously.

Her little face lit up. 'Really? In a proper frock and everythin'?'

'A pink frock and a ribbon in your hair, and there's going to be a bunch of flowers for you to carry. You'll be like a princess in a story.'

'And can Maggie be one too?' Connie was more tenderhearted than her sister, but they were loyal as dogs to each other all the same. Peter saw the look of hope on his wild sister's face. Her mop of red curls was still in want of brushing, but there was a beauty to her, a waywardness that men would find a challenge.

'Maggie will definitely be one too, of course.' May smiled.

Connie beamed, and Maggie looked shy; she wouldn't show her delight, but Peter knew she felt it.

'Can Maggie have a pink dress as well?'

'I'm not wearin' pink. With me hair I'll look like a butcher's apron,' said Maggie belligerently.

'You're quite right, Maggie. You obviously understand your colours,' said May kindly. 'Green is your shade, but we can't have that – it's unlucky at weddings – so how about we compromise with pale blue? And, Kathleen, since I don't have a sister, would you be maid of honour?'

Kathleen looked quite overcome, mumbled she'd be delighted and ducked her head over her apple pie, and Peter felt a wave of affection for May. She really was a powerhouse once she decided she wanted something. And maybe she was right; maybe she was the perfect person to have by his side.

'YER NOT TO GO DYIN' on us now, d'ya hear me?' Maggie nudged his ribs as they walked to the boat. 'We only have two brothers.'

'I'll do my best.' He smiled and put his arm around her shoulders. Maggie was not as tough as she liked people to think, and last night she'd cried in his arms, begging him not to go back. So many boys and men they knew never returned, and she was terrified he'd be next.

'You better do better than your bleedin' best. I seen what your best looks like, and that's not good enough at all,' she scoffed, to hide her pain.

'Just if they say you have to go out, to where the Germans are, just say you have to go to the toilet or somethin', right?' Connie slipped her little hand in his.

'Don't you worry, Connie. I'll do that,' he promised. 'I'll come home in one piece, don't worry.'

Nick detached himself from the wall and came to meet them, and Peter introduced him to May, who asked him if he'd managed to meet up with his Alicia Shaw. He admitted he had and thanked her for her help, but he wouldn't say any more about it, which she clearly found a bit frustrating.

The boat was here, and the gangplank down, and Nick disappeared up it with his kit bag and a small suitcase. But May held Peter back for ages, in floods of tears, and in the end, he had to gently disengage himself. 'Will you take the girls to get a cream cake each and maybe a lemonade?' he asked her, taking a shilling from his pocket. There was a woman selling cakes and drinks from a table on the quayside. 'While I have a last word with Eamonn?'

She smiled tearfully and gave him a last kiss and hug, then took the girls by their hands and led them away, chatting brightly to them.

Eamonn punched him on the arm. 'Mind yourself, d'ya hear me?'

'All right, and if…well, if you get a telegram, tell May in person, yourself, all right?' He didn't like to dwell on the prospect of his death, but the reality had to be faced. 'And tell Ma and the girls that I love them, and you mind yourself too.'

'Sir, yes, sir!' Eamonn laughed as he stood to attention and gave Peter a salute, clicking his heels as he did so.

'Eejit,' Peter said, picking up his kit bag. 'But seriously, no acting the clown and getting yourself shot. They're not messin', Eamonn. It's not a game. All right?'

'Don't worry about me. I won't take any chances I don't have to, alrigh'?'

Peter nodded and hugged his brother.

'And keep an eye on May for me, will ya?'

'I will, of course. Just come back in one piece.'

Over at the stall, his sisters and May had bought a box of cakes tied with twine. He hoped they wouldn't turn around and see him still there; he couldn't face any more tears. He slapped Eamonn on the shoulder, then hurried up the gangway without looking back. He was surprised to realise he wasn't at all unhappy; in fact he was looking forward to seeing Nick. The French-speaking, piano-playing posh boy might be hiding a lot about himself, but Peter still felt as close to him as he did to any of the loved ones he'd just left behind. Closer, really, because whoever Nick really was, at least he understood the hellish reality of France.

CHAPTER 14

NORTHERN FRANCE, SEPTEMBER 1917

 ETER

PETER LAY on his wire mattress in the dugout, smoking, taking a moment of rest before some bloody officer asked him to run anywhere else. His stomach growled; he was starving. The shelling had been very intense that week, and rations weren't getting through. There had been pea soup on offer for dinner apparently, but it had run out by the time he'd got back from delivering messages, and even the fresh water with which he'd quenched his thirst smelled of petrol and tasted worse, having been transferred in petrol cans. Enzo, who had just finished a back-breaking day filling sandbags, had shared a can of bully beef with him, but it hadn't satisfied him at all.

He closed his eyes, tried to block out the endless thuds and bangs of the battlefield from down the line.

It was harder this time. The damp of the earth beneath him created a seeping, unrelenting, all-pervasive cold that went into his bones; it was as if nothing would warm him. He had almost forgotten what a warm, dry bed felt like. He lit a cigarette, inhaled and then exhaled deeply. He shouldn't smoke, he knew, because he could feel a tightness in his chest that wasn't there before, but it was all there was to do sometimes. He shifted slightly and heard the ominous sound of scratching and then a scurry as a rat sat up on its two back legs and gnawed at something.

What on earth had possessed him to sign up for this? Or come back again instead of just running away? He asked himself these questions over and over. It was indescribably awful. And the Germans they were meant to hate, whenever they got a glimpse of them, were lads just like them, just as woebegone, just as bewildered, just as lonely for home. But yet some bloody generals or politicians or someone decided they should keep battering each other until one of them fell down. For what?

Large assaults were relatively rare, but here in the trenches, they took their lives in their hands every day. Patrolling, working on the wire out in No Man's Land, taking pot shots at the enemy, and them sniping back, not to mention the endless artillery harassment that went on all day, every day. The bigwigs would get wind every so often that the men weren't being aggressive enough, and they'd order a raid or a targeted attack just to build morale and the offensive spirit in the men. Of course, it did the complete opposite, cementing the futility of it all in the hearts of the soldiers, but nobody bothered to check on how the orders affected morale.

He knew a whole lot of the English Tommies were disgusted with the generals, at how long this was taking. The army were getting wise to fellas deliberately injuring themselves to get a pass home. A shot in the hand or the foot was a famous one, or pretending to be insane was another, 'pulling a blighty', as they called it. It was a risk because such acts, if discovered, were deemed treasonous and could result in the perpetrator being court-martialled and shot for cowardice, but such were the conditions here that every week a few lads chanced it.

'Gawd, I'd take anywhere on earth over this hell.' Enzo yawned. He was stretched out on the other bunk and clearly thinking along the same lines as Peter. 'They go on about the 'orrible 'un and what they did to "poor gallant little Belgium" and that bloke called Franz Ferdinand who copped it in some place out foreign. But is that why the whole bloomin' world is at war? Somehow I don't think so. Nah, more like a bunch of fat old blokes sittin' drinkin' port in a club in London, or Berlin, doing it for the lark. Playin' soldiers. But it isn't them getting blown to kingdom come or worse, is it? And they don't even 'ave the decency to feed us edible grub.'

Enzo grumbled endlessly about the army food. He'd spent his childhood holidays in Italy, and apparently for Italians, food wasn't just sustenance – it was the very essence of life and joy and love and belonging. It broke Enzo's heart that the so-called chef they had to put up with was a man from Brixton in London who'd been an accountant before the war and who knew as much about cooking as Enzo reckoned he himself did about debits and credits. Though clearly that little detail didn't bother the British army.

'My *nonna*, my Italian granny, she'd make this ragu,' he said wistfully. 'It was the most delicious food on earth. It was made of beef, all tender and succulent, cooked in tomatoes and garlic and onions, all served over fresh pasta she made from this special wheat...' He closed his eyes and inhaled deeply through his nose, as if he could smell the aroma of garlic and onion frying in olive oil. 'Oh, lawdy, my mouth is waterin'...'

'Ah, stop it, Enzo,' Peter said furiously. 'I'm starving, and you're making it even worse. Damn it, I'm getting out that packet of biscuits.' He'd been saving it for emergencies. It was the only remaining treat he had left from the last parcel May had sent him. Too many people knew about her packages now and were always cadging. He'd have to get her to send bigger ones. Bless her, she probably would if he asked.

As he opened the box, he let drop the last letter she'd sent him, with the photograph of David – 'In case you hear anything,' she'd said – and he remembered what he'd said to her about asking Enzo. Tricky, though, because Enzo was so touchy on the subject.

He brought the photo with the packet of biscuits over to Enzo's bunk. 'Irish butter shortbread good enough grub for ya? Or will I eat them all myself?'

'You will not.' Enzo sat up, his feet dangling over the edge of the bunk, and grabbed two from the open packet Peter held out to him. 'Who's that fella?' He nodded at the photo. 'Your brother?'

'No, my girl's brother.'

Enzo took it and studied it. 'Nice-looking guy. Hope he gets out of there alive.'

Peter stared at him. 'Out of where?'

And Enzo looked equally startled. 'Didn't you say he was a prisoner of war?'

'No?'

'I'm sure you did, mate, ages ago. How else would I 'ave known?'

'Yeah, I guess I did then…' Peter left a couple more of the biscuits with Enzo, took four for himself, then packed the rest away again. He retreated to his bunk and lay staring at the ceiling.

Had he told Enzo? He supposed it was possible, although he thought it was more likely he'd have told him David was dead, which was what he personally believed.

'Well, I'm off to see Nick and Two-Soups,' announced the Londoner, rejuvenated by the biscuits. 'You comin'?'

Their dugout had been badly damaged in last week's raid and one half of it had collapsed entirely, so where all four of them had slept, there was now just room for him and Enzo. Nick and Two-Soups had been moved to another dugout twenty yards up the line, where two bunks had come free in the same raid, for the usual reasons.

'Nah, thanks, Enzo. I'm gonna stay here and read me book.' He waved the other man off and turned onto his front to read.

It was a novel he'd got from the library someone had set up in the rest area behind the lines. He still wasn't much of a reader, but it was something to do, especially now the gramophone had been destroyed along with half the dugout, and it had captured his interest because it was about the Roman circus. The main character was a gladiator and had to fight wild animals. He didn't know the name of it because the cover had been torn off, but it was good. Exciting. And it took him away from here.

He wasn't reading just for fun, though. May had assured him that together they would achieve great things and he was inclined to believe her, so he was constantly trying to better himself these days, to make himself more like May and her folks, to extend his vocabulary, to rid himself of his uneducated, inarticulate roots. Not that he was ashamed of his family, just their lack of education. It was a work in progress, but he was improving.

The place was still for once, the guns fallen briefly silent, and he soaked up the silence like a sponge. It was great just to get a bit of peace and quiet. In fact, when the guitar music started up, his first instinct was to yell at whoever it was to shut up, but something about it was compelling, hypnotic almost. He lay there listening. He didn't recognise the tune, but it sounded foreign somehow, not like the music he was used to hearing.

Finally he closed the book, rolled off his bunk, and went outside to take a closer look at whoever was playing a melody so haunting and beautiful.

A slight young man, tanned skin and straight dark hair oiled back from his forehead, in the uniform of a British Tommy, was sitting on the smoking platform next to the dugout, a small guitar held like a lover to his heart, the neck sticking straight up in the air.

Peter stood with his back to the sunset, watching. The man wasn't just strumming chords; he was picking each note individually with the fingers of his right hand, while his left moved with effortless speed and dexterity up and down the upright neck of his instrument, some-times so far down that his fingers rested on the soundboard. The effect was sharp, nasal almost, with no reverberation, and Peter was fascinated.

No one else was around – the dugouts to the left and right had been destroyed along with the half of Peter's own – and they were all alone in the fading light. Peter felt there was a plaintive melancholy to the scene, the man, the music, the location.

When the man finally finished the tune with a flourish of single notes picked out at such velocity it was hard to see what his fingers were doing, he looked up, and seemed surprised to have an audience.

'That was amazing,' Peter said. 'Is that a French guitar or something? I've never seen one like it before.'

The man smiled. 'No, it is flamenco, Spanish. I'm from Spain, not France.' His English was accented but good. 'I hope you don't mind me using this platform to sit on. I was walking up and down the line, looking for somewhere peaceful to play. I thought all these dugouts were abandoned.'

'Still enough of this one left to fit me and my mate Enzo into, though our two mates had to move further along. So you're Spanish then?'

'I am.'

'Why are you here then? Spain is neutral, isn't it?'

'Sí, Spain is, but I'm not.' There was something about the way he said it. Something burned in his eyes, a kind of zeal that Peter never saw out here, only dull acceptance.

'I'm from Ireland. Nice to meet you.' He offered the Spaniard a cigarette, which the young man accepted and lit with his own matches.

'So not British either?' There was a devilish gleam in his almost-black eyes.

Peter grinned back at him. 'That's right, though try telling the Brits that. They think they own the place, but that's not going to last for much longer. Part of the reason I'm out here is Mr Redmond said we'll get Home Rule because of it. I'm Peter Cullen, by the way.'

'Ramon Wilson.' He stuck his cigarette into the neck of his guitar to shake Peter's hand.

'OK, call me nosy, but…what's your story then?'

Ramon took back the cigarette and placed his guitar gently on the platform beside him, leaning it against the wall of the dugout. 'Well, I found this guitar – well, not found, I bought it.' His Spanish accent was pronounced. 'I saw it in the window of a house in Marseille, and the woman agreed to part with it when she heard me play.' There was no arrogance in his statement – he was gifted and he knew it.

'All right, but what's a Spaniard with a guitar doing in the British army?'

'Ah, *amigo*, that is a longer story.' He nodded and stroked the neck of the guitar. 'It's not a beauty. I had a better one at home in Valencia, but it is much better than nothing.'

'When did you get here?'

Ramon looked about his age, eighteen or so, but he still had flesh on his bones; he'd not got the look of a man who'd spent much time at war.

Ramon shrugged. 'About three weeks ago, I had to come up from Spain. It was difficult.'

'You volunteered?'

'*Sí*, yes, I volunteered.'

And there Peter had been, not half an hour ago, thinking it was the most stupid thing he'd ever done, even with the Home Rule thing. 'Why on earth did you do that?'

'Join up, you mean?'

'Well, yes.'

'You don't like fighting the Germans?'

Peter laughed. 'Well, put it this way. When I was a kid, there was a dentist who lived near us – well, people called him a dentist, but I doubt he was trained or anything. And when you got a toothache, they'd send you to him. And he'd kneel on your chest and get out these big old dirty pliers, and he'd pull the tooth out. No medicine, just pull and go. Well, most days here are worse than that.'

Ramon laughed, and his black eyes gleamed again. 'So you don't see why I volunteered, no?'

'Frankly, mate, I do not.'

'OK, it's like this. Like a fairy tale actually.'

Peter was intrigued. He took a seat beside him. 'So go on then, tell me your fairy tale.'

Ramon inhaled and composed his thoughts. 'My father was English, from Bristol. He was maybe the best stonemason in Europe – everyone wanted him. He could repair sculptures like new.' Ramon used his hands for emphasis, a very continental way of talking, Peter thought. 'So when he was called to Valencia to fix the nose of St Nicholas and also some fingers, he named his price, the city fathers said yes, and he went to Spain. He'd been many times. Spain has a dark history, you know, the Crusades, the destruction of the Moorish ways, then big Christian churches on the sites with many statues – lots of work for someone like my father. But this was his first time to Valencia. He thinks he will stay one, maybe two weeks.'

'So what happened?' Peter found himself enthralled.

'He met Conchita Suarez, and he was lost. She was the woman of his dreams, a dancer from Granada but visiting family in Valencia. They fell in love and got married, and then I was born. My mother grew up under the walls of the Alhambra palace. Her mother, she was descended from a courtier – they say her people were entertainers all the way back to the court of Ferdinand and Isabella. You remember, they were the ones that sent their daughter Catherine from the Alhambra to the court of King Henry the Eighth?'

Peter didn't – he hadn't even finished primary school – but he nodded for the story to continue.

'My grandmother would tell me how the story of Catherine and Henry went, that Catherine thought England so cold and backwards and she hated it and begged her mother to be allowed to return home to the Alhambra. The Alhambra has gardens where the most beautiful and succulent fruits and flowers grow, and so elegant the architecture. Pools, hot water, everything. And she was brought to medieval England, and she nearly died, it was so horrible.'

He grimaced as if he had personal experience of such a terrible contrast.

'Anyway, I digress. So coming from a long line of musicians and dancers, the music and dance was in my mother's blood, in her bones. My father said he knew he was in love when he saw her dance, flamenco, you know? The elegance, the power, the beauty – he was lost. And we were happy. We lived beside the sea, on the *playa*. My father was in much demand, so we had lots of money and a nice house, and my mother paid a great flamenco player to teach me to play the guitar so she could dance, and I loved it.

'My mother had a best friend, Gabriella Gonzalez. She was a dancer too, and they performed together sometimes. And oh my, the way they danced together, their backs arched, their bodies so tight and controlled, their long arms and graceful hands, and their feet, like lightning. Gabriella has a daughter, Aida, and we grew up together, like brother and sister. I learnt guitar and she learnt to dance.'

This life, so exotic and peppered with a fascinating cast of characters, made Peter realise just how boring most people were, including himself. If he survived this bloody war, he would get out of Dublin, he would travel, he would do great things with his life. 'Go on,' he urged.

'Then my mother started to get sick. We didn't know then what was wrong, but her muscles got weaker and weaker, and soon she couldn't stand. All our money started going to doctors. My father turned down every commission – he didn't want to leave my mother and Valencia until she was well again. Gabriella had stopped dancing as well. She taught small children, and it didn't pay much. So Aida and I – we were fourteen then – we needed to make extra money for our families, so we decided to perform for the tourists in Valencia. We made enough money for food and rent, and our parents were grateful.'

'And did your mother recover?' Peter felt like he almost knew these people.

'No. She got weaker and weaker. We had to take her to many doctors. Nobody knew what it is, but she gets worse. Like she starts to find it hard to swallow – we feed her soup… Every day a bit worse. My father spent all our savings to pay the best doctors in Spain, but nobody could help her.'

His face darkened with sadness. 'Then my father was summoned by the German government, the Kaiser himself. He wanted the best man for the job, to repair and restore the sculptures of the Berliner Dom. It was a big contract, and my father decided he had to leave us. He said to me that he would make a lot of money and this time we would take my mother to Harley Street in London, to see the greatest, cleverest doctors in the world, and she would be well again. So he left, and I stayed behind to care for her, with Gabriella and Aida to help me. He thought it would take only a few weeks – he said he would work night and day to get home to us as quickly as he could. But each restoration he did, they had another one for him to do. He said he needed to go back, his wife was sick, but they would not pay him until he did the next one and the next one.'

Ramon's voice faltered, and Peter stole a sidelong glance at his face, which was dark with hatred. 'That's cruel. Your poor father must have felt so trapped.'

Ramon nodded. 'Yes, and he had no money to send to me, and Mama couldn't be left. It was so hard for her to breathe. I kept watch over her every night, so I couldn't go out to play guitar with Aida. Gabriella tried to help us from her little bit of teaching money, but I knew she needed it for herself so I said I had enough, and I sold our furniture to pay for food. Then one day we get a telegram to say my father is dead. He fell from a scaffold when working and was killed instantly.'

'Oh, Ramon, I'm sorry for your troubles.' God got everything the wrong way around, Peter thought. Killing Ramon's father, who was needed and wanted by his family, while Kit Cullen's fall at work had left him alive, no longer a threat but still a millstone around his mother's neck. 'So then what happened?'

'Then we have no money, and the Germans won't pay for his body to be brought back to Valencia – they say it's not their problem. They ignore when I write. Gabriella and Aida and I, we go to Madrid, to the German embassy, ask them to help, and they laugh in our faces...' He shrugged and rubbed his knuckles across his eyes. 'So now my father is buried in a pauper's grave in Dorotheenstadt Cemetery in Berlin. That's all they would do. Nothing more. They would not pay us what he was owed. They said he was paid already, but I know he was not.'

'And your ma?' Peter asked, fearful of the answer.

'She stopped being able to eat, and then she fought for breath...' Ramon shut his eyes tightly, as if trying to block out a memory. 'And now she is dead.' He mumbled the next bit, so Peter had to strain to hear. 'So now, because of my father, I am here.'

'You were conscripted because your father was English?' Peter was puzzled.

'It's true my father was English, and so I am a mixture of Spain and England. But the reason I came here...' Ramon paused. He turned to face Peter, and his eyes blazed with dark intensity. 'I came here because I want to kill Germans. They have taken my parents from me, destroyed my life, and so I want them to suffer.'

CHAPTER 15

ETER

THE ORDERLY BROUGHT a forty-eight-hour retreat pass for Peter and Nick from Major Billingsley, with instructions to fall back to the rest area that Friday and put on another show at the Aigle d'Or. Apparently the major and his fellow officers thought the Tommies needed cheering up ahead of the serious fighting that was coming, and Marine had last week run off with a deserter, which was causing problems all round.

It was the chance Peter had been waiting for.

'What about Enzo and Two-Soups? We c-c-c-can't leave them,' Nick said, worried. The dugout had been repaired now, and the three of them, and Two-Soups, were back living together.

Peter, Nick and Enzo and the Scotsman had become very close. Peter, being a runner, was gone most of the day, but the other three were often on the same team, delivering supplies, filling sandbags, pumping the base of the trench to rid it of water. Endless hours of boring back-breaking work in between manic periods of terror when the Hun attacked.

'Yeah, you're right, we can't.' Peter nodded.

'Nothin' to do with me, mate. Take it up with Major Billingsley if you've got a problem.' The orderly left.

'D-d-do you think the major might let them c-c-c-come if we asked him nicely?' said Nick. 'I mean, I'd feel better if they were in the audience. Those English T-T-T-Tommies can be a bit intimidating.'

'Hmm. Leave it with me,' Peter said.

The following evening, after a long day running messages up and down four different communication trenches, he stopped off at Captain Edgeworth's dugout with a small bottle of Calvados, a local apple brandy, which he'd spotted in one of the better-stocked dugouts earlier that week; he'd traded two bars of Cadbury chocolate May had sent for it. The captain's wife's brother was a doctor in the United States, so she was good for sending over high-quality American medical supplies.

He found Edgeworth polishing his rifle. As captain he could have had one of his subordinates do it, but the boredom in between the bouts of chaos were so hard to endure, and everyone had to have something to do to fill in the time. Normally an upbeat sort of man, these days Edgeworth looked pale and haunted. He'd been rattled badly last week when his brother was killed by a mortar in front of him, and Peter had heard he was waking, screaming a lot. There was a very noticeable tremor in his hands. Another man might have tried to get home on sick leave, but the captain wasn't like that. He was very straight and 'stiff upper lip'.

'How's it goin', Captain?' Peter asked. The formality of the army was lax in the front line with most officers, and Edgeworth had a reputation among his men for being a decent fellow.

'All right. Have you a message?' The captain answered in a dull monotone, a far cry from his usual cheery tones. He was balding and wore a thin moustache.

'No, sir, I do not, sir, but I did bring you this?' He pulled the naggin-sized bottle from his tunic.

The man's eyes flickered with a spark of hope at the sight of the booze, something that could dampen his mental suffering and send him to sleep. But then a shadow passed over his face. 'Why?' he asked, suspicious now.

'Thought you might need it?' Peter shrugged.

'Who are you exactly?' Edgeworth looked him up and down carefully.

'Private Peter Cullen, sir, Irish Rifles.'

'And you just came here to give me that? A man you don't know?'

Peter smiled. 'Well, sir, the brandy is yours either way, but if you could give me some of that American medical foot powder I hear you have, I'd be grateful. I'm scared stiff of trench foot, what with all the running up and down the line in the wet, and my mate lost his whole foot to it last winter.'

The captain observed Peter for a moment, and there was a brief second where Peter thought the man might accuse him of black marketeering, something that went on wholesale but was against the rules.

'Irish, are you?' he asked instead.

'Yessir, from Dublin.' Peter took care to stand to attention and use a deferential tone at all times.

'So you volunteered for this?'

'Yessir.'

'I suppose they told you you'd see the world?' His voice dripped with heavy irony.

'They did, sir, but I think the next world is more likely the one I'll see the way things are goin' here.' Peter kept his eyes front and centre and gave an involuntary start when the captain laughed loudly.

'The next world. Very good, private.' The man patted Peter's shoulder in a fatherly gesture. 'Hold on, let me see what I can find.'

He pulled out a canvas bag from under his bunk, undid the buckles and took out a pair of hand-knitted socks, which he held to his nose and mouth and inhaled. 'Gladys, my wife, she wears rosewater scent, and she sprinkled some on these that I might be reminded of her when I wear them. I miss her...' He sighed deeply, misty-eyed. War did funny things to men, Peter observed for the millionth time. He could never imagine the captain admitting something so emotional in his civilian life. The captain then returned the socks to the bag and took out a quarter-pound tin of foot powder made by the Manhattan Soap Company. Peter handed him the Calvados in return, and immediately the man opened it and took a big slug.

'Thank you, sir. Much appreciated,' Peter said, backing towards the doorway.

'Right-o. Er...what did you say your name was again?' asked Edgeworth, then took another long swig.

'Cullen, sir, Private Peter Cullen.' He wanted to get out of there before the man became maudlin and started weeping on his shoulder.

'Good man, Cullen. Must keep one's pecker up, eh? King and country.' He held the bottle aloft as if proposing a toast.

Peter repeated, 'King and country, sir!' before scarpering out of there.

As he ran back down the trench, the world around him banged and crashed. The sky was lit up like a city tonight, shells and machine-gun fire. There were rumours of another Big Push, and he hoped it was planned for when he and Nick got sent back on rest that weekend.

He leapt sideways to avoid an unexploded mine, narrowly missing it. Two lads carrying an injured man on a stretcher were running towards him, and he called out a warning. 'Watch out there! That one's not exploded yet.' He pointed at the mine lying menacingly on its side.

'What, mate?'

They rushed past him, and the next moment there was a terrible explosion. Something hard hit him in the middle of his back, winding him and sending him face down in the mud. When he scrambled to his feet, he found the object that had struck him was an army boot, with a foot still in it. The stretcher bearers and the man they'd been carrying were all blown to bits. It had been quick at least. He didn't wait around. After checking himself for injury and finding he was all right, he kept running. The horror was daily, relentless and defied description, yet he found himself emotionally numb to it all after the first week or so. Everyone did, it was the only way to survive.

The major was in his office, which was little more than a shed cut into the trench and covered with corrugated iron and earth. He could have been billeted further back, in much more comfort, as most of the officers did, but apparently he'd chosen not to out of solidarity with the men, though it felt a bit stupid to Peter. If he had the chance to get out of here, or get back behind the lines, or just move in any direction away from No Man's Land, that was exactly what he would do.

He had even considered pulling a blighty himself, or sleeping with one of the madame's girls and catching the clap, though he'd decided against it. He'd done it honourably this far, so he might as well see it through to the end, the same as Captain Edgeworth.

There was a gas lamp on the battered table, and the major sat there, writing a letter.

Peter stood to attention at the threshold.

'What is it, private?' The major never looked up.

'Permission to enter, sir,' Peter said, saluting him.

'Oh, it's you, Cullen…' The other man finally gave him his attention. 'Put your arm down, boy. We don't know who's watching.'

'Yes, sir.' Peter did as he was told. A lot of the officers didn't like to be saluted in the trenches in case a German sniper was watching and realised the man being saluted was high-ranking and therefore a prime target.

'So what is it, private? What do you want?' He sat gazing at Peter. His large moustache grew down over his mouth, giving him a hangdog look. Despite the poverty of his surroundings, his uniform was immaculate, his tunic spotless and the buttons almost sparkling. His three stripes and crown insignia indicated his rank. His Sam Browne belt was as shiny as a conker, and the brass buckles gleamed. On his feet, the leather boots shone, but Peter knew the major's feet had been troubling him.

'Sir, I heard that your feet were bad, sir, so I got you some dry socks and some foot powder, sir.' Peter proffered two pairs of May's warm, dry, hand-knitted socks and the tin he'd got from Edgeworth.

Billingsley's eyes never left Peter's as he tried to size him up. He didn't take the offerings. 'Where did you find these?' he asked directly.

'The socks were knitted by my girlfriend, and I got the powder in exchange for a bottle of brandy I swapped for some chocolate, sir,' Peter said truthfully, eyes straight ahead.

'You know you already have a forty-eight-hour pass for this Friday? Didn't the orderly tell you?' Billingsley frowned.

'Yes, sir. Me and my friend, Private Nick Gerrity, we're hoping to get some sleep, sir, on the Friday night. And we'll do the show on the Saturday.'

'Ah yes, good stuff, cheer everyone up. The men have had a lot to put up with of late. Still, though, we must keep the bright side out, eh, Cullen?'

'That's right, sir. We'll do our best, sir.'

'Might even come by to see you myself, see how you're managing.'

Peter's heart lifted. Maybe May's idea was coming to fruition. Maybe there were more weekend passes to be had. 'Was hoping you might, sir.'

'So then.' The major sat back on his chair and took his pipe from his pocket, slowly cleaning the bowl, blowing up the mouthpiece, then examining it before taking a leather tobacco pouch from his inside pocket and filling it with his head bowed. He was thinning on top, though the army haircut was so short, it didn't make much difference. 'What is it you do want?' His voice was low, and at the same time, there was a softness in it, something un-officer-like, Peter thought. The major seemed to have that shred of humanity the previous adjutant had lacked.

'Honestly, sir, nothing,' Peter answered. He placed the quarter-pound tin of foot powder and the socks on the desk.

The major picked up the tin. 'Manhattan Soap Company... American? Who gave you this for the brandy?'

Peter shrugged. He didn't want to get Edgeworth into trouble for black marketeering, if that's what he'd been doing – it was a fine line.

'Just some Tommy, don't remember his name. But I think it's better than our stuff, sir.'

'And you don't want payment for this?' He still sounded sceptical.

'No, sir.'

'Hmm...' He stood now, placing the powder and the socks in his bag. Then using his cane, he limped painfully towards Peter. 'Good man, Cullen. I won't forget this.' He clapped him on the back with surprising force. 'Enjoy your rest, and I'll see you at the show.'

'I will, sir. Thank you, sir. And if you need anything else, I'm a runner, as you know, so I can usually help out. You can let my other friends, Private Lorenzo Riccio and Private Baxter Campbell, know. We're mates, sir, and they'd be great at entertaining the troops. Private Riccio is a professional acrobat, and Private Baxter is a well-known comedian in Scotland. But unfortunately they didn't get a rest pass to come with me and Nick.'

That glimmer, the glance at the foot powder and socks and a tiny stretch at the sides of his mouth, under the drooping moustache. Peter knew he'd got away with it.

'Very good, private. Dismissed.'

'Sir.' Peter nodded and took his leave. Then decided to push his luck and turned back. 'And if you are coming, sir, there's another act you might enjoy – Private Ramon Wilson. He plays the flamenco guitar. It might be a bit sophisticated for the Tommies, but if you and the other officers are good enough to come, I could put him on for five minutes so you can enjoy a bit of culture.'

Again, that hint of humour and the almost invisible smile. 'And I suppose Private Wilson needs a rest pass as well, does he, Cullen?'

'Gosh, sir. You're right, sir. I hadn't thought of that, sir.'

'Oh, get out of here, Cullen.' And this time the major did laugh.

CHAPTER 16

 ETER

PETER WAS HOLDING a conference in the dugout with his mates. 'Enzo, Two-Soups, I've got you a rest pass for Friday. Me and Nick are putting on another show in the Aigle d'Or, and this time you have to join in.'

Two-Soups and Enzo looked at Peter in astonishment, and Nick listened with interest.

'What you on about?' asked Enzo, bewildered. 'I can't sing, you know I can't…'

'My Betty says I sound like a tomcat on the prowl,' added Two-Soups.

'You can do acrobatics, though, can't you, Enzo?' Peter said calmly. 'That's what I told Major Billingsley, that you're a professional acrobat. And, Two-Soups, as far as the major is concerned, you're a well-known comedian in Scotland.'

'But I've never been on stage!'

'And there ain't no trapeze in there, is there?' protested Enzo.

'They'll love your jokes, Two-Soups, you're a natural. And, Enzo, I seen you do tumbles and handsprings and backflips and cartwheels in the air. Trust me – they'll love you.'

'This is mad,' Enzo insisted. 'I ain't...'

Peter drew the two of them in closer, a hand on each shoulder. 'Listen, lads. I've a plan to get us out of this hell a bit more often, and it involves this, so just go with it, all right? My girl, May, is always telling me I should get a troupe together and go around entertaining the troops, and maybe that's what the major is thinking too. Nick on piano and singing, Enzo doing some acrobatics, Two-Soups telling his jokes, me doing compere and introducing you all or whatever. We impress the major, and he tells the bigwigs behind, and they let us start doing shows up and down the line, in huts or halls or places like this, to raise morale. May told me there was a visiting troupe in Ypres last year, brought out from England, and they thought it did the men great good. We could prove we can have the same effect but much cheaper.'

'So you want me to tell a few jokes, that's it?' Two-Soups's eyes were beginning to sparkle at the thought.

'And all I'd 'ave to do is jump about a bit?' Enzo was incredulous.

'Well, we'd have to put on a good show, but yeah. The major likes me and Nick already, and if you all row in behind, I think we might be able to pull something off.'

'Well, I think it's a b-b-b-brilliant idea,' said Nick firmly, ever ready to back Peter to the hilt.

* * *

THE CHANT HAD BEGUN: 'Cull-en, Gerrity, Cull-en, Gerrity.'

The bar was bursting at the seams, a sea of khaki. Word must have got out that Peter and Nick were performing, and it had drawn in more soldiers from the other drinking establishments. At the very back sat a table of at least five high-ranking officers, Major Billingsley among them. And...was that the commander?

Peter felt a twinge of stage fright but swallowed it.

'Nick, take it away,' he said. Nick wouldn't let him down. He was the quietest of them all by miles but much more confident about his talents. In fact he seemed to get the opposite of stage fright, being much calmer on stage than off it, to the point of not stammering at all.

As for himself, he knew these songs backwards, and as Nick played and sang and the Tommies joined in, the stage fright quickly disappeared, and soon he was acting his way through their repertoire, marching up and down the little stage, his hand on his heart, a tear in his eye. In between two of the songs, he amused himself and the troops by doing a bit of introductory patter in the style of Lord Kitchener, pretending to twirl his moustache and roaring, 'Your country needs YOU!' And after the next one, he brought the house down by mimicking the crazy German Kaiser, Wilhelm the Second, bursting out in a perfect German accent, 'Ze English, zey are mad, mad, mad as ze March hares!'

After five or so songs, he clasped Nick's shoulder. Nick lifted his hands from the piano as Peter turned to the crowd.

'And now, for the first time in the Aigle d'Or, the famous Scottish comedian, Baxter Campbell, more popularly known to his fans as' – he looked at Nick, who mocked up a little drum roll on the piano – 'Two-Soups!'

Two-Soups looked paler than usual as he made his way to the stage, but the Tommies, softened up by Nick and Peter, were in a generous mood, and Two-Soups was so tall and so red-haired, he was compelling before he ever spoke. Then once he got cracking jokes in his melodious Scottish accent, it only took a moment for him to have the audience howling.

'What's Beethoven doing in his grave? Decomposing! Did you hear about the bear that walks into a bar and asks for a whiskey and' – Two-Soups paused for several seconds – 'lemonade? "Why the big pause," asks the barman? The bear looks down. "No idea, mate. I was born with them."'

The Scotsman was really enjoying himself, one crack after another, feeding off the roars of laughter. It wasn't because his jokes were that funny, and they certainly weren't original. It was because of the way he told them, the innocent face, the mop of red hair. Something about him was highly comical, and Peter had known he'd go down a storm. He was clean too, so Peter had no concerns about causing offence to the officers at the back.

'What's the best thing about Switzerland?' Two-Soups asked the crowd.

'Nothing!' several of the soldiers roared back at him. Switzerland's neutrality was a bone of contention with the English soldiers, and the mood in the bar soured slightly.

'How dare you, private! There's nothing good about Switzerland at all!' shouted Peter in a posh English-officer accent, over the strong yelps of disapproval.

'No, sir, of course not, sir.' Two-Soups picked up on Peter's reading of the crowd. 'But its flag is a big plus.'

And straight away, everyone was roaring with laughter again.

It was clear the Scotsman could have gone on all night; he had so many jokes at his fingertips. But after a while, Peter decided the room needed calming a little, so he nodded at Two-Soups to wind it up and the Scotsman bounded off the stage to deafening whoops and shouts of approval.

'And now…' Peter stepped forward, raising his hands up and down to quieten the crowd. 'And now, another first for the Aigle d'Or. All the way from sunny Spain, a man who is definitely not neutral – he's here to fight the Hun to the death. But in the meantime, here he is with his amazing flamenco guitar…Ramon Wilson!'

It hadn't been as easy to persuade Ramon to join them as Peter had imagined it would be; there was a push against the Germans coming that weekend, and the crazy Spaniard really wanted to be a part of it. But he'd received his rest pass, whether he liked it or not, and Peter had promised Major Billingsley something with a bit of culture, so Ramon reluctantly obliged.

Peter loved hearing and watching Ramon play, watching his fingers pluck the strings like a harper while his other hand flew in a blur up and down the neck of the guitar. His intricate melodies were haunting and powerful, and at the back, the group of officers paid attention. The commander leant his elbows on the table and put his chin in his hands.

The Tommies were starting to look a little puzzled, though, and Peter touched Ramon on the shoulder after a pause in the piece. Ramon looked up inquiringly, his finger hovering.

'That was beautiful, Ramon,' Peter said. 'Stand up and take a bow.'

'But it is only half the piece…' the Spaniard said, with a resigned shrug of his shoulders, but he did as Peter asked and left the stage to the loud applause of the table of officers, one of whom came over to say something to him. The officer then called to the daughter of the house, Celine, for a pitcher of wine, which Peter could see cheered Ramon up to no end, as well as Two-Soups, who was with him, and Enzo, who poured himself a huge glass.

'Better get Enzo going before he starts drinking that,' Peter said. 'Nick, fill in for me, would you, while I sort him out.'

He jumped down off the stage, while Nick got the audience going again by launching into 'It's a Long Way to Tipperary', which the English soldiers loved so much even though they had no idea where Tipperary even was.

Enzo had been acting very jittery, and as soon as Peter sat down, he started coming up with excuses, like he had a bit of a bad foot or something, and in the end, Peter decided to allow him a glass of wine after all and let him calm down a bit.

Up on the stage, Nick was hammering out more old favourites and even a few hymns that had the whole place in tears. *Soldiers love a bit of sentimental old twaddle*, Peter thought to himself, looking around at their maudlin faces. Celine went on stage and placed a large glass of wine on the piano. Nick smiled up at her and started playing the wartime favourite 'Madelon', only this time he sang it in French.

'*Pour le repos, le plaisir du militaire, il est là-bas à deux pas de la forêt, une maison aux murs tout couverts de lierre, Aux Tourlourous, c'est le nom du cabaret.*'

On the floor, the Tommies sang heartily along to the familiar tune, in English.

'There is a tavern way down in Brittany, where weary soldiers take their liberty. The keeper's daughter, whose name is Madelon, pours out the wine while they laugh and carry on…'

Celine stood smiling down at Nick as he sang to her in her own language, and as he reached the chorus, she joined in.

'*Quand Madelon vient nous servir à boire, sous la tonnelle on frôle son jupon, et chacun lui raconte une histoire, une histoire à sa façon…*'

Peter was pleasantly surprised, because though she was a quietly spoken French girl, her singing voice was gravelly and sultry, and the soldiers in the bar fell silent as she and Nick sang together in French.

The owner's daughter of the Aigle d'Or was held in almost saintly status among the men. She didn't flirt or entertain their advances at all, and she was permanently under the watchful eye of her father, and that rebuffing made her all the more alluring.

Several lads had tried their luck with her, but all had failed. She'd tell them that she'd a boyfriend in the 11th French Army Corps defending the Ardennes and that she was waiting for him. Nick had whispered to Peter that Celine was lying; he'd overheard her talking about it in French to her father. Antoine was dead for the last year. He'd trod on a mine and lost most of his legs and spent four days in a field hospital, but the injuries got infected and he died. Just as well. The poor bugger wouldn't have had any life left like that.

Peter supposed it was as good a way as any for Celine to keep the men from harassing her. They all had wives and sweethearts at home, and so they respected her loyalty and hoped Gladys or Cynthia or Dolly or Gwen back in Blighty was being as faithful to them as Celine was to poor old Antoine.

Now the men gazed in reverential awe. Her strawberry-blond hair framed her oval face, and her amber eyes with flecks of gold, making her look almost like a tiger, rested calmly on them as she sang. Celine was nice enough looking, Peter supposed. She had a pretty face and didn't look like a kipper, but she was no oil painting either.

She was as flat as a washboard, everyone was thin, but her body had none of the curve of womanhood, yet up there on stage next to Nick, she had every man in the place in the palm of her hand. There was something pure about her, something unsullied by the horrible war, that perhaps reminded them of their mothers and sisters.

Enzo seemed calmer, so Peter put his hand on his arm and said, 'Come on, let's get it over with.' The Londoner winced but stood up and allowed Peter to escort him through the crowd to the double doors at the back, just near where the officers were sitting. God knew how this would go, but Enzo was naturally comedic, so it would either be a display of skill or so bad he was funny. Either way, Peter hoped it would work.

Up on stage Celine and Nick had come to the end of their duet, and Celine got down off the stage.

'Now, ladies and gentlemen,' Peter called over the clapping crowd from the back doors, 'all the way from Italy, via Clerkenwell Road of course,' that got a cheer, 'we have a very special guest, the amazing Enzo. If you can squeeze up there, give him a bit of room...' He walked into the crowd, clearing a pathway to the stage, shooing soldiers out of the way, then looked back and...Enzo was gone.

Peter panicked. Surely he hadn't bottled it? He looked despairingly towards Nick, but Nick just winked reassuringly at him and played a riff on the piano, gradually building suspense. Then, to everyone's delight, and Peter's relief, Enzo threw open the double doors, burst in and somersaulted his way to the stage.

Soldiers scattered out of his way as he bounced effortlessly, head over heels, barely touching the ground each time, and landed with a flourish beside Nick. After that he bounced from the floor to the top of the piano, and then to the exposed beams in the roof of the inn. There he performed the most incredible flips and turns, looking like he might fall but never doing so. The men were entranced. He was so dexterous and flexible, they couldn't take their eyes off him, following him open-mouthed as he swung all over the inn. Nick vamped to keep the tempo going, and everyone clapped in time.

Gasps and groans ensued at the deliberate near misses as Enzo then skipped like a monkey along the top of the shelves behind the bar, pausing only to help himself to a swig of the best brandy that the owner stored there, to everyone's delight.

Enzo put down the brandy and climbed up to the roof beam, where he joked around, making gestures like he was diving into a swimming pool. He pointed at a pole in the middle of the room. He must have been twenty feet off the ground. The audience held their breath, sure it was too far; even the officers seemed mesmerised. Enzo playacted being terrified, did several false starts, blessed himself repeatedly and mopped his brow. Nick changed the music accordingly – suspenseful, panicky…

And then Enzo leapt, flying through the air like a bird, and he landed, wrapped both arms and legs around the pole, slid down and, after kissing his hand to his adoring audience, somersaulted out the door.

CHAPTER 17

MAY DAY, 1918

ETER

'Billingsley wants to see you, Cullen,' the orderly said as he passed through the trench, on his way to the communication trench that linked Oxford Circus with Tottenham Court Road. Each section of the line was given its own name by the Tommies to differentiate one from the other.

'When?' Peter looked up from polishing his Lee-Enfield. There was an inspection later, and woe betide any man whose kit wasn't in tip-top condition.

'Now.'

Peter put his rifle back together and trudged exhaustedly towards Billingsley's dugout, passing men on sentry duty and some just sitting around playing cards. There had been very little in the way of rest recently, and the men's eyes were hollow with tiredness. Sleeping was so difficult. Every day, death and destruction, exhaustion and hunger, were their ever-present companions. Peter and his mates had incredibly stayed in one piece. But so many others had been killed or injured. But Peter was worried the tiredness would cause them to get careless. His own eyes were gritty from lack of sleep.

The fighting had been savage since the last German offensive in April, when forty-six divisions of the German 6th Army pushed them back at Ypres. It had been very demoralising, because the Hun managed to reclaim the Passchendaele ridge so hard-won last year. If not for the reinforcements from the French and Australians, the war might have ended with a German victory, but once again the whole thing had turned on a sixpence and the Germans bore even heavier losses than the Allies. Someone said it was almost half a million of the Hun had been killed.

In some good news for a change, they'd had word that the infamous Red Baron was shot down. That caused jubilation among the troops, because the flying ace was credited with shooting down countless of their aircraft.

Things were on the turn, if you could believe the top brass, which Peter didn't really.

The papers were reporting strong Allied advances, and that both the Germans and the Turks were on the back foot, but the fighting was still fierce. They weren't going to give up, it would seem, while there were any men standing.

Whatever about Turkey, Peter didn't think Germany was going down without a fight. They'd decimated the French 6th Army and had blocked supply lines so that food and ammunition, even medical equipment, were dangerously undersupplied. Still, the American troops were in France now, and everyone was saying that it was just a matter of time till victory was theirs. Peter wished the Americans would get on with saving the day. He was sick to death of the whole bloody mess and longed for it all to end.

The bit of canvas that served as a door to Billingsley's dugout was in shreds, and Peter knocked on the upright beam holding back the wall of mud.

'Ah, Cullen, come in. At ease.'

'You wanted to see me, sir?'

'I did.' Billingsley beckoned him in. 'I've had a communication from London. They said they want some of the troops to put on a sort of variety show for the Americans behind the lines, and I was asked if I knew of anyone. Direct from the front sort of thing to boost morale, maybe by proving to them that we're all in one piece and still singing and dancing and all jolly hockey sticks or something.'

Billingsley's tone suggested that he thought it was the most ignorant thing he'd ever heard from the top brass but didn't want to say. 'So what do you think, Cullen?'

Peter struggled to keep his face neutral. Looking too enthusiastic about anything in the army, he'd learnt, led to immediate suspicion. Everyone did everything with a sullen acceptance, no delight. Could it be Billingsley was about to suggest he organise the show himself? Surely not.

Before the April push, he and the others had been performing in the Aigle d'Or every weekend, and he was glad of it, but he'd given up on the idea of Billingsley allowing them to travel away from the front. Being sent back to entertain the Americans, well, this was beyond his wildest imaginings. He couldn't be that lucky...

'Yes, sir,' was all he said.

'So?' Billingsley seemed impatient now. 'Will you organise it?'

'A whole show, sir?' he asked, barely able to breathe normally with the potential joy about to erupt inside him.

'Yes. Yes, you and those other chaps, you know, the acrobatic one and the one that makes everyone cry when he sings.' He furrowed his brow, clearly trying to remember something. 'Oh, and that funny red-haired Scot.'

'Of course we will, sir. We'd be delighted to. How' – dared he ask? – 'how long would we be going for?'

Billingsley shrugged, his lugubrious bulldog face blank, as if the thought of singing and dancing shows for Americans was so far from his remit that he resented spending another moment on the topic.

'No idea. You'll report to a' – he checked the paper on his desk – 'Captain Olsen. Just get ready to leave.'

'Yes, sir. We will, sir.'

'Not the Spaniard, though. Far too sophisticated for the men.'

'That's not a problem, sir. Private Wilson wouldn't want to leave the front anyway, too keen on killing the Hun.' Ramon had continued to do the occasional short guitar solo at the Aigle d'Or, and had even gained some fans among the English Tommies, but he always seemed to resent getting dragged away from his sworn duty of killing Germans.

'Dismissed.' Billingsley returned to his desk duty, and Peter saluted and turned to leave.

'Oh, and Cullen?'

Peter turned, his heart sinking. There was going to be a but, and it wasn't going to happen. He just knew it.

'If I hear that "Charlotte the Harlot" is part of your repertoire, I will not be pleased, understood? We want to put on a good show for the Yanks, make them realise they made the right move coming over here, not have them turn on their heels and head back to New York. So best foot forward and all of that.'

Peter let out an involuntary laugh that Billingsley met with the faintest of smiles.

The last night they'd been in the Aigle d'Or, in March, one of the men had insisted on singing the very bawdy song as his party piece. Peter had been off stage having some food when the man took it upon himself to go up, and his performance, complete with actions, had elicited much appreciative bellowing and roaring from the gathered men. It had been impossible to stop.

'I don't know it, sir,' Peter said. 'And nobody in our group would play it.'

'Very good. Enjoy your sojourn. God knows you need a break from this.' The major waved his hand around vaguely to suggest the trench, the front, the entire war. 'We all do. But now the Yanks are here…' He sighed and returned to his notes. 'Lieutenant Hodges will have all the paperwork you need to be on your way. He's preparing it now, so it should be ready for you tomorrow. Report back here once you've gathered your men.'

'Yes, sir, and thank you, sir.'

A harrumph was the only response he got.

Peter made his retreat through the trenches with a lighter step than he could ever have imagined an hour earlier. He would need to round up his troupe and get them out of there before the top brass changed their minds.

CHAPTER 18

UBLIN, IRELAND, OCTOBER 1918

MAY

MAY HAD Peter's letter on her lap under the breakfast table, reading it eagerly while she ate.

Dear May,

So your plan worked! Me and Nick and Enzo and Two-Soups are putting on shows for the American soldiers where they're camped behind the lines, and telling them how great life is at the front, as if.

May, you won't believe what happened with Nick. You know how I always suspected he was a posh boy? Well, I was saying how much better the show could be if we had our own piano and if we could build a bit of a trapeze thing for Enzo to swing on, but then we'd need a lorry for transport. I was just dreaming aloud, and the next thing is, Nick says he has some money 'put by for a rainy day', like there's a single day out here that hasn't been rainy. And he did! He had a hundred-pound note in his cigarette case, May, and he insisted on giving it to me for anything I wanted. He said the show was his future now, so it was an investment.

May felt a twinge of jealousy; she preferred to be the one always coming to Peter's rescue. But that was a selfish thought, so she put it out of her head and carried on reading.

I wonder who gave it to him? My money is on this Alicia Shaw when he met her in Dublin, which blows up your idea of her being a lady's maid.

That was true. The most she'd ever had to offer Peter was five pounds. Again the jealous little imp whispered in her ear. 'You're not the only girl in the world with money, are you?'

So we bought an old lorry in Poperinge and a second-hand piano, and the shows have been great. I'm getting the Yanks to sing along even though they don't know the words, and we've learnt some of their songs, which goes down a storm. I write up the lyrics on a big white sheet that we hang at the back of the stage or the canteen, wherever we are, and I use a stick to point to the words as we go along, like a schoolteacher, which they find hilarious. The Yanks love Nick, and they think Two-Soups is gas – they've never heard his jokes before, can you believe? And Enzo is an absolute star. We got this frame made with a trapeze, and he has ropes hanging everywhere, and he does mad stuff on it.

We can't bring Ramon with us, sadly, as he's too highbrow for us. But he doesn't care. He says he signed up to fight Germans, not to entertain Americans. Celine can't come either. Nick is really upset about that, but her father won't let her go; he needs her serving in the bar. It's a shame. You'd like Celine. She's not pretty in the conventional sense, but there's something attractive about her all the same.

May sighed quietly to herself. Why was Peter wasting his time writing to her about some other girl when all she wanted was to hear about how he felt about her.

Anyway, Nick suggested to both of them that if this bloody war ever ends, we all meet up back in the Aigle d'Or while we're waiting around to be demobbed, and Celine's father said we'll be welcome to stay in one of his guest rooms for free because we've brought him so much custom. Isn't that nice of him?

May frowned. He'd have to wait to be demobbed? It was the first time she'd realised that Peter might not be on the first boat back to Ireland the moment the last shot was fired.

I'm sure you're wondering what I do in the show. Well, I sing along a bit with Nick, but mostly I do the introducing and stuff. I've learnt off the American accent, and I do a line mimicking Woodrow Wilson saying, 'My fellow Americans, our sworn duty is to make the world safe for democracy,' and the Yanks all laugh and clap.

That was better. She liked hearing about how clever her fiancé was.

The billets are better back here. We get to sleep in wooden huts, and there are beds with woollen blankets and even pillows. It's funny – we haven't had this luxury for so long, we were a bit reluctant to put our heads on the pillows at first. The Americans have really great quarters; they have no idea what's going to hit them. Some of them did fight in the Fourth Battle of Ypres in April, but mostly they haven't started yet. They still think war is a great lark and are very patriotic. Anyway, thank you so much for pushing me about putting on a show. This all goes back to that first night at the Aigle d'Or, when your idea came into my head. This place feels a million miles from the trenches, and I honestly can't believe my luck.

May, this is all down to you, and I'm forever grateful. You will always be my sweetheart.

All my love, Peter

She looked up with a smile, happy now and dying to tell her parents Peter's news. But her father was reading from his newspaper to Mother an article about what looked like the regrouping of the Volunteers.

The newspaper article said that Mr Redmond had promised a free state for Ireland if they got behind the war, but the reality was that many Irish boys had never come home and the war that was meant to be over by Christmas of 1914 was still dragging on, as it was now the autumn of 1918. The British talking about conscripting men did nothing to help, and then when the bishops came out against it, so many people like the Gallaghers were so conflicted. Nobody should be forced, of course, but so many of their boys had died. It was all for nothing if Germany won the war, and the army badly needed men. The idea of conscription would never gain traction, knowing how the Irish would react, but even the thought of it had driven even more people into the arms of the rebels, and it was all looking very worrying indeed. Ever since Mr Redmond died last March – the poor man was only going to have a routine operation, but he died – the move towards an independent republic was gaining momentum.

Father had been furious when de Valera, Countess Markievicz and Cosgrave were arrested on totally spurious charges of trying to collude with Germany, not because he was a supporter of de Valera and the like, but because such action drew the lines of demarcation deeper, and more and more moderate people were moving to the side of those seeking a free and totally independent Ireland.

'The Allied offensive is really routing them now. I feel like the end might be in sight,' he said as he balanced the paper on one side of his plate and spread marmalade on his toast.

'Please God, it will be. Father O'Reilly is doing a special novena to bring about a speedy conclusion,' Mother replied.

May bit back a response along the lines that if Father O'Reilly's special novenas worked at all, the war would have been over four years ago and nobody would describe an Allied victory as a speedy conclusion.

'Mother, Father, wait till I tell you about Peter…'

But now Mother was busy telling Father some long, winding story about Father O'Reilly being confronted by some rough types and told he should not be offering Masses to bless the troops when those were the very same men who were inflicting misery on fellow Irishmen. 'They even threatened the poor man, can you believe it?'

Father O'Reilly loved to have the ladies of the parish fuss over him, and May suspected this latest dramatic outburst would no doubt turn out to be not as menacing as the priest had claimed. But her mother was clearly looking for a sympathetic response, so May made tut-tutting noises. 'That's terrible, Mother.'

'What do you think, Michael? Do you think it's terrible?'

May fought the urge to roll her eyes. She longed to tell her mother that the reason the priest was so bland and mildly pompous was because Olive deferred to him in everything. When May and Peter were married, she wouldn't be like that. She would be her own woman and have her own opinions.

She waited for Father to say something soothing to pacify his wife, but to May's surprise, he voiced his own opinion for once, not just what was in the paper. 'Things are changing, and Father O'Reilly would do well to keep his great loyalty to the Crown a bit quieter,' he said.

Her mother looked personally offended. 'Michael,' she exclaimed, 'how on earth could you say such a thing when it was Father O'Reilly who blessed our David and who says the Mass for his safe return each month? And who'll marry May and Peter, please God, when Peter comes home safe and sound? He's a wonderful support to us all, everyone who has boys over there. Elsie Sheridan got word that her Billy was lost at sea, somewhere out by Turkey, I think, and he was straight around their house, offering condolences and arranging a Mass.'

Her father immediately relented, as he always did in the unusual advent of his wife showing the slightest displeasure. 'Of course he's a fine man and fine cleric. I just mean things are going to become nasty here – everyone says so. They should never have shot those men who signed the Proclamation of Independence, and shooting Connolly in a chair, for goodness' sake. They were asking to make martyrs of them, and that's exactly what they did. And then the rest of them, the ones the British imprisoned, well, it seems they put that time to good use and are now a much more disciplined army. They'll strike again, mark my words, and this time it won't be poets and teachers and shop-keepers but properly trained men.' He took a sip of his tea and an angry bite of his toast; he was having an opinion again. 'Men who were trained by the British themselves, coming home and taking up arms against the very army that made soldiers of them in the first place.'

'They wouldn't surely?' Mother clutched the string of pearls at her throat in horror.

'They have and they'll continue to do so. The rebels came close last time, but that was only round one. They're determined to break Ireland away from Britain, and all I'm saying is it might be prudent to remain silent on the subject of loyalties.'

'Poor David. I hate the thought of him coming home to such a sorry state of affairs.' Mother's voice quivered at the mention of her son. 'He'll be horrified. He'll hate it, won't he, Michael?'

May shot a furtive glance at her father, who said nothing.

Father had long ago decided that David was dead. May had told her parents about Enzo knowing David was a prisoner of war without being told, but her father didn't believe in 'feelings', he believed in facts, and the fact was they had never had a letter from David even though the Germans did allow POWs to write. Friends of the Gallaghers, a judge and his wife, had a son who'd been captured, and they heard from him regularly and could send him parcels. So as far as Michael Gallagher was concerned, his wife was deluded if she ever thought she would see their son again, and he refused to encourage her fantasy by referring to David as if he were alive, even though he hadn't the heart to stop her doing so herself.

'David will hate it, Mother,' said May, filling in the sad silence.

'So you've a letter there from Peter, May?' her father asked, changing the subject.

'I have!' She was relieved to have something more hopeful to talk about. 'And he's got such exciting news!'

'Oh really, dear? Are they driving the Germans back?' her mother asked, as she often did, to demonstrate her knowledge of the war.

'No, Mother, not that.' She placed her knife and fork side by side on her plate, though she had not managed to finish the huge pile of eggs and bacon her mother had placed in front of her, saying she was too thin and not eating enough. 'Remember when I met Peter he was in the Gaiety, acting in Macbeth?'

'Yes, dear.' Her mother was clearly confused as to what this had to do with driving the Germans here, there and everywhere.

'Well, he and some of his chums have put together a show. It went down very well in their local…um…theatre…' She didn't think her mother would approve of the sort of establishment Peter had described to her in a previous letter, with jugs of wine and loose women lining the bar. 'And so now they're performing it regularly for the American troops, to cheer them up. Isn't that marvellous?'

'A theatre performance, excerpts from Shakespeare, is it?' Olive was doing her best to understand, but this was so far beyond her experience or comprehension, she was struggling. May didn't think her mother had ever set foot in a music hall in her whole life.

'No, more singing and dancing, and a comedian, and an acrobat… things like that.' May spoke with as much confidence and authority as she could muster, as if she was describing the pinnacle of highbrow art. Not that she was ashamed of what Peter was doing; after all, it had been her suggestion in the first place.

'Oh…and the army allows that, do they?' Her mother sounded very doubtful.

'Oh, Mother, the army have asked him to do it. It was the adjutant to the commander who asked him to manage it. It's cheering up the American troops and encouraging the war effort, so it's really a wonderful thing they're doing.'

'Well, of course I'm firmly behind supporting the war,' Olive said tentatively. 'But, darling, you did say when we were so worried about Peter being only an actor that he only performed in proper plays. What you're describing, well, is it quite…seemly?'

'War changes everything, Mother,' said May firmly.

'Does it, darling? What do you think, Michael?'

Already May could see the cogs of her mother's brain moving. What would people say? What would the women on the flower-arranging committee say? What would Father O'Reilly say?

'I think if the army have asked him to do it, they see some merit in it, and then what else could he do, dear?' said May's father, removing himself from the conversation by returning to his morning paper.

'Well, I suppose we don't need to broadcast it.' Olive smiled at May to take the sting from her words, while her daughter quietly seethed. What would her mother say if she found out Peter was from Henrietta Street…

Well, May thought, she would have to make sure she and Peter were safely married before that happened.

CHAPTER 19

OCTOBER 1918

ETER

Major Billingsley had sent notice to Peter of his arrival at the American camp and had requested Peter to come and see him at the officers' headquarters there.

The summons had made Peter's blood run cold. He knew the Fifth Battle of Ypres was raging, looking no doubt like the first four, carnage, slaughter, blood, rats, cold. He shuddered at the idea of going back to fighting again, but the American troops were moving forward now and no doubt the patriotic major wanted all hands on deck.

The private serving as a secretary directed him to an office in the depths of the building. Peter knocked on the door.

'Come.'

Peter opened the door and saw his old commanding officer sitting alone behind a desk piled with buff-coloured files, his cane resting against the wall beside him. He looked more or less the same as the last time Peter had seen him, in his always perfect uniform with the shining buttons, although one of his hands rested awkwardly on the table, as if it had no power. He remembered hearing that the major had taken another bit of shrapnel, to the shoulder this time. It had been only a few months since he'd seen him, but the major had aged.

'Hello, Major Billingsley, sir.' Peter saluted. He was in uniform for the visit today, and the fabric felt so scratchy and hard compared with the evening suit he wore on stage.

'Ah, Cullen.' The major smiled beneath his bushy moustache. 'Come in, come in. Good to see you.'

'Thank you, sir.'

'Had a few days' leave and wanted to see how you were doing. The Americans gave me this rather grand place to conduct my business. Fancier than what I'm used to. At ease Cullen.' He stood in the small room with one tiny window. 'So I hear you've had them rolling in the aisles,' Billingsley remarked as he cleaned his pipe.

'Well, it's been a great success, sir…'

'Been?' Billingsley raised one hairy eyebrow. 'Past tense?'

Peter hesitated, confused. 'Well…' Wasn't the major here to order him and his mates back to the front?

'I take it you've been keeping abreast of what's happening, Cullen.'

Peter's heart sank again. So he'd guessed right – the major was planning on sending him back into that hell. 'Yes, sir, but I've been so focused on what we're doing here, I don't know much about the detail, sir.'

'The Germans brought in reinforcements we didn't know they had really, to try to stop us crossing into Belgium. We lost something in the region of five thousand men in that scrap alone, and that's not including the two thousand dead Belgians and many more thousands wounded.' Billingsley showed no emotion as he talked about the losses. No matter how hectic the battle got, the major was the epitome of calm under fire. Nothing seemed to rile the man. 'But we did advance in that push, Cullen, took ten thousand Hun captive and liberated quite a bit of hardware as well, so while it's not over, it soon will be.' His eyes sparkled as he contemplated victory at last.

Peter remained silent, standing, awaiting his orders.

'The Americans, the Canadians, the Australians, they're all doing their bit. It's very heartening to see. And the navy are scuttling the U-boats at a great rate.' He looked at Peter, as if expecting an answer.

'That's good to hear, sir,' Peter replied.

A hint of a smile played around the other man's lips. 'So you're probably eager to know if I'm sending you, Riccio, Campbell and Gerrity back for the last hurrah, I expect.'

'Well, yes, sir, I suppose I am.' Though eager wasn't the right word.

'I expect you want to see it out, don't you? You did a lot of fighting, so you have a right to be there for the victory. It wouldn't seem fair for you to end your war singing and dancing when you all put in the hard yards for so long. And God knows, it was a long, hard slog, Cullen, but we're moving now, en masse, and though it's hard-won, we are getting there.'

Peter hoped his heart wasn't beating in his chest as loudly as he felt it was. So Billingsley was concerned they'd be missing out if they didn't get to be there for the capitulation of the Germans. The major was clearly looking forward to it, but to Peter, the very idea of going back to all that death and destruction… Well, he could hardly bear the thought. To say so, however, would be unpatriotic and a total anathema to Billingsley.

'I suppose it would be a shame, sir,' he said sadly. Every fibre of him longed to beg Billingsley to leave them where they were, and he knew the others felt the same. But it wasn't an opinion he could voice to a career soldier like the major.

Billingsley didn't speak; he was contemplating Peter with his head to one side.

Eventually he said, 'You're a good lad, Cullen, and a brave soldier. You did your bit, and you have nothing to be ashamed of, but I'm sorry to disappoint you. I'm afraid now the troops are moving, the top brass want you to take your show around the base hospitals behind the lines. It's not ideal, I know, but I see their point, I suppose. Poor buggers recovering from their wounds could use some cheering up. Something like you chaps turning up might be just the ticket. It will mean you'll miss the end, and that doesn't seem fair, but then nothing about this bloody war is fair, is it?'

Relief flooded Peter like the opening of a dam. 'Of course I'll be sad to miss the end, but it can't be helped, sir, and I'm sure my mates will agree to it, yes. It might take some modification of the set, but yes, it is very doable, sir, especially as we have an old truck for getting around.'

The major nodded and stood. His limp was more pronounced than ever now, and his left hand hung by his side; perhaps he'd lost the use of it. 'That's very good of you, Cullen.' He clapped Peter on the back with his good hand. 'Anything you need that I can help with, like a bit of fuel for the lorry, let me know.'

'Thank you, sir. We'll do our very best to bring a bit of fun and a few smiles to the faces of the wounded, sir.'

'I'm sure you'll succeed. Now I've a meeting with my American counterpart to attend, so I'll let you see yourself out.'

Peter saluted him, and the major suddenly offered him his good hand to shake.

'Good luck, Cullen. I appreciate this. Try not to regret not being there at the death. There are more ways than one to win a war, old chap.'

'Thank you, sir.'

It took him all he could do not to skip down the corridor, bellowing at the top of his lungs for joy.

CHAPTER 20

ETER

FOR THE NEXT FEW WEEKS, the logistics of getting his troupe all around the place from one base hospital to the next and putting the act together every day took all of Peter's organisational skills. They travelled all over Normandy and Brittany mostly, and despite the horrible nature of the injuries they saw, they were greeted with so much enthusiasm, it was hard to feel down in the dumps.

Then came the last day of October 1918, and the newspaper headlines were full of how the Ottomans had signed the Armistice of Mudros, thus ending hostilities between them and the Allies.

Sitting in the canteen of the hospital where they were performing, Peter looked at the grainy photo of the Ottoman Minister of Marine Affairs, a man called Rauf Orbay, on board the *HMS Agamemnon* off some Greek island. Royal Navy Admiral Sir Somerset

Arthur Gough-Calthorpe, who accepted the armistice, looked exhausted.

Less than two weeks later, the war was over at long last, the final armistice with Germany signed on the eleventh hour of the eleventh day of the eleventh month. How very poetic.

Peter wondered what the future held for them now. The thousands of wounded would take a while to be moved, and the able-bodied troops, now with time on their hands, weren't going to be going home any time soon – demobbing would take months – so as far as he could see, it made sense to keep the show going for the next while, entertaining the troops wherever they were stationed. Thanks to Nick, they had their own lorry and gear, so hopefully the army would just let him and his mates keep on doing what they were doing until they got their walking papers, which might not be until after Christmas or even next spring. Everyone said they'd be demobbing the useful workers first, like miners and brickies and men like that, and probably nobody thought actors were useful to the economy.

Major Billingsley was no longer around; he had succumbed to the flu and died three weeks before the end of the war, missing the end. His pointless death made Peter genuinely sad, but at least nothing had changed for his troupe; no one had issued fresh orders, and he and his mates were still getting their army wages for putting on their shows. Peter figured they might as well keep going until someone noticed and told them to stop.

But first they had a date to keep. The four of them piled into their ramshackle lorry and drove over the muddy potholed roads back to Poperinge, where they found Celine and her father had mercifully survived the war, with their precious hotel intact. Everyone shed tears of joy, including Madame Picot's poor malnourished girls. Peter and his mates had a great few days eating and drinking, spending the dollars the American soldiers always insisted on giving them, and then to their joy, Ramon turned up as promised, full of bloodthirsty stories about killing Germans up to the last possible minute.

Of them all, Ramon was the only one not exhilarated to be out of the trenches. His zeal for the war made him stand out among the other soldiers. There was something vengeful about the Spaniard that unsettled Peter slightly. He was brooding – that was the word for it – a deep-thinking man, and Peter felt those thoughts were not necessarily benign. Still, Ramon was a mate, and Peter felt a duty to look after him, which in his mind meant bringing him into the troupe.

The problem was how to make Ramon a bit less brooding and 'highbrow', as the major had put it, and a bit more 'music hall'. Nick could capture an audience's heart, Enzo entertained and amused, and Two-Soups had them in stitches, but while Ramon's superb, complicated guitar playing was mesmerising to Peter, it wasn't going to work for a bunch of demob-happy troops.

'It's because I need a dancer to do the performance,' Ramon explained when Peter raised it with him, sitting with the others at the table in the nearly empty bar while Celine served up plates of eggs and chips and apple juice and a jug of wine. 'Flamenco is the marriage of both, you know? Music and dance, they are interchangeable. The feet are part of the rhythm. What I need is my flamenco partner, Aida, to work with me, but she hates me because I left her side to fight the Germans. And anyway, I can't ask her here – too much mud and wounded men. She hates misery. She says she's had too much pain in her life already.'

'Maybe Celine can dance for you?' said Nick hopefully. Nick was always trying to persuade Monsieur Ducat to allow Celine to come with them when they went back to entertaining the troops. Celine was keen – she wanted to get away from bar work – but Monsieur Ducat was convinced that if he put his daughter on the stage, she'd never get a husband.

Peter suspected Nick would happily offer to marry Celine himself, but probably he didn't have the courage to say so, and maybe never would.

'*Pouvez-vous dancer, Celine?*' Nick asked the girl, blushing furiously as he always did when he talked to her.

Celine laughed and shook her head, but then Enzo, who was a little drunk, jumped off his stool. 'You know what, mate, I know all about flamenco dancing. It's simple, ain't it? I seen it in Italy – a Spanish troupe travelled with us in the circus for a while.'

He placed one hand behind his back and the other in the air, clicking his fingers and stamping his feet. Ramon grinned wickedly and began to play, something slower this time, more deliberate, and Enzo swirled around like a seductive but drunken woman, bending his spine so far back, Peter was alarmed it might snap.

'Stop, stop…' Ramon's black eyes were glittering with glee. 'Aida would scream in horror if she saw you, but it is very funny. We should do this. It will make the Tommies laugh.'

He placed his guitar by his chair, then jumped up to show Enzo a few moves, his narrow hips pivoting in a perfect arc, looking something between raffish and dangerous as he demonstrated the moves of a female flamenco dancer. He adjusted Enzo's hands and fingers, pushed him here, pulled him there, and then they had another go. The better Enzo got – and it was incredible how quickly he picked it up – the funnier it was.

'He cannae do it wi'out a dress,' howled Two-Soups, weak with laughter.

It was like a light bulb had gone on in Peter's head. 'You're right. Hang on.'

One of Madame Picot's young girls was sitting at the bar, wearing a shabby pink crinoline dress, which May would have criticised for being very old fashioned; apparently those big-hooped dresses were out of style now and the simple, shorter, less fussy but more elegant fashions were all the rage.

As he approached the girl, he wondered if she was older than he'd first thought or just worn down by the ravages of war and her work. She was rake thin, and her cheeks were lined, and she was pouring brandy from a small bottle into a chipped cup.

''Allo, dear, you want?' she asked him in quite good English as he joined her; lots of the girls had picked up the language from the Tommies. She pushed the bottle towards him, and her eyes, the one part of her that hadn't aged, were kind.

'No thanks, mademoiselle. I don't drink. But I do have a favour to ask…'

Enzo looked very flushed and apprehensive when the prostitute beckoned him upstairs, to the slow handclapping of Two-Soups and Ramon while Nick and Celine looked aghast. But then Peter whispered in Enzo's ear, and Enzo grinned and nodded and bounded after the girl.

By now the other tables were filling up; it was getting towards dinnertime. Soldiers shouted to Celine to bring them beer and wine and chips, so she got up and ran off to the bar.

Fifteen minutes later, Enzo descended the stairs again in the pink frilly crinoline; the girl had even managed to unearth a black curly wig and had painted his lips bright red, and he was pouting comically. Ramon sat smoking a cigarette and looking on in bemusement, his guitar on his knee as he absentmindedly tuned and plucked. But the newly arrived soldiers whooped and shouted with laughter and burst into a round of applause.

Grinning hugely at them, Enzo jumped up on the small stage and struck a pose, his arms in the air and his hands folded over his head, like the wings of a swan. Ramon rolled his eyes and began a flamenco tune of wild intricacy and rhythm. Somehow Enzo was able to keep up, and the boards were soon reverberating to the sound of his hobnailed soldier's boots. The music was pure and passionate, and the dancing tribal and furious, although at the same time hilarious since it was obvious that Enzo was a man.

Peter watched the faces of the soldiers for their reaction; they seemed both amused and enthralled. Enzo stamped and twirled and arched his back, his hands creating graceful shapes in the air. Ramon's fingers flew all over the guitar as if on fire, and the melody conjured up a time and place far away – hot nights, orange-scented air, crashing waves, sultry women with kohl-ringed eyes – and the whole strange tableau was so compelling that hardly anyone spoke. As more and more soldiers drifted in, every eye in the bar was on the stage.

CHAPTER 21

AY

DEAR MAY,

Sorry I didn't write earlier. I've been doing shows for the wounded and everyone stuck away from their families still. As you can see, I've enclosed some silk stockings some American GI gave to Celine and she gave to me. It makes a change for me to be sending something to you, doesn't it?

So what news do I have for you...let's see.

Ramon is going down a storm – all we needed was a dancer for him. He has a flamenco partner in Spain, Aida Gonzalez is her name, but they fell out and he doesn't know whether he dares ask her over. She's very fiery apparently. Anyway, guess who's filling in as his dancer? Enzo! It's a right laugh, as Enzo would say. So we get the highbrow flamenco thing, but Enzo manages to drag it down to lowbrow, and somehow it all works.

Celine's father finally relented and let us take her with us. The way it happened, she and Nick told Monsieur Ducat they were engaged, which I think Nick would love in real life, but as far as Celine is concerned, it's an 'engagement of convenience'. Two-Soups thinks she's stringing poor old Nick along, nothing like his wonderful Betty. I'm dying to meet his Betty some day. She sounds like an absolute gem.

May sighed deeply, sitting at her dressing table, brushing her hair as she read Peter's news. He was at it again, singing the praises of other women when she'd rather he was praising her.

I'm sort of glad you're not here with me, May. It would break your heart to see the lads in the base hospitals here, so many of them so badly wounded, you wonder if they'd have been better off to cop it. They put the worst injured or horribly deformed men at the back of the audience when we're performing – the nurses push their beds into the hall – but Celine has started going back through the rows to sing, and the men love it. She sings and sits on their beds, or perches on their knees if they're in a wheelchair, and she jokes and flirts with them, and they are delighted with her. Her English is quite good now, and she has this breathy French accent that drives the men mad! She's a piece of work, our Mademoiselle Ducat, nothing like the sweet little French country girl she presents herself as. She's much more confident and full of fun –

Oh, Celine, Celine, Celine! Why did he think it was all right for Celine to be there with him, living that life, and not her? Did he imagine she was some silly pampered girl, destined to turn into her pearl-clutching mother? Wasn't she also 'confident' and 'full of fun'?

We've had a lot of talks about what to do when we're demobbed. All the soldiers will get a month's extra pay and a rail ticket and civvies.

I thought at first everyone would want to go to their own homes when they got their walking papers, but it seems Nick isn't keen – he's so mysterious – and Ramon says he's nothing to go back to, and Enzo thinks we should all go to London for a while and maybe audition for some of the variety shows. He reckons there's money to be made there. So anyway, we're thinking about it.

Well, that's all my news, May. I hope you're keeping well, and I'm looking forward to seeing you again whenever I get back to Ireland. I enclosed a letter to Kathleen as usual, and can you forward Nick's letter to Alicia Shaw – he wants her to know he's not coming back to Ireland and he'll send her his address when he's settled. I wonder who Alicia is? I know you think maybe it's a lady's maid in the house or something, but he's so stuck on Celine, I don't think it can be that. Unless he's two-timing Alicia, but he doesn't seem like that sort of man, much too shy.

~~All the best,~~

~~Peter.~~

Don't stop reading yet! Just as I went to give this letter to be posted, I was handed my walking papers! The Royal Irish Rifles is being demobilised and sent back to 'civvy street', as they say. I checked with Enzo, Nick, Ramon and Two-Soups, and sure enough, they've got them too.

So we'll be out of commission by the middle of February, and then the army wages will stop. So now we're agreed – we're off to London to see if we can make some money. We've got some of Nick's hundred pounds still to see us through, and we'll sell the lorry and piano and just bring the costumes and see if we can get some paid work.

Celine is determined to come with us. She's seventeen and old enough to make up her own mind, she says, but we'll see what her father says. Maybe her and Nick will have to have a 'marriage of convenience'. And Ramon has decided to risk writing to the fiery Aida to join us, and we had a whip-round of money for her and her mother to come to London. Ramon says Enzo is fine dancing for the soldiers, but in London he wants to do things properly. I don't know. I think Enzo is brilliant, but maybe Ramon's right. In London we can afford to go a bit more sophisticated maybe. But maybe Aida and her mother won't come at all, so we'll see.

Two-Soups is writing to Betty even as I'm writing this. He's going to ask her to leave the farm for a bit and come down to London. Apparently she's a darling and gorgeous as well –

Another gorgeous girl, thought May crossly.

– and also a dab hand with a hammer and nails and even knows how to weld metal, so maybe she can help Enzo build a set for his acrobatics. I'm so excited, May! It's all coming together!

I'll let you know as soon as I know where I'm living.

All the best,

Peter xx

As she read and reread the letter, May twisted the ring on her finger that she'd bought for herself with the five-pound note Peter had rejected. He'd promised to buy her a ring 'when he could afford it'. She knew it didn't make any difference, they were engaged anyway, but she had to have something to show her friends from the tennis club and to discourage the overeager Mr Swift. She had settled on a thin gold ring with a tiny diamond, which she would put away when Peter bought her a new and better one.

She'd thrown away the silk stockings. She had plenty of her own and didn't need Celine's castoffs, thank you very much. She was inclined to send them back again, but she supposed the war made everything different, and Peter was always trading, so maybe he'd forgotten presents were supposed to be special and personal.

It was so disappointing Peter hadn't asked her to meet him in London, even though she knew it was because he'd promised her father that he would never make his precious daughter live in poverty. This Scottish comedian called Two-Soups could have his girlfriend there apparently. Mind you, she sounded very rough. And then they had invited this French girl along. Goodness knows what sort of a person she was, very unsavoury and used to the gutter by the sounds of it, flirting with strangers.

I'm sort of glad you're not here with me, May…

He was as bad as her parents, wrapping her in cotton wool like she was a china shepherdess on a mantelpiece. But she wasn't breakable. She was tough, she knew she was, and besides, she could be more help to Peter than anyone.

Auntie Maura in Stillorgan had finally died three weeks ago and had left her grandniece more money than May could have imagined inheriting in her wildest dreams. Nearly two thousand pounds, an enormous sum. It made her feel guilty for not going to see her aunt more often, even though she was a dreadful bore.

Mother had been equally astonished. Her maiden aunt had been a recluse and a bookworm, and they had no idea how Auntie Maura had amassed so much money. Nor had the aunt been particularly affectionate. She was nice enough and gave May and David a gift of a book on their birthdays and at Christmas, but when she died and the will was read, the Gallaghers were totally taken aback. It turned out that Maura Longford used to play the stock exchange, and her solicitor, a man in Parnell Square, told them that she had been a shrewd but creative investor.

The money was to be held in trust until May's twenty-first birth-day, which was only eighteen months away. So never mind flirty French girls and hammer-wielding Scotswomen. If Peter wanted to get ahead in his musical hall career, then he didn't have to look any further than the resourceful and soon-to-be-wealthy May Gallagher.

May drew her silver inkwell and fountain pen and lavender-scented writing paper towards her.

My darling Peter,

As soon as you are settled in London, let me have your address. I have such a wonderful surprise for you. I won't tell you right now because I want to tell you in person, but be sure it will change our lives. I can't wait to see you, darling. I miss you so much. I'm enclosing a ten-pound note to help with your expenses in London...

She wrote on and on, praising him, loving him, supporting him, being his perfect sweetheart.

CHAPTER 22

ICK

THE DAY CELINE had asked him to pretend they were engaged in order to pacify her father and convince him to let her travel with the troupe around northern France had been the happiest day of Nick's life.

Peter had been annoyed about the lie at first. He seemed to feel responsible for all of them, like they were children under his care. But Nick had been determined to bring her. He loved being part of the troupe, but for him the high point was singing with Celine. So he stood his ground and reminded Peter that Celine was a civilian and therefore entitled to do as she pleased. And the others all agreed, saying it was important to have a pretty girl in the show along with all their ugly mugs.

So Peter had given in, but he'd made Nick promise to make sure no one took advantage of her.

Of course Nick would protect the innkeeper's daughter. Deep down he knew that's why she'd picked him as the one to become 'engaged to'; it was because she felt the safest in his company. She probably couldn't even imagine him plucking up the nerve to ask her out, let alone 'take advantage' of her.

Two-Soups warned Nick that Celine was stringing him along. The Scot wasn't the most diplomatic person you could meet, and their so-called romance was compared very unfavourably to his and Betty's. But then Betty was above every other female on earth, it would seem. Maybe Betty was that gorgeous, though Nick found it hard to imagine anyone lovelier than Celine. As for being faithful, that wasn't a fair comparison. Two-Soups and Betty were engaged for real, but Celine had never given any indication that she was interested in Nick romantically, and it wasn't her fault that she was all he dreamed of.

When she'd come up onto the tiny stage that night in the Aigle d'Or and he sang to her in French and she joined in, he'd known then that she was the girl for him. But he'd had no idea what to do next, or how to progress the relationship further. Peter said they had great chemistry on stage, and off stage, Celine assured him he was her *bon ami*, but that's where it stopped, because he'd never got up the guts to ask her out.

At least she wasn't seeing anyone else. On tour with the troupe, she was the darling of the forces. She was charming, funny and flirty with everyone, but she wasn't easy. She never seemed to go on dates with any of the men, always making the excuse she was engaged to Nick – he seemed to be the new Antoine, the dead boyfriend she'd used as her cover for so long – and when Enzo batted his eyelashes at her, she didn't even seem to notice.

Nick envied the ease his mates had around women, Enzo especially. The Londoner was always chatting up the nurses in the hospitals, and they loved him for it. He knew exactly what to say to make them giggle and blush. He did it with all women, even that matron who was a terrifying-looking dragon with a bushier moustache than poor Billingsley. She scared the living daylights out of all the nurses and patients, the doctors too, but Enzo made her simper like a lovesick schoolgirl. Nick had studied him, trying to see how he did it, what made it so effortless, but it was impossible to emulate.

One disastrous night – and he burned with hot shame at the

memory – he'd decided Dutch courage was what was needed to ask Celine out, so he drank as much red wine as he could as fast as he could. He'd made a total fool of himself, and just barely stopped himself from bleating to Peter about what a sad, lonely childhood he'd had and giving the game away about who he really was.

Peter didn't drink so was never out of control. He had tried to rein Nick in and make him sit down and sober up, but Nick wasn't having it. The rest of the night was hazy, but apparently he'd tried to dance with Celine, who just wanted to go to bed, so he'd ended up dancing flamenco with Enzo instead, then falling over and cutting his head on a chair. His only real recollection was the miserable vomiting for hours and wishing he could just die.

Maybe in London, back on familiar territory – because he'd often holidayed there and in Brighton with his grandmother – he would get up some normal courage and manage to ask her out then.

In the meantime, Celine had told her father that she and Nick would be married in London as soon as Nick had the money for a gold ring. Poor innocent Monsieur Ducat had believed her and had come to Nick, telling him he trusted him not just with his daughter but with his life.

Nick thought it was strange and embarrassing how people always seemed to trust him, because he'd lied about everything to his mates. He wasn't who he said he was, so his entire existence was predicated on a falsehood, and yet people seemed to believe in him instinctively.

Up to now, he'd got away with it. There had been one or two slips. He'd mentioned how the food in the army was no worse than school, and Peter had seemed confused. 'They fed you at your school, did they? My ma just gave us a chunk of bread and a bit of jam or butter to take.'

'Yes, they used to give us a bit of bread and a cup of cocoa some days,' he'd said hastily, and Peter seemed to accept it. Boarding school would have been a dead giveaway.

Though now it was dawning on him that in London he might see someone he knew, and he would be found out, just like he'd nearly given himself away to Peter when he was drunk.

Joining the army as Nick Gerrity, making friends for life and now performing with them was like a dream come true, except he would never have even dreamed of such a wonderful thing. But he'd not thought it through, he now realised. Should he confide the truth now, before it was too late? His instinct was to keep up the charade, but supposing someone in the street recognised him? Or came to one of their shows? Not his parents, obviously – they'd never darken a music hall with their presence – but one of their staff?

He hated the idea of his parents finding out where he was and what he was doing; it didn't bear thinking about. His father's fury, his mother's disdain, Wally's sneering laugh – little N-N-Nicolas is in the music hall. How he'd howl. And his parents would insist he embarrass them no longer and leave the theatre and return with them in shame to Brockleton to live the life of a gentleman and never have any fun again.

And even more terrifying was the idea of his friends finding out. He'd lived such a solitary childhood, his brothers only seeing him as a punch bag, but now everything was different. Peter and Enzo were his sworn comrades, and Two-Soups and Ramon were his mates, and Celine…well, she was the love of his life.

He couldn't see how any of them would ever be able to trust him again if it emerged he'd told such a huge lie. They might even be so angry that they'd reject him. And then there was Celine… How could he ever marry Celine, in real life, if she didn't even know who he was? To get married, you had to have birth certificates and witnesses and things.

On the train to the Normandy coast, where they would be embarking from Cherbourg, Nick made his decision. Ramon, Peter, Two-Soups and Enzo were engrossed in a round of cards, but Celine was sitting gazing out of the window at the green countryside and ruined villages passing slowly by.

'Celine, w-w-will you come to the d-d-dining car with me? For a c-c-coffee?'

'I will. I could do with a warm drink – this train is so cold,' she said obligingly, getting up. She was wearing a lovely dress under a fur coat, midnight blue with a lace collar and buttons down the front. She'd told him she had made it herself out of an old piece of fabric she'd found in her late mother's sewing box, and the coat had been her mother's as well. Her hair was elegantly pinned, and she wore a small cloche hat. She was perfect.

As she walked with him down the corridor, she hunted in her purse for coins.

'P-p-put your p-p-purse away. The c-c-coffee is m-m-my t-t-t-t...' He blushed furiously as his stammer got worse. She kept swaying against him as the train rattled along, and her physical proximity was making him more nervous than any German sniper or shell.

She looked at him with pity, the expression he most hated to see on other peoples' faces. Nurses at school, some teachers, even his grandmother had all looked at him that way at times as he struggled to form a word, and he wished they wouldn't. He didn't want to be a figure of ridicule or pity; he just wanted to stop stammering.

'T-t-treat.' *There!*

'Poor Nick. Is very bad today.' She slipped her hand into the crook of his arm as they walked, and this, the first act of intimacy between them, off the stage, took the sting from the words. Was this happening? Was Celine Ducat really linking him as they walked? Though probably it was just to keep herself steady as the train went around a long corner.

'Y-y-y-y-yes.' *Damn it.*

'And there is nothing, no doctor, can do?'

Her gentle pressing didn't make him want to run away like it did when anyone else mentioned it, but he still hated this conversation.

'But not when you sing? No?'

He shook his head, afraid to speak.

'It does not matter to me, but I see it is making you...what is word...*frustré.*'

'F-f-frustrated.' He wished they could change the subject, and he knew he was blushing; he could feel his face burning.

'It doesn't matter to me, in case you worry.' Her English had improved so much in the months she'd spent with him and his mates.

She refused to let him speak in French to her, even though he'd have preferred it; he seemed to stammer less in French. Maybe because he was talking in a foreign language, he could pretend to be someone else entirely, someone suave and handsome and attractive to women, just as he did when he was singing.

'I'm g-g-glad,' he managed.

'I just wanted you to know that.' She smiled, and he was sure she could hear his heart beating out of his chest.

In the dining car, they sat opposite each other, and Celine ordered two coffees, which seemed to come in soup bowls, the way the French liked it at breakfast time, and two big flaky croissants. Nick picked up his coffee as Celine sat crumbling one of the croissants over hers, then put it down again. He was fighting the nerves that were threatening to overwhelm him.

'So, you want to tell me, Nick?'

He blushed, startled. 'Oh…' He'd just been thinking he might put this confession off for a while longer.

'Because *je pense*…I think you do want to tell me something?' Her cheeks were too thin for dimples, but her eyes twinkled at him so kindly and so trustingly, he felt he might blurt out his feelings there and then, in the dining car thronged with people.

Instead, he took his life in his hands and told her everything.

CHAPTER 23

VALENCIA, SPAIN 1918

IDA

AIDA GONZALEZ LOOKED through her four flamenco dresses hanging on a rail in the corner of the bedroom and wondered if she could sell them for enough to pay for her mother's funeral. But how could she bear to part with them? They had been handmade by her mother, herself a dancer, with lace from Andalucía and fabric from a special manufacturer in Málaga. Every stitch had been done with love, and since she was fourteen and started dancing for the tourists, Aida had cared for these dresses as if they were her children.

A lump formed in her throat, and hot tears stung at the back of her eyes. No, her mother had told her never to part with these dresses, so that while she was dancing, her mother's spirit would always be with her, dancing with her.

She returned to her mother's deathbed and just sat there on the wooden chair, holding Gabriella's cold, stiff hand, as she had done all the previous day, and then the night, without sleeping. 'Mama, what can I do? How can I get money?'

Ramon had gone to the war. He was so obsessed with his hatred for the Germans since his own parents died that he'd forgotten everything he owed to Aida and her mother. Since he'd left, Aida had had no accompanist, and dancing without music was not an option. She would never, ever understand how Ramon could abandon her so cruelly when she'd thought of him all her life as a brother.

After he'd left, Gabriella Gonzalez continued to teach flamenco dancing to a handful of children, which brought in just enough week to week to pay for rent and food if they ate very little, so for a while they survived.

But last week Mama got sick, and when the doctor came, he'd just said there was nothing to be done. Gabriella Gonzalez had the Spanish flu that was wiping out all of Europe. He advised Aida to leave her mother, as she would die soon anyway, and not risk being infected herself, but Aida would never do that. They had been a team, just the two of them, all of her life.

So she stayed by her mother's bed, in their fourth-floor apartment in Valencia, bathing Gabriella's forehead with a damp cloth. Gabriella was pale and shivering but at the same time soaked with perspiration. Savage cramps seemed to twist her insides, and for an hour, she cried out repeatedly, then she lost consciousness. Half an hour after that, she was dead. Leaving her daughter numb, shocked, terrified. Nothing to pay the rent, no food in the house and, above all, facing the unbearable prospect of burying her beloved mother in a pauper's grave.

As she sat holding Gabriella's hand, there came a knock at the door of the apartment. She heard it open, and then a short, fat figure appeared in the bedroom doorway.

It was the landlord's son, a self-satisfied spoiled brat. 'Your next-door neighbour tells me your mother died yesterday?'

Aida looked at him expressionlessly.

He gave a callous little shrug. 'I'm sorry for your loss, but I need to know what arrangements are in place to remove the body. We can't take chances with the health of other residents.'

Like this fat little monster cared about the 'health of the other residents'. He and his father were slum landlords who had made a killing of late as people from the countryside flooded the cities in search of work. Political and social unrest, strikes and rising poverty made people desperate, and vultures like the Dumases capitalised on it, charging extortionate rents. What this vulture wanted her to do was leave the apartment so he could rent it to several tenants, cramming them in together, making more money.

'I...I haven't made any arrangements,' Aida managed.

'Well, can I engage an undertaker on your behalf?'

'I don't think... I can't afford that...' she said, never feeling so alone. Why wasn't Ramon here to help her? The war was over, wasn't it? Selfish fool, he had probably been blown to pieces in Flanders.

'Well, we can't have a dead body just lying in the building, you know, contaminating...' The fat young man made a face as if he'd just drank sour milk.

Aida looked at the still, silent face of her mother. Such a lovely person, who had the misfortune to waste her love and life on the pursuit of Rafael Narro. She had been a beauty; she'd had such talent as a dancer. Tía Conchita, Ramon's mother who had died two years ago, always said that Gabriella had something special, more so even than Conchita herself, who was a famous dancer. But Gabriella was a delicate flower in a hard, hard world. She was too soft. She believed lies. She was exploited by men, men who said they would make her famous, like the promoter who said he would put her on the Liceu de Barcelona. He did, but he stole her money and was never seen again. Or Rafael Narro, who gave her a daughter but not much else except empty promises and a visit every few months. Time and time again, Gabriella trusted and was hurt.

Even as a child, Aida could see all this and wished her mother would learn, but she never seemed to. She loved, saw the best in people, was always kind and gave what she had, even to people who were not in such dire straits as she herself was. And what was her reward? A pauper's grave with her daughter the only mourner.

'I will go to Paterna now, ask…' she replied, with as much poise as she could muster. She'd heard her mother and Tía Conchita saying how the poor were put in a plot at the back, no markings, no marble headstones. She decided then and there that she wouldn't ask anyone to the funeral. Their neighbours had always looked down on her mother, and she would spare Gabriella the final indignity of those nasty gossips witnessing how the city of Valencia disposed of their rubbish.

'Well, there is a way I could let you have the money for the funeral,' said the landlord's son, coming closer to the bed.

Aida looked at him. What was his name again? Raul Dumas? Pedro? Something like that? Her brow furrowed as she tried to remember, but then it struck her. Yes, he was Pedro. And she knew exactly what he was suggesting. She looked at the four flamenco dresses hanging in the corner. The last thing she had of her mother. And then back at Pedro.

'How much?' she asked coldly, laying down her mother's dead hand.

'Enough to pay for a funeral. A hearse, a plot and a gravestone.'

'I need money for rent and food.'

The transactional nature of the exchange was the only thing that made it bearable.

'One week's rent and food.' He licked his red lips and his eyes shone; he was like a fox just about to enter the chicken coop.

'Give me the money now, first,' she said calmly.

'Don't I get a smile?' he asked as he reached for his wallet.

Aida observed him coolly as he counted the notes into her palm, pausing once and then counting again as she continued to hold out her hand. He'd been collecting rent, so he had plenty of cash.

Once she'd taken what he had, she left the bedroom where her mother's body lay and went to the living room. Before he had time to follow her, she buried the roll of money down the side of the small oven.

She turned to face him as he entered, saying nothing.

'Here?' he asked, looking around at the sparsely decorated room. 'That sofa doesn't look very comfortable.'

She went back into the bedroom and brought out the rug she used as a blanket on cold nights, laid it on the floor and stood on it. Her dark eyes never leaving his, she dropped the shoulder straps of her light cotton dress and allowed it to fall to the floor. He watched, mesmerised, as she removed her slip and underwear and stood completely naked before him.

She held her hand out to him, and he took it, kissing her roughly, his hands roaming her flesh. His face became dark and predatory, and he reminded her of a storybook her mother used to read to her about a little girl who went to visit her grandmother in the woods but was met by a greedy wolf. He pushed her down on the blanket, and she focused on the story of the little girl with the red cape all the time he was on top of her.

He was a clumsy and inexperienced lover, and the entire encounter was over in minutes. Once it was finished, he looked dejected, as if he had expected more. She lay there, not moving, impassive and aloof. He might have bought her body for a brief few moments, but that was all he would get.

'Can I see you again?' he asked, his voice gruff with passion and satiety.

'No,' she replied, getting up and quickly dressing.

'But what about next week's rent and food?'

'I'm leaving.'

'Don't leave. I thought we could be friends, like you were with that guitar player before he left you. I bet you didn't charge him a king's ransom.'

She made no response as he stood, fumbling with his shirt and pulling up his trousers. Despite the obvious disparity in their circumstances, she knew he was just a pathetic schoolboy really, who didn't have the strength to push his luck.

'What's wrong with you? Don't you speak?' he grumbled.

'Not to the likes of you. Goodbye.'

He muttered, 'Not worth it,' as he pushed past her, but he left as she demanded.

She stood at the sink, washing herself thoroughly and praying she wasn't pregnant. She didn't think she could be; it wasn't the time of the month when it was likely – Mama had explained all about it when she was younger – so she just had to hope for the best.

She then dressed and took the roll of pesetas that she'd stuffed down the side of the stove.

In the bedroom, her mother looked serene, all sign of pain gone, and Aida thought she looked so much younger. She crossed the room, her long dark hair still wet – she'd scrubbed herself head to toe – and kissed her mother's forehead. 'I'll be back soon, Mama,' she said quietly.

At the undertaker's off the Plaça de la Reina, she gave a solemn-looking man her money and he offered his bland sympathies in return, and later that day, Gabriella Gonzalez had a modest but dignified funeral with flowers and a priest and a small headstone, so at least, after her short, sad life, the broken-hearted dancer was buried with dignity.

Aida was glad she was able to do that much for her mother. But now she felt truly alone. The last person who had loved her, as the child in her craved to be loved, was gone.

CHAPTER 24

ICK

THE DAY after his confession to Celine in the dining car of the train, he stood with a fast-beating heart on the deck of the ferry crossing the channel, waiting for Peter and Enzo to join him. Celine had suggested she send up his oldest friends first to hear his story. She didn't think they'd be angry with him; she was sure they'd understand, as she had done, holding his hand as Nicholas cried, hearing about his awful family, and Brockleton, and how he missed his grandmother…

He gazed into the grey distance while he waited, a grey sea bumping up against a grey sky, trying to figure out where the horizon was, anything to take his mind off his confession. He'd never before had friends, and the thought of telling his two closest friends that he'd been lying to them all this time made his guts churn. What if they were so disgusted that they didn't want to be friends with him any more, or threw him out of the theatre company?

But it was only a matter of time before he was found out, so it was best to be honest.

'Nick!'

He looked around at the shout; they were climbing the companionway. He raised his hand to wave, and they smiled as they made their way towards him through the strolling crowd of demobbed soldiers, some in their civvies, some in uniform still.

'So apart from this lovely old pals' reunion, what's this meetin' all about then?' Enzo asked as they reached him.

'I-I-I-I...'

'Take your time,' said Peter calmly, leaning on the rail beside him. 'There's no rush. This crossing will take hours.'

'I was t-t-talking to Celine on the t-t-train yesterday...'

'We noticed. You 'aven't finally persuaded the mademoiselle to give in to your lust, 'ave ya?' teased Enzo, hands in pockets.

'Not lust, love. And no, I didn't.' He had long ago given up pretending Celine wasn't the love of his life with his mates, though they were all under oath not to tell her.

'So what is it then?' Peter asked, giving him a searching look.

Nick breathed deeply. This was going to be so, so hard, and his stammer was going to be impossible to control. He opened his mouth, but as hard as he tried, no sound came out at all. It was like he was being strangled.

'Sing it,' Peter suggested gently.

Nick looked at him, still struggling for the words.

'Seriously, Nick, you don't stutter when you sing. So sing whatever you want to say. You don't need to bellow like you do up on stage. Do it quietly, so just me and Enzo can hear.'

'That's genius.' Enzo was very impressed. 'Go on, Nick, give it a whirl. Tell you what, do it to that song the troops all love so much, that one from *The Pirates of Penzance*.'

Peter laughed. '"I Am the Very Model of a Modern Major-General?" No, that's crazy fast.'

And yet as soon as Enzo suggested it, it felt right to Nick. He had memorised the original lyrics so well, he could perform it faultlessly at breakneck speed, and now what he had to tell his friends started falling into place in his mind, in time to the music.

The bell for the first sitting of dinner had just gone, so a lot of the soldiers were disappearing down the companionway and the deck was relatively empty.

'It's all right, take your time. We'll wait for the second sitting,' said Peter, seeing Nick glance anxiously towards the exodus.

'Yeah, I don't mind starvin' to death,' said Enzo cheerfully, 'if it means hearing you make a fool of yerself singing out yer troubles.'

Nick laughed and tried to relax a little. 'A-a-a...' *Damn.* He was still so nervous, he couldn't even get out the words 'all right', so he took a deep breath and closed his eyes, and to the tune of the famous light opera, he sang.

'I know I told the lot of you that my name is Nick Gerrity, but that is not the truth because it's not my true identity. The Honourable Nicholas Vivian Shaw, well, that's the real me. My father is a baron, and he's very, very posh you see.'

Peter and Enzo were open-mouthed, half amazed, half laughing.

'My brother Wally is the heir because my brother Roger's dead. My father said I'm useless, so I left and went to war instead...'

It was strange. He hadn't set out to make his story rhyme, and yet it kept on doing so.

'I signed up as a private from Waterford in Ireland. In fact I come from County Cork, where my parents own a lot of land.'

His two friends were laughing uncontrollably.

'The only one who loves me is my grandmother Alicia, and that is why I write to her in secret when I'm missing her. I don't want Father finding me, he'll only drag me home again, so please don't be upset with me because I have a stupid name.'

It was as far as he could get – he was running out of ideas now – and like the other two, he collapsed into helpless laughter.

'Are you serious?' gasped Peter, wiping his eyes. 'I knew you weren't from Waterford, and I thought you sounded fierce posh altogether, though I didn't like to say anything...'

'R-r-really?' Nick was shocked and mortified. 'Everyone g-g-guessed all along?'

'Not me, mate. All you Paddies sound the same to me.' Enzo

grinned as he recovered from his fit of laughing. 'Same with Two-Soups and Ramon – they'd never notice the difference between a shop boy from Waterford and a lord from Cork.'

'It was only you who knew?' He was impressed by Peter's ability to keep a secret. 'And you never t-t-told?'

'Not my secret to tell, Nick. So you're actually some lord or whatever?'

'Well, just an honourable, b-b-because Wally is the heir, so he'll be the sixth b-b-baron when my father dies.' He was so relieved they didn't appear to be mad at him; it made him a lot less nervous and tongue-tied. 'Thanks for not being c-c-c-cross with me. I thought you would be.'

'Nah, mate, but I reckon we need you writing songs if you can rhyme like that on the 'oof. Imagine what you could do if you 'ad a bit of time, eh?' Enzo chuckled.

'You might be on to something there.' Peter grinned. 'So, Nick, when we went home to Dublin that time, where did you go?'

'Stayed in a hotel and m-m-m-m-met Floss – that's what I call my grandmother. I slept and ate and had a great t-t-time. It was she who gave me the hundred p-p-pounds. It was mine from before.'

'I did wonder if it had something to do with that woman you were writing to.'

'It was the last of my m-m-money, though. I'm not holding out on you. B-bank account's closed for g-g-good.'

'You reckon you'll get back in touch with your folks now the war is over?' Enzo asked, but Nick shook his head.

'No, I don't want to go home. I want t-t-to stay with you and the theatre. I'm just scared someone will recognise me,' he admitted.

'Well, they can be recognising away,' Peter said, patting him on the shoulder. 'You're Nick Gerrity from Waterford. I know your mam and dad, and your two brothers and three sisters. So I'll vouch for you.'

'Grow a beard. I'm thinkin' I'll do it too, to disguise myself from all the girls who are waiting for me back in London,' Enzo moaned.

'No sympathy, Enzo.' Peter grinned. 'You draw all your romantic entanglements on yourself.'

197

'A b-b-beard.' Nick looked thoughtful, stroking his chin. 'Good idea. Maybe I will.'

'Hey, Nick,' said Enzo as they strolled back towards the companionway to go down for the second sitting. 'If you don't want to go back to Brockleton and be a rich boy, have you got a sister I could marry and get the money instead?'

'F-f-fraid not, Enzo, and the g-g-girls don't get any money anyway – they have to marry rich.'

'Pity.' Enzo sighed, his hopes dashed. But then his face brightened. 'We'll just have to get Celine to marry Wally!' And as Nick made a show of threatening to thump him, he grabbed the stair rail, slid down it, did a somersault at the bottom and raced off to the dining room, laughing his head off.

CHAPTER 25

IDA

SHE'D TOLD the landlord's disgusting son that she was moving out, but that was a week ago and the rent was due again, and now she sat in fear of Pedro Dumas knocking at her door, come to claim his due. But where could she go to escape him? She had no money.

She knew who her father was, and he was wealthy, but she would never go crawling to him.

The Spanish Naval Admiral Rafael Narro lived in a fine villa in Madrid, but he was married to the daughter of a count and had several well-brought-up children. Aida's mother was just his portside dalliance.

Gabriella had thought Rafael Narro loved her and would marry her if he hadn't been married already. It was nonsense, but she kept on dreaming and letting him into her heart and bed. The people in their building shunned her, a woman without a husband but entertaining a regular gentleman caller; she wasn't someone they wanted to associate with. Gabriella told Aida to ignore the poisonous gossips. Love was what was important in this life, she said.

Every time Rafael Narro visited, he left behind a sum on the table, 'to treat yourselves'. Gabriella never complained that he should give them more, because she didn't care about his money – she cared about his love.

Arthritis made her feet swell and stiffen, and professional dancing was no longer possible for Gabriella, but she delighted in Aida's grace and technique. Gabriella still made a small income from teaching, and she was a good teacher. She made all of the little girls in her class feel so special, like they were going to be the best flamenco dancers, even if they had two left feet. And she wouldn't just teach them the dances; she would tell them all of the stories of Andalucía and the legends and myths, and they would hang on every word. But the teaching didn't bring in enough. The wealthy families had their daughters learn ballet. Flamenco was the dance of the *gitanos*, and not of nice girls with ideas of gentility. The girls who wanted to dance flamenco were all from the poor south, and their families had next to nothing. And Gabriella, with her gentle unworldly soul and broken heart, barely bothered to charge their parents any money and always forgave their debts.

She and Aida managed to get by. Neither of them had a big appetite, although they enjoyed one treat, a cornet of gelato from an Italian man who sold his home-made ice cream in the piazza each Friday. They had an odd combination, a scoop of pistachio and a scoop of raspberry, but they had the same thing each time. He knew their order and always gave them a little discount.

Conchita would have helped them, but she was already sick and the Wilsons had fallen on hard times. So fourteen-year-old Aida had had to step up.

She and Conchita's son, Ramon, played on the streets, him on guitar as she danced for coins from the tourists. They were successful, and every day they would set up in the Plaça de la Reina, and within minutes large crowds gathered to watch. They passed around a hat, an old one from Ramon's father, the Englishman, Edward Wilson, and soon it would be full. Notes too, not just coins.

And then Edward and then Conchita died, and Ramon had gone to war to kill Germans and left her in poverty, and he hadn't even written to know if and how she was managing without him.

There was a knock on the door. She feared it was Pablo, the landlord's son, come to demand his 'rent'.

She sat there, trembling, as the handle turned and the door opened, but to her relief, it was Carmen, the tiny old woman with streaks of grey in her hair who lived on the ground floor. Carmen was the only neighbour in the building who had sympathised with her when her mother died. She'd stopped Aida when Aida was leaving the building two days ago to see if she could buy some stale bread with her last few cents. 'I heard about your mother. She was a wonderful soul, may she rest in peace,' she'd said in her soft, twittery voice.

Tears had formed and spilled over Aida's lower lids at Carmen's kind words. She hated to appear vulnerable in public, but at that moment, she couldn't help it; she had never felt so bereft. And Carmen had simply put a kind hand on her arm and said nothing, then turned away and left her alone.

Now the little old woman stood at the door with a fat brown envelope in her hand. 'The postman left this for you, dear. It's come from England.'

'Thank you, Carmen.' She stood and crossed the room to take the letter. Who could be writing to her from England? She knew nobody there. But then she looked at the handwriting of the address and her heart faltered. Only one person she knew had a hand like that, a handsome swirling style, inherited from his artistic father…

'I'll leave you to open it, dear,' said Carmen, who, unlike the rest of the neighbours, was no gossip, and she retreated and closed the door.

The letter was from Ramon. It was very short and formal; the only reason the envelope looked so fat was that it was stuffed with money in different currencies.

Dear Aida,

The war is over, and I am no longer a soldier. I hope this makes you happy and that you can forgive me for abandoning you when you said I should stay. I expect you think I should come home, but I have joined a company of entertainers and we are heading for London to make our fortune in the music halls. I am sending this money from the company so you and your mother can join us in London if you wish. There is no need to return the money if you do not come. Aida, I apologise for leaving you. I was half mad with rage. I still think of you as my sister and hope you can think of me as your brother again. Please join me. We are planning to stay at a YMCA hostel in London. It is a place known to my friend and fellow performer Lorenzo Riccio. He is not sure of the street number, but it is called the Shakespeare Hut, and it is on the corner of Keppel Street and Gower Street in Bloomsbury, which is in central London. There is an underground train station nearby called Russell Square.

Peter Cullen, our manager, is trying to arrange an audition for us at the Acadia Theatre in London. He is confident we are good enough, but, Aida, I need you. The guitar alone is not enough.

Give my love and respect to your mother, and I trust all has been well with you since we last spoke.

Love, Ramon

His letter astonished her in one way...and in another it didn't.

As she lay dying, Gabriella had told Aida that she would never really leave her. 'My mama never left me, though she went home to God when I was just sixteen, and I will never leave you, my darling,' Gabriella Gonzalez had wheezed.

Aida was sure Ramon's invitation and gift of money was her mother's doing from beyond the grave, of that she had no doubt. He had even apologised and said he needed her, despite his ridiculous pride. He and she were so alike in that way; they hated to back down. Her own heart still burned with rage against him for deserting her, but as she read the letter again, the flame smouldered less hotly. If this was her mother's doing, which she was certain of, then Gabriella wanted her to take this chance. Maybe she could swallow her pride, as Ramon had swallowed his.

Another knock on the door, and this time it *was* Pedro. When she handed him the money for the week's rent, in American dollars, he grabbed it and stormed off in a frustrated rage. Aida went to the window, raised her eyes to the beautiful blue sky and thanked Gabriella Gonzalez for her heavenly intervention.

* * *

FIRST SHE CAREFULLY FOLDED HER dancing dresses into the bottom of her green carpet bag, placing tissue paper between each one. The letter from Ramon, and most of the money, she tucked into the torn lining of the bag, then stitched up the tear with needle and thread. The only other thing she brought was a photograph taken of her, her mother and Tía Conchita dancing together at the Villa Antonio Tablao Flamenco in Granada. It was in a brown leather frame, and she'd always cherished it. Flamenco was all about control – control of the body, the movement, the feet and the face – but in this photo, they were all smiling, a most unusual thing to see.

She picked up the picture and kissed it. 'Be with me, Mama. Whatever happens now, stay with me.' Then she put it on top of the dresses and closed the lid.

She took one last glance around the small apartment where she had lived with her mother all her life, then put on her coat. It was a black one of her mother's, with ribbon embroidery on the cuffs and hem. The buttons too were ornate and made of ebony. It fit Aida like a glove. Underneath the coat, she was wearing her best day dress, made by her mother four years ago when she was fifteen and which still fitted her perfectly, a slender dark-red sheath that hugged her figure and reached to her black button boots. Her black hair was plaited and pinned up under her black hat.

She wondered about the neighbours watching her leave, and in a moment of rebellion, she took the red lipstick she normally only wore when dancing the flamenco and applied it to her lips. She would never let them imagine they'd driven her out with their gossip, or that she was too poor to continue to live among them. And then, after putting the lipstick in her pocket, she left the apartment and carried her bag down the stairs.

Carmen was the only person she paused to say goodbye to, knocking on her door on the ground floor.

'You look like your mother, so beautiful.' Carmen smiled as she opened the door.

'I've come to say goodbye, Carmen. I'm going to England. This is my address.' She gave Carmen a slip of paper with the location of the YMCA written on it.

The old woman took it and tucked it into the pocket of her apron. 'As long as I live, I will visit your mother in the graveyard every Sunday after Mass, Aida, and I will say a prayer for her. She was such a gentle soul, and she had such a soft and open heart.'

CHAPTER 26

ICK

THE LAST HALF of the trip from France had been horrendous; the channel turned choppy, and it poured rain. Two-Soups was sick as a dog, leaning over the railing on deck as he got wetter and wetter without his soldier's greatcoat, which had to be handed back in when they got demobbed, though what the army was going to do with those filthy, bloodstained, ripped and flea-ridden coats was anyone's guess.

The storm was still raging as they arrived to Folkestone, the ferry spending ages trying to dock, the stern swinging wildly as the gang-plank went down. Nick and Celine supported Two-Soups down the ramp, their arms around the tall, gangly Scot, whose flaming red hair was hanging down in strings and who was still retching and wishing he was dead.

'This is the worst day of my life,' he groaned.

'You'll feel better soon,' Nick said soothingly, 'as soon as you get on dry land.'

'Baxter Campbell, you beauty!' roared a huge voice from below on the quayside.

'Betty!' roared Two-Soups, miraculously transformed. 'This is the best day of my life!' He threw off Nick and Celine's supporting arms, bounded down the rest of the gangplank like a gazelle and threw himself into the arms of a massive, big-boned girl who lifted him up and spun him around while both of them brayed with laughter like donkeys. *This must be the gorgeous Betty*, Nick thought.

Beauty was certainly in the eye of the beholder, because Betty was not classically beautiful. She had mousy-brown hair that was neither curly nor straight but definitely could have used a brush, broad shoulders and a strong, stocky body. Her face was a mass of freckles, and her green eyes sparkled with merriment. The love of Two-Soups's life had come down from Glasgow to meet them off the boat.

All the way on the slow train to London, Betty and Two-Soups clung to each other like a pair of overgrown limpets, while the other lads rolled their eyes and pretended to gag at all the loud kissing and snuggling and Celine discreetly read a book.

Nick, though, was secretly fascinated by how love could make the plainest of women seem like a beauty to the man who loved her. Two-Soups had told him that Betty was more beautiful than Celine, so he must genuinely think it was true. And it didn't just work one way either. Two-Soups was no oil painting, but Betty obviously thought he was a Greek god or something.

Eventually, Two-Soups and Betty detached themselves slightly from each other, and she took a box of home-made oat cakes out of her big black valise and handed them around with lumps of a cheese she called Dunlop, like a soft, sweet cheddar, and a bottle of Irn-Bru each, an orange-coloured fizzy drink that none of them had ever tasted before but which turned out to be absolutely delicious.

After that, Peter made a hilarious welcome speech in a perfect Glasgow accent, saying the 'beautiful Betty' was 'one of us' now, and Two-Soups wiped tears from his eyes, overcome with pride.

'So have you t-t-two really g-g-got a farm up there in Scotland?' Nick asked as the train trundled on through the streaming wet countryside. Coming from the landed gentry, he was interested to know how many fields they had and what they grew. 'How many acres do you have?'

'Fifteen,' said Betty, glugging loudly from her bottle of Irn-Bru.

'Fifteen hundred? That's a nice manageable size. Do you grow wheat or barley? Do you have any cattle?'

'Fifteen acres, ye dafty. Ten acres for the sheep, three acres for the oats and two acres of thistles.'

'Aye, and Betty's amazing the way she's been keeping it all going.' Two-Soups nodded enthusiastically. 'Betty's da is elderly and has rheumatism, so he cannae do a lot, and her ma died when she was only a bairn, and so there's only her. I grew up in the Gorbals, the tenements south of the Clyde, so I never saw a sheep in me life, but then I met Betty and she opened my eyes to the farming life. I love it so, I do, and I'm not a bad hand at it either, am I, love?'

'Yer a wee natural with the sheep.' She smiled. 'My da was fearful I'd not find a chap at all to help him with the farm, being as I am, but I told him not to worry – a woman with a farm is always attractive. And my da always said farming and everything else is not about how much you want somethin' but how hard you're willin' to work to get it. I went to the Albert Ballroom every Friday and Saturday night for two years, trying to get a lumber.' She laughed.

'A what?' Nick asked, bewildered. Her accent was so strong, he had to concentrate hard to stay with her.

'A date, a lad, someone to squeeze.' She turned to Two-Soups with a grin. 'I dinnae know how they teach them down here – can they speak English at all?'

'Go on,' Nick urged, smiling.

'Well, on my lonesome, every weekend I went, and every weekend came home empty-handed. Couple of boyos tried their luck, but I knew they weren't what I was after, so I dinnae bother wi' 'em. And then just when I thought I might have to give it up as a bad job, in he comes.'

She was thrown against Two-Soups as the train shuddered to a halt at a small country platform, and the Scotsman's arm went protectively around her and remained there once the train got going smoothly again.

'And you knew he was the m-man of your dreams just by looking at him across the room?' asked Nick, fascinated. It reminded him of when Celine came up on stage – that had been the moment for him. He'd thought Celine was very pretty, but it was when she started to sing with him that he gave her his heart and she became the most beautiful woman in the world for him, like Betty was to Two-Soups. Had he also been blinded by love? It was a mystery, and maybe it was best not to think about it.

'I did know. And I asked him to dance, crossed the floor in front of everyone and asked him up.'

'In front of all m'pals too, she dinnae care.' Two-Soups beamed with pride.

'And I told him about the farm and asked if he'd like to come and see it. He got the bus to Bishopbriggs the next Saturday, and after he looked around and took it all in, I asked him to marry me.'

'You did?' Nick was amazed. He had never heard of a woman proposing before. It was quite common among the aristocracy to marry for land, without any love at all involved, but there was usually some show of the man wooing the woman.

'I bloody well did.' She guffawed. 'But he said no.'

'He…what?' Nick stared in growing confusion at the blushing and beaming Two-Soups.

'I did say no,' admitted the Scotsman. 'But that next week, I worked overtime every night down the dockyard, and I borrowed some money from my mum, and I went to Laings and bought Betty a ring. I never wanted her to feel like she did all the running – I was very happy to run to her too.'

Betty held up her hand with the small single diamond solitaire.

'That's b-b-b-beautiful.' Nick smiled, not just at the modest ring but at the love story.

'So now I just need to get him up the aisle and into my bed,' Betty finished, nudging Two-Soups hard in the ribs as they both brayed like donkeys again. 'We'll be wed in Scotland, won't we, Baxter? And we've a farmhouse that needs filling with bairns and a farm that needs workin' – Da cannae do it all alone. I can be up and down all summer to sort him out while you're making your fortune in the shows, but I'll need some help with making the bairns.'

She guffawed once again, and though her humour was raucous and certainly unbecoming of a lady, there was something endearing about her.

'I'm your man,' Two-Soups said proudly, so red with joy he actually did look like a tin of tomato soup.

'You certainly are,' she said, softer now, and the look that passed between them was so tender and full of love and admiration, Nick felt a pang of jealousy.

'I'll bring him to you m-m-m-myself, so long as I get an invite to the wedding.' He smiled at them again.

'Bargain.' She shook his soft hand with her hard, meaty one, and he felt a wave of affection for them both. He thought that one day Two-Soups and Betty should get to fill that farmhouse with 'bairns', as they called them.

CHAPTER 27

ETER

HE'D NEVER GONE near a YMCA in his life – he thought of it as a Protestant organisation – but Enzo seemed to think the one in Bloomsbury, on the corner of Keppel Street and Gower Street, was for everyone and did well by returning soldiers. 'It's where the Kiwis all go to get a bish-bash-bosh and some fresh clobber before they head on back down under, and they say it does nice grub and is dead cheap.'

Celine rolled her eyes. Enzo's English bewildered her at the best of times.

Cheap was important to Peter, who was in charge of the money. Everyone still had some of the month's paid leave to go, and he had fifty pounds left from selling the van and piano, but they'd need to conserve it, especially if it was going to take them a while to get a gig. It had taken forever to get from France, so much paperwork, the army loved that nonsense, but they had to do it properly so what should have taken weeks ended up taking months. Still, they were here now and the weather was getting nicer and the future was hopefully, bright. He had an audition lined up at the Acadia, a slightly run-down but busy theatre in the West End, but if they didn't get that, then they were going to fall on hard times. He'd had to pull a lot of strokes, and the owner, Teddy Hargreaves, had a reputation as a skinflint, but he'd hung around the bars of the theatre district until he found out who was looking for new acts and had got some names of people to drop when applying for the audition. He only spoke to a secretary in the Acadia but led her to believe they were coming from much higher heights of the theatrical world than they were, citing all his experience in Dublin and France and even adding in a fictitious trip to America to perform off-Broadway. He flirted outrageously with her, and eventually she agreed to add them to the list for the open auditions.

Enzo was saving them even more money by staying with his family, and he'd suggested Ramon could share his old room. They were quite the double act these days, always clowning around together and play-fighting like puppies. 'I can't take everyone to mine, though. My mum would 'ave an 'eart attack, so the rest of you will 'ave to stay at the place in Bloomsbury. I'll take yer there first, of course. Yer'll never manage to get there without me to guide you.'

They had just got off the train at Victoria Station. The huge vaulted train station was teeming with khaki, and everywhere was still plastered with posters supporting the war.

'But Betty and I, we cannot stay in place for young men?' protested Celine. She had only just found out from Betty what YMCA stood for – Young Men's Christian Association.

Peter's heart sunk slightly. How stupid of him not to have thought of this before. But Enzo said airily, 'Don't worry, we'll find a boarding house for you two luvverlies nearby – there's loads around there. So we'll give the place a butcher's, eh?'

'A butcher's? *Un boucher*? But I don't wish to stay at a butcher's...'

Enzo threw back his curly head and laughed, and so did Celine even though she didn't understand what he was saying; the Londoner was permanently upbeat, and it was infectious. 'It's more Cockney slang, ain't it? 'Ow we Lon'uners talk – like a butcher's hook rhymes with look, so to take a butcher's means to take a look, see? Like, if I said, "Alrite, gotta scarper, 'ere comes the trouble and strife," then my mates would know I mean I better leave quickly, here comes my wife.'

Celine still looked confused, though she was smiling. 'That seems very complicated.'

'Oh, you don't know the 'alf of it, 'cause then what 'appens is the word that rhymes often gets left out. Like a stairs is apples and pears, but then we drop the pears out of it, so it's just goin' up the apples.'

'I will have some difficulty understanding this London English...' She looked nervously at Nick, who smiled and squeezed her arm and mouthed, *Don't worry.*

'Go down the market, and you'll be bewildered, darlin'.' Enzo chuckled. 'Right, come on, we'll take the Tube to Russell Square. This way.'

He marched down a long downward-sloping tunnel, and they all followed him into the bowels of the earth – like the rats after the Pied Piper, Peter thought.

* * *

THE TUBE WAS hot and exhausting, and it was hard to find seats, but when they arrived at their destination, Peter was delighted by the sight of Russell Square gardens, a big stretch of trees and grass surrounded by fancy houses. Civilians in nice clothes and Tommies in uniform were stretched out on the lawns, listening to a brass band, and he could see plenty of American, Australian and New Zealand uniforms too, all the soldiers making the most of the spring sunshine.

The YMCA turned out to be a beautiful Tudor-style building, with the name 'The Shakespeare Hut' painted over the door.

He liked that name; it reminded him of his brief career in Macbeth. Funny to think how back then he'd believed he was going to make his fortune as a Shakespearian actor rather than as the manager of a music hall troupe. He didn't mind, though. He'd long since stopped caring about the supposed difference between high and low art. It was all entertainment and gave him the same buzz, whatever he was doing.

'Do you think this place has got a room where we could do a bit of rehearsal this evening, Enzo?' He was already worrying about the calibre of the show they had cobbled together. Maybe it was good enough for soldiers stuck far from home, with no other access to entertainment, but not up to scratch for a London audience.

'A rehearsal, this evening? I was going to go out for a few pints with Ramon and my bruvvers and my dad?' Enzo looked horrified. He'd clearly been planning on a big homecoming celebration.

Peter hesitated as all eyes went to him. He knew they looked to him for leadership, so he had to sound like he knew what he was doing. 'OK, one night off, but then we have to get serious. Banging out a few tunes and messing about a bit for the troops was one thing, but this is our big chance. We need to make a good first impression. We need to present ourselves with a watertight semblance of unity or cohesion, and it's going to take a lot of practice.'

Enzo and Ramon looked relieved and headed off with cheery waves back down to the Tube and off to the East End, while Peter and Nick and Two-Soups and the two girls stepped into the splendid building, looking around with interest.

Inside the entrance hall, nice ladies were handing out tea and buns, and soon the five of them were sitting on their luggage, hungrily eating sandwiches and accepting slices of cake from passing women in long aprons. After they'd eaten, the boys were shown to a corner where they could sleep, in a large room that seemed to serve as both a common room and sleeping quarters.

Enzo was right about the Kiwis, Peter noticed. There were lots of New Zealand servicemen there. The place was packed. There were so many young men who needed accommodation on their way back to their various countries from France, it was floor space only, but the atmosphere was jovial, and the aromas of baking coming from the kitchen beyond were tantalising.

Back out in the entrance hall, after dumping their bags, they found one of the tea ladies giving Betty and Celine directions to a suitable bed and breakfast on a side street just a few minutes' walk away. 'Just past the British Museum, dearies, you can't miss it.' And Two-Soups announced he would accompany the lovely ladies there and make sure they were settled. Nick looked crestfallen, so Peter suggested he go too, and his friend rewarded him with a huge smile.

Standing alone on the front steps of the Shakespeare Hut, watching the four of them walk off towards the British Museum, Peter hoped Celine wouldn't break his friend's heart by finding herself a new man among all these demobbed soldiers with a month's cash in their pockets. Not that she seemed particularly interested, and not that she was a beauty who could have anyone she wanted, but he could tell the chemistry between her and Nick was only on stage, not in real life, whatever his friend liked to believe. Nick had fallen for Celine because of the singing – he was sure of that. If she hadn't had such a wonderful, come-to-bed voice, he didn't think Nick would have got stuck on her. But he had, and Peter just hoped it wasn't too late to fix.

And then he thought about May, and worried whether he was going to break her heart one day, like Celine would do to Nick. He really should write her a letter and let her know his new address.

As his friends disappeared from view through the jostling streets, he noticed a tall, slender, very striking young woman moving towards him across the street, carrying a green carpet bag. Two expensive open-topped cars had stopped to let her cross, their leather-gloved drivers staring at her through their driving goggles. She had on a black coat, buttoned up all the way despite the heat, and as she drew closer – because she seemed to be coming his way, almost as if she wanted to meet him – he saw she was wearing black button boots.

She paused before him as he stood on the steps. He realised his heart was beating very strongly, and he worried he was blushing. She wore a little black hat and red lipstick, and if she moved on, he had a feeling he would have to follow her. But she didn't move on. She just stood there, saying nothing, with her dark, liquid eyes fixed on him.

'Can I help you?' he asked stupidly, after what seemed like a long time, during which every sound of the noisy city seemed to fade and they were left in a zone of silence.

She put her carpet bag on the step beside him, opened it, pulled at a few loose stitches in the lining and took out a letter, which she handed to him.

He looked at it but only recognised his own and Ramon's name from the short note in Spanish.

Astonished, Peter raised his eyes and looked at the girl's beautiful, proud face, a slight flush on her high, fine cheekbones.

'Peter Cullen,' he said slowly, pointing to his own name in Ramon's letter and then to himself. Then at her. 'Aida Gonzalez?'

She smiled then, and the sun shone even brighter. 'I am Aida,' she agreed, in sweet, halting English. 'And I am… I good…to be here you, Peter Cullen.'

CHAPTER 28

 ICK

As THEY PASSED the British Museum, trailing the besotted Scottish couple who had eyes only for each other, Nick turned and asked Celine, 'Are you still glad you decided to come to London? Not too worried about your father?'

'I am glad I'm here, yes,' she said with a smile. 'And Papa understands, and he trusts you to look after me.'

'Of course I'll look after you! We're engaged, aren't we?' he said lightly.

He was carrying her small valise, swinging it as he walked, and she tucked her arm into his for the first time since they'd walked down the train in France. 'You're so nice, Nick. It is as if you are another father to me.'

'Hang on, I'm not that old!' He laughed to hide his hurt.

'A brother then. Poor Papa will miss me, I'm sure, but who knows – perhaps I will be back sooner than I think if they don't want our show for a long time.'

'Peter has great p-p-plans, and honestly, if anyone can p-p-pull it off, it's him,' Nick reassured her, but he trembled at the idea of her returning to France without him.

'Peter is very good at – I forget the word – negotiation?' She pronounced the word the French way, and his heart melted. He loved to hear her speak her native tongue, and to speak it with her.

'*Oui, bien sûr, il est un entrepreneur…*'

'English, Nick, please, or I will not ever learn.'

'He's w-w-what we call in Ireland a chancer,' Nick translated, back to stammering again.

'It is bad, this chancer?' Her brow furrowed.

'No, not bad, but he's a man who gets things d-d-done.'

She smiled and squeezed his arm in hers as they continued their walk.

The tea lady was right; the bed and breakfast was only a little way beyond the magnificent façade of the British Museum. The door was opened to them by a big bustling woman in an apron.

'Are these your two young men then?' she asked crossly as they crammed into her hallway.

'This is my fiancé,' said Betty in her loud voice, clutching Two-Soups's hand firmly and showing the landlady her ring.

Nick hoped Celine would say the same about him, especially as she was wearing the expensive emerald ring he had bought her for their 'engagement', but she just murmured, 'Nick is a friend,' which made his heart break a little.

'Very well then. We have two rooms available, but I cater for single girls only, and there will be no gentleman callers, fiancé or not.' She gave Nick and Two-Soups a disparaging look up and down, then turned back to Betty and Celine. 'Curfew is at ten sharp every night, no exceptions for weekends, and breakfast finishes at nine on the dot.'

'Oh, but…' Nick began, realising this wouldn't work. If they got the job at the Acadia, they wouldn't be out of there until midnight. But Celine jumped in.

'Madame.' She turned on the full blast of her French charm,

speaking in her most purring voice. 'Thank you so much for the offer of the rooms, but unfortunately we have a little problem.'

'Oh yes?' The woman's brows practically disappeared into her hairline as she glanced uncertainly from one to the other of them.

'Betty and I, we will be performing at the Acadia for the next six weeks. We are both singers and have just come from touring Europe entertaining the troops and the injured. We have been invited to perform here in London, so we won't be able to make the curfew.'

Betty, who clearly knew she had a voice like a donkey, started giggling despite a quick frown from Celine, and Nick fully expected the woman of the house to shoo them all out onto the pavement. But to his surprise, she didn't. Instead she looked thrilled at the prospect of having two famous singers in her establishment.

'Really? Goodness me, I do love that Pearl White. I saw her in *The Iron Claw* last year, frightfully good it was. And I saw that Laurette Taylor in *Peg o' My Heart* up the West End last year – it was ever so romantic.' The change in her tune was so profound, Nick wondered if he'd imagined the dour, cranky woman who'd opened the door. 'And that Basil Hallam! I know they called him Gilbert the Filbert, but he really was wonderful. Poor man, he was one of those balloonatics, you know? Killed falling from a balloon on the front. Did you ever meet him?'

The diatribe was interrupted by the question, fired directly at Nick, who unlike Two-Soups was still wearing his uniform. Nick was nonplussed by it. The famous actor Basil Hallam, known as a bit of a dandy, had captured the imagination of the public in that someone as famous and good-looking as he was would go and fight and die just like their sons and husbands.

'No, ma'am, I never d-d-did,' Nick answered. It was startlingly apparent that the British home front hadn't the faintest idea of what life on the actual front had been like. As if he'd just casually bump into a famous actor while taking tea or having a sherry on the Messines ridge. Maybe they were as well off in the dark; knowing what had happened to all their young men wouldn't do people like this landlady any good.

'Ooh, I would have loved to have met him, poor soul. But oh yes, I love them all. Lily Langtry, even that Vesta Tilley, though she's a touch on the odd side and no mistake, dressing up as a man – I mean, did you ever? She's got a pretty face if only she'd dress properly.' She took a breath and went on. 'My sister Mabel was at the Royal Command Performance back in 1912, and she told me that poor Queen Mary nearly needed the smelling salts when she saw Vesta in her trousers. But fair's fair, and I won't deny it – that woman did more for our boys on the front than anyone. She was called the best ever recruiting sergeant, you know? Singing those lovely songs about our country, all dressed up like yourself, and honestly any young man who ever saw her was right down the recruitment office the next day, keen to get over there.'

'Ah, that's wonderful, madame...' purred Celine, with a warning glance at the others not to say anything negative about encouraging innocent boys to go to war and lose their lives.

'Juddy, dear, Frances Juddy. Me and my Stanley run this place, and I'm delighted to have someone from the theatre staying. Anything you need, you just let me know. This way, dear, you first...' She ushered Betty deeper into the house, with Two-Soups tagging along behind; apparently the woman didn't mind bending the house rules on male callers for a famous singer. Then she returned for Celine, who winked at Nick as they followed the woman's large floral bottom up the stairs.

'This is the best room in the house!' declared the landlady, unlocking the last door on the landing with a brass key and throwing it open with a flourish to reveal a room that looked more like a bordello than a respectable B and B. The cerise and aquamarine counterpane, curtains and lampshade all matched, but the bed was large and looked very comfortable. There was a washstand with a pitcher and ewer and a little locker beside the bed.

'Bathroom's down the hall, breakfast in the morning, but I know actresses keep late hours, so don't worry – I'll have a listen for when you and your friend are up and you can let me know. Boiled eggs and toast and marmalade all right, dear?'

'Thank you so much, Madame Juddy. The room is beautiful.'

Celine gave her a winning but innocent smile, and Nick could see the poor landlady becoming even more smitten, almost as much as he was himself. '*Alors*, I must be alone now. I need to rest. I must be fully prepared for my performance.'

'Oh, I'm sure you'll bring the house down, dear. What's your name again?'

'Celine Ducat, *enchantée*.' She took the woman's hand and shook it warmly. 'And this is my friend and other co-star Nick Gerrity. He's from Ireland.'

Did Nick notice a slight wince from the landlady? He'd heard from other enlisted men who had been to Britain about the anti-Irish sentiment, but he'd never experienced it in London himself. But then he wouldn't have, coming from the Anglo-Irish ascendency as he did, he supposed.

'Well, you're very welcome, Miss Ducat. I'll leave you to settle in.'

She withdrew then, leaving Celine in the room and Nick in the hallway, and took up a position at the top of the stairs, waiting for Nick to follow her. He suspected something about him being Irish was making her sterner with him than she had been with Two-Soups, who she'd left alone with his Betty.

'Well, I'd b-b-better get back,' he said through the open door of Celine's room. 'I s-s-suppose you need time to get w-w-washed and changed. I'll c-c-come back to t-t-take you out to d-d-dinner if you like.' Watched by the beady eyes of the landlady, he was straining to speak. His stammer always got worse under pressure, and he wished more than anything he could control it.

'Oh, I don't have another dress to change into, so it will have to be this one. Does it look enough for going out to dinner?' From the sultry charmer, she suddenly looked uncertain, and he longed to take her in his arms, kiss her and tell her she was the most beautiful girl on earth and that if she wore a grain sack, she'd still be stunning.

'It's f-f-fine,' was all he could manage. He didn't want to try another long sentence.

A shadow of something passed over her face – humour, disappointment, he had no idea. Had he said something very stupid? He knew literally nothing about pleasing women or girls. His mother had been a cold person to be around. His grandmother was lovely, but she was American and they seemingly did everything differently there. The only women at his boarding school were the women who came in to cook and clean, and they were behind closed doors mostly anyway. And he'd never had a sister.

He leant in to place her small valise on the floor just inside the door while she turned to examine her face in the speckled mirror over the table. She grimaced a bit but then smiled brightly over her shoulder at him.

'All right, Monsieur Gerrity, you may come back later to take me to dinner.'

'I-I-I…' He gave up and just waved goodbye.

The landlady accompanied him downstairs, then bustled off along the hallway and knocked loudly on a downstairs door, from which Two-Soups presently emerged, straightening his tie and looking rather flushed. 'No gentleman callers, not even fiancés,' the woman reminded him archly. 'Now off you go, you two. Let the girls have some well-earned rest.'

He enjoyed the stroll back to the YMCA with Two-Soups, who was in tremendous form and already planning to bring the girls out for a curry later. He'd heard about the Indian restaurants in London and thought curry sounded exciting and like something a Scotsman would enjoy.

Nick knew about Indian food because he'd been taken to Delhi when he was twelve. They'd stayed in the city for two nights while his father did some business, but his mother complained constantly about the smell and the noise, so they withdrew to a place outside the city called Shimla, which was beautiful. It was in the foothills of the Himalayas, and he remembered seeing animals and plants he'd never seen before. They stayed at the Viceregal Lodge, a sprawling building where white-clad servants teemed, just desperate to attend to one's needs. It was a wonderful summer and he'd loved it, but his parents seemed to hate the heat. He wondered if the culinary pleasures of the viceroy's kitchen could be replicated here in London? Somehow he doubted it.

'I don't know if Celine would like such spicy...' His voice trailed off in surprise. 'Who is that Peter is walking with?'

Their troupe manager was strolling towards them down the pavement carrying a green carpet bag, and with him was a young woman who even the infatuated Nick might have to admit, under heavy questioning, was almost as beautiful as his Celine.

'Well, would you look at her,' said Two-Soups, equally thunderstruck. 'She's almost as gorgeous as my Betty.'

Peter came to a halt in front of them, blushing and smiling. 'Hello, you two. This is Aida Gonzalez, Ramon's flamenco partner. She came as soon as she got his letter from France. Isn't that brave of her? Especially as she is having to learn English from scratch. So were there rooms at the bed and breakfast?'

Nick stood there, transfixed, but no words came. The young woman was stunningly beautiful, but she also looked fierce, and he felt oddly intimidated.

Two-Soups, who didn't suffer from nerves around women at all, stuck out his hand. 'Name's Baxter Campbell, but they call me Two-Soups, and this is Nick Gerrity. There were two rooms free, and Celine and Betty have them. There's a spare bed in my Betty's room, and I'm sure she wouldn't mind sharing. She's my fiancé, and she has a heart of gold – you'll love her to bits.'

Aida's liquid-black eyes turned inquiringly to Peter; even if her English had been perfect, Nick imagined the Scot's Glaswegian accent would be too much for her, as it often was for Celine.

'Come with me,' said Peter to Aida, smiling back at her, and he led her away past his mates without sparing them another glance. For a long moment, Nick stood looking after the pair of them.

'Come on, hurry up. Let's get back. I want some more of those YMCA sandwiches,' said Two-Soups, who was always hungry.

'Sure, coming...' Nick pulled his gaze away. As he walked with

Two-Soups back through the fine streets of London, he found himself thinking of a girl he'd never met: the lovely May, who wrote Peter all those long letters, and knitted him socks, and stitched him shirts, and spent her every penny on sending him gifts of tea and chocolate and cigarettes. She'd have her work cut out for her to keep Peter Cullen's eyes on her now.

CHAPTER 29

AY

MAY STOOD IN THE HALLWAY, staring at the postcard that the postman had just delivered. It was a picture of the Tower of London, and on it were two scrawled sentences.

Dear May,

If you want to write, my address is the Shakespeare Hut YMCA, Gower Street, Bloomsbury. Audition at Acadia this week, holds three thousand, rehearsing hard, very busy, all my love, Peter x

She stuffed it into her pocket and went back into the breakfast room.

Her mother looked up with an inquiring smile. 'What did the postman bring, darling?'

'Just a long letter from Peter. I'll finish reading it later upstairs. It's so full of news, it will take me a while.'

'Has he found a job yet?' asked her father, glancing out from behind his newspaper.

'Oh yes, at a very important theatre called the Acadia, and they're staying in a hotel called the Shakespeare Hut.'

'He's in a play by Shakespeare?'

She couldn't be bothered to contradict him or explain. 'Hamlet.'

'Ah, the Dane.' He went back to reading the news.

May sat down and buttered herself a piece of toast. 'I thought I might go over there, to watch the play. Peter needs me by his side, and there is a very respectable hotel where I could stay with the actress playing Ophelia.' She tried to let the words trip nonchalantly off her tongue, as if popping over to London was something a person could do at the drop of a hat.

Her father looked up and laughed, and her mother, who had been instantly horrified, relaxed, relieved by her husband's smirk, clearly assuming, like him, that their daughter was joking.

'Don't laugh at me. I'm not joking. I want to go.' She hated that her voice came out petulant, making her sound young and peevish instead of like the mature, sensible adult that she had become. She was nearly twenty years old, no longer a child, yet still they insisted on treating her like one. If only David would come home, as Peter's friend Enzo had said he would. Maybe then they'd stop smothering her. Though it had been months since the end of the war…

'Oh no, dear, definitely not. No, it wouldn't be right, or safe even. Oh no, we couldn't allow that, not at all. Michael?' Olive looked appealingly at her husband, giving him the eyes, the ones that said 'jump in here and support me'.

He buried his head back in his paper. 'Your mother's right, May. It wouldn't be suitable.'

Gratified, her mother leant forwards, patting her daughter's hand, saying soothingly, 'But maybe Peter could come and see you here? It would be nice to see him again, wouldn't it, Michael? Wouldn't he like to do that, May?'

'Obviously he would, but he's very busy!' May bit her tongue. She knew she must try not to sound angry, but the postcard had really upset her. Still, it was true, he'd said he was very busy. And he'd signed the card 'All my love, Peter', so she was still his sweetheart. 'Of course he would love to come to Dublin, but Hamlet runs seven nights a week. He can't come over here.'

'Ah, that's a pity. Perhaps when the run is finished? Before his next role? I've asked Father O'Reilly to meet with you both before the banns are read, so it might be a nice opportunity for him to do that.' Olive was twittering now, the way she did when there was any kind of awkward moment.

May fought back tears of frustration.

'Mother, Father.' She forced a steadiness into her voice, though a seething fury was threatening to bubble up inside her. 'Peter is my fiancé and I'm a grown woman, so I am making the decision to go and see him in London. It will all be perfectly respectable, but I am going.'

'No, no, oh my goodness…' Olive glanced at her husband in panic. 'Michael!'

Her father folded his newspaper with a heavy sigh, resigned now to having to spend his time dealing with this nonsense between his wife and daughter.

'May,' he pronounced in his deepest, most authoritative voice. 'I know you think you're an adult and capable of making decisions for yourself, but you are not yet of age. And perhaps we do treat you like a child, and I'm sorry if that offends you, but you are so precious to us and we love you, so we have to protect you. Peter wouldn't be best pleased with us now, would he, if he thought we weren't caring for his darling girl properly until he can take over the job? So please now, May, let there be no more talk of this silly plan. I'm sure Peter doesn't want you over there either, bothering him while he is building his career. So no, best you stay here, and Peter will appear in due course, no doubt.'

And he went back to his paper once more, giving it a firm shake as if to say 'and that's my final word on the matter'.

May exhaled in fury. 'Have you not heard that women are no longer subservient? We will not be downtrodden any more and made to feel like we go from being our father's property to our husband's. It's not right and it's not' – she searched furiously for the word – 'con-stitutional! We got the vote this year…'

'Only respectable women over thirty with property,' her father murmured from behind the broadsheet. 'Not a young chit of a girl like yourself.'

May felt like punching him right on the nose. A chit of a girl, was she? 'Don't forget I have my inheritance from Auntie Maura, so I'm financially independent.'

He said, without even looking at her, 'And it is wonderful that Maura chose you as her heir, and that money I will take care of for you until you're twenty-one. Which, may I remind you, is over a year away.'

May folded her Irish linen napkin with the hand-embroidered daisies in the corner and placed it on top of her barely touched bacon and eggs. She pushed her chair back and stood, leaving both her parents sitting in the heavy silence that followed.

She waited until she was in her bedroom before allowing the tears to fall. Hot, fat drops rolled down her cheeks, not just because of the way her father had put his foot down but because of something specific he had said. That Peter wouldn't want her bothering him.

CHAPTER 30

 IDA

SHE'D THOUGHT she'd never sleep. It was spring, and in Spain the weather would be glorious and the flowers blooming, but here in England, she was cold all the time, though in the streets she kept seeing people walking without their jackets, as if the day was hot. The huge brown-haired woman, Betty, didn't seem to feel the cold either, walking around the room they shared almost naked, which Aida wished she wouldn't do. Her body was at least three times the size of Aida's, and she was not one bit self-conscious about it. She was kind, though a little loud and irritating. When she saw Aida shivering, she gave over her second blanket, which she wasn't even using, so Aida had three now but still she was freezing.

She wished she could have a room of her own. The Scottish girl was big and clumsy and snored like a trooper. And she kept trying to teach Aida English in her big donkey voice, but Aida wasn't inclined to learn.

What did she need to learn English for? Soon she would go home.

Coming here had been a terrible mistake. She was broken-hearted, her mother's absence was a sharp pain that sometimes took her breath away with the intensity of it, and she missed the sun of Spain, the sounds and smells of her home. She despised British food; it was revolting. Stodgy, greasy stuff that felt like it sat in your stomach like a stone, no fresh fruit or salads. And it was bad for her. She had to maintain her dancer's body by eating well, and nothing in this country seemed to make that easy.

She'd thought Ramon would make things better when she met him, but he'd changed. He was too friendly with that Enzo, with his flashy Italian looks, who held her gaze too long and seemed to always be performing even when he was off stage. Enzo's family lived in this busy, bustling city, and Ramon stayed with him rather than at the YMCA.

Ramon had told her that Enzo always had a few women on the go at any one time, and he sounded like he admired him for it, even though he knew what had happened to her own mother, being strung along by the man she thought loved her. Aida wished he would be more friendly with someone like Nick, who treated Celine so kindly, even though the French girl was playing with him as a cat plays with a mouse. What was it with these men, that Two-Soups was another one, foolish for his ugly fiancée. She hated the idea that Ramon was influenced by Enzo, who was clearly the worst kind of man, more like the disgusting Pedro Dumas, who thought it was all right to treat women like objects or fools.

Pedro Dumas... The memory made her cringe and sweat. Would her mother have been angry with her for giving her body to that disgusting person? Would she have understood?

Thoughts of her mother flooded her once more, and the permanence of her passing hit Aida like an icy wave. She would never see her again. If Ramon's letter with the money had only come a week sooner...

As Betty snored in the other bed, she soaked the pillow with her tears. She felt so cold, so sad, so lonely, she would never sleep.

But she must have done, because she was startled awake by Betty shaking her by the shoulder and saying in a loud voice like the foghorn at the port of Valencia, 'BREAK-FAST,' while making eating gestures and gobbling noises. She was already dressed in what looked like men's trousers and a knitted sweater the colour of a puddle, her brush-like hair pulled back in a ponytail.

Sighing, Aida got out of bed, washed and dressed in her red dress and followed Betty down for breakfast in the small dining room. There were four tables in the dining room as well as a large sideboard and a set of shelves. Mrs Juddy loved china ornaments, and so on every surface were shepherdesses with lambs, ladies in crinoline, cherubs, gentlemen in plus-fours and a variety of animals and fowl, all made of hand-painted china.

'Good morning, girls.' The landlady greeted them as she came out to check what they wanted. 'Good morning, Betty.'

'Guid mornin', Mrs Juddy,' boomed Betty in a completely different accent from the landlady.

'Good morning, Aida.'

Aida smiled at the landlady but then realised she was expected to reply. 'Good morning,' she said carefully, trying to speak more like Mrs Juddy than like Betty, who she knew was from a different country than England.

'Oh, well done!' Both Betty and the landlady clapped, and Aida smiled politely while she inwardly seethed. She couldn't bear to be treated this way, like one of those china shepherdesses, something pretty to be put out on display.

'Did you sleep well?' asked the older woman, pronouncing each word carefully.

'Yes. Thank you.' She had picked up some English without even wanting to. Even Ramon insisted on speaking it to her, which she hated him for doing.

'Tea?' Mrs Juddy smiled at her approvingly.

Aida shuddered and shook her head. 'No. Thank you.' In Spain people only drank tea when they were sick.

'Tea for me,' said Betty, with lots of enthusiasm, trying to make up for Aida's shudder. 'You make lovely tea, Mrs Juddy. AI-DA, DO YOU WANT COFF-EE?'

Aida hesitated. 'Yes. Please.' She had been utterly shocked at first by the disgusting brown liquid that Mrs Juddy called coffee – it was like someone had heated up a pot of canal water – but it was better than the hot boiled weeds they called tea.

'And what will you have to eat, my dearies?' asked Mrs Juddy cheerfully.

'Porridge for me, Mrs Juddy.' Betty beamed, and Aida shuddered again. The substance they called porridge reminded her of the paste they used to hang wallpaper. Grey and lumpy, it smelled bad and looked worse, and she had no desire whatsoever to taste it a second time after Betty had forced her to try a mouthful.

'WHAT DO YOU WANT, AI-DA?'

Such a difficult choice; all English food was disgusting. 'Egg. Please.' She didn't mind the eggs too much, even if Mrs Juddy boiled them until they were rock-solid and the whites had turned grey. She hated the stodgy white toast they came with, though. It was nothing like the beautiful bread of Spain, and what Mrs Juddy called 'butter' tasted like engine oil. And the marmalade was made of oranges from Seville, which everyone in Spain knew were bitter and horrible, which is why they palmed them off on the English.

She thought longingly of the sweet Valencia orange tree that grew on the balcony outside her bedroom, how she would open her window, lean out and pluck one for her breakfast. She salivated at the memory. An orange, a cup of rich black coffee – that was what she liked for breakfast. Maybe once a week she and her mother would treat themselves and bake *ensaïmada de Mallorca*, the spiral-shaped pastry that melted in your mouth. Her grandmother came from the island of Mallorca, and she had taught Gabriella how to make them, the exact recipe unchanged for centuries.

The dishes arrived, and soon Betty was eating the horrible food with gusto, covering the gloopy grey stuff with honey and milk and tucking in.

And then the tall Scottish man they called Two-Soups knocked on the door of the dining room and came in, smiling. He'd started joining Betty for breakfast in Mrs Juddy's, and the landlady didn't seem to mind. He was wearing his soldier's uniform like he often did, his red curls springing around his head now that the military haircut was growing out. He had to duck coming into the room so as not to hit his skull on the door frame. Aida had never seen such a tall man, and she couldn't help staring every time she saw him.

'How do you make a tall person look more awkward?' he asked her now, and Aida was startled. He had never directly addressed her before.

'I…I not know,' she replied, unable to understand what he was saying.

'You can't.' He winked.

And while Aida tried her best to work it out, Betty's braying laugh filled the dining room. Mrs Juddy roared with laughter as well as she brought out a spare cup for the Scotsman. It seemed Two-Soups was a brilliant comedian – everyone seemed to find him very funny and howled with laughter at him whatever he said – but so far Aida had not understood a word of it.

'You been out already, my flower?' Two-Soups asked, sitting down at the table with them and helping himself to a cup of the awful stewed weeds, into which he slopped milk and sugar.

'Aye, I woke at five, so got up and went out' – Aida noticed Betty pronounced it like 'ooot' – 'and walked all over the city.'

'Well, ladies, time to get going again. Peter sent me to fetch ye down to the YMCA. He wants us to sort out our costumes before the audition tomorrow, maybe a last practise.'

Aida listened quietly, picking up every other word. Audition…like *audición*. Practice…*práctica*. So more dancing with Ramon and that foolish, horrible Enzo prancing around and pretending to dance too, making Ramon laugh and mess up his guitar playing. Ramon had told her that the clownish Londoner had pretended to be a flamenco dancer for the troops. Ramon had thought it hilarious, and even dared suggest to Aida that maybe for the *audición*, the two of them could dance together.

He'd backed off quickly at the fiery look in her eyes. Flamenco was an honour, her people's tradition, a subject of pride and passion. How dare Ramon allow it to be mocked and degraded.

* * *

THE REHEARSAL SPACE was a big room in the basement at the YMCA, a storeroom of sorts. There were boxes neatly stacked at one end and a big boiler at the other, and there was just about enough space for them all to rehearse.

Enzo was already there, looking flashy. His curly glossy hair shone like a chestnut. And he had an absurd moustache that he waxed in a small curl either side of his full mouth.

'All right, my old muckers, 'ow's it goin'?' He grinned and whistled and then turned round and began play-fighting with Ramon as usual. Aida shuddered. They were like a pair of puppies, constantly clambering over each other and playing the fool. The Ramon she'd known all of her life was not this man. She hated that she was losing him to this ignorant show-off. Once, she and he saw the world the same, but he was becoming more like Enzo every day. She should never have come here.

Seeing her watching him, Ramon stopped playing the fool and came over, his eyes kind for once.

'Good morning. Did you sleep well?' he asked in English.

'Not really,' she replied in Spanish. 'Betty snores, and I was hungry but not for any of the food they have here. I want oranges and olives and some *ensaïmada de Mallorca*.'

Ramon laughed, replying once again in English. 'Don't be such a misery. It's London! Go out, explore, have an adventure.'

'Why don't you speak to me in Spanish?' she asked, refusing to use the hated language.

'Because we are here and it's rude to my friends and you need to practice. And if you don't speak to anyone in English, how will you improve?' Ramon replied in Spanish this time, dark eyes snapping, a growing frustration in his voice.

Rude. How dare he call her rude. Ramon, who had been her brother, her best friend, the only one who knew who she was and where she was from – how could he take the side of these people over her? These strangers with their pasty skin and horrible food?

'I'm going home,' she said flatly. She hadn't quite made up her mind until he'd accused her of being rude, but now she knew what she had to do.

'To the bed and breakfast? What about rehearsal? The audition is tomorrow.' He still spoke in Spanish, and he looked disgusted with her.

'Don't glare at me like that. I don't like it when you're –'

'When I'm…what?' he asked dangerously, his head to one side. The army had cut his straight hair, but it was growing back, the same as the other boys, softening the harsh military look of him, but his near-black eyes were hard in a way they'd never been before the war and all the killing.

'You're someone different now. I don't feel like I know you any more.'

His lip curled, and she heard the sneer in his tone. 'And who should I be, eh? The poor boy back in Valencia, playing his guitar for the tourists, being patted on the head for his trouble, all excited they fill up his father's hat with coins and even notes… That boy?'

'At least that boy didn't follow around a clown like your new best friend Enzo.'

Enzo glanced across the room sharply, hearing his name. Peter was also there, and he was watching as well. She turned her back on them both and faced the man she'd once thought of as a brother.

Ramon's black eyes had narrowed to slits, and he jabbed his finger in her face. 'Don't you dare be rude about my friend.'

That word again. Rude. She knocked his hand aside. 'I should not have come.'

He smirked arrogantly. 'I agree, but you're here now, so I suggest you make the best of it.'

'I've no intention of making the best of this horrible country. I'm going home to Valencia.'

The push in her chest that followed caused her to totter backwards before righting herself. Instead of apologising for laying a hand on her, a stream of rapid angry Spanish left his lips, accompanied by wild arm and hand gesticulations and the slamming of his fist into his palm for emphasis. He ranted about her being ungrateful and haughty and thinking she was better than his friends, when all they'd ever done was try to make her feel welcome. He told her he was embarrassed by her rudeness and her terrible attitude, and that while she was a good traditional dancer, he was better off with Enzo if she couldn't fit in with the troupe. He shouted that she had no idea, none, of what he'd endured in the trenches, how proud he was of what he'd done and how now he had a chance to make a life for himself. He yelled that he'd offered her a part of that, and if she wasn't interested, then she would be better off back in Valencia.

She stood there and let him rant, forcing her face into a bored expression, acting like she didn't care what he was saying, while acutely aware of all the others looking on in astonishment, wondering what was happening between the two Spaniards.

He spat that he was sorry her mother had died but that it wasn't his fault – it was the fault of the flu that had killed so many of the young men who had fought alongside him in the war; it was horrible, but that was life.

When he finally ran out of words, his breath was heavy, his nostrils flaring, and he reminded her of the infuriated bulls in the Plaza de Toros as they charged at the matador and he swirled his cape and avoided them. Anger and frustration pulsed through his veins, and she could see the dark rage in his once-loving eyes. Eyes that now were full of contempt.

Like the eyes of the man who had used and abused her mother. Like the disgusting Pedro who had violated her body. She'd thought Ramon was different, but he wasn't. He was just like every other member of his gender. A bully who sought to control and subjugate women.

'I will not see you again,' she said quietly, and left the room, the others stunned into silence, watching her as she went.

235

She met Celine on the basement stairs. The French girl had gone upstairs to use the toilet.

'Aida, *que se passe-t-il…*'

Aida walked past her, up and out of the building. She had no idea of her next move. She'd not spent all of the money Ramon had sent to her, so at least she wasn't destitute, but if she had enough to get back to Spain, and what she would do when she got there, she had no idea.

She swallowed back the tears as she marched down the street. She would not cry in public. She would leave with her head held high and figure things out on her own, like she always did.

* * *

As she placed her hand on the door of the bed and breakfast, she heard someone come running up behind her. She spun around with a snarl on her lips, expecting Ramon.

It was Peter.

'Aida, please, can we talk for one minute?' He spoke gently, slowly and clearly, and she understood him.

'I have nothing to say,' she answered, with as much dignity as she could muster.

His shrewd blue eyes met hers. 'Can we speak in private? Please, just one minute?'

She sighed and opened the front door and listened for movement. Nobody seemed to be around. Mrs Juddy had a strict 'no men in the women's quarters rule'…but what did she care? She was leaving anyway. She stalked down the corridor to the room she shared with Betty. If he wanted to follow her, that was his business.

He did, coming into the room after her and closing the door behind him.

She sat on her bed and studied him, waiting for him to speak. Strangely, she had no fear of him being in her room. There was nothing threatening or predatory about him, and though she knew it wasn't seemly for a respectable woman to be with a man in her bedroom, she didn't care.

He sat down on Betty's bed, saying nothing. He was dressed casually in dark-grey flannel trousers and a dark-blue pullover that matched his eyes. His sandy-blond hair was swept back from his forehead, and there was a delicateness to his features that was unusual in a man; with his high cheekbones, slightly slanted eyes, straight eyebrows, long lashes and cupid's bow mouth, he would have been an exceptionally beautiful woman. He wasn't physically big; he was slender and about the same height as Ramon.

Finally he looked at her and spoke. 'You and Ramon, you had a bust-up, am I right?'

'Bust-up?'

'A fight?' He said in French, '*La guerre?*' which she understood; it was very like the Spanish word for war, *guerra*.

'*Sí.*' She shrugged and kept her face impassive.

'And now, *vous departez?*' He was sitting back against the pillows, his hands in his pockets, one eyebrow arched.

His French accent was remarkably good – he must have picked it up in France – and he obviously had a good ear. She herself under-stood a little French; there were many French people in Spain since the war began.

'*Sí.* I hate him. And I hate England,' she said bluntly.

He smiled and nodded sympathetically when she said she hated England, which surprised her. Wasn't he English himself? If he wasn't, he spoke it very well, better than Mrs Juddy.

'Please stay, Aida,' he said in English.

'Why?' She lifted her chin, her attitude defiant.

He smiled. '*Parce que je veux que tu restes.*' Because he wanted her to stay.

She shook her head. Ramon didn't want her, that was all there was to it. There was no going back from what he'd said.

'*Non, ce nest pas possible,*' she said in French. Then, continuing in French, she said, 'Ramon is lost to me, and he says I am rude.'

'Ramon is…*comme votre frère?*'

She nodded miserably. Ramon was like her brother, yes.

'Ramon loves you, Aida.' He put his hand on his heart, pointing at her.

'No.'

'Yes.' He nodded firmly, then pointed to himself. 'Me...*moi*... My sister...*ma soeur*...' He sprang to his feet, placed himself in the space by the door and did a really amusing mime of two people fighting and then making up, which made her laugh and feel better for the first time that day.

'He does love you, Aida.'

This time she didn't contradict him, but she pulled a face.

'He does. And when you and Ramon...' Again he resorted to mime, first being a wild Spanish guitarist like Ramon, and then her, spinning and clicking her fingers, and then the audience, applauding wildly, and then himself, falling to his knees with his arms stretched out in gratitude. And then with a wallet full of money, greedily counting notes and handing them out.

She laughed again; he was so funny and talented. He stayed on his knees, his arms held out towards her, smiling, with a question in his eyes, and she could feel herself blushing.

'Please, Aida,' he said sweetly. 'Stay with me. Stay with me.'

Should she say yes? At the thought of it, relief flooded through her. Ramon had been horrible to her, but Peter was nice, and in one thing Ramon was right – she should get out and explore. Yes, the food was awful, but she could maybe try to go to a market and buy things she wanted to eat, like oranges.

'Yes.' She gave him a shy smile.

He leapt up from his knees and did a funny triumphant little dance with his arms by his sides, lifting only his feet, grinning as he did it. On the spur of the moment, she joined him, imitating him. He laughed loudly at that, and so did she.

In the distance, the front door opened, and the two of them stopped dead and looked at each other in alarm. Mrs Juddy's voice came down the hall, chatting to someone called Stanley, her husband no doubt, and then they both turned into the kitchen and the door closed after them.

Finger to his lips, Peter held out his hand for Aida to take, and together they crept down the hall and out of the front door, which they closed ever so softly behind them. Then they ran as fast as they could down Great Russell Street, past the British Museum, giggling like a couple of schoolchildren.

It wasn't until they'd got back to the YMCA that Aida realised they were still hand in hand, and she pulled away sharply with a fierce glance at the blue-eyed boy. Was he trying to take advantage after all? At nineteen she was a beauty, and she knew it. But good looks and flirting had been the undoing of her mother, and it would not be the rock she'd perish on.

Peter didn't seem to mind her reaction or even notice; he just smiled and patted her shoulder and pointed up the steps into the building. Aida relaxed. All was well. She and Peter Cullen were friends. Just friends. And that's all she wanted. A friend.

They entered the room they were using to rehearse. When he saw her, Enzo jumped up and went out. He returned a few moments later with a covered bowl and a spoon.

Ramon stopped playing his guitar, looking confused, but he translated for his friend despite still being angry.

'Enzo brought you this. His father makes gelato, and he thought you might like this. He asked the ladies here to keep it in the icebox.'

The Italian handed her the bowl, and when she removed the cover, she saw one scoop of pistachio and one scoop of raspberry. She looked at him, then at Ramon. She'd never told Ramon about her ice cream treat with her mother – it was special and just for them – so how did Enzo know?

She gazed in wonder. *Accept the gift graciously and say thank you*, her mother's voice whispered in her ear.

'Thank you very much, Enzo. I like very this.' She smiled and he winked.

'You're welcome, Aida,' he replied, no trace of flirting or joking.

CHAPTER 31

 ETER

WHEN HE ARRIVED BACK in the storeroom, having had a cigarette break to restore his composure, everyone was sitting around, looking glum. Celine was examining her nails, and Nick was slouched against the wall, fed up, smoking a cigarette. Only Betty and Two-Soups seemed content, but that was no good because they were huddled on a box together in a world of their own, as if they were already back on their farm in Scotland and none of this was anything to do with them. There was something going on in the corner with Aida, Ramon and Enzo, and he hoped it wasn't going to lead to more fireworks.

Peter knew that how he presented himself now was vital to restore morale. He marched into the centre of the room and clapped his hands. 'All right, ye miserable little men,' he shouted, mimicking one of the most hated officers at the front, Major Stubbs. 'Heads up and no smoking, you horrible little lot! Jerry's getting active tonight!'

It got the laugh he was looking for, and he smiled and dropped back into his own voice. 'I've persuaded Aida to come back and join us, because I think she is vital to the show. She and Ramon are a big part of what makes our set-up unique. When they perform together, when they're on stage, it's magical – no offence, Enzo.'

The Londoner grinned. 'None taken.'

Aida even smiled, and amazingly Ramon had his hand on her shoulder as she ate something with a spoon from an earthenware bowl. Whatever it was must have been delicious, because she was clearly in ecstasy.

'Look, tempers get frayed sometimes. We've all been through a lot, and we're tired and anxious about the future. But if we are serious about making a go of this, we have to pull together.' He saw with relief that Ramon was murmuring in Aida's ear, presumably translating. 'It's vital we all get on together and don't just split off into our own little corners.'

The Scottish couple flushed and looked guilty.

'Now most all of us, me and Enzo and Nick and Two-Soups, and Ramon and even Celine too really, we were already kind of bonded by all we saw, all we survived, and there are special individual bonds between us as well. But we have to make space in our group for Aida also. We're all in this together, and every one of you is equally important, and I'm sure she knows that too.'

They were all looking at him now, focused on what he was saying.

'Now I could tell you it's because I care about you all that I want you to get on together, and I do care about everyone in this show. But I care most of all about the show itself, and so should you. And we have something special here, something unique, just by virtue of who we are. Enzo is half Italian, Two-Soups is Scottish, Nick and me are Irish, Celine is French, and Aida and Ramon are Spanish. It gives the whole thing a' – he shrugged – 'a kind of exotic flavour, and I think people will like that, so I don't want to mess it up by any of us falling out. I've big plans, really big plans, and if we can all stick together, I can promise you…well, maybe not a life of luxury just yet, but some day in the future. And on the way to the top, we'll live a good life, with a regular wage, and enjoy the companionship of some great people, doing what we love.'

He paused and looked around. He had everyone's attention, and Nick was smiling and nodding, which was a good thing, because he trusted Nick most of all.

'Now today what I want to check is costumes. We have a great show, I think, and we don't need to rehearse any more, just sort out the clothes and then relax and enjoy the spring sunshine. The slot for the audition is twenty minutes, which gives Nick and Celine two numbers. They'll be doing "If You Were the Only Girl in the World" and "It's a Long Way to Tipperary". Two-Soups, five minutes – I'm expecting at least fifty punchlines in that time – and then Ramon and Aida, do your magic. Finally, Enzo, a five-minute routine. Play it for laughs if there's nothing to swing on.'

He smiled around at them, certain of their talent. It would be all right tomorrow, he was sure of it. Ramon and Aida were friends again, and anyway they were perfectly in sync musically even if they seemed to drive each other daft. It had been annoying him how they were constantly rubbing each other up the wrong way, but maybe the fight had cleared the air.

'And what about you, Peter?' asked Nick.

'I'll introduce everyone, that's all.' He wasn't planning to do anything himself for the audition, just direct his troupe and make sure to keep it tight. If – and it was a huge if, but he was banking on it happening – they got a start at the Acadia, then he'd have scope to expand his own role. 'Now I have no concept of how good the other acts might be at the audition, I just know we are good – and we're going to look our best. Aida has her flamenco dresses, so she's sorted, and Celine's blue dress is lovely, and I'll wear my uniform. So really it's just Ramon, Nick, Enzo and Two-Soups. Now I've been scraping some costumes together from the jumble sales. Nick, let's start with you...'

He handed Nick a black dinner jacket and wide-leg trousers with a silk stripe down the side of the leg. He'd been delighted when he'd found the suit. 'It might have to be altered a bit, but these should be OK.' He pulled a white shirt out of the same large paper bag and a tie that was the same midnight blue as Celine's dress. 'You can use that space behind the boiler to get changed.'

As Nick disappeared around the corner of the boiler, Peter produced a red silk shirt and a pair of tight black trousers and handed them to Ramon. 'I asked Lady Appleton, who serves the tea and buns above – she was in Spain on her European tour as a girl – did she have anything a flamenco guitarist might wear, and this is her idea of it. The red silk was a skirt her lady's maid turned into a shirt, and the trousers are her son's.'

A few of the women who volunteered at the YMCA came from the wealthy aristocracy who lived in the surrounding neighbourhood of Bloomsbury, and Peter had made sure to rally them to his cause.

Ramon seemed satisfied with the outfit, but when Peter pulled out a stripey Edwardian bathing suit with long legs and arms for Enzo, the Londoner and his Spanish friend both cracked up laughing. 'Yer not serious, mate.'

'Just try it on, Enzo. I think we can make it look like the sort of thing an acrobat would wear, but if you hate it, we'll have to put you back in your crinoline.'

'Bloody hell, a swimsuit or a dress. All right, give it 'ere. I'll try it.'

'I'm the only one wi'out a fancy costume now,' Two-Soups grumbled good-naturedly, standing in line.

'Don't worry, I have you sorted too.' From another paper bag, Peter produced a proper top and tails, like a butler or doorman would wear.

Two-Soups looked very impressed. 'Where on earth did you get those? They must have cost a fortune.'

'Not at all. Lady Appleton's best friend has a giant of a butler who was complaining his uniform was getting threadbare, so she bought him a new one and this is the old one.'

Two-Soups clapped his hands and said, with a delighted grin at Betty, 'It'll do for our wedding, my flower!'

'You'll look like a lord.' She beamed, then insisted on trying on the top hat to Two-Soups's cries of admiration.

There was a lot of huffing and puffing going on behind the boiler, and then Nick re-emerged, his face creased with anxiety. 'I don't know, P-P..eter. Maybe I'll stick to my uniform.'

Peter studied him critically. The trousers fit his waist, but the legs were far too short. The jacket fit on the shoulders, but the sleeves didn't even reach his wrists. 'No, it's perfect. Keep it on.'

'But, Peter, I know I look r..r..ridiculous...'

Aida stepped forward, examined the sleeves, looked critically up and down at Nick and said something in rapid Spanish to Ramon.

'She can fix it. If you can find her some black silk, she can lengthen the sleeves and the legs of the trousers and put a panel in the back of the jacket so he has more room.'

'Wonderful. I'm sure Lady Appleton can get something suitable.'

Peter then called the other women in. There were too many aristocratic ladies for the work in the YMCA, so they were delighted to be asked to help. A gaggle of women followed him happily down the stairs, dresses fluttering, producing things from bags of donated clothing.

Nick – who did look ridiculous – almost panicked as Aida descended on him. She knelt at his feet with a mouthful of pins and quickly let down the hem of his trousers, and then she ripped the lining of the jacket in order to access the sleeves as he stood with his arms stretched open like a scarecrow.

Enzo was the next to emerge from behind the boiler. His hair was growing out, curly and shiny, and he grinned and pranced around the basement, showing off his lithe body in his stripey Edwardian swimsuit, to Ramon's shouts of amusement and the giggling of all the girls, including Betty and Celine and, to Peter's amazement, Aida.

'He needs a sash and some decorative beading!' declared Lady Appleton, clapping her hands, and before long there were all sorts of alterations being made, and tight black slippers like ballet shoes were found for the acrobat. Then the next problem was Two-Soups, whose tailcoat and waistcoat and trousers were just about long enough but far too wide; he was swimming around in the outfit.

Peter was tempted to leave the comedian's suit as it was – there was something clownish about it – but Two-Soups had said he wanted it for his wedding and it seemed wrong to deny him, and anyway the daughters of the aristocracy and their lady maids were already fussing about him. Soon the Scotsman's suit was a perfect fit, and Aida worked a miracle on Nick's. Ramon's costume didn't need much work, just a bit of leather cord to tie to the top of the shirt, a wide belt for the trousers and a pair of boots with a heel, which one of the maids was sent running for, and the end result was a very dark and brooding but devilishly handsome pirate. Meanwhile a blue silk flower was found for Celine's hair, and the most amazing dowry shawl, black lace threaded with actual silver. She and Nick looked perfect side by side. A red rose was found for Aida's hair, and all was done.

'Right, Mr Cullen, I believe your friends are looking splendid,' Lady Appleton announced, with her hands on her hips, as they surveyed everyone in costume. Her assistants applauded their own efforts as Peter's troupe lined up for inspection. 'Break a leg, as they say,' added the middle-aged aristocrat, and she tittered like a girl, then blushed at her own enthusiasm.

'Thank you so much.' Peter smiled, and the woman blushed even deeper. 'It's up to us now. If they don't like us, it won't be because we don't look the part.'

'Oh, they'll love you, Mr Cullen, I just know they will. Come on, ladies!' And she ushered the giggling throng out of the basement and up the stairs.

Peter looked around proudly at his splendidly attired troupe. Betty was in fits of joy over how handsome her beaming Two-Soups looked in his soon-to-be wedding suit, and Nick and Celine were perfectly matched in their midnight-blue outfits. Enzo was hanging upside down from a beam in the centre of the basement, trying out his moves in his now glittery outfit and tight black slippers.

And Ramon and Aida were in the corner speaking quietly in Spanish. Peter had had a word with Ramon before running after Aida, so he knew he'd paved the way for this reconciliation. As he watched, the two took each other's hands, and he felt an odd little pain in his heart. Ramon had insisted Aida was like a sister to him, nothing more – but was that really the case? There was such tension between them, especially when they danced.

Ramon had said his father was English, but Peter thought he must be the spitting image of his mother, because no Englishman Peter had ever met had that dark hair and those flashing black eyes. Lady Appleton's girls had hardly been able to contain their excitement as they were dressing him in his red shirt and tight trousers.

Peter fought back a surge of envy and told himself sternly that he was happy that he'd forced the couple to make up their stupid argument. The show needed them. They would be a big hit with the audience, and his job wasn't to pay special attention to a lost little Spanish girl – it was to keep everyone together and with their eyes on the same prize.

CHAPTER 32

ICK

THE FOLLOWING AFTERNOON, they got out at the Kensington High Street Tube station and walked the ten minutes to the theatre. Peter led the way, carrying all their stage costumes folded carefully in a hessian bag that had been found by Lady Appleton to replace the paper bags. Two-Soups walked with his arm around Betty, who had come to cheer them on, Ramon strutted along with his guitar case between Enzo and Aida, and Nick and Celine brought up the rear.

All the lads were in their uniforms, a bit red in the face as the day was hot, and the girls were in light summer dresses except for the mysterious Aida, who was buttoned up to the chin in her black coat and shivering like it was winter still instead of a glorious spring day.

'You look b-b-beautiful,' Nick said encouragingly to Celine. It had been a tiring and stressful day, tempers were frayed and tension was high. They'd put so much work into preparing for this audition, all of them, and she looked exhausted and nervous; he was pretty anxious himself. 'How do you feel?'

'Not perfect,' she said, giving him a sweet smile and tucking her hand into the crook of his arm as she often did now. 'How about you?'

'I'll think I'll feel b-b-better once I'm out there on stage.' They were walking through Kensington Gardens, and up ahead, the Acadia stood before them in all its glory. 'Did you know Rachmaninoff himself p-p-performed in the Acadia seven years ago?' Floss had brought him to see the great man during one summer holiday.

Again Celine smiled sweetly at him, but he suspected she didn't know who he was talking about.

They went around to the stage door entrance, and Peter knocked while giving them all a big thumbs-up. 'This is going to be great!' He was acting with his usual bonhomie, but Nick knew him well enough by now to know that the wide smile was forced and that underneath he was quivering too. Even the confident Ramon looked pale, his knuckles white on the handle of his guitar case, and Enzo kept fidgeting, and even Two-Soups and Betty were silent for once.

This was their chance, thought Nick, gazing around at his friends. They had survived the war uninjured and alive; they'd cheated the inevitable. But had they used up their luck? Like cats with nine lives, down to the last one. And if they were rejected, then Celine would return to the Aigle d'Or and her papa, and Nick would never see her again. The thought was unbearable.

After what seemed like an interminable wait, a doorman let them in, looking them up and down with bleary eyes without saying anything, then pointing the way into the depths of the building.

Once inside the dun-coloured hallway with doors off either side, they were approached by a man in a three-piece suit, shiny with age, and with his sparse hair combed back over his bald head. He walked with a distinct limp and had a clipboard. He snapped, 'Which lot are you then?'

A less glitzy setting you'd have trouble to find, Nick thought. *So much for the glamour of show business.* The place smelled of body odour and a sickly flowery scent.

'Cullen's Celtic Cabaret,' Peter said with authority, though it was the first time Nick had heard him call their little company anything official.

The man ran his nicotine-stained finger down a list, frowned and got to the bottom. 'No...never heard of yer.'

Panic rose inside him as Peter protested and told the man to look again. Were they not even going to get to audition? Was the dream ended, and all their luck used up, and Celine going to return to France? Oh God, his hopes and dreams were crashing down...

A woman came up behind the man, dressed in what looked like a long silver stocking. Her hair was pulled back tight and fastened in a bun. She wore a full face of theatrical make-up and looked kind of alarming. Ramon and Enzo grinned, eying her up and down, but Nick hastily averted his gaze; the dress didn't leave much to the imagination.

'Charlie, the bloomin' light's blown again,' she complained loudly. 'It's like a cave down there.' Her Cockney accent was just like Enzo's.

'Right, hold your horses. I'll be down – I've just got to find this lot...'

'Oh, get me a bulb and we'll do it ourselves. You know Teddy will go mad if we're not all ready to go when he calls us later,' she said in exasperation, and then looked at Nick and his mates, rolling her eyes. 'You don't wanna work here. Get out while you still can. Bloomin' theatre's held together with bits of twine and glue. That Teddy Hargreaves is too stingy to pay for proper repairs, so poor Charlie here has the job of keeping everything going. Leaking gas pipes, naked flames, bare electrical wires...'

'Put a sock in it, Mabel.' The man sighed in frustration and balanced the clipboard on the wainscoting. 'Wait here, you lot. I'll be back.'

He limped after her down the corridor and in through one of the doors.

Once he was gone, Peter picked up the clipboard, slowly scanning the list, running his fingers along under the names, mouthing them to himself. Nick stood close behind him, reading the list a lot faster. The man was right – there was no mention of Cullen's Celtic Cabaret.

'We're not there, Peter,' he said softly.

His friend and manager went white. 'I don't understand. I spoke to the woman in the ticket office – she swore blind...'

Nick took a deep breath. He had too much to lose – not just the show but his new life away from Brockleton, his beloved Celine. Several names had a green tick in pencil beside them, but several didn't. He selected one of the names from the list with his finger, not yet checked off.

He and Peter exchanged a look and wordlessly decided they'd do it. Peter replaced the list on the wainscoting.

Before there was time to argue the wisdom or morality of claiming to be a group they weren't, the man reappeared and grabbed the clipboard, scanning it. 'Right, you lot, not on my list, so you'll have to 'op it, right?'

'Maybe we're listed as the Peckham Players? I sent my secretary to book us in and that was our former name before the war, so maybe she put us under that... Women!' Peter rolled his eyes, and the man nodded.

Women really were a pain in the neck, he agreed, the silver-stockinged Mabel being a case in point. He picked up his clipboard again and ran a finger down the list, stopping and ticking them off with a green stubby pencil that was tied to the clipboard with a piece of twine.

'Right. You're far too early, but never mind. There's been a no-show from the Clapham Kickers, so we'll fit you in. Second door on the left, wait there. We'll call you shortly.'

They piled in and immediately began to dress. Nick marvelled at the job Aida had made of his new suit and hoped he could do it justice. The women hadn't oohed and aahed over him as they'd done with Ramon, or giggled and flirted as they had with Enzo, and he wished he looked exotic like the Spaniard and half-Italian boy, but they were his friends; they couldn't help being how they were, could they? Peter at least had the same Irish colouring as him, but he didn't blush every two minutes, and he was slender and as beautiful as a girl, where Nick felt like an elephant, all bulky and ungainly.

'Right.' Peter gathered them all together for their marching orders. 'We'll open with Nick and Celine, then Two-Soups, then Ramon and Aida, then you, Enzo, acrobatics, tumbles, all of that. Nick'll back you on piano, big finale. Enzo, I know it will be hard when you don't know what you have to work with out there on the stage, but if anyone can improvise, it's you, my friend. And we're all under pressure, but this is our big chance. If this works out, all of our lives could go in a totally different direction, so let's give it our best shot, all right?'

Nick swallowed his fear and nodded. Celine looked up at him and gave him a smile that, if he hadn't been terrified, might have reduced him to a puddle.

'You're ready?' The man with the limp popped his head around the door.

'Yes, sir, we are,' Peter replied confidently.

The man opened the door a little more and studied them for a moment. 'You look better than the last lot, that's for sure. Teddy only listened to about thirty seconds of them. Auditioning all week with blokes who reckon doing a funny walk or singing off-key cuts the mustard 'asn't done much for 'is temper, so you're gonna get one shot and one shot only. Make it work.'

'We will,' Peter replied silkily, and Nick was relieved that his friend had regained his composure, especially as Nick was rapidly losing his.

As they followed the man up the stairs to the wings of the enormous stage, Nick struggled to breathe evenly. What if he opened his mouth to sing and no sound came out? Or if it did but he stammered? And Celine was left there, singing alone, and he like a big gangly fool beside her doing nothing? As he fought the urge to bolt back down the stairs, he felt a small hand in his, then a squeeze. He looked down and she met his eyes.

'*Bonne chance.*' She winked.

Then he was on the stage, and there was a grand piano – not a battered old upright but a concert Steinway like he'd had in Brockleton.

Peter had come on with him and walked to the front of the stage, peering into the dark. From where Nick was standing, there was no way to know how many people were down in the auditorium, as the stage lights were blinding.

'And you are…?' A bored Cockney accent carried across the still, greasepaint-scented air.

'Peter Cullen, manager of Cullen's Celtic Cabaret, formerly known as the Peckham Players, and our first act is Nick Gerrity with Celine Ducat.'

'More bloody singers?' asked the person wearily.

'Yes, and following them, a comedian, then a Spanish guitar player and flamenco dancer, and finally a comedic acrobat.' Peter spoke clearly into the void, and Nick noticed he had adopted a middle-class British accent.

'Right, let's be having you then. But I warn you, if I say stop, you stop immediately and get the hell out of my sight, because frankly, I need a large brandy and no more blasted warbling.'

As Nick sat down at the grand piano, he caught Peter's eye, and their manager gave him an encouraging wink as Nick launched into the introduction to the hit from the show *The Bing Boys Are Here*.

Celine moved towards the front of the stage, smiling, waiting for him to start singing. He opened his mouth, gazed at her slender figure and waited for the words to come.

Nothing.

His heart turning over, he played the intro again, as Celine pleaded with him with her eyes. *Do it for Peter, for his friends. They're relying on you…*

He swallowed and forced the notes from his throat.

'Sometimes when I feel bad and things look blue, I wish a pal I had…say one like you. Someone within my heart to build her throne, someone who'd never part, to call my own.'

Everything was OK, he wasn't stammering, he was no longer frozen. He was singing about his love to Celine, and that was all that mattered, not the Acadia, not success, not money, not the bored voice, nothing but Celine.

'If you were the only girl in the world and I were the only boy,

FOR ALL THE WORLD

nothing else would matter in the world today. We could go on loving in the same old way...'

Celine took over then, in her sweet throaty alto, such a surprisingly large voice from such a dainty young girl.

'A garden of Eden just made for two, with nothing to mar our joy. I would say such wonderful things to you. There would be such wonderful things to do. If I were the only girl in the world and you were the only boy.'

Then together, Nick playing melodically.

'No one I'll ever care for, dear...but you. No one I'll fancy, therefore, love me do. Your eyes have set me dreaming all night long. Your eyes have set me scheming, right or wrong.

If you were the only...'

Peter gave him another thumbs-up from the wings as the number came to a close and mouthed, *Well done. At least we're still here.*

Before they could go into their second number, the disembodied voice spoke again. 'Right, the rest of the act?'

Nick's heart sank. Did that mean he and Celine weren't good enough? On the way out, walking with his arm around the French girl, who was trembling, he passed Two-Soups jittering behind the curtain, looking positively sick.

'You can do it,' Nick whispered in his ear as he passed him.

'I've nae got much of a choice, do I?' the Scotsman said with a watery grin as he headed onto the stage after Peter, who had stepped out to introduce the next act.

In the wings, Betty grabbed Nick in a painfully big hug. 'I been sobbing me heart out,' she hissed in his ear.

'There weren't a dry eye back 'ere when you two was singin' Enzo added, 'even Aida wiped away a tear.'

The Londoner nudged the Spanish senorita, who gave him a reluctant smile. Whatever war had been raging between them seemed to be over.

Hoping it was true, and also hoping Enzo would stop swinging Celine around like that – she seemed to be enjoying it far too much – Nick turned to watch Two-Soups being introduced by Peter as 'our best loved Scottish comedian'. He hoped the Scotsman would get over his fit of nerves as quickly as he himself had, but it really didn't matter if Two-Soups took a moment to get going. Nick had always thought there was something comical about Two-Soups before he ever opened his mouth. His mop of red hair, his freckles, his big frame – something funny yet vulnerable too.

'Hullo,' Two-Soups began. 'High up here, isn't it? I had to come by the stairs, but I don't trust stairs – they're always up to something.'

A titter from the darkness seemed to encourage him.

'I'm from Glasgow, and things have been very hard. My dad got the sack. He worked on the roads, you see, but he got the sack for thieving. I didn't believe it at first, but when I got home, the signs were all there.'

A laugh now, possibly even from the disembodied Cockney voice.

'So I was on the front, fighting for king and country. And sometimes it's right boring, so me and the lads had to come up with ways to amuse ourselves. Racing snails was a favourite pastime of ours. I had a really fast one too, but I thought I'd take his shell off, less to carry, you know? Didn't work, though, just made him a bit sluggish.'

Several voices from the darkened auditorium were laughing now, and Two-Soups was in his element.

'My childhood wasn't all bad, though. Sometimes my dad would put me in a tyre and roll me down the hill beside our house. Ah... those were Goodyears.'

The ripple of laughter echoed around the empty theatre.

'All right, I've heard enough from you, Mr...?' There was humour in his voice, though.

'Baxter Campbell, sir, but like Peter – our manager Peter Cullen, that is – like he said, everyone calls me Two-Soups.'

More laughter at his explanation. 'I'm sure they do, Mr Campbell. Right, Mr Cullen, your next act?'

'All the way from Spain...' began Peter, moving to the front of the stage again as Ramon strutted over to the piano stool and put one foot on it and Aida stalked out into the lights in an incredible crimson dress with such a perfectly fitting bodice that Nick felt his eyes grow large. As Ramon had explained on her behalf, Aida had been worried she would damage her dresses if she danced in the basement, so this was the first time he'd seen her wearing one.

There were so many flounces and ruffles on the dress, he could hardly believe how it had fit into the green carpet bag she'd brought with her to England. And she didn't only have the one, apparently. As Betty had told them all in awe, there were four of them in there, folded in tissue paper, and over the last two weeks, Aida had washed them one by one by hand in warm sudsy water, then rinsed them in basin after basin of cold water, removing all soap residue, then hung them to dry on a line across the bedroom, which made everything permanently damp.

Mrs Juddy had been most put out that Aida wouldn't allow her to hang her dresses in the yard with all of the other clothes, and even more offended when Aida had said in her terrible English that the London air was 'too dirty' for them. Betty had had to jump in and explain Aida hadn't meant Mrs Juddy's yard was dirty, that Aida was just worried the lovely hot English sun would fade the colours, but Mrs Juddy had taken a while to calm down.

Without saying a word, Ramon swept into the wild music, and Aida clapped her hands and stamped her feet and spun with pinpoint precision, her dress swirling around her. After a minute or so, she clicked her fingers and summoned him to her, and Ramon took his foot off the stool and walked towards her. He played and Aida danced, both with their black eyes fixed on each other, and then he knelt, his guitar on his knee, his hands flying over the instrument, gazing up at her with a strange demonic smile, and the stage filled up with heat and passion and desire...

Nick's heart was hammering. This was nothing like the wild, funny dancing of Enzo. This was... Well, Nick had never seen such a thing, such a fiery relationship. It seemed like some kind of unexpressed passion...an unspeakable passion, fully on display in this theatre in London. Outside it was warm enough, but in here the heat blazed.

When the tune ended, there was nothing but silence. For a

moment, both guitarist and dancer remained frozen in position, and then Ramon got to his feet, offered Aida his hand and walked her off the stage. The movement broke the spell, and scattered applause broke out in the dark auditorium.

'Right, the next thing, Mr Cullen, please,' came the bored voice again.

'All the way from Italy, via good old London Town...'

Nick walked onto the stage and sat at the piano again, and he began playing the popular song 'Take Me Back to Dear Old Blighty'.

Enzo, in his new costume that now looked a lot more like an acrobat's costume than an Edwardian swimsuit, somersaulted out of the wings and bounced all over the stage like a jackrabbit, doing flips and cartwheels. As the tempo sped up, so too did his routine. He was as flexible as rubber and quick as lightning, but lacking the beams and rafters of the Aigle d'Or, or the metal frame they'd made for him to tour Normandy, he wasn't showing his talents to the maximum.

As Nick glanced up from the piano, worried, he saw a surprising sight. A six-foot square platform on wheels was parked behind the curtains in the wings, a huge thing, which he thought must be used to put the light rigging in place. Betty had her shoulder to it and was pushing it slowly out onto the stage.

Just as Nick noticed what was happening, so did Two-Soups and Peter, and after a startled glance at each other, they joined Betty in putting their weight behind it and shoving it into the centre of the stage. Enzo understood what they were doing at once, and without hesitation, he swarmed up the structure like a monkey. Then Two-Soups and Betty, as if it was part of the act, cranked the axle, and the platform rose higher and higher, until it was fully extended and Enzo was close to twenty feet in the air. He teetered at the top, playacting that he was too scared to jump, clinging to the bars, and Nick made the music reflect his exhilarated terror. There was a sharp intake of breath from the auditorium as Enzo made like he was about to fall. He even slipped down a little and dangled for a moment or two, his legs hanging in thin air, before scrambling back up. Then, with impeccable timing, he leapt, spun in the air and landed on his feet with a thump.

Spontaneous applause erupted from everyone in the wings, and some from the auditorium as well.

'Call your troupe to the stage, Mr Cullen,' said the bored voice as Enzo dusted himself off, and for a moment Nick's heart sank. The man didn't sound that enthusiastic.

With the others, and with Celine holding his hand, Nick moved centre stage, trying not to wince in the spotlight as Peter stepped to the edge of the footlights.

'Right, Mr Cullen,' said the voice. 'Your troupe are in. You need to polish up those acts, but we open in three days' time, so you don't have much in terms of rehearsal opportunity. But I think you'll be fine. See Charlie about all the details, and welcome to the show. Next performer, please.'

CHAPTER 33

 AY

SHE'D WRITTEN IMMEDIATELY to the YMCA, and then weeks had passed, during which she sent him another ten letters, one every other day. Then finally, this morning, his reply. At least it wasn't just a postcard. Heart beating, she took the flimsy brown envelope up to her bedroom, sat at her dressing table and devoured every word.

Dear May,

Thank you for your letters. I got a whole bundle of them this morning from Charlie, the stage manager, forwarded from the YMCA, with a bark that he wasn't my secretary. I haven't had a chance to read them all, but I will try to get around to it this week. Life is so busy here. We perform every night and do matinees as well at the weekends. Weekdays we are up at twelve for breakfast, which must sound lazy to you, but wait till I tell you. We have to be at the Acadia for four thirty each day, and when we're there, we iron out any little glitches from the night before, then we get into costume and make-up and do the performance, so we are ravenous by the time the curtain goes down every night around ten thirty.

We get the Tube back and all go to a place nearby our digs that serves fish and chips and beer – and milk for me and Aida, as she and me don't drink – and by the time that's all done and we are in our beds, it's well past midnight. Then I am usually on a high and can't sleep for ages, which is how I have the time to write this letter now. I finally remembered to bring a pen and paper to bed. Sometimes I don't drop off till two or three in the morning and then up again at twelve, and at weekends it's worse – we have to be up at nine. Teddy Hargreaves is an absolute tyrant. When I have my own theatre, remember our dreams, May? I won't treat people like he thinks he can and get away with it.

Our landlady, Mrs Juddy, is a nice old dear, and she loves the shows. We give her free tickets when we can, though they're hard to come by because the show is sold out every night. It was meant to run for six weeks, but there's talk of it going on for longer and even touring it around the country. There were other performers, of course, but our troupe make up the most of it now, and so we're getting famous, May – who'd have predicted that?

You'd like Mrs Juddy. She is very respectable –

May frowned as she read, she didn't want to hear about old women who ran boarding houses in England.

– so she just took in the girls at first, Celine and Betty (she's Two-Soups's girlfriend, but she's gone back to Scotland for a bit to help her dad on the farm – the goodbyes between her and Two-Soups were more emotional than if he was sending her to the front!) and Aida, who I'll tell you about in a minute. But some more rooms came up, and Celine moved in with Aida, and Mrs J. knows us all so well by now that she sort of relaxed her rules about not having gentlemen and ladies, as she calls us, in the same house, but she made us promise to be good!

He was sharing a house with two women. May's heart sank.

Mrs J. took a while to getting around to Nick because he's Irish. She hates the Irish because her nephew was shot in Dublin the week of the Rising. But Nick explained he's not from Dublin, and as for me, I don't mention my Irish connection. I've had to adjust my accent a bit. You won't recognise the boy from Henrietta Street when you see me next – I've gone right posh English altogether.

So anyway, Mrs Juddy is like a mother to us all, and she doesn't mind us sleeping all day and coming in at all hours.

It is so good to have a proper place to stay after the bunks on the front and then blankets on the floor at the YMCA. But now we get paid a nice wage for the show, so we can afford a bit of luxury. Mrs Juddy works miracles with the ration books. We don't have much meat, except on a Sunday morning, she makes us bacon and eggs, but she's a great cook and we do all right. My favourite thing she makes is potted cheese. She often waits up for us and makes it for us when we come in. It's a little bit of cheese mixed with mustard and then baked, and then served on toast she makes with a toasting fork by the fire. It's lovely.

We all miss Betty, not just Two-Soups. She taught Nick how to dance in Mrs Juddy's front room. Poor old Nick is scared stiff of girls. He grew up with just brothers and went to a boys' school, so never knew any. He's got a stammer too, so he's very self-conscious, but he's a great lad and what a voice. Betty is the kind of person that puts everyone at their ease. No airs or graces, just a genuinely nice person.

Enzo is a wild one. Gaggles of girls hang around the stage door at night waiting for him, and they give him gifts and giggle if he speaks to them. His particular interest, though, is not them, funnily enough. He prefers older ladies and cares not in the slightest if they are married. In fact, he confided to me, he prefers when they are. It's less complicated apparently. His parents came to the show along with his six older brothers. They seem very nice and so proud of him. His father was pumping his hand and speaking so fast, it was hard to follow, but it was clear how much seeing his son perform to rapturous applause on the stage of the Acadia meant to him.

I don't know what that's like, but it must be nice.

Now I promised to tell you about Aida. I think I said to you before that Ramon asked his childhood friend – she's his flamenco partner – to join the show. I wasn't that enthusiastic at first because Enzo was so hilarious, but once we saw her on stage, I was so glad I agreed, and Enzo is delighted too because it means he can concentrate on his own act and not have to perform with Ramon as well.

May, you should see Aida – she's amazing. She's tall and slender, and her dark hair is back in a tight bun the way they do, and she has these amazing outfits, and she has the whole place enthralled, so she does. She'd remind you of nothing so much as a beautiful dark snake the way she writhes and twirls and twists.

Ramon plays guitar for her, and he wears a tight pair of black trousers and a red silk shirt that Lady Appleton made, with puffy sleeves and leather cord instead of buttons, so he looks 'devilishly dashing', according to Mrs Juddy. Aida wears dresses the likes of which you've never laid eyes on, May. My favourite is red with black polka dots, tight on the body, but it goes out into a full skirt with layers of ruffles of lace and fabric. She paints her fingernails red too, and so she's totally co-ordinated. They make some pair. You'd stand up to look at them.

Aida is a quare one, though. She speaks English a bit now but with a heavy accent, and unlike Celine, she isn't warm. She seems watchful, obser-vant kind of, but when she dances, May, she has the whole place mesmerised. You can't help but watch her, and every eye in the whole place is transfixed. It's like she weaves a spell or something.

Funny, in the beginning I thought maybe she was Ramon's girlfriend and that he was trying to get her to London for that reason, but she's not. They seem more like a brother and sister if anything. They speak in rapid Spanish to each other, and nobody has a notion what they say, and they're always bickering, which is annoying, but then they make up. Whatever way it works, though. She's sensational. I'm so glad she's part of it.

Teddy, may the divil roast him, as my mother might say, was being most obstinate about paying us more than the original rate, what with us packing his house out every night and making him a fortune when he never spends a penny on fixing the theatre. It's a death trap. He never fixes the wires or the gas or anything. He's a tight-fisted bugger, May. But anyway we had strong words, and the upshot is we're being paid properly now.

See you,

Peter

He hadn't even signed it 'love'.

As she studied his words, she tried to fool herself, to find signs of affection, longing and romance, but it was time to face reality. Whether it was just that they hadn't seen each other in so long or because his new life was so exciting and he thought she was too respectable for it and so had put her behind him, the fact was she loved Peter Cullen far more than he loved her, if he'd ever loved her at all.

Since he'd been here on leave and they'd become engaged, she'd had a lot of time to think, and she knew that she'd more or less bamboozled him into the engagement. However, that didn't mean she was going to let him go. But she'd have to move fast.

Because this Aida... Oh, the pain of how he spoke about her was like a burning in her chest. Such admiration he had for her, how compelling he found her, and worse news, Ramon wasn't her beau but her sort of brother. And even if it wasn't Aida, somebody would get her hooks into him. No, it was too much, the temptation was too great, and she was sure that all the pretty girls of London, with all the latest fashions and manners, would be head over heels for her fiancé. He was so handsome anyway, but now he had star quality too. She had to go there and make her mark on him. Let the world know he was hers and she wasn't going to allow anyone to get in her way.

Then and there, May made up her mind. Peter Cullen would be her husband or she'd die trying.

* * *

THAT NIGHT, she stashed her bag in the shed at the bottom of the garden and nearly jumped out of her skin when busybody Madge stuck her nose inside wondering what she was doing in there. She made up some story about looking for a paintbrush, but the nosy old bat didn't believe her, she could tell. She'd put the bag under some old sacks Mother used for the clippings of the garden, so out of sight. She just had to pray Madge didn't go snooping.

The next morning she got up and dressed for work as always.

'Will you be able to finish early today, dear?' asked her mother, looking up from the breakfast table where May found her parents sitting every morning, day after day, always so respectable. In half an hour from now, her father would set off to walk the thirty minutes to the bank, as he did every morning, leaving at 8:46 on the dot. And today her mother had a Legion of Mary meeting, which she wouldn't miss, although she would fuss and worry and say maybe this once she would stay at home because she found Mrs Cuddihy so stressful with her ideas about sweet peas and lily of the valley, which gave poor Father O'Reilly hay fever...

'Quite the opposite, Mother,' said May firmly. 'I told Mr Swift that I'd work very late. Gladys and Christina are both gone down with this Spanish flu, and they're very ill, so we're very short-staffed in the office as well as on the factory floor.'

Her mother panicked, blessing herself. 'May God spare them. So many people are falling foul of it. I fear for you in that factory, May, I really do. No, I insist you call Mr Swift and say you have to give up your job immediately and stay at home.'

May also panicked, but for a different reason. She'd forgotten to never mention illness to her mother. 'Or it could be Mrs Stapleton or Mrs Lynch or Charles Barry, or anyone in the choir could also have it and give it to you, Mother,' she snapped fiercely. 'So we can either sit in here, terrified to go out and breathe, or we can get on with our lives and hope for the best.'

'I only meant...' Her mother did that wounded expression, the one May hated.

'I think your mother is just concerned for you, May dear. She doesn't want you to get sick, and I support her in that.'

May modified her tone and played to her father's weakness, which was snobbery. 'Father, I can't hand in my notice with no warning. I would be letting down Mr Swift, and you know he went to your old school, Belvedere. You wouldn't want me to be disloyal to a Belvedere man.'

'You're right.' He nodded, stroking his moustache, allowing his wife and daughter to wait breathlessly for his judgement. 'Maybe I should have a word with Swift myself. It might be best to avoid the factory for now – I mean, the war work is over, isn't it – until the bug or whatever it is dies down?'

The rage bubbled up again. Here they were, smothering her once more. She couldn't breathe in this house.

'No, Father, we are short-staffed. Now I must go.' She stood up, squeezed out around the breakfast table and made for the door, while her parents stared at her in horror, their mouths open. She experienced a rush of triumph and then fear. It was the first time she'd openly defied them, and she half expected them to call the police or something. But of course what could they do aside from locking her up? They couldn't even threaten to cut her off any more, not with Auntie Maura's inheritance coming to her in a year's time.

Suddenly feeling a pang of guilt at the distress she was about to cause them, she relented and returned, kissing them each on the cheek. Mother blushed and Father beamed. They were easily pleased after all.

She waited in St Fiachra's Park, where she had walked with Peter all that time ago, and she could have sworn it was the same old man and his dog who passed her by. When she was sure her parents would be gone, her mother to her church meeting, Father to work and Madge to do the grocery shopping, she returned to the house, ducked through the side gate and skirted down to the shed, being careful to avoid the line of sight from the kitchen window just in case Madge returned unexpectedly.

The bag was where she'd left it mercifully, so she grabbed it and let herself out, then walked quickly to the tram stop, praying she didn't run into any nosy neighbours who would question her about where she was going with her luggage.

Her urge was to run, but that would definitely draw attention. Mrs O'Donnell waved as she passed; she was out deadheading her roses as usual. How boring was her life to be gardening at ten in the morning, May wondered.

Boring but respectable.

But May Gallagher wasn't respectable. Not any more. She was an independent woman. Well, she didn't have her inheritance yet, but ever since the war had ended, she'd been saving her wages and allowance in case she had to travel to see her Peter, and she had plenty enough to be going on with.

A fizz of excitement rushed through her veins. Soon, very soon, she'd be away from this dull, predictable life. She'd be in London, with Peter. The thought made her heart sing, and she felt light with optimism again. As soon as he saw her, his old feelings would come back, she was sure of that. He had loved her. Of course he had. Waiting in St Fiachra's Park and seeing the old man and his dog had brought it all back to her. That was the day they were engaged…kissing in every doorway, all the way back home to Ranelagh.

She'd seduced him before, and she'd seduce him again.

How could he prefer a bad-tempered foreign girl who could barely speak English over a beautiful, wholesome, clever, sensible Dublin girl like herself who could be his eyes and ears, his right-hand woman, his genie in the bottle?

Once he saw them side by side, her and this Aida Gonzalez, he would know. And if he didn't, she would make sure he chose her.

Then they'd get married over there and they could openly share a room. She had every intention of sharing his room anyway, at least some of the time, however 'respectable' this Mrs Juddy was – probably not very – but to do it legally would be wonderful. She felt her face flush with embarrassment at the ideas in her head. Her parents would be appalled – worse, they would have no idea how to react because if they knew that she and Peter had already gone all the way, it would confound them. Girls like their daughter barely held a boy's hand before the wedding. It just wasn't the done thing. But they were the old world and she and Peter were the new.

A niggle of doubt, ever present, forced its way to the surface of her mind again, trying to spoil her mood. She dismissed it with a mental stamp of her foot, crushing it under her shoe. Of course Peter would be happy to see her, thrilled even. She was his fiancé. He loved her. Had he ever actually said those words… Who cared! He was a boy – they weren't good at expressing their feelings. And she knew, she just knew he felt it. Why else would she have been the one he came to after running away from home all those years ago? She was the one he'd come to when he came home on leave. He wrote to her, even though he wasn't much of a letter writer – but that wasn't his fault. It was because of his upbringing, or lack of it. Of course he loved her.

Anyway, she had enough love for both of them.

The tram came on time but was absolutely packed, so she had to squeeze on and endure the smirk of two lads, clerks or shopkeepers, who had no choice but be crushed against her. She gave them an icy stare, and the younger of the two had the grace to look ashamed.

She got off in town, much to her relief, and hoped the smell of bodies from the warm morning on the tram didn't cling to her outfit. She'd packed her nicest dress, coat and hat for the trip in her bag. She would find a place to change into them, but not until she got to London; she didn't want to risk her clothes getting smutty or dusty on her travels.

The boat was due to depart from the quays at ten thirty for Liverpool. How close Liverpool was to London, she wasn't sure, but she assumed she would need to take a train, and if there was time, maybe she could change in the toilet on the way.

As she walked towards the Ballast Office on Westmoreland Street to buy a ticket, she fought back the nerves. It was true that she'd never been anywhere without her parents, and they never went anywhere. When she and David were children, her parents used to take them to Bray to the seaside, visiting Auntie Maura on the way, and Father took them with him once when he went to Cork for bank business. But other than that, they'd never ventured beyond the south side of Dublin City.

The man sold her a ticket without paying any attention whatsoever to her and, to her immense relief, didn't seem to think there was anything untoward about a young lady going to Liverpool alone.

'Just to Liverpool, is it?' he asked, glancing up from his book for the first time.

'Well...I am... I...ah... I'm going to London, but I'll need...' She wished she could sound more sure of herself.

'You can get a ticket to do ya for the train to London as well. It's cheaper.'

'Oh, right...yes. Then yes, please.'

'And when you coming back?' he asked, his demeanour suggesting he hadn't time to be dilly-dallying.

'Ah...I'm not sure. Can I get an open-ended ticket?'

He shrugged. 'It's dearer.'

'I don't mind,' she said, smiling.

He gave her an odd look, as if to say who on earth doesn't mind how much something is, then said, 'Well, if money's no object, then can you afford first class? It will add fifteen shillings to the trip, but it's safer for a young woman travelling alone?'

'I can.' She was grateful for his gruff concern about her welfare.

He filled out the ticket and handed it to her. 'Custom House quay. You'd better go now.'

'Thank you.' She took it and placed it in her purse.

The boarding process was simple, and a very nice young man in a navy jacket with gold braiding showed her to the first-class section of the boat. There were no cabins – it was only a four-hour journey – but she was given a very comfortable seat with a porthole, and as soon as she was settled, a waitress offered her tea. As the ship pulled away from the quay, the happy murmur of her fellow passengers filling the bright airy cabin to the fore of the ship, she sat back and took a sip of her tea.

She'd done it.

She'd escaped. But that was the easy part.

EPILOGUE

$\mathcal{A}$s May Gallagher sailed across the Irish Sea, a man she'd never met before bided his time. The plan was simple, but the slightest whiff of him being overeager would raise suspicion in the wily old fox, Viscount Banting White, known to everyone as Blimpy.

The murmur of conversation in the Trinity Club off Stephen's Green in Dublin, the Chesterfield wingback chairs, the glitter of twelve-year-old malt in cut-glass tumblers, was this man's natural habitat, but if his fortunes were not supplemented, and soon, things could start looking very different indeed, and he wasn't having that.

Viscount Banting-White was clearly in foul form, and though this was his customary demeanour, today felt even worse than usual. To approach or not, that was the question.

Everyone knew the viscount had shot a groom last year an hour after Maud, Blimpy's wife, declared herself in love with the poor young chap. Blimpy claimed it was an accident, of course, and the family were paid off. The chap survived, just about, and nothing was made of it. The family knew better than to make a fuss.

Viscountess Maud Banting-White, if she were of a different class, would be what was known as a good-time girl, but nobody would dare attribute such a title to one so highly bred. But nonetheless, she loved a party and a flirt, and being thirty years her husband's junior and decidedly better looking, she marched to the beat of her own drum. It drove her grouchy husband mad. He was obsessed with her, and rumour had it he had the entire household spying on her, convinced she was bestowing her favours on other men.

The man decided to give it a go. After all, they'd known each other for years, since Eton.

'How goes it, Blimpy?' he asked, standing beside the viscount's chair. He used the nickname the other man had had since he'd turned up at boarding school as a rather chubby five-year-old, clinging to his mother's skirts. By the time they'd grown, he'd slimmed down a bit. Alas, the nickname stuck.

'Ah, it's you.' He looked up.

Time had not been kind to Blimpy. His jowly face in permanent scowl, his thinning hair and his rounded belly did not endear him to anyone. He'd inherited the estate much too young when his father was killed in India. They'd all been heirs, their set, and of course they all wanted it, but not too soon.

While the man was doing his grand European tour and having all manner of adventures, poor Blimpy had to go back to Tipperary at just seventeen to take over the huge Ardrish Castle.

Blimpy's first marriage to some horse-faced third daughter of an earl from Yorkshire was not one of love, but she failed to produce issue and so helpfully died in the attempt. Blimpy had remained single for years and years, and despite his somewhat toad-like features, people were surprised someone hadn't snatched him up. Goodness knew the ambitious mothers of London and beyond did try, but it was Maud Blackwell who took his fancy, and so her mama, the most ambitious of them all, engineered the match quick smart.

She was so far out of his league, and she'd grown up in Osterford Hall, a magnificent place outside Bristol. Rumour had it the Blackwell money came from coal. His seat and lands didn't impress her, and he was destined to spend his life terrified of being cuckolded. She did give him an heir – well, a daughter, but still, better than nothing.

'Might I join you, or would you rather be alone?' The man asked.

'Hrrmph.' A wave of a hand at the other leather wingback meant he could sit.

'How's things? I hear you had a nice win at Ascot? Fleet of Foot was bred by you, was she not?' He accepted a glass of whiskey from the liveried waiter.

Blimpy nodded. 'Out of Jessop's Fancy and by Kitingan. Bound to be good.'

'Still, well done.'

He nodded, gave another harumph of acknowledgement. Even at school Blimpy had been dour and uncommunicative.

'And how are the family? Well, I hope?'

The man needed to get the conversation naturally around to the rumours he'd been carefully planting for weeks now, but slowly and gently.

The viscount eyeballed him then, searching for meaning in his words. The man kept his face neutral and pleasant.

'Fine, fine. Thinking of sending them to Warwickshire to my mother, though. Things are getting a bit…' He waved his hand again.

Getting a bit…was exactly right. People like them were on borrowed time here in Ireland, and anyone who thought otherwise was deluded. The rebels were not going to take no for an answer this time, and they seemed determined to drive every Protestant landowner back into the sea.

'Might be wise.'

'Will *you* stay?' Blimpy asked then.

He wondered if Blimpy knew that, unlike other members of his class, the man didn't have a selection of other houses to go to, no hunting lodge in Scotland, no townhouse in Bath, no charming old pile in the home counties.

'For now, but…' He shrugged.

Another nod. Things were going well.

'You know Wally Shaw, of Brockleton, Walter's middle son? You've a connection there don't you?' Blimpy asked.

Yes. This was exactly how he wanted this to go.

The man nodded his head, carefully nonchalant.

'A tenuous one, yes, on my mother's side. I heard their eldest Roger died in France and the youngest Nicholas was killed too by all accounts. Wally is the only one left. Why do you ask?'

'No reason.' Blimpy looked wretched again.

Now was his chance, now or never. His whole future relied on this moment and how Blimpy reacted.

'I saw him recently actually, Wally I mean, now that you mention it. Where was it now...' He paused to contemplate. 'Oh yes, actually it was at a party in Chelsea. He was there. We exchanged a few words. I knew Roger better and the youngest one Nicholas not at all, I think he was a bit sub-par mentally if I recall, a dreadful stammer, almost unintelligible. But yes, I saw Wally with Maud actually. They seemed to be enjoying themselves, though I was trying to wangle an escape – costume parties are not my forte. Fine for the young people but...'

The glower gave way to a flash of rage. 'When?' Blimpy asked, his voice low, even and furious.

'Oh gosh, I don't recall... Was it last month? I think the sixteenth... I could be wrong, but off the top of my head.'

'Was that the only time you saw Wally Shaw in the company of my wife?'

Mock shock, followed by friendly concern, the man said smoothly, 'Oh, Blimpy, now you mustn't jump to conclusions. I'm sure it was perfectly innocent – they were just having some fun. Goodness knows the young need that after all they've been through. Besides, a man of your standing need have no worries on that score.'

'Shaw never saw combat,' he spat. 'And he's set to inherit the Barony of Simpré so he's a much better prospect than most, so forgive me if I don't share your optimism, Now I'll ask you again, have you seen Wally Shaw and my wife together other than on that occasion?'

He furrowed his brow. 'Look, Blimpy, they're young, she's beautiful, and they need to have some –'

'Is that a yes?'

He gave a reluctant sigh. 'Maybe once or twice, I can't remember. But in a group, not alone or anything. They are around with the same crowd, Dickie Proot's boy and the Gillingham sisters, you know. I'm sure there's nothing more to it.'

Blimpy threw back his drink and held his glass out for a refill, which came in seconds.

'You are not at all sure, and neither am I, but nobody will take my wife from me, I will make sure of that.'

Discretion being the better part of valour, the man remained silent. The seed was planted, and now all he had to do was sit back and watch it germinate. He'd not seen Wally Shaw since he was a child, but that was not important. What was important was removing Walter Shaw's heir, the only hurdle between him and the barony. And Blimpy was just the man to help him.

Checkmate.

The End

I SINCERELY HOPE you enjoyed this book, and will be glad to hear the sequel, *A Beautiful Ferocity* is available to preorder HERE for release at the end of September 2023.

If you can, I would also really appreciate a review on Amazon, here, it helps enormously.

Thanks so much for your support,

JG - 2023

ABOUT THE AUTHOR

Jean Grainger is a USA Today bestselling Irish author. She writes historical and contemporary Irish fiction and her work has very flatteringly been compared to the late great Maeve Binchy.

She lives in a stone cottage in Cork with her husband Diarmuid and the youngest two of her four children. The older two come home for a break when adulting gets too exhausting. There are a variety of animals there too, all led by two cute but clueless micro-dogs called Scrappy and Scoobi.

ALSO BY JEAN GRAINGER

The Tour Series

The Tour

Safe at the Edge of the World

The Story of Grenville King

The Homecoming of Bubbles O'Leary

Finding Billie Romano

Kayla's Trick

The Carmel Sheehan Story

Letters of Freedom

The Future's Not Ours To See

What Will Be

The Robinswood Story

What Once Was True

Return To Robinswood

Trials and Tribulations

The Star and the Shamrock Series

The Star and the Shamrock

The Emerald Horizon

The Hard Way Home

The World Starts Anew

The Queenstown Series

Last Port of Call

The West's Awake

The Harp and the Rose

Roaring Liberty

Standalone Books

So Much Owed

Shadow of a Century

Under Heaven's Shining Stars

Catriona's War

Sisters of the Southern Cross

The Kilteegan Bridge Series

The Trouble with Secrets

What Divides Us

More Harm Than Good

When Irish Eyes Are Lying

A Silent Understanding

The Mags Munroe Story

The Existential Worries of Mags Munroe

Growing Wild in the Shade

Each to Their Own

Made in the USA
Columbia, SC
24 August 2023